# ONLY THE
# WICKED

# BOOKS BY GARY PHILLIPS

## NOVELS

*The Jook*
*The Perpetrators*
*Bangers*
*Freedom's Fight*
*The Underbelly*
*Kings of Vice* (as Mal Radcliff)
*Warlord of Willow Ridge*
*Three the Hard Way* (collected novellas)
*Beat, Slay, Love: One Chef's Hunger
    for Delicious Revenge* (written
    collectively as Thalia Filbert)
*The Killing Joke* (co-written with
    Christa Faust)
*Matthew Henson and the Ice Temple
    of Harlem*

## SHORT STORY COLLECTIONS

*Monkology: 15 Stories from the World
    of Private Eye Ivan Monk*
*Astonishing Heroes: Shades of Justice*
*Treacherous: Grifters, Ruffians
    and Killers*
*The Unvarnished Gary Phillips:
    A Mondo Pulp Collection*

## ONE-SHOT HARRY NOVELS

*One-Shot Harry*
*Ash Dark as Night*

## IVAN MONK NOVELS

*Violent Spring*
*Perdition, U.S.A.*
*Bad Night Is Falling*
*Only the Wicked*

## MARTHA CHAINEY NOVELS

*High Hand*
*Shooter's Point*

## GRAPHIC NOVELS

*Shot Callerz*
*Midnight Mover*

## GRAPHIC NOVELS CONT.

*South Central Rhapsody*
*Cowboys*
*Danger A-Go-Go*
*Angeltown: The Nate Hollis Investigations*
*High Rollers*
*Big Water*
*The Rinse*
*Peepland* (co-written with Christa Faust)
*Vigilante: Southland*
*The Be-Bop Barbarians*
*Cold Hard Cash: A Martha
    Chainey Escapade*

## ANTHOLOGIES AS EDITOR

*The Cocaine Chronicles* (co-edited
    with Jervey Tervalon)
*Orange County Noir*
*Politics Noir: Dark Tales from
    the Corridors of Power*
*The Darker Mask: Heroes from the
    Shadows* (co-edited with Christopher
    Chambers)
*Scoundrels: Tales of Greed, Murder and
    Financial Crimes*
*Black Pulp* (co-edited with Tommy
    Hancock and Morgan Minor)
*Black Pulp II* (co-edited with Tommy
    Hancock, Ernest Russell, Gordon
    Dymowski & H. David Blalock)
*Day of the Destroyers*
*Hollis for Hire*
*Hollis, P.I.*
*Culprits: The Heist Was Only the
    Beginning* (co-edited with Richard Brewer)
*The Obama Inheritance: Fifteen Stories
    of Conspiracy Noir*
*South Central Noir*
*Witnesses for the Dead: Stories* (co-edited
    with Gar Anthony Haywood)
*Get Up Off That Thing: Crime Fiction
    Inspired by the Songs of James Brown*

# ONLY THE WICKED

## GARY PHILLIPS

SOHO
CRIME

Soho Press
227 W 17th Street
New York, NY 10011

Library of Congress Cataloging-in-Publication Data

Names: Phillips, Gary, 1955- author.
Title: Only the wicked / Gary Phillip.
Description: New York : Soho Crime, 2024.
Identifiers: LCCN 2024003780

ISBN 978-1-64129-445-4
eISBN 978-1-64129-446-1

Subjects: LCSH: Monk, Ivan (Fictitious character)—Fiction. |
Murder—Investigation—Fiction. | Civil rights movements—Fiction. |
Baseball stories. | LCGFT: Detective and mystery fiction. | Novels.
Classification: LCC PS3566.H4783 O55 2024 | DDC 813/.54—dc23/
eng/20240129
LC record available at https://lccn.loc.gov/2024003780

Interior design by Janine Agro, Soho Press, Inc.


Printed in the United States of America

10 9 8 7 6 5 4 3 2 1

*To the ones who have died or been imprisoned by cruel hands, for the ones who have toiled ceaselessly, and the ones who sought neither fame nor fortune, but that which is the most precious and the most elusive, freedom.*

*Mainstream America is counting on you to "draw your sword" and fight for them. These people have precious little time and resources to battle misguided Cinderella attitudes: the fringe propaganda of the homosexual coalition; the feminists who preach that it is a divine duty for women to hate men; Blacks who raise a militant fist with one hand while they seek preference with the other; New Age apologists for juvenile crime who see roving gangs as a means to only the merchandising of violence as a form of entertainment for impressionable minds; and the gun bans as a means to only the Lord-knows-what. We have reached that point in time when our social policy originates on 'Oprah.' It's time to pull the plug.*

—Charlton Heston,
President of the National Rifle Association,
from his speech before the Free Congress Foundation

# CHAPTER 1

"I can't think of anything better'n pussy."

"You can't think of anything better, unfortunately, it just don't think of you too much."

"Now, Willie," Johnny Patterson responded paternally, "you know you doin' good if you manage to stay awake past them *Sanford and Son* reruns you watch on BET. Let alone be out at night doing any shark hunting."

"Yeah Willie," Kelvon Ulysses Little chimed in. "You ain't even sniffed none since that chick you was seeing was managing the bowling alley over on Gage." Little, co-owner of the Abyssinia Barber Shop and Shine Parlor on South Broadway, adjusted the blinds to shunt some of the morning sun beaming through his dingy picture window.

Globules of sweat gathered on Willie Brant's hairless head. He closed the *Jet* magazine he'd been looking at, careful to keep his thumb on the page where the tender young thing in the bikini could be found. "Look here, that Doris could make a stuttering man speechify like James Earl Jones. You know she had some Spanish blood," he leered.

"Nobody's arguing that, Willie," Abe Carson added. The rangy carpenter had his long legs stretched out as he leafed through a back issue of *Car Craft*. "The point was, when was the last time you got up close to some?"

"That is if you can remember what it looks like," Patterson chuckled.

Brant snorted like a cornered ram. "I've turned down more pussy you silly motherfuckahs would sell your mama's gold teeth for."

"Nigga, please." Little's laugh melded with the others for several moments.

Old Man Spears ambled out of the restroom in the back, hitching up his slacks. He did a final adjustment with his suspenders and took up his usual position next to the Trumanera Philco radio. He passed a callused hand over the curvature of its peeling walnut veneer as if it were an ever-constant pet. He'd turned it on before going to the bathroom, so in the five minutes it took him to return, the instrument was sufficiently warmed up to receive a signal.

The shop contained a TV plugged into cable, which perched overhead in one corner. The device was handy for the basketball games, tractor pulls and the other pursuits of mass entertainment afforded on such venues as the Speed channel and the various incarnations of ESPN. But something about Saturdays and Old Man Spears made the use of the reliable Philco the right combination of sound and imagination, the TV too distracting at times to the conversational flow of subjects of import to the mind, and lesser regions of the body.

"What about you, Abe?" Little winked to the gathered men as Darsey Wiles sat in the chair to get his haircut. "Didn't I see you in a three-piece going into The Hightop the other week? Try'n to be all *GQ*-like you don't work with your hands."

"You wouldn't see me where I go, good brother," Carson drawled in his baritone. "I keep my business on the quietlike."

"You mean in your dreams," Brant needled. He leaned forward to look down the row of seats. "What about you, Monk? You ain't got nothing to offer?"

Ivan Monk was browsing through a copy of the *Watts Times*, a neighborhood free paper that carried news from an angle the white press often missed. He'd been perusing an ad for an upcoming blues show at the Olympic Auditorium. The event featured some local talent he wanted to see. "I'm just a man who tries to keep the lawn trim, and the grout clean."

"You had all kinds of pussy when you was in the merchants, didn't you, Monk?" Patterson inquired sincerely, his Kool dangling up and down as he spoke.

Monk turned a page. "I don't like to be so crude, Johnny."

The men all made noises of disbelief.

Spears looked at Monk. His deep-set eyes were steady and clear, the years of living and the years of could-have-beens evident in their depths. "You scared your Japanese honey has got this place wired, huh?" The old man smiled, revealing dull-colored false teeth. He leaned toward the Philco's speaker, tuning in on the baseball game with the precision of a safe cracker.

"Yeah, man," Brant went on, "how come you don't never brag about all that Turkish and French pussy you got overseas? You know, I had me a French girl once," Brant gloated.

Little pushed out his bottom lip with his tongue, but said nothing as he clipped Wiles's hair. His current customer, a beer truck driver, questioned Brant's veracity.

"Willie, the only thing you ever had that was from France is that super-size order of fries you get at McDonald's."

"Just 'cause you got a ball and chain, Darsey, you ain't got to take your jealousy out on the rest of us," Brant cajoled.

"You know Monk's a circumspect dude," Carson said, steering the attention back to the private detective.

"'Cept we talkin' 'bout the past, man," Patterson exclaimed. He held his smoke in one hand and drank from a bottle of orange juice with the other. "Now, what you trying to hide, Virgil Tibbs?"

"I don't want to embarrass you fellas with my—how shall I say it?—my achievements. 'Cause I know how fragile your egos are."

"Shee-it," Brant exhaled. "That must mean your sorry ass never got off them tubs you was a grease monkey on."

Another raucous chorus preened through the warm air of the barber shop. Spears abruptly stopped laughing as he all but shoved his ear into the Philco.

"I'll be goddamned with grandma's hogs," he said.

Monk peered at the older man curiously. "What is it?"

Spears didn't respond. He sat tensed and hunched in front of the radio's speaker like an athlete whose prowess had long since faded, but who still knew the moves. The old man was rigid and his face a map of contradictory emotions. Everyone stared at him as a voice came from the radio.

". . . Yeah, yeah, I guess you could say we made the way for these youngsters today. These million-dollar stars who got to have their face upside every boxa Wheaties or name slapped on a tennis shoe. When I played for the Black Barons, we was doin' good to get four, four and a quarter a month, you hear me? And man, we played some ball in those days. Didn't have no massager, none of that spinning water bath thing for sore muscles. What liniment couldn't take care of, you better hope sleep did."

"You know who that is?" Monk asked Spears.

Spears's dentures clacked in his mouth as he worked his jaw. "Kennesaw," he said, barely audibly. "Kennesaw Riles."

The name rolled around in Monk's head. Something

vague tickled at the edges of his memory but he couldn't form a picture to go with the name.

"You knew him when he played ball? Did you play, Spears?" Brant jumped in.

Monk got up and walked toward Spears, who was lost again in Riles's words. He gently touched the older man's arm. "Did you play in Black ball?"

"Southern League, Negro Nationals," Spears rasped, locked in another realm. His long, knotted fingers turned up the volume.

Monk reflected on the old man's words. Riles was his mother's family name, and he was sure this Kennesaw was related to him, that it wasn't just a coincidence Riles had the same name. The more he concentrated on it, the more he was convinced that as a child he'd met this Kennesaw once or twice. Visualizing, he reconstructed Wrigley Field as it had once existed at Forty-First and Avalon. A band playing on a platform, and his father taking him and his sister there to see Kennesaw play? No, he wasn't certain. He still couldn't conjure up a physical characteristic or a memory of a voice to flesh out the amorphous concept of this supposed relative.

"You played ball with this guy on the radio?" Monk prompted again.

Spears was breathing through his mouth. He attempted to wet his lips with a dry tongue. "Sure did. We was even roommates on the road."

Wiles stepped out of the chair, running a hand over his close cut. "Had me a play uncle who was on the Kansas City Monarchs with Satchel Paige. Said Satchel threw so hard his balls streaked like little meteors." Wiles paid and tipped Little.

Carson unlimbered his tall frame and ambled over to take his place in the barber chair. Little let the chair down.

"I promised the kids I'd take them to Knotts Berry Farm today," Wiles continued. "Some damn new ride that goes straight up, loop-the-loop, then curves back around like a bigass snake." He mimicked the action with the flat of his hand. "I'll see y'all later."

The men said their goodbyes as the driver left.

"How come you never told us about your playing days?" Carson asked Spears.

Spears didn't answer. He dug a faded blue handkerchief out of his pocket and worked at his face. He got up and went over to the Ramona water cooler. The ex-barnstormer poured himself a cup and gulped it down. He was working on a second one as Riles began to stammer on the radio.

"... Ah, that's not what really happened. Y'all press boys get the story wrong all the time. I ain't saying I didn't do it. But there was reasons. See, what I'm saying is, soon I'm going to set it to right, and you'll see."

"He's still lying, mostly to himself." Spears shook his head in indignation. He was standing at the cooler. The old man had one hand on the top of the plastic bottle, the other holding his cup at chest level. "What he better be doing is lookin' out for Malachi. Kennesaw's train is comin' back to the station."

Monk hadn't caught what the question was that Kennesaw was responding to, and definitely was lost as to what Spears was referring to about Malachi. "What do you mean, the chapter in the Bible?" he asked as Spears returned to his seat. Wasn't the older man moving slower? Maybe it was the temperature. Despite the door to the shop being open, and some movement of air, it had gotten stuffier.

"What about an answer, Monk?" Brant chimed in again.

"I believe we've moved off that topic, Willie," Monk said wearily.

"Not me," the retired postman said. "Ain't too many things hold my attention the way women and what they do to a man do."

"It would seem," Carson commiserated. "Here we have some living history, and all you can go on about is sex."

"What can a Black man call his own, Abe?" Brant pleaded. We ain't got no say in who runs the country, the foreigners got our jobs, and none of you cats in here can rub three quarters together to call his own."

"Abe's a contractor," Patterson said, lighting another cigarette in defiance of state law. "You sittin' in Kelvon's business, and Monk's got a donut shop," he added.

"You know what I mean, " Brant said icily. "We can't put up one of those big-ass high-rises like them Koreans do up and down Olympic. So what do men like us have? What makes us the same as men like Michael Jordan and Denzel Washington?"

"They can get any woman they want if they had a mind to," Little advised.

"All right," Brant allowed. "But under the right circumstances, so can any of us. You'd be surprised what I experienced when I had a route on the west side."

This engendered another round of incredulity. Monk had tuned them out, waiting for another opportunity to talk with Spears. Here was somebody he'd known only from the barber shop for years. Just, an old man, who, he figured—well, he didn't know what he figured. Spears was a fixture, someone he thought about when he occasionally reflected on Abyssinia's regulars, not somebody he socialized with or had reason to talk to outside of the camaraderie of the barber shop.

He'd been over to Patterson's place with some of the others to watch pay-per-view boxing matches a couple of times. And he and Jill Kodama, his girlfriend, had been at the Mint, once a live music club in the Pico-Fairfax section of town, and run into Carson—who'd been perched in a corner metering a Budweiser and eyeing a healthy woman in a too-tight tube top. Maybe Brant was right after all about men and the basics.

Nonetheless, Carson had spotted the couple, and they'd hung out together through two sets. Monk had also been over to Carson's house a couple of times. The last time was when the builder's pickup truck had broken down and he needed a ride home.

And some of the barber shop crew also frequented Monk's donut shop on the edge of the Crenshaw District. But Continental Donuts had its own collection of regulars and Monk realized he knew less about them than the ones in the room. Obviously those folks, like Spears, like all of them, had a life beyond these walls.

The older man was working at his brow again, leaning back in his chair. He looked tired. The interview with Kennesaw Riles had ended. A commercial for auto insurance played while Brant and Patterson continued their gentlemanly jousting.

"You saying you'd choose Halle Berry over Salma what's-her-name, the one who was in the *Wild, Wild West* movie?" Brant all but fell out of his chair he was so stunned.

"Ain't nothing wrong with preferring a sister, Willie," Patterson intoned, couching his prurient interests in nationalist trappings.

"That's cool, brah," Brant retorted, "but Salma's got a body, man. Halle's cute, but she's too much on the thin side for my tastes."

"For somebody who's always complaining about foreigners," Carson joined in, "you really dig women with Spanish in them, don't you, Willie?"

"Yeah, so?" Brant asked rhetorically. "I tell you what, you get rid of the men, and let their women stay. Fact, that should be our state policy."

"Open borders if you fine and got a nice booty, the Willie Brant law," Little joked.

The men started laughing again. Underneath the cackling, Monk could hear Spears hacking. The older man sat upright and the younger man reached out to him. Spears went slack and dripped to the floor like liquefied vinyl.

"Oh shit," Brant exclaimed as he erupted from his seat.

Monk kneeled beside Spears, tilting his head back. He opened his mouth, checking for any obstructions.

"I'll get an ambulance," Little shouted. He whirled and snatched the phone's handset mounted next to his picture mirror.

Carson had removed the barber's shroud and moved toward where Spears lay. "Come on, y'all, give Monk some room," he boomed.

"Hey, should you be doing that?" Brant inquired in his bothersome voice. "I worked with a dude named Fowler who gave this big-titted transvestite mouth-to-mouth at Tommy Tucker's Playroom one night and he—"

"Shut up, Willie," Carson ordered. Nobody snickered at the sight of his unevenly clipped hair; one side of his medium salt-and-pepper Afro looked like an untended hedge.

Monk pinched Spears's nose, and breathed into his mouth three times. He then forcibly pressed on the man's chest three times. Concern frosted his eyes as he repeated the CPR technique for several minutes. The men in the shop stood in a semicircle around the two on the floor. A mortal quiet gripped the gathered. Everyone could tell it was too late. They knew Monk's efforts were futile, yet he had no choice but to continue.

"Paramedics are here," Patterson said unnecessarily. The emergency vehicle's siren had been apparent for some moments. He had raised the blinds to see out into the street. The auto parts clerk stood there in sunlit relief, his ever-present cigarette unlit between his compressed lips.

Monk looked at Carson, and the contractor shook his head. The PI felt cheated. Here was a man who had stories to tell, anecdotes about his personal struggles and triumphs to relate. And none of them had known that. Who would tell them about the life of Old Man Spears? And would the men in this barber shop, like many in other parts of the city, fade away without anyone championing their accomplishments on this planet?

He stood as two paramedics rushed through the Abyssinia's front door. Patterson was holding it open for the techs, their gurney surging forward on well-oiled wheels. Monk fumbled with the keys and wallet he'd taken off the dead man. He managed to hold onto the items behind his back.

Carson glanced at Monk, tilting his head slightly downward. He didn't hide the accusatory glare he leveled at Monk.

# CHAPTER 2

"So that's all you know," the paramedic declared perfunctorily. Her umber eyes, behind modified granny glasses, drifted from Carson to Monk. The woman, a Chinese-American, had done her hair short, and the strands adhered to the contours of her head. She was left-handed, and made notes on a clipboard encased in a slim, rectangular metal container.

The second paramedic was a stout blond man with a brush mustache and tawny skin from off-hours spent on the beach. As was required, even though he'd checked for a pulse, he'd placed an oxygen mask over the still man's unmoving mouth. Now he was guiding Spears toward the door on the collapsible gurney.

"Yes," Carson repeated. "We only knew Mr. Spears from seeing him around here." He flicked his long fingers at the ceiling, as if seeking to pull descriptions from the stratosphere. "Can't say I know anything about his family or where he lived. Sorry."

"That true for you gentlemen, too?" she asked, swiveling her head and upper body to address the others.

"Yep," Kelvon Little corroborated. "He's been coming here

'bout eight years, and this was the first time I knew he'd played in the Negro Leagues."

"He must live around here," Patterson concluded. "He always was on foot."

The woman had already closed her clipboard carrier and had retrieved her small plastic case of medical supplies.

"Take this if you need us for anything else." Monk handed her a business card. "Where will Spears's body be?"

She glanced at the card and was putting it in a pocket of her overalls when she looked at it again. She read it carefully as she talked. "California Hospital on Grand. At least for tonight. We'll try to contact a family member or relative, of course." The woman exited, climbed behind the wheel of the ambulance, and sped off.

Monk, crowding with the others in the doorway, made a note of the vehicle, a Med-Trans van. As one, the quartet went back into the shop.

"THEY AIN'T gonna be able to find any relatives, are they?" Carson twisted his bottom lip, fixing Monk with a snide glare.

"My mother's an RN, Abe. I know all about how wallets and keys disappear from hospital bedsides." He lifted the wallet to eye level. "And don't tell me you're not curious like I am about Spears." What had he meant about Malachi?

"Yeah, and it shouldn't be strangers goin' through his stuff anyway," Brant rationalized.

"I suppose," Carson amended. Little indicated for him to get back in the barber chair. The contractor did so. "So Monk, did the old man have a driver's license?" Brant wanted to know.

"We'll see." He had the thin wallet open and was going through its contents. There was $23 in cash, no ATM card, a Kaiser card, a two-jumbo-jacks-for-99¢ coupon, no credit cards, an NAACP lifetime membership card, some loose receipts, and no driver's license. "That's it," Monk announced, looking up. He was seated and Patterson and Brant stood near him.

"His social security number's on the Kaiser card," Brant stated. "I belong, too."

Monk read the number on the medical card. It began with 4-2-6, and the letter A came after the nine digits.

"That means," Brant said, poking the letter with his finger, "he worked for the railroad."

Patterson took the Kool out of his mouth and pointed with it. "You sure about that, Willie?"

Offended, Brant merely bugged his eyes at Patterson.

"And these first three numbers of his social security ID indicate Mississippi," Monk noted.

"Ain't you the Simon Templar," Patterson flattered him.

"His first name was Marshall, and his middle name was Adam," Brant announced, tapping the Kaiser card in Monk's hand.

"But what about where he lived?" Little snipped at the back of Carson's head with a pair of his long scissors, finishing the haircut.

"You would bring that up," Monk fretted. He went through the receipts. There was a recent one from the Ralph's Market not too far away on Fifty-Second and Main, one from Gadberry's Bar-B-Que on Broadway near Slauson—did he walk or did he ride?—a couple from liquor stores for chips and sodas, and a large rectangular NCR receipt from Lordain's Hardware folded in four.

"You know this place, don't you?" Monk stood close to Carson, extending the receipt.

"Sure. I trade there all the time." He was also standing,

and he began to brush loose hairs from his pant legs with his large hands.

"Then you two ought to get on your horses and find out where the old man lived." Brant also came over.

Carson shrugged a shoulder and Monk nodded. "I'll drive. Can I go in front of Johnny for my haircut?"

"Ain't you on a mission, man?" His cigarette tilted sideways as he grinned.

"Gotta look clean, baby."

Monk was allowed to bump the others, and soon he and Carson were in his cherry '64 Ford driving over to Lordain's Hardware. The business was on Main Street in the 6700 block. The building it was housed in also contained a furniture store and a chrome-plating service on the ground level. In its second story were the cursory ghetto apartments that were hot and sticky in the summer, and inadequately heated in the surprisingly cold Los Angeles winters. Yellowed curtains blew from weathered sashes and Monk could hear *norteña* music over an infant's cry coming from one of the windows.

"You should do the talking, Abe," Monk said as they entered Lordain's.

"Yep," he responded. "One of these fellas ought to know Spears."

The two were near a collection of rakes whose tines stood ready in industrial green and glossy black. Off to the side from the rakes was a row of shelving containing bins of nails, hooks, wood screws, carriage bolts and the like. Opposite that row was a stand-alone counter where a heavyset man in a striped shirt was measuring a piece of glass. On the owner's side of the counter, an older man sipped coffee noisily despite the heat.

"See, it's off by a quarter of an inch," the man in the striped shirt growled.

"That was made 'cordin' to the measurements you gave us, Blass."

"It's a quarter inch off."

The other man produced a small piece of paper from underneath the counter. "You tell me."

Blass picked up the paper and scrutinized it for too long, like he was working out his best excuse. "Well, you can see this here is a three, not an eight." Even he didn't sound like he believed what he was saying.

"That's an eight," the other man said, enjoying his coffee. He acknowledged Carson's presence. "Tell you what, Blass, I'll charge you half for that glass and you pay me cost for the other'n."

The lower part of Blass's face contorted and he leaned heavily on the counter. He looked as if he were going to get into it, then gave himself an out. He made a production of looking at his wristwatch and sighing. "All right, Price," he said, shifting his weight on tiny feet. "What can I do, I've got to get this pane in."

Price gave Carson a dry look and took the pane into the back. He returned momentarily. "It'll be out in a minute, brother Blass." He sipped and said over the rim of his cup, "What's on your plate for today, Abe?"

Carson put a hand on Monk's shoulder. "This is Ivan Monk, Price. He's that detective I've mentioned now and then."

"Pleasure," Monk said, returning the other man's assertive handshake.

"Same here."

"Without getting into a whole to-do, we're trying to find out where one of your customers lives." Carson was careful to use the present tense.

"He steal some drywall from you, Abe?" Price asked half seriously.

"Nothing like that," Carson replied. "His name is Spears, and he was in here"—Carson took out the receipt—"day before yesterday. He bought some Clear-All and a whisk broom."

"What does he look like, Abe? A lot of folks come here to buy the real stuff once they find out that advertised shit can't unclog nothing. Now how in the hell anyone expects people to get a drain backed up with that conk, wave, Jheri Juice, straightener, and what all men and women be putting on their hair with that weak-ass gel crap they sell them dupes, is beyond me. 'Course, if people just used some plain ol' Ivory Soap and a spot of Brill Cream, then they wouldn't be having such problems." He touched his fingers to the side of his receding hairline.

Monk was hoping Carson could get Price back on the subject.

"That might cut down on your business, Price," a new voice said. He was an older man, and he walked slowly through a doorway leading from an area where the sign EMPLOYEES ONLY was tacked overhead. He had on matching green khaki shirt and pants, and there was a white handkerchief protruding from one of his back pockets. He was above medium height, and his graying hair had a reddish hue at its roots.

"Least I got some people who come in here to buy something now and then, Dellums," Price responded.

"I bring in new customers, man." Dellums stopped at the counter and leaned against a fly-fishing decal. "How you gentlemen doing today? Now who you say you were looking for?"

"Why don't you go on back there and finish counting the bags of peat moss like I asked you?" Price folded bony arms.

"Thirty-seven, Price. I told you it was around that 'fore you had me count them 'cause I knew how much was unloaded last week. And I knew roughly how many bags had been sold since then."

"That's 'cause you ain't got no place to be 'cept here." Price picked at the space between his teeth with the edge of a matchbook cover.

"Mr. Dellums," Monk started, "we're trying to find out where Mr. Marshall Spears lived." He purposely used the past tense reference. "He was about this tall"—Monk leveled a hand two inches below the top of his own head—"dark complexion, had a scar on the right side of his nose. He wore suspenders, the button-on kind, not clip-ons. He—"

"I know who Spears is, mister," Dellums interjected. "He lives up the block from me on Stanford."

A middle-aged woman in a jean skirt entered, and Price moved from around the counter to assist her.

Dellums regarded Monk and Carson with a fixed interest. "I've seen you in here a time or two," he shook a finger at Carson. "How come y'all're looking for Marshall?"

Monk and Carson exchanged a feeble look and Carson spoke. "He just died, wasn't an hour ago it happened in the barber shop me and him go to."

Dellums lowered his head and shook it from side to side. "Son of a gun, son of a gun," he repeated, then blew his nose on his handkerchief

"We're sorry to tell you like this, Mr. Dellums," Monk offered quietly. "Do you know if he had any family? Anybody we should call to let them know what's happened?"

The older man took out a pair of horn-rimmed glasses from a breast pocket. He didn't put them on, but handled them like prayer beads as he spoke. "There's one family member, I think. But I don't know how to contact her. We weren't the best of friends, you understand, but I've known him for quite a while, I guess you could say."

"Did you know he played in the Negro Leagues?" Monk asked, aware he was digressing, yet eager to know something more about Spears.

"Oh yeah," Dellums beamed, "he was very proud of his scrapbook." The old man composed himself and put the glasses back in his pocket. "If you want, I can show you where he lived."

THE TRIO got to the duplex on Stanford in the 5300 block in less than ten minutes. Like a lot of Los Angeles' plaster-and-wood duplexes, it had a square front and was long down the sides. Running below the roof line was a wide arabesque of acanthus scrolls and swags. The building's only other nod to style were the doors, which were rounded on the top and recessed in the doorways. The small overgrown lawn was choked with alligator weeds and was bifurcated by a seg-mented walkway. A looming maple tree took up most of the space on the left area of grass, and there was a child's wagon upended on the right-hand side. A high shrub ran perpen-dicular to the duplex on one side, separating the place from a two-story house.

"He lived in that one," Dellums pointed at a black security screen on the right side of the common porch.

"Ain't there something about using a dead man's keys?" Carson mumbled.

"Don't make this harder than it needs to be, Abe," Monk chided. He got the security door open on his second try and then got them through the inner door. The room beyond was spacious, and light came in through the clean front windows. There was a couch underneath the windows, and two mismatched end tables in opposite corners. An ancient floor lamp in a third corner had a crooked shade perched on it at an angle. There was a coffee table with a scarred top in front of the couch. A copy of a recent *Ebony* lay open upon its surface.

Spears's apartment looked comfortable. It was a home waiting for its occupant to return. Monk knew the other two felt as uneasy as he did as they stood there, uncertain of what to do next.

"Let's close the door at least," Carson said. "Just our luck the cops will roll by and we'd have a hell of a thing to explain."

Dellums eased the door shut. "I been in here plenty of times, but it feels funny now."

"I'm sure," Monk said. "But we should try to find a number for a relative if we can."

An open archway let into a dining room with a built-in sideboard and drawers. To the left of the sideboard was a doorway presumably leading to the bathroom and back bedroom. On the sideboard were a stack of magazines. The dining room also contained a drop-leaf table in the center that had four chairs placed around it. Two of the chairs matched. In one of the walls of that room, there was another open archway.

Carson peered at a poster taped to the wall near him. "What's with this?"

"Yeah, he got that the other week," Dellums said.

The poster depicted an attractive Black woman with streaming bejeweled braids in a tight, short skirt, her legs wrapped around a giant can of a malt liquor. It was a brand sold exclusively east of La Brea, in the 'hood, the ghetto delight of eightballers and shot-callers.

"She's the relative I mentioned," Dellums illuminated. "That's why he put it up."

"You got a name for her?" Monk inquired, anxious to look around and get out.

"Well," Dellums mused, scratching at his chest. "I met her over here once, and he's mentioned her name a couple of three times and all."

Monk squinted at Carson as the old fella worked up to giving them a complete answer.

"See, he called her name, but it wasn't normal. It was like, oh, you know that tall black-haired woman who's Italian or something? She goes by one name like that singer, the one who plays in movies. Always dressing kinda loose, even though she must be over fifty by now."

Carson grinned and said, "I'm going to start looking around." He walked toward the sideboard, leaving Monk to play *Jeopardy!* with Dellums.

"You mean like Madonna or Cher?" Monk hazarded.

"Right," Dellums snapped his fingers. "This child got a name like that. Yeah, she's some kind of Hollywood model."

"Maybe we'll find a phone book," Monk said, touching the old man's arm as he moved past him.

In one of the drawers Monk found several paper bags folded over and kept shut with rubber bands. The bags each contained a wealth of receipts from the grocery store, drugstore, and so on. There didn't seem to be any particular order by dates, as the receipts went back past the last two decades.

Monk crouched down to a lower drawer under the yellow-and-white tile counter. A throb lanced his lower leg, and he winced, sinking to a knee. It had been more than nine months since he'd been shot in the Rancho Tajauta Housing Projects. A burst of high-velocity slugs had shattered part of his tibia and his leg had required reconstructive surgery. The case had started with the firebombing murder of several members of an immigrant family, and ended with him and Lt. Marasco Seguin of the LAPD fighting for their lives in an abandoned part of the projects.

He was in good condition for a man his age, and had healed satisfactorily. But, as the doctor indicated, the two areas on his torso from previous gun wounds years earlier, and a calcified lump behind his ear from one beating or another, there was a cumulative effect of violence to the body. Pro football and hockey players, boxers with their *dementia pugilistica* and street fighters after enough brawls, suffered such effects. There was only so much resiliency to the flesh, the doctor had warned Monk. The older you got, the more knocks you took, it added up. And there were the psychological ramifications, too.

Monk focused and got the drawer open and looked through its contents.

"Spears had more receipts in this drawer, too." Garson held up several more packets where he leaned over the sideboard. He turned and straightened. "Why in the hell did he keep all these? I keep mine for taxes, but I bunch them by year. And I sure don't have them going back all those years like he's got. And some are from out of state."

"What if he got audited once and swore it wouldn't happen to him again?" Monk was looking through more drawers in the kitchen, occasionally massaging his lower leg.

"Mr. Dellums, any idea on that?" Carson asked.

Dellums was standing in the doorway, his hands in his pockets, watching the two intrude in his friend's home. "Not a one, really. Marshall wasn't the most talkative of sorts."

"That's for damn sure," Monk said. "Did Mr. Spears work for the railroad?" he asked Dellums, stepping into the dining room.

"Yes, but me and him mostly talked about baseball, Doan's pills, and argued about what was the best way to change a sink trap." A rueful look crossed the old man's face, the significance of the loss of his companion coming on him in increments, deepening his melancholy.

"We'll find something," Monk said, trying for a reassuring tone.

Back in the kitchen, in a drawer underneath the counter he found some tools, a potholder and electrical tape. No phone book. He looked about and spotted a phone attached to the wall in the breakfast nook. Scribbled on the wall next to the phone were several telephone numbers. Monk got a piece of paper and recorded the numbers.

"Hey, anybody look in the closet?"

"Not yet," Carson replied to Dellums.

"I think that's where he kept one of his scrapbooks." The older man crossed to a closet along the northern wall of the dining room. He opened the door, revealing a compact cubicle.

Two suits and several white shirts hung on a wooden rod spanning the length of the small space. On a shelf above the clothes was a large cardboard box. A green BEKINS logo was stenciled on its side.

Dellums started moving the box off the shelf and Carson came over to help him. They got it out and the carpenter put it on the dining room table. Among the items in the box were two photo albums containing old newspaper clippings and original shots.

There was one sepia-toned picture with a ruffled edge that got their attention. In it stood a man in a Homestead Grays' uniform and cap, dark piping running down his half-sleeves, a bat cocked back waiting for the pitch, the muscles rigid on his exposed forearm. He had one of his feet slightly off the ground, as his body leaned back just so.

It was evident from the picture the stadium was small since large poplar trees could be seen behind the stands. The audience behind the ballplayer had their mouths closed, quiet with anticipation. They, like the batter, were Black.

"That's Marshall in '46," Dellums said, tapping the image.

Monk catalogued the blurry features in the photo and tried to reconcile them with the old man who used to hover near broadcast baseball games like he was waiting for winning lottery numbers to be announced.

"Goddamn if that ain't something," Carson admired.

"He played for the Birmingham Black Barons and the Cuban X Giants, too," Dellums recounted. "But he always said of the three teams he played for, he liked being on the Grays the best."

They leafed through the rest of the photo album, attempting to outguess each other as to which Black baseball player they were viewing.

"Sam Bankhead, player-manager until the Grays went bust in 1950, I think," Dellums recited, as they came upon a particular photo.

"That's Cool Papa Bell," Carson said with conviction, jabbing his finger on a brittle newspaper clip.

"I can read too, Abe," Monk chortled. There was another newspaper clipping about the Kansas City Monarchs and the piece included a photo of Bell, complete with identifying caption, showing some rookies how to steal a base.

The three remained hunched over the album until they got to the end. The trio had been lost in the faces, and the suggested stories, of men whose lives of triumph and sacrifice and disappointment were overwhelming.

Carson opened the second album.

"We better get back to work," Monk reminded the two.

"There'll be time to look through this stuff later."

"Okay," Carson replied reluctantly. He stacked the second album on the first and lovingly put the two in the center of the table.

"Look at this," Dellums said, pulling out a framed

photograph of more baseball players. The group was posed in the outfield of a large stadium. Their uniforms were crisp and each had a large five-pointed star over the left breasts of their long-sleeved shirts. The words TOWNE AVENUE were reversed out in the center of the stars.

"The Towne Avenue All-Stars at Wrigley Field," Dellums provided.

Marshall Spears was easily identifiable in a hound's-tooth suit, standing to one side of a group of younger men. The cut of the suit and flare of his hat set the era of the photograph as somewhere in the late '50s. Next to Spears was another Black man in a zigzag-patterned sport coat and open collar. On the opposite end of where the team either stood or crouched, were two more men in suits. One white, the other Black.

"Did he ever tell you who these other men in the suits were?" Monk pointed at the All-Stars photo while addressing Dellums.

At some point Dellums had put his glasses on and he shifted the heavy frame on his face as he answered. "The man standing next to Marshall was Harvey Lyle, a numbers man."

"Yeah?" Carson exclaimed.

"Oh certainly. Fellas who operated on the tougher side of life were quite prevalent in Negro sports. Who else had the cash?" Dellums pushed his glasses on the bridge of his nose with an index finger. "If I'm not mistaken, I seem to remember one of his girlfriends was conking his hair one time, and deliberately poured the chemicals into his eyes. Half-blind, he stumbled out into the middle of Hoover waving his switchblade, trying to kill her. She then ran him down in his own powder-blue-and-white Mercury Montclair. That girl didn't stop driving until she got back to Galveston."

"So he was the team's backer?" Monk asked, attempting to get Dellums back on track.

"Along with that man." Dellums pointed at the white man on the other end. "That's Ardmore Antony. He had a club on Towne Avenue called The Nile. I think it stopped operating sometime around '69 or '70. But in its day, that was one of the spots, I'll tell you. I was in there one night and Dorothy Dandridge came in. Now you got all them young things these days shaking their rump and what-not on them videos, but Dorothy was class, man. She was one beautiful woman, in here," he put a hand to his chest. "But what white movie boss was going to let a Black woman, who should have been as famous as Elizabeth Taylor or Jean Harlow, get the kind of roles she deserved?" He touched his frames again, holding his head at an angle.

Carson's eyes twinkled at Monk as the two listened to the old man go on about the actress whose life had imploded. Dandridge was a woman driven by talent and ambition, only to be stymied in her career by the racism at work in Hollywood's apothecaries of fantasy. Color, it seemed, was just too real for the studios to deal with.

Monk also removed from the box an award in a matte-black frame, a crack in the glass like an electric pulse running diagonally in one corner. "Look at this." He showed the award to Carson.

"*From the United Alliance of Churches for his steadfast dedication to civil rights and the betterment of mankind in Coahoma and Bolivar Counties. We humbly bestow on Marshall Adam Spears this award of recognition.*" *Mound Bayou, Mississippi, 1967. —Reverend Amzie R. Teasdale.*

Carson read the award again silently.

"He didn't go on about it all that much," Dellums began, "but Marshall did his share of strugglin' for colored folks where it mattered most, down south."

Monk asked, "Was he from Clarksdale?"

"Your mother's people are from there, aren't they?" Carson finished.

"Yeah."

"No, he wasn't born there," Dellums answered. "I believe he was originally from Chicago. But he got a job when he was just a teenager working on the railroad. Gandy-dancing, you fellas know what that is?"

"Laying tracks," Carson contributed.

"Uh-huh, putting down the line in a road gang. You got one who calls the time, the rhythm boss, so to speak. He calls and taps out the beat the men using the hammers and spikes do their work to. From them cities like Chicago and Detroit, all through there, the south, on past Ohio, Arizona, that was working, man."

"What'd you do for a living, Mr. Dellums?"

"I worked for Pacific Motor Trucking for thirty-six years." He took a seat at the table, resting one of his elbows on its Pledge-scented surface.

"They used to be out there off Mission Road, the trucking arm of the old Southern Pacific Company," Monk recalled.

"Back when SP was the biggest landowner in California," Dellums contributed. "I was a refrigeration mechanic on the yard. It wasn't building bridges, but what with the union wages, I bought my house"—he pointed toward the north wall—"and put two kids through college. That kind of work ain't around no more."

"Brother, you ain't never lied," Carson agreed. "Make a man want to holler it's so tough sometimes."

As the two talked, Monk pulled a thick file folder from the box. It was as if he were on an anthropological quest, and each item in the simple cardboard container revealed more and more of Marshall Spears's layered, rich history. Monk felt cheated that Spears had been so circumspect he'd never regaled the barber shop customers with what he'd gone through.

Conversely, Willie Brant could go on for hours about some insignificant aspect of his life, and too often embellish the tale as he did so. Yet here was an individual who had vibrant anecdotes and insights, but was content to let them dwell in his mind. Or more likely, spend a quiet evening with Dellums and maybe a couple of older gents talking away the hours.

Who was he to say? How one man chose to relive the past was no one's concern but his. In an age of twenty-five-year-old pop stars writing their autobiographies about how much money they've made because they're so gifted and how and where they've banged their groupies, there was an honorable genuineness to Marshall Spears's humility.

"What is this?" Carson spread his crooked fingers on several sheets of paper Monk had taken out of the file.

"Stuff on Damon Creel. His trial and"—he lifted several sheets—"and his political battles. I think he was convicted of murder that some say the crackers down there framed him for."

"Who was this guy?" Carson sat down.

"He was a well-known activist on the scene in the late sixties and early seventies." Monk paced and held onto the file, drawing up memory from the well. "He'd been in 'Nam, from out here, I think, originally."

"You mean L.A.?" Carson asked.

"Yeah, Compton or Long Beach." He placed the file on the table. "He was organizing down south. In fact"—Monk slapped the table for emphasis—"he was running for mayor in Memphis when the murder beef was slapped against him. I believe he was tried for killing two white girls."

Carson whistled. "In the south? Back then? I'm surprised he didn't get the gas chamber." Carson glanced at the article. "This says he was put away in 1974."

"I'm sure he ran for office sometime in '71 or '72," Monk said.

"And he's been in prison all this time?" Carson pulled out an article from the sheaf on the table stapled together on slick stock.

"Why did he have this, Mr. Dellums?" Monk asked, pointing at the stapled magazine article.

"Why don't you keep this stuff together so we can read it later?" Carson advised.

"Did Mr. Spears have something to do with Creel?" Monk gathered the materials and put the items back in the file folder.

"I don't know. The first I ever seen of that file or heard about this man is you two going on about him right now."

"So Mr. Spears didn't mention Creel?"

"Not that I recall. That don't mean he didn't, it just means you're dealing with an old man's recollection." He snorted through his nose.

"Maybe Spears worked with Creel," Carson ventured.

"It would seem so, Abe. But he's got items on Creel going back to when he first got out of the service and decided to organize in the south. Then the trial and all these recent articles on him, too."

"What exactly was the trial about?" Carson leaned back in his chair.

"I don't remember the details. I was still in high school when it originally went down."

"Thought you was born with a copy of *Das Kapital* in your left pocket and *The Soul of Black Folks* in your right one," Carson joked.

Ignoring the comment, Monk said, "Spears had a lot to tell us."

"Everybody's got stories," Dellums hinted.

"Yet he didn't mention Creel to you," Monk said to the older man.

"Everybody's got their secrets, too," Dellums observed.

"I'll give you that. Do you know what Kennesaw Riles looks like?"

Dellums cleared his throat. "He's in that picture you two was looking at. The one with the All-Stars." The retiree dug the photo out of the stack and pointed to a man standing toward the back of the players. He was above average height and his high cheekbones accentuated the almond shape of his eyes. His full mustache glistened with wax even in the black-and-white photo; his jaw tapered to a planed-off chin.

There wasn't much in the face to tag Riles as in the same lineage as his mother. If he'd passed him on the street, Monk wouldn't have given the man a second look. "I'm going to hold on to this for awhile, if you don't mind, Mr. Dellums."

"Why you askin' me?"

"Who else is there?" Carson said.

"That girl on the poster," Dellums mentioned.

"I'll take good care of it. I want to show it to someone—"

"Well, it ain't for me to say. But you two knew the man, helped him the best you could today. So I guess you're the responsible kind."

Carson winked at Monk. "He is, Mr. Dellums, he is."

Another hour of searching turned up more receipts, several trophies, and an extra pair of reading glasses. But no phone book. Monk figured he could always trace the woman through the beer company if that was his only lead. He'd returned the Damon Creel file folder to the Bekins box after first debating with Carson whether he should take it or not.

Carson had convinced him if he should find a relative, it was best not to have to explain why most of Spears's things weren't where it should be.

They walked Dellums to his house down the block, and Monk drove Carson back to the barber shop. Brant, as Carson had prophesied to Monk on the way over, had stuck around to see what they'd found.

"Damn," the former postman proclaimed. "And you two just left his things there?"

Monk resisted looking at the silly smile he knew to be on Carson's face. "What were we supposed to do, Willie, take all the man's possessions out of his pad like they belonged to us?"

"Who's going to take care of his valuable items, Monk? You can't replace those pictures, you know that. Ain't nobody there now."

"If I find this young woman, Willie, she might not see it that way. It's better the way we left it alone."

"I'm going to drive over to the hospital and see about Spears's body." Carson made for the door.

"I guess it might be up to us to get a funeral together for him." Little was incising a *Z* onto the side of a young man's head. The teenager's long feet stuck out over the footrest.

Only the sound of his clippers could be heard as each stood mute for several moments.

"Well, Monk could find this girl in time," Brant stammered.

The idea that he would have to lay out money for somebody other than himself was enough to motivate the talkative, and thrifty, ex-civil servant to scale city hall with fishing line if he thought Spears's relative could be found.

Monk said to Carson, "Why don't we talk on Monday afternoon? I doubt if I'll have anything on this young woman before then, seeing as how I can't call the beer company until Monday morning."

Brant looked anxious.

"Then one of you call me," Little put in. "I feel like I want to do something. He did die in my place, and I was used to him coming around."

The kid's eyes widened at Little's reflection in the mirror, but he said nothing.

Monk also made to leave. "I know what you mean, Kelvon." He tapped him lightly on the back.

HEADING BACK to his house in Silver Lake, Monk occasionally glanced at the aged photo of the Towne Avenue All-Stars lying face up beside him on the bench seat. He'd laid it upside down, and the man Dellums had told him was Riles seemed to be returning the look. His mute form betrayed neither family ties, nor what he knew of the life of Marshall Spears.

# CHAPTER 3

"Ivan, would you pass the macaroni and cheese?"

"Here you go, my dear." Monk handed the casserole dish to Judge Jill Kodama and continued to savor the piece of smothered steak he was chewing with enthusiasm.

"Have you tried to get hold of Kennesaw, Ivan?" his sister Odessa asked him. She sat next to her younger boyfriend, Frank Harris. Once again, as she'd done several times since they'd sat down to dinner, she'd cut a piece of his meat and fed him as if his arms were malfunctioning. Then they would both giggle.

Monk had stopped finding it cute the second time she'd done it. "Nope. I was hoping Mom might be able to help me in that department."

Frank Harris made a loud sucking sound as he maneuvered his tongue to retrieve a morsel of meat trapped between his gums and the inside of his mouth.

Nona Monk, nee Riles, concentrated on spearing several green beans onto her plate. She'd set the table with the Lenox china she and Josiah Monk had gotten for wedding presents more than forty years ago, the pattern of wheat in gold leaf around the edges of the plates still bright with promise, belying their age.

Languidly, she chewed on the vegetables while everyone waited for her reply. "I haven't made an effort to see Kennesaw in more than twenty years."

"But we met him a few times when we were kids, didn't we?" Odessa asked, rubbing her hand along Harris's forearm.

"Oh yes," her mother answered blandly. "Joe took you two to a few of the games of the All-Stars over at Wrigley Field. I believe Kennesaw was a coach then." She forked in a mouthful of macaroni.

Kodama got up from the dining room table. "Anybody want a beer or something?"

"I'll take one of those Weinhard darks if there's any left." Harris leaned back in his chair, stretching and expanding his well-built chest.

Kodama went through the swing door. Monk dabbled at the corner of his goatee with a napkin. "Did you ever meet Mr. Spears, Mom?"

She indicated negative with a shake of her head. "Not that I remember, Ivan. 'Course it was your dad who followed baseball, not me. But you'd think if that man who passed away yesterday had known your father, he would have mentioned it to you."

"Maybe he didn't remember," Harris contributed. "He probably met a lot of people in his baseball days. Your cousin and him might not have been real tight." He ate his remaining piece of steak, and crisscrossed the knife and fork on his plate.

Kodama returned with two beers. She placed one in front of him.

"Thanks," Harris said, taking her in as she sat back down.

Monk tabulated a few remarks, but settled for staying on subject. "Yet Spears also goes back down south after Kennesaw does."

Odessa cackled. "Ivan, since we were small you always wanted to fit things together when most times they had nothing to do with each other."

"Like the time you took apart your Tonka dumpster truck and tried to attach your rocket, oh what was that show you always watched on the Sheriff John program?"

"McCloud, *Scott McCloud the Space Angel*," his sister yelled, clapping her hands together once in triumph. "Ivan saved up his allowance all that summer and with some money from you and Dad, bought himself that ship that cartoon spaceman flew. What was that thing called?"

"The Starduster," Monk said proudly.

"That's nice, baby." Kodama puckered her lips at him across the table.

"So Ivan," his mother went on, "had the idea of hooking his rocket to the cab of the Tonka truck. He was going to make an all-purpose vehicle that could fly and when it landed, drive over the rocks of the moon. He cut a slot in the rocket, used glue and screws, I mean he really went all out." She smiled warmly at her son.

"Which only goes to show you how stubborn you can get," Odessa opined.

"Meticulous," Monk interpreted. "But nonetheless, how come you haven't mentioned much of Kennesaw all this time to us, Mom?"

Odessa was pouring Harris's beer for him in a short, stout glass. He rubbed her neck affectionately.

"What was there to say?" Nona Monk replied. "I was born in Clarksdale, but my folks came up here when I was eight. That was before the war. I didn't see Kennesaw again, except for two summer vacations, until I was a teenager. There was a funeral for one of my aunts, and I saw him then. 'Course, when Jackie broke the color barrier in '47, I remember my father getting a call from Kennesaw. We were living on Wadsworth, just west of Central. And you could hear whooping and hollering up and down the Avenue. You'd of thought Jesus had returned, and brought Moses with him. Men and women took part of that day off to celebrate Jack Roosevelt Robinson's victory. Our victory."

"Jackie played in Montreal the year before," Monk said.

"That's right. We all knew it was going to happen, it was just a matter as to when. April fifteenth, opening day the following year after he returned from Canada. That was the day. White fellas in the stands hollered 'Hey Snowflake,' and 'nigger go back to the cotton field.'" His mother set her jaw in a determined fashion. "It didn't matter. It was like when my father and his friends would huddle around the radio and listen to one of Joe Louis's fights."

"Or Ali predicting what round he was going to win." Monk clasped his hands together and leaned forward on the table.

His mother ran a finger over the gold leaf of her plate. "Some of the Black players had pools going, you know, would it be Satchel or Josh White ... but history and circumstance decided, and gave us Jackie Robinson." His mother's eyes glistened. "You can't imagine what it was like then. Jackie maybe wasn't the best, but he was damn good enough."

"Satchel Paige went to Cleveland the following year, I believe," Kodama added.

"That's right," Nona Monk concurred. "Anyway, around 1950 or so, I was fourteen ... yeah, and Kennesaw was still playing ball, though he was getting up there for an athlete. By then you had forty or so Black players in the white leagues. They paid the money and could attract the young up-and-coming talent."

"Killing the Negro National League," Monk lamented.

"The Negro American League kept going, but things had changed," Nona Monk remembered. "Kennesaw's time had passed, too. Then I don't see or hear from him again until back here in L.A., and he's coaching the Towne Avenue All-Stars in '60 or '61, I guess." She started to salt her beans, but stopped at a stern glare from her son. "Really, we weren't all that close. Like I said, it was your father who was a bigger fan of baseball than me. It was like with Tiger Woods now. People who never had a thought about golf in a hundred years starting to watch the game. Kids taking it up. That's what Jackie was then."

"So you didn't talk to him again after he went back down south?" Odessa rose, gathering her own and Harris's plates. He leisurely drank his Weinhard's.

"No." She sighed. "There was no reason to." Impatiently, she snapped, "Can we talk about something else?"

Monk looked at Kodama, who stared back. He put his attention elsewhere. "You got it real good there, Frank," Monk said between tight lips. "I've never seen Odessa pay that much attention to one of her beaus before, not even her ex-husband." He ignored the implication of Kodama's raised eyebrow.

"We do for each other, Ivan," Harris said evenly.

"Why are you so nosey?" Odessa challenged, having stopped at the kitchen door.

"Observant." Monk tapped the side of his eye socket.

Their mother and Kodama exchanged head nods and kept on eating. Odessa went into the kitchen, mumbling a reply she chose not to make too audible.

Monk got up and leaned over the table, slicing off a second helping of steak. "Anything for you, my love?" he asked, turning to Kodama.

"I'm fine." She smiled sweetly at him.

Monk sat and ate and contemplated.

"Excuse me a minute," Harris said, leaving the room and going through the kitchen door.

"You're hilarious," Kodama hissed at Monk.

His mother laughed softly into the napkin she held to her mouth.

Monk looked up at her quizzically, gnawing on his food like a bumpkin.

Kodama shook a finger at him like a school marm as the two returned from the kitchen. Odessa carried the pineapple upside down cake she'd baked and brought with her. Harris held a tray with coffee, cups and saucers.

"Let me clear a space for you there, Frank." Monk jumped up and bused plates out of the way.

Harris put the tray down, a bemused twist to his mouth.

"So, Mom, did you tell Ivan?" Odessa deposited the cake on its plate in the center of the table and began cutting slices.

Monk sopped up gravy with a piece of bread. "Yes . . . ?" he drawled.

"I want to get my finances in order so I can retire this year." Nona Monk poured herself a cup of coffee. "I'll be sixty-five, that's enough work for one person."

"That ain't the point, Mom." Monk poured coffee for him and Kodama. In his, he added a healthy amount of milk and a little sugar. "You got your good looks and the house is paid for. You got the union pension and those whopping social security checks George W. Bush and Arianna Huffington want you to have."

"Shut up," his sister teased him.

"But the reality is, what would you do? You've been working for a long time. And I know from Dexter, if you don't find something to keep you busy, you'll go nuts with boredom."

"You want me to do something," she put a hand on her still-slim hip. "Give me a couple of grandchildren, and I'll have plenty to do." She waved a hand at her daughter. "Coleman's pretty much grown, and at your lousy pace, he'll be having my great-grandchildren before you step up to the plate."

"How clever of you, Mom. Using a baseball metaphor to tie in with our previous conversation."

"Jill's right, you think you're too doggone smart." She reached over and playfully slapped him with the linen napkin.

"We're getting there," he said evasively.

"Your son's not kidding you," Kodama said, stirring her coffee for a long time. "We did talk about children last weekend." She lifted the cup, pausing halfway. "We even fooled around with some names."

Nona Monk was on her feet, gathering up what was left of the meat and the empty casserole dish. "Now we're talking." She drifted off.

Monk got up and went into the living room. He searched through the rack of CDs on a black tubular shelf from IKEA. He found what he wanted to hear, and inserted the disk in the CD player.

As Etta James sang "Rather Go Blind," he passed by a sitting Kodama. He leaned over and kissed her on the mouth. She grabbed his shirt front and kissed him on the cheek. "Nona," Kodama said, watching Monk take his seat again. "I've got a guy I use who helps me with my investments."

"I don't have your kind of money, Jill." Nona Monk devoured a piece of pineapple cake.

"No, no," she said. "He's not some Century Park East stockbroker. He's got an office not too far from Ivan's in Culver City. He works with middle-class folks to put something away and get better returns than a bank."

"You mentioned him to me before," the older woman admitted.

"And now's the time you should see him," Kodama said. She retrieved her purse from the sideboard, and dug in the stylish Gucci clutch bag. "Here," she wrote a number and name on a scrap of paper, and handed it to Monk's mother. "I'll tell him you're going to call."

"Sweetheart," his mother began to protest.

"Even with my Siberian camp wages, I've been able to save something with Mel's help." Monk wrestled with having another piece of cake. He silently voted yes, and pledged to himself to do extra sit-ups at the Tiger's Den, the gym owned and run by ex-middleweight Tiger Flowers on West Forty-Eighth Street.

"Listen to Jill, Mom. Mel's a good guy. He won't put you in anything that will send you to the poor house." He eagerly shoveled another piece of cake onto his cake plate.

"I can always live with one of you if I'm broke." She drained her cup.

Monk tried to catch Odessa's attention, but she was brushing crumbs off Harris's shirt. He let a small smile pull back one side of his goatee. He hoped his sister's boyfriend saw the action. "Maybe Coleman would rent you space in his room."

His mother slurped her coffee noisily, not amused by the idea.

LATER, IN the Ford on the way home, Monk complained to Kodama. "What in the living hell was all that about?"

Kodama, sitting close to him on the bench seat, fell over toward the passenger door laughing. "Shee-it, you're just mad 'cause I don't dote on you like that." She giggled some more.

Monk patted her thigh. "Listen here, Your Honor. I been

knowin' that girl all my life. I'm the one talked her into marrying Nelson Gardner when my mother said to hold off."

Kodama straightened up, slapping Monk in the shoulder with an open hand. "That proves you don't know what's good for your sister."

"If I could make my case without being interrupted," Monk implored. The Ford went past a tangle of vines crawling up two sides of a red brick house; he turned right, heading east on Third Street. A man in kilts and a space helmet did a dance in the glassed-in bus stop in front of the vine-covered wall. Kodama and Monk barely noticed him.

"The thing was, she was crazy for Nelson. He drove mail trucks, the eighteen-wheelers, from the old downtown annex to the airport. He was a man, you know what I'm saying."

Kodama tapped her sternum with her fist several times. "Kong, son of Kong."

"She couldn't go to bed at night 'less she knew his socks didn't have holes in them, and he had a good bowel movement. See? She was that concerned about his well-being. But I never once, not once, saw her fuss over Nelson the way I've seen her act around Harris." He came to a stop at Western. "You remember last month, when the four of us went to see Jimmy Smith at the House of Blues?" Monk rambled, jerking the car forward on the green light. "A couple of drinks in her, and every five minutes she was getting up to wipe pretzel crumbs off his mouth."

Kodama made a face, watching the cars pass alongside her window. "This is the first time she's been with a younger man. Maybe Odessa feels she has to do more to keep him."

"She ain't got an aluminum leg."

"She ain't no kid."

"Meaning you think it's all right for her to act like some lovesick debutante with that dude?"

A blue-and-silver garbage truck barreled south on Westmorland in front of the pair. The Ford was waiting in the left turn lane to turn north on the same street. Plastered on the side of the truck was a cartoon logo of a buck-toothed possum in top hat and tails. Beneath that image, the words SHINDAR L.P. could be discerned by the truck's running lights.

"You're not trying to talk me into doing that with you, are you, Ivan?"

The veins on the back of Monk's hands stood out like thick speaker wire as he gripped the steering wheel. "No."

She slid close to him, rubbing his inner thigh with her hand. "Sure about that, baby?"

They kissed quickly, and Monk took the Ford toward Beverly Boulevard. Once there, he swung east on Beverly and took that street until it branched off onto Silver Lake Boulevard. "I don't want to see my sister getting in so deep she can't see which way she's going. She hasn't exactly had a great record with men and relationships."

Kodama touched the back of Monk's neck. "I don't think Frank is using her. He seems to have genuine feelings for her."

"This from a modern woman."

"People express their love in all kind of ways, Ivan."

"Huh," he rumbled.

They rode along for a few minutes. Eventually Kodama broke the silence. "And what's up with your mom avoiding talking about your cousin?"

"Another goddamn mystery," Monk groused.

Soon he parked in the driveway to their Richard Neutra-style, split-level two-story house on a hill overlooking the Silver Lake Reservoir. At the door, Monk nuzzled Kodama from behind. "Love is something, isn't it?"

Inside, Monk began to unbutton his shirt, Kodama tugging on the tail. "What about kids, Mr. Monk?"

Monk continued removing his shirt. He then bobbed his head like a fighter warming up, or ducking an opponent. "How many you thinking about?"

"Two," she said adroitly. "I'm an only child, which was cool, but I think a kid should have a brother or sister. When the old folks are gone, they should have each other."

Monk scratched his exposed belly. "Assuming they still talk to each other when they're grown. I know some siblings who just as soon not make the effort."

"But we do agree on having children?" Kodama took a few steps up the stairs.

"Well, yeah, at some point."

"Some point is now, sport."

Monk also started up. "Like right now?"

"I'm pushing the time clock, baby. If children are to be in our lives, I've got to get crackin' pretty damn quick."

Monk leaned against the wall, next to a Noah Purifoy found-objects sculpture in a Plexiglas frame. "I kinda figured we'd plot this out, Jill."

She started walking upstairs again. "I'm not going to have to draw you diagrams, am I?"

"You know what I mean." He followed her.

"We've talked about it for several months. We both want children. If your mother retires, and what with my folks having extra time, it does seem like this is the best opportunity to get the show on the road."

"My dad used to say that." Monk caught up to her on the landing.

"Scared, huh?" Her gaze dissected him.

"I'd be lying if I said I wasn't," Monk admitted. "It's a serious move, Jill."

"We've talked about the angles, Ivan. For the last two years you've made the most money you've ever made in your business. You're doing more research, and are getting more referrals from lawyers."

"Get myself a couple of youngsters to do the leg work and an office a little closer to Santa Monica." Monk switched on the light in the bathroom.

"Is that so bad?" She knew about his "crash," his and Marasco Seguin's psychological after-shocks following the shootout the two were involved in at the Rancho Tajauta Housing Projects not too long ago. After the rush wore off, after the heady feeling of bullets whizzing by you and challenging death, and surviving, there's the inevitable toll on the psyche. The sudden anxiety attack walking to the 7-Eleven on the corner or the apprehension that dances with your nerves when you're taking out the trash. You can't predict when it will hit, just that it will.

Delayed stress, emotional come-down, or combat fatigue, as the head doctors called it in the old days; it was the mortal certainty the body's capabilities were finite. The concept wasn't new to Monk, but it took an incident like he and Seguin had gone through to reel in his ego, his feeling he could go forever. The cumulative effect of being hit, stabbed, shot at and kicked for twenty-something years exacted a heavy price on your mind and body.

"Maybe not so bad," he said. Six years ago he wouldn't have entertained the idea of being desk-bound.

She undid her skirt and Monk leaned against the bathroom's doorjamb, watching her undress. Slowly, she wiggled the skirt down over her hips, and then kicked it away as it fell to the ground. She took off her blouse, and unhooked her bra, letting it slip down from her body as she turned in profile.

Then Kodama, clad solely in black sheer panties, walked over to him and unbuckled his pants, pushing his boxers down below his hips. He stepped out of them, and she elevated herself, wrapping her legs around his torso. Monk put his hands under her firm backside, easing her down. Kodama took his penis, positioning him around the material of her underwear. He gently shoved her against the bathroom wall. She arched her back upon contact with the cool plaster. Monk entered her. Kodama latched her arms tight around his flexed shoulders, the muscles in her legs bunching as he worked himself in her.

As they made love, somewhere above the house on the hill, he heard a coyote howling. The creature's yelping matched the rhythm of their hearts.

# CHAPTER 4

The funeral for Marshall Adam Spears took place the following Saturday. Afterward, the wake was held at the Abyssinia Barber Shop and Shine Parlor. Food from Yank's Texas Bar-B-Que was laid out on two long tables set in the far end of the shop. The catering tins of beef hot links from San Antonio, fried turkey, greens with pebble-sized chunks of ham hock immersed in their mass, and other savory items of sialagogic value rested on pressed, brocaded linen. Juice, alcohol, ice and paper cups were laid out on a card table. Cold cans of beer were below the table in a metal washtub.

Little had KLON, the jazz and blues station, playing softly on his speakers. Several members of the Rakestraw Methodist Church were in attendance. Dellums had informed Pastor Breedlove, at the church, of Spears's passing, and he had been the one to do the eulogy. The story persisted about a daughter and an older sister, but neither the pastor, his congregation, nor Monk, had uncovered either as of yet.

Along with the church-going folk, the men who had been present at Spears's demise were also in attendance. Added to their number were some of the surviving teammates of the Towne Avenue All-Stars, along with members of their families. Monk had been able to contact a few through the community self-improvement organization—100 Black Men—and contacting the Negro Hall of Fame in Kansas City.

"This is nice," Willie Brant enthused while chewing on a slice of hot link.

"That's the first time I ever heard you give a compliment, Willie," Abe Carson said.

"Man can appreciate things, can't he?" Brant wandered off.

"I'm glad Spears had burial insurance." Kelvon Little munched on a plate of red beans and rice. "Paying for the spread between all of us wasn't so bad though. Even Willie kicked in something. But I hope this doesn't start a trend."

"Haircuts and send-offs," Monk remarked, taking in the people milling about. "Might get you new business, Kelvon."

"The octogenarian trade, and they don't tip so good," the barber lamented, shoveling down more chow.

Monk had spent extra effort in trying to locate Kennesaw Riles. Had wound up talking with another relative, on whose side of the family, and specific extraction, he wasn't sure. This one, who lived out in the desert community of Perris, thought he had an old number for the former ballplayer, and had promised to look for it. He hadn't called back, and Monk was so busy getting things in order, he'd forgotten to get back in touch.

"Gathered," Pastor Breedlove announced, wiping at his trim mustache with a paper napkin. He put his previously full paper plate on one of the barber chairs. The clergyman brushed at the front of his blue serge Zegna three-piece suit, the material beginning to tug across a stomach that had apparently grown since the suit was fitted.

"Gathered," he repeated. "I didn't know brother Spears as well as I would have liked. But he came to our church off and on for some three years past. He may not have been a steady visitor to the house of the Lord, but how one comes to Jesus is not for us to say."

Somebody said, "Amen," and Monk and Carson turned to see Brant shaking his head in the affirmative. They exchanged incredulous glances.

"We don't know when our number will be called, when we'll round home plate for the last time," Breedlove intoned. He pivoted about in semi-arcs and shifted on his feet as he talked. "We only know we must be prepared for the time our savior decides to bring us home." He was a good-sized man, and he used his hands as if he were scooping out mounds of earth.

"Marshall Spears had a long and good life. He went past his three score and seven, and, really, can any of us ask any more? He was a professional athlete, a fighter for our people's rights in the deep south, but first and foremost he was a worker."

A man in a vintage tan Vicuna sport coat and a ratty flat-brimmed cap sauntered into the shop. His pants were pressed corduroy, and his saddle-brown cap-toes were military shiny. He wore a pair of sturdy glasses and walked with the aid of a gnarled swagger stick with a gold orb for a top.

"The railroad, the playing field, the road to freedom and the rails on which the powerful locomotives carried many of our kin up north to a better life—these were the outward manifestations of Marshall Spears's life."

The newcomer plopped into one of the empty barber chairs, wincing as he got his left leg onto the foot rest. This man and one of the old-time ballplayers exchanged nods as the minister continued his impromptu sermon.

Breedlove folded his arms, palms flat against his wide chest, a pharaoh in repose. "We can only ask to do what we know is right by our fellows. We can only do what we can do to ease suffering and injustice in this most imperfect of worlds. If we can do that, if we can keep our Father close to our hearts, then surely only God can call us to account. As the last book in the Old Testament promises, 'Behold I will send my messenger, and he shall prepare the way before me.' We know the way has been prepared for brother Spears."

There was a round of "Amens." Breedlove was handed a small paper plate of the sliced beef links by a woman of ample hips in a hat of many angles. He kept his grin on her as he devoured his snack between his next plate of food.

"Man gets hungry working for the Lord," Carson said sarcastically.

"You should watch that, Abe," Brant cautioned.

"When you get so full of the Holy Ghost?" Monk asked.

"It ain't that," Brant shot back. "But when someone you know goes, that's a sign, man. A sign the higher power is marking all our time." Brant looked solemn, stuck his hands in his pockets and walked outside.

"Hey, Kennesaw, you looking pretty fit." Lamarr Cedras, who'd played on the All-Stars and the Cuban X Giants, greeted the newcomer.

"Goddamn, ain't that you, Lamarr?" the other man chuckled.

The two hugged and laughed boisterously, and walked over to the beverage table. Cedras poured invigorating doses from the Gentleman Jack for both of them. Monk let the two reminisce and stamp their feet for several minutes before he introduced himself.

"Kennesaw, I believe we're cousins," he said, after the two older men sat down.

The old man gazed into the face beaming down at his.

He had some more whiskey. Then he put the cup down on the black-and-white tiles Little had waxed that morning, all the time not taking his gaze off Monk. "You're Nona's boy You kinda got your mama's face, but you're sturdy-like, like I remember your daddy the mechanic was."

"Yes, sir." They shook hands. "My name's Ivan." The old man's hands were surprisingly smooth, the grip sure.

Kennesaw Riles got back up, listing slightly on his elegant walking stick. He put a hand on Monk's shoulder. "Did your mother come?"

Embarrassed, Monk ad-libbed, "She didn't really know Mr. Spears, and wasn't sure you'd be coming today."

Anticipation fled his face, and he removed his hand from Monk's shoulder. He looked down, his long fingers caressing the small gold orb topping his cane. Riles angled his head up again. "I ain't seen you since the time your father took you and your sister—what's her name again?"

"Odessa," Monk said.

Riles peered at Cedras. "This boy's mother was always something. Always had her own mind on things. His daddy wanted to call him Earl, but she wasn't having that." He sat down heavily, tilting his head back and exhaling softly.

"You know why she gave 'em those foreign-soundin' names, Ivan and Odessa?" He was looking at Cedras, but jerked his head at Monk.

"She's from Canada?" the old ballplayer asked blithely.

"Canada?" Riles chortled, tapping his cane on the floor as if invoking a familiar. "Negro, what's that got to do with—look, the reason she insisted on them names is kinda very fascinating." He had another helping of the Jack as he settled in to regale his former teammate.

Monk noticed another newcomer just entering the shop. She was a young African-American woman in a black maxi-length skirt combined with a top of some clinging material that swept up and around one of her muscular shoulders. There was a silver lame sash tied around her trim waist. She wore oversized dark glasses, and her hair was done in an elaborate combination of plaits and braids.

He was aware he was staring too hard at her, but not, he justified, simply because she was fine. It did seem like he'd seen her before.

"Hi," he said as she stood munching on a radish she'd plucked from the salad tin. "I gather you knew Marshall Spears?"

The face behind the big shades was impassive. Her jaw worked in efficient motions as she consumed her vegetable.

"I'm not trying to be funny," Monk reacted. "I didn't know him well, but he was a regular here like I am."

She swallowed. "Your name is Monk, isn't it?" Her voice was smoky, like aged bourbon on ice.

"Sikkuh," he shook an index finger at her. "I tracked down the photographer who shot the poster you were on."

She displayed her white teeth, slipping the glasses down on her nose. "I don't know what you thought when you saw me draped over a giant malt liquor can."

"I thought Mr. Spears had, well you know, good taste."

She scratched at a spot on her forehead. "He told me he was happy I was getting work. That sometimes you had a whole lot of ties to put down before the train could roll through."

Spears's life was revealing itself to him as if it were a series of boxes, one inside the other. And the various people who knew him far better than Monk and the men from the barbershop were the locksmiths undoing the containers. "How were you two related?"

"He was my great-uncle. The brother to my father's mother."

"Ah."

"I do some modeling and like every other chick in this town, I'm trying to get my big acting break, too. I know how trite that sounds."

"Some make it," Monk conceded.

"I've been at it for about five years now." She retrieved another radish. "After I got out of Spellman, my parents had a fit. Here I was with a degree in marketing, and I'd made up my mind to be the next Tyra Banks."

"Are you from Atlanta originally?"

"No, Philadelphia. Although my folks and Uncle Marsh came from Arkansas back in the day. Before they moved to Chicago."

"I'm sorry you had to hear about your great-uncle second-hand."

"Yes," she lamented, "but he had a long, full life." She brightened. "Anyway, the photographer described you accurately." She straddled the glasses on top of her head, cocking one of her expertly plucked brows.

"When was the last time you saw your great-uncle?"

Husky laughter turned the duo's heads toward Riles, Mr. Dellums, Cedras and two other old-timers who were now standing near the beverage table, the Jack and cans of beer held aloft.

"For Piper Davis, the best of the rest," one of the older men said.

"He should have been in the majors, not that damn farm team of the Red Sox," Riles commented.

"Yes," another one nodded. "And so should have Nate Moreland, Jackie's teammate at Pasadena City College."

"Yep," mumbled another. "He pitched ten years for the El Centro Imperials, and should have been doing it for the Dodgers, too."

The men all agreed and drank some more.

"About a month ago," Sikkuh responded. "I came by to see him and saw that he'd put up that poster. I did the job last year, and had forgotten about the gig." She looked off, then back at Monk. "He told me he'd spotted the poster in the liquor store he frequented, and convinced the owner to get another copy from his beer distributor." She put a hand to part of her face. An ornate silver ring was on her thumb and a simple gold one around her forefinger. "Gawd," she complained, peeking at Monk.

"Couldn't help but hear you were related to Mr. Spears."

Monk introduced the newcomer. "Sikkuh, this is Abe Carson, another man who knew your great-uncle from the barber shop."

"Pleased to meet you."

"Likewise," Carson said, exchanging a quick grin with Monk. It was the kind of look men get when in the presence of good-looking women—that feeling equally charged with sexual current and junior-high awkwardness. "We just recently learned he played baseball with Monk's cousin there." He tipped his plate of food in Riles's direction.

"Oh yes, many a night Uncle Marsh would go on with the menfolk about those times. Cool Papa Bell's running ability; Lou Dials's skill; he had a steamer trunk full of stories he liked to tell," Sikkuh said.

"You said Cool Papa, miss?" Kennesaw Riles inquired from across the room. "Don't you know he once stole home plate and was in the showers by the time the ball bounced off the second baseman's glove."

One of the men snorted, "He never got past me. I hugged third like she was Lena Home in a sarong."

"Billy Timms," one of the other men scolded, who was wearing a hearing aid, "you confusing my stats with yours again."

The old men kept their cajoling and reminiscing going, entertaining themselves and several others moving in and out of the barber shop. Though embellished upon, their firsthand accounts of life in Black baseball were like exploring a treasure cave with many alcoves.

"Listen, I have to get to a shoot out in the Valley." Sikkuh had finally relented to the call of hunger. She'd sated her appetite with two bites of potato salad and one drumstick she'd peeled the skin off of and placed in a crumpled napkin.

"Guess that was a feast for you," Monk observed.

"It's crazy, I know," she said. "Thin is not simply a physical state in the modeling world, it's a religion."

"You know your great-uncle's stuff is just sitting there in his duplex," Carson said. He bestowed another smirk on Monk.

That was because Monk still had Spears's keys and wallet sitting on his dresser.

"Oh Lord, I can't deal with that right now. On Monday, I've got to go out of town for a small part I've got in a Morgan Freeman film."

"Well," Monk ventured, "we do have a set of his house keys. Frankly, I wanted to turn them over to you." He didn't look at Carson. "And his wallet."

"Didn't seem right leaving his personal items on him, us not having a relative for Mr. Spears at the time," Carson elucidated.

She touched Carson's forearm. "Oh, no, I appreciate what y'all have done for Uncle Marsh. If you could get his stuff together and store it, I'd be really thankful." Sikkuh shifted her hips, glancing up into the tall man's face.

"Of course," he all but stammered.

"I should be back by next weekend. Then I can get in touch with you guys to get my uncle's things."

Carson produced a business card and handed it across. "That'll be no problem."

"Cool." She smiled at both of them and walked out the door. Both men watched her go.

"You're a magnanimous man," Monk said.

"Truly," Carson replied, watching the woman go. He ambled toward the entrance, too.

"So that fine young honey is Marshall's niece?" Kennesaw asked.

"Great-niece," Monk corrected.

Riles, Dellums and Cedras were sitting down, plates of food balanced on their laps or held shakily aloft by trembling hands. "Kind of a day for long-gone family," Riles said to Monk around a mouthful of greens. "I ain't seen your mother in more than, hell, I guess it's been more than twenty years."

"You moved back down south after the ball club folded."

"The club didn't end, exactly," Cedras said. "It was Wrigley Field that got closed."

"After O'Malley brought the Dodgers west," Dellums contributed, "and they did all that mess to build Dodger Stadium out there in Chavez Ravine. So Wrigley Field, and the teams that used to play there like the Pacific League and the Triple-A Angels, became a casualty of war in our part of town."

"'Course when Autry, the Singing Cowboy, bought 'em, the Angels became a pro club."

"Dodger opening day in '58 was in the Coliseum, the place they had to use until O'Malley built their park," Cedras recalled. "I believe they beat the Giants."

"O'Malley worked the swap of Wrigley to the city in exchange for the land out there in the ravine," another old-timer put in from a corner. "And the city let our stadium go to rot."

"And now O'Malley's done sold the Dodgers to that Murdoch, a foreigner."

That got a round of heads shaking side-to-side.

"Let's face it," Kennesaw added, "who was gonna pay to see the farm team when the big boys were in town? All the sharp colored boys who could were playing in pro teams, or trying to by then."

"Integration ain't never done us no good." Dellums set his plate down and wiped his mouth with a floral-patterned handkerchief.

"Central Avenue and its businesses, the Negro Leagues ... when we built up our own, we couldn't wait to tear it down so we could go chase after the white man's approval." Cedras also put down his plate, and took a drink from his cup.

"I hope you don't mean all white men." The speaker was a portly individual in a military-green three-piece suit with a maroon-and-white polka dot tie and pocket square, with brown-and-white Stacey Adams. He wore rimless glasses, and there was a beneficence to the grin encased in the all-white, neatly trimmed beard.

A chocolate-brown-hued woman heavy in the hips but thin in the face stood next to the man. She wore a dark gray, pleated skirt and same-colored tunic top. Perched atop her head was a black slouch hat with a bright red feather sticking out of the crown. Though the years had marched her along, she was still a handsome woman who didn't hide her age behind vain attempts at too much makeup.

An awkward silence descended as the three older Black men, and all the other Black folks in the shop, stared at the stranger. It was like a scene from an old west movie when the outsider comes into the bar and the piano playing and conversation stops. Who was the stranger, and what did he want?

"I'll be shot and goddamned," Cedras proclaimed. He got up and came over, Monk watching and waiting. The two men faced each other, then Cedras threw his arms around the man, hugging him. "You know I didn't mean the ones who'd crossed the tracks, man."

The white man had his arms around Cedras and roared. "And never looked back, baby."

Riles had also gotten up and was slapping the bearded man on the back. "Ardmore, man, how the hell are you?" He didn't wait for an answer and addressed the Black woman. "Good to see you, too, Clara." He kissed her on the cheek and she squeezed his shoulders.

"You too, Kennesaw." She regarded him with an emotion Monk couldn't identify. Suddenly, she seemed to become aware of the expression on her face, and recomposed it into a cheerful appearance. "I was sorry to hear about Dora passing."

"Yes, thank you," the old ballplayer said. "She was a terrific woman. I want you to meet this young man, here. He's a cousin of mine on my mother's side of the family." He extended an arm like a maître d'. "This is Ivan Monk."

"Ma'am." He shook her hand with its set of long, fresh-crimson nails.

She shook a finger at him. "I've heard of you. Or read about you, I should say. You're some kind of detective, aren't you?"

"Uh-huh, private."

His cousin and Dellums opened their mouths in mild shock. "Just like Jim Brown in them Slaughter movies?" Dellums exclaimed.

Monk grimaced. "Not really. It's much more ordinary than that. I can't be blasting at people in restaurants and airports like big Jim does in his flicks."

"You carry a rod?" Cedras asked.

"I have a permit, yes."

"I'll be goddamned twice today," the one-time catcher said. "Got us a hawkshaw and the one white man who's been better to me than some of my own." He clapped Monk on the back, and looked at the one they called Ardmore. "Come on, let me buy you fellas a drink." And he led the way to the Old Grand-Dad, the Gentleman Jack having been exhausted.

THREE BELTS of bourbon and numerous tales of days past later, Monk was leading his cousin and Mr. Dellums out of the Abyssinia Barber Shop and Shine Parlor.

"Both you fellas got nice wheels," Dellums exclaimed. He was walking with the careful exaggeration of a man who'd been bedridden for months, the use of his legs having suddenly returned. He put one foot assiduously in front of the other.

Monk ambled over to the 1958 Chevy Bel Air ragtop coupe parked a car down from his Ford. The classic was bronze-colored with silver-and-white trim, the leatherette seats the hue of dried oxblood. Ardmore and Clara Antony were exiting the shop too, heading toward the finely redone '50s Detroit iron.

The portly man had been the owner of the Nile, a jazz and supper club on Slauson near Towne Avenue back in the day. The Nile had opened in the waning days of club life along Central Avenue, the Stem, in the mid-'50s. Monk, had learned this from his cousin and the other ex-ballplayers conversations over the past few hours.

The Nile's line-up of talent had represented the next phase of jazz. The mid-'50s gave birth to the hard driving, bebop era as exemplified by the warriors of cool such as Miles Davis and Dizzy Gillespie, and L.A. natives Dexter

Gordon, Eric Dolphy, William "Budd" Collette and near-native Charles Mingus, born in Nogales, Arizona—but raised in Watts, California. Their tunes permeated the scene of clubs and records, and seeped under the skin of hipsters and squares. This jittery pulse was a reflection and a response to the oppressive Red Scare, and the stuffiness of Jim Anderson, the model patriarch of TV's *Father Knows Best*. But ol' Jim had one thing going for him: He was all reet in his snap-brim hat. And it was this insurance man's chapeau the jazz cats and beats would appropriate to wear on their wigged-out heads as they jammed or lolled in other night spots besides the Nile, like the Gas House in Venice or the original Parisian Room on La Brea and Washington.

The fifties was a time when you had to work to show you weren't a fan of Uncle Joe Stalin. One way to prove you weren't a pinko was to rat out a pal so you could keep your public teacher gig or get your name taken off The List. And it was in this environment that the wail of these jazz messengers could be heard, a signal that things were gonna change.

These cats were telling in their music, but few were listening, that they were part of a people that expected allegiance from the government and the people down south and up north, not to loyalty oaths worth their weight in toilet paper, but to a piece of paper with some real weight called the Constitution. That being a good American wasn't about denouncing your fellows to political poseurs like Tricky Dick Nixon and closet gay bully Roy Cohn, but upholding ideals like equality and fairness.

As these jazz players came of age in that time, it was no surprise that mid-to-late-'50s jazz would blow the stanzas of the freedom suite. Collette and Mingus would integrate their musicians' local in Hollywood. The music had an edge, and the Nile was one of the venues where one could come and commune with the masters who laid it all out in tumbling, preening notes and innovative musical annotations.

Monk halted his ruminations, paying attention to Ardmore Antony, who was talking to his cousin. Clara Antony had the passenger door open to the Chevy, starting to get in the seat.

"You and your cousin tight?" she asked Monk abruptly, stopping midway into the car.

"Fact is, I haven't seen or heard from him since I was a kid." She considered his words, then sat heavily in the Bel Air. Monk closed the door for her.

"But you know about him, right?" she asked, rolling down the window. She rested her head on the back of the seat. She removed her hat and fanned her face, which was warm from the booze.

Her tone told him she wasn't talking about baseball. He was about to inquire further when her husband and Kennesaw Riles wandered over.

"We got to talk, you know what I mean?" Riles slapped a large hand on the Bel Air's fender. He leaned in to the car on his cane as if a harsh wind had suddenly whipped down from the San Gabriels. "I want to tell my side." The older man was staring at Clara Antony, and she was making an effort not to return the look. "I need to," Riles pleaded.

The fat man stood on the driver's side of the car. "We'll talk, Kennesaw, really, we'll talk. Now don't forget, I gave you my card." He pointed at Riles's breast pocket. "I've got a concert coming up at the Olympic next month I want to give you tickets for, all right?" The round man squinted at something that wasn't sunlight. "I know where you've been, Kennesaw." Antony got in the car and ignited the fine-tuned engine.

"I think he said his office was in the Dunbar," Dellums mumbled, rubbing his head with both hands.

The Chevy melded into the light traffic on Broadway.

Kennesaw had Antony's card out, holding it far from his face. "Says the Somerville Two on it." He looked blankly at Monk.

"Those're new buildings the economic housing people built after taking over Dunbar," Monk illuminated. He unlocked the car for the men.

"Hey," Kelvon Little called from the doorway. "Why don't you gents take this, otherwise it will just go bad." The barber came over with one of the serving tins that he'd folded over to hold its contents inside.

Dellums took the food and got in the back behind Riles in the Ford. Monk waved goodbye to Little and drove away.

"Them 'Killin' Blues' is playin'." Riles was slumped in the seat, his right leg moving with nervous energy. "Marshall is gone and Charlie Patton is strummin' for me."

"What's all that about, Kennesaw?" Monk continued piloting the car south along Broadway.

"Testament and sacrifice."

"Whose sacrifice? Yours or Patton's?"

"The people who cared."

"What people?" Dellums chimed in.

Riles rubbed a hand over his whiskered jaw and began to sing softly, "*The leg done gone bone dry, the fields lie fallow like a virgin's heart, them cries are in the woods, I can hear my name an the steel.*" Kennesaw's voice was steeped in the sound of the Delta and its jukes.

"What is that, Kennesaw?" Monk asked. "That a song by Patton, that the 'Killin' Blues'?" Monk was booming his voice in an effort to cut through the man's melancholy and whiskey stupor.

The PI reached El Segundo, then turned east, heading toward the address his cousin had given him earlier. They were now in Willowbrook, an area of the city lying between Watts and the city of Compton. It was straight out of Compton where Iva Tagorl, better known as one of the Tokyo Roses during WWII, went to high school; and, more recently, the city was infamous for gangsta rap. Riles was moaning and at first it seemed as if he might be crying. But he was singing again, slurring and whispering the refrain. Minutes went by as Monk drove.

"What's he goin' on about?" Dellums barked from the rear seat.

"The 'Killin' Blues'; you ever hear of that, by Charlie Patton?" Monk reached San Pedro and made a right.

"No. You?"

"That's why I asked . . . no," Monk said exasperated, "I haven't, either. But I'm more of a jazz man than a blues collector, so I'm no expert."

He looked over at Riles. His cousin's mouth was agape and his eyes shut. "Kennesaw," he hollered, "why are the 'Killin' Blues' after you? Because of Marshall Spears?"

There was no answer as Monk continued driving. He got to 138th and made a left. He slowed and found the modest house his cousin said once belonged to an old girlfriend. The abode was one of a variety of California Craftsmen that were ubiquitous in older neighborhoods. This one had a peaked roof reminiscent of a Swiss chalet with a touch of Japanese influence exemplified in the ornate upswept eaves. There were white security bars on the windows and a matching heavy mesh screen door over the entrance. Water stains had oxidized to rusty brown on the metal door, making it look like a pelt left too long in the sun.

"This is it, right, Kennesaw?" Monk peered at the house.

"I think he's asleep," Dellums said.

Monk looked over. Riles was slumped against the door, his head pressed against the glass. He shook the older man's arm. Nothing. "Kennesaw."

The moan gurgled up from the other man like a desolate wind seeping through the reeds along the Mississippi's banks. Riles grabbed at his head, crushing his cap in his workman-like hands. He pulled the hat down across his face, sobbing as he did so. "I got to rest."

"You going to be all right?" Monk asked, concerned. He looked hard at Dellums.

"I can stay with him tonight," the other man said, reading the intent in Monk's face. "As long as he's got a TV in there and I can catch an old shoot-'em-up on it."

"I'd appreciate that, Mr. Dellums. I can come back for you in the morning."

"Good. Help me get him inside."

"I will make sure I pay my debt," Riles said as Monk supported his cousin to the door.

"Your riddles are startin' to bug me, cuz."

Kennesaw Riles settled bleary eyes on him. "You and your mama close, Ivan?"

"Yes," he confirmed proudly.

Awkwardly, the two ascended the steps, Dellums behind them.

Riles leaned against the door, digging his walking stick into the toe of his left shoe.

"Why don't we get inside," Dellums said to no one in particular. He came forward and placed a hand on Riles's shoulder. "Give me the keys, huh?"

Riles had his head down, watching the tip of his cane scuff the finish off his shoe. He had his cap in his other hand, kneading it in his fist. He dropped the cap and rummaged in his pocket. A crooked smile on his face made it appear lopsided. It took several moments to get his set of keys free.

The two got the drunk man inside and onto the couch.

He stretched out, holding onto his cane with both hands as if it were a talisman he needed to lead him out of the depths of the pit. Monk put his cousin's cap on an end table. Riles's eyelids were lowered, and he talked quietly to himself.

Dellums walked into the kitchen, and put the tray of food Little had given them in the refrigerator. He returned to the front room. There was a portable TV on a circular table in the corner of the small and cluttered living room. There were too many chairs, as if they'd been hoarded against a time when such items would no longer be manufactured. Dellums sat in a rocker with paisley padding near the TV. He turned it on.

"I'm going to leave my home number on this paper, Mr. Dellums," Monk said. "I'll be there the rest of the evening."

"Okay." The older man was clicking through the various channels, settling on a war picture on KCAL 9. He was quickly becoming lost in its progress.

"If you need me for anything, call at any time." Monk placed the paper underneath the hat on the end table. He crossed to the door. Nearby on the wall was a small frame, dingy glass partially obscuring the photo inside. He peered closer and could discern Kennesaw Riles, Central Avenue hip in a bulky sport coat and broad-brimmed hat in hand. He was wearing the same coat now. Riles had his foot on the front bumper of a '53 dark-colored Kaiser, four-door. Behind him Monk could make out part of a neon sign, off, on a building. It was the Nile. Worry and burden were far from the unlined smiling face in the picture. The club's façade had an Egyptian-moderne panache. A light-skinned woman showing big teeth stood next to him. There was a lot he had to catch up on with his cousin. He wouldn't make the same mistake he'd made with Spears.

"I'll see you tomorrow, about ten, Mr. Dellums."

The old man waved listlessly as a blazing Thompson raked a Quonset hut.

# CHAPTER 5

"That's workin' real good, chief."

"Certainly," Monk said, effort in his voice. "This stuff you got is all that." He stopped rubbing, studying the refurbished sheen of the leather he'd been buffing. A lustrous area had been revealed among the dull pallor of the booth's padded back. The patch was like an eye gazing out on the early morning environs of Continental Donuts.

Elrod, the six-foot-eight, 325-pound ex-burglar and current manager of the facility, picked up the pale green plastic bottle of leather cleaner. He poured an amount on his rag and went to work on the bench seat opposite. "Not that the regulars will notice." His powerful strokes cleared a swath across the booth's leather like a scraper across an icy windshield.

"You know our customers expect the best, even if they don't say it all the time." Monk smiled, soaked his rag, and continued rubbing. "How's that night class of yours going?"

"Cool. Being adept with tools gives me a confidence in working with refrigeration and compressor units," he replied laconically. The bench seat he was working on was nearly clean.

Monk remembered when he'd first hired Elrod. He'd been

warned against it by his mother and Dexter Grant, the ex-cop and former PI he'd gotten his license under. They told him it was good of him to want to help a man like Elrod, but Elrod's size and usual unreadable demeanor didn't instill serenity in the wary.

Monk never did decide why he'd been willing to take a chance on the big man, since he did share his mom's and Dexter's misgivings. But he'd already been through three managers, including one who turned out to believe that maple bars contained secret messages from the netherworld. What the hell was there to lose? And a brother from the 'hood, who wanted to turn his life around, seemed a good fit for a part-time capitalist with a small business on the edge of the Crenshaw District.

"See you been hitting more than just the text books," Monk commented.

"Been readin' Ralph Ellison's *Shadow and Act* like you suggested." Elrod poured some more solution on his rag and started on the next booth.

The bell over the door jingled and a square-shouldered Black man in a dark blue three-piece pin-striped suit with an open-collared shirt walked through the door. He had a Strike Anywhere Diamond kitchen match dangling from one corner of his mouth, a hint of a smile on his lips.

It took Monk a moment to recognize Roberts. He was a plainclothes homicide detective he'd met a few years ago on a case involving a buried body at Florence and Normandie.

Monk kept working but said, "What brings Hollywood Division over to see me, Sergeant?"

Roberts sat with his back to the counter, swiveling back and forth on a stool. "I'm over at Southwest now, Mr. Monk." He worked the wooden match from side to side. His knees would point left, the match would go right.

Monk raised an eyebrow but kept silent. The cop would get to it.

Roberts aimed a thumb at the just-brewed pot of coffee. "Mind if I pour myself some?"

Elrod started to speak, then looked at Monk, who inclined his head. "Knock yourself out," the manager said ruefully.

Roberts did so, tossing his chewed match in the wastebasket after he poured some coffee in a Styrofoam cup. He stood at the window, looking out at the haze lifting off the morning. "When was the last time you saw your cousin, Kennesaw Riles?" He turned, blowing at the steam rising from his cup.

So that was it. "Are you telling me he's been murdered?" Monk finally stopped cleaning.

"'Fraid so, Monk. He was found by a Mr. Dellums yesterday morning in his bathroom."

"Shit," Monk threw the rag on the booth's table. Somewhere a mooring had broken loose. He sat down heavily. "Burglary?" He sensed Elrod flinching.

"Yes and no," Roberts said, moving forward a few steps. "It looked like natural causes, an old man collapses in his robe and pajamas, draped over the bathtub." Roberts made a semicircular motion with the cup.

"The ME would be obliged to do an autopsy." A clinical detachment colored Monk's voice.

"It looked like a heart attack," Roberts said. "And that's what she confirmed after her first examination."

"So where did you come in?"

"The old man, Dellums, insisted there was one of those firesafe boxes under Riles's bed that was missing."

"But that could still have been a burglary and unintentional manslaughter," Monk countered. "Say some cat surprised Kennesaw, he keels over, and the dude takes off with the goods." Monk paused, then went on thinking aloud.

"And what the hell could have been in the box? Probably personal items some stupid neighborhood thief thought would be hundred dollar bills." The waste of both lives made him shake his head.

"Uh-huh, that ain't a bad scenario. I knocked it around myself in my head a few times." Roberts put his cup on the table in the booth where Monk sat.

Elrod went to work on another booth.

"Fact, I probably would have gone with that notion, except of course no forced entry, which could still mean somebody he knew."

"Or answering a knock," Elrod put in.

Roberts's lizard-lidded eyes briefly flashed wide. Normally, he usually seemed half-awake, as if missing or not comprehending events around him. But Monk knew from the past Roberts assessed and weighed every word and action, and their nuances. "But then there is the old man."

"Dellums," Monk supplied.

"He's wearin' my ear out about how Riles had been going on about his sins catching up to him. I guess y'all had been at a funeral last Saturday?"

"That's right," Monk said. "I dropped them off at Kennesaw's place afterward in Willowbrook. Mr. Dellums was kind enough to stay with him." Recalling his own fuzzy awakening Sunday, he added, "We'd all been sampling the joy juice at the wake."

"And you never saw your cousin after that?" Roberts had more coffee.

"I came by and got Mr. Dellums the next morning. Kennesaw was on the couch, but not in too good a shape. He said he wanted to talk with me about Mississippi, but later when he wasn't hungover. He went back to sleep, and Mr. Dellums and I left."

"This is Friday," Roberts said unnecessarily.

"I had to go out of town on Tuesday to finish up a chickenstealing matter in Flagstaff," Monk offered without further explanation. "I got back yesterday, and intended to call Kennesaw today or this weekend."

"His phone records indicate he called your office on Tuesday, and he talked for about three minutes." Roberts's hooded eyes disappeared in a ribbon of vapor as he held the cup to his lips.

"Yeah," Monk answered, fingering the cloth. "He talked with Delilah, who told him I would be in today. I have my hotel receipt, Mr. Roberts."

"I'm sure you do. But you ain't my suspect anyway."

Elrod kept buffing.

Roberts returned to the counter.

A customer entered and Monk filled his order for a bear claw and a large hot chocolate. He started to sit down, but the three pairs of baleful eyes drove him out the door. The PI sat next to the cop at the counter, placing his elbows on its just-polished surface. Behind them, Elrod moved silently and efficiently in his task of restoring the sheen to the leather.

"I had the medical examiner do a chemical analysis on your cousin, after talking with Mr. Dellums some more." Roberts had his notepad on the counter, open. His handwriting was compact, controlled, suggesting a linear personality. "There was an overabundance of a substance called Digoxin in his system. It's a prescription medication for a heart condition. Too much at any one time speeds up the heart , which could cause it to give out."

Monk realized where he was going and said, "Old folks get confused about their doses all the time."

"Yes, this is so," Roberts conceded. "When I visit my dad

I always go over with him what he needs to take and when. I make a little chart for him to help avoid mistakes."

"But you think otherwise with Kennesaw," Monk declared.

Elrod stopped rubbing.

"I found some empty gel capsules in a trash container two houses down. Good thing, too. We found 'em around five A.M. At six-thirty, the trash was picked up. Anyway, there were traces of Digoxin inside the capsules. No latents, though."

"Thorough investigation," Monk admitted. "A lot of cops would have stopped at just Kennesaw's garbage."

Roberts closed the notebook. "You wouldn't have." He sipped some coffee and swung toward Monk. "The glasses had been washed in the kitchen, but there was a fifth of Old Crow in Kennesaw's trash. I figure the killer chatted him up about the good old days, the two of them having a few drinks. He played in the Negro Leagues, I understand."

"Yeah. But are you saying he was killed for whatever he had in that fire box?"

"He was slipped that speedball for some reason."

Monk was trying to make sense of the data. "You said he was found in his bed clothes."

"ME estimates the stuff might have taken awhile to work its way to the pump. Depending on how diluted it was in the booze, how much, you know." He watched Monk, the veiled eyes missing nothing. "Your mother's a nurse, isn't she, Monk?"

"Kind of a reach there, ain't it, Sarge?"

"Dellums told me that last Saturday night Kennesaw was moaning and groaning and fretting something fierce with his drunk on. Talking about how he needed to make it plain before the 'Killin' Blues' came to claim him. About how he needed to explain things to your mother."

"You talk to her?" Monk asked. He wouldn't admit it to

Roberts, but he was curious as to what her reaction might be to her cousin's murder.

"Oh yes," the plainclothes cop said. "She was properly shocked, but 'fessed up she'd been finished with him for some time. She told me about his testifying against Damon Creel and what not." Roberts's eyes took on a dreamy quality. It was as if his mind were floating in several realms at once, assaying information of a physical and ephemeral nature.

"When's the last time Dellums saw Kennesaw?" Monk tried to sound professional, not indicate the surprise the last bit of information had been to him. It was logical that Roberts would assume he already knew his cousin was the reason Damon Creel was in prison. And that this was the family disgrace his mother had been unwilling to share with her family at dinner.

A tight smile pulled Roberts's face, automatic cop resistance. "Since you're gonna ask him anyway, I'll tell you. He saw him on Wednesday. He called him to see about the two of them getting together to watch a baseball game on Thursday."

"So he does drive," Monk confirmed.

"Daytime, not at night." Roberts got up, producing another kitchen match. He busied it between his substantial thumb and forefinger. "I've been going at this strong since I got the call. I'm gonna go home and hit the sack." He put the match in the side of his mouth, where it bobbed as he talked. "You might want to have a conversation with your mother, Monk."

"You can't believe what you're thinking," Monk said.

"I believe a lot of things, brother." He nodded at Elrod and strolled out.

MONK HELPED Elrod finish cleaning the booths. He needed to do something mundane while he tried to make sense of what had happened. That Saturday, Kennesaw had been going on about setting the record straight. He'd figured it was just the liquor making an old man contend with his regrets, a room full of should-have-beens-and-dones all of us have. Only his cousin maybe had one big regret: he'd sent a man to prison under possibly questionable circumstances. Had someone finally exacted a payback on his cousin for what he'd done? And if so, why now? Could it have been one of the old-timers at the shop, men who hadn't seen Kennesaw in decades? Without a doubt, he had to talk to his mother.

Later, he went back to his office file room rather than call her from the phone on the wall behind the donut case. As he'd hoped, the message machine was on. His mother's cheery voice was a sharp contrast to the concerns festering within him. He quietly replaced the receiver, and considered what time to call her at Cedars-Sinai.

He'd recently hung a print of John Biggers's "Harriet Tubman and Her Underground Railroad" in his research room. The courageous Tubman stood, arms outstretched bearing a flaming torch, leading runaway slaves to freedom. In the left quadrant of the illustration, there was a Black man, head hung low, brow deepened by years of burden and abuse. He was struggling mightily with a cotton sack, full of the fiber, its rope around his neck holding up the bag. He looked as if his labors would never end, as if fate had intended for him to forever travail in back-breaking endeavors.

Monk smiled sardonically at the idea.

KODAMA BENT down and picked up a copy of *LA Parent*. She smiled at Monk, folding the free tabloid in half the long way. The judge tucked it under her arm. Impulsively, Monk kissed her and they nuzzled faces and continued past the newsstand after leaving the Nuart movie theater.

"Did you realize *The Armored Car Robbery's* plot was about a heist at the old L.A. Wrigley Field?" Kodama asked.

"Yes. After all, he is the unrecognized king of the taut, terse, B-gangster epic."

"Especially when the movie featured yours and Dex's favorite actor, Charles McGraw." Kodama said, in a passing imitation of the tough-guy-actor's gravel voice.

They went to a coffeehouse around the corner from the theater. They ordered a regular and a café au lait. Sitting outside in the warm evening, Kodama thumbed through the *LA Parent* magazine.

"Is that supposed to be a subtle hint, dear? Looking for tips on how to balance career and kids?" Monk asked, noting Kodama was reading an article with interest in the magazine.

"It's about women my age and what happens once they decide to have children." She didn't look up. Her café au lait rested near her hand, untouched.

"Just what is your age?" Monk inquired seriously.

"You know us Asians, like some Black folk, never show, honey." She kept reading the article. "And I suppose I'm to believe you've never sneaked a peek at my driver's license when I've been asleep?"

Monk made a tsk-tsk sound. "How could you think that about me?"

She raised an eyebrow, and finally had some of her coffee. "Anyway, older women turn you on."

Monk drank and started to unwrap a petite cigar as quietly as possible.

"Don't even," Kodama warned.

"You're not pregnant right now, are you?" Monk asked, the cellophane wrapper shaking in his unsteady hand.

"No, darling, but one must lead by example." She closed the magazine.

"Parenting advice from Chairman Mao." Monk replaced the wrapper, and put the cigar back in the pocket of his jean jacket.

"Hey, did you talk to your mother yet?"

"I called over to the hospital once, but her station said she was busy."

"You sound glad about that."

"Do I?"

She slapped his hand. "Your mother ain't a killer."

"She didn't like him. She didn't want to talk about him."

"There seems to be good reason, Ivan. Anyway, that's not exactly a motive, Nick Charles." Monk grunted. "For your own peace of mind, let's find out," she said.

"YES, YOUR buddy Roberts talked to me yesterday, Thursday." Nona Monk took off her reading glasses, placing them on the chart she'd been making notes on. She pinched the bridge of her nose. A soda machine hummed in a corner, providing a background cadence in the nurse's lounge.

"Mom, you're a natural suspect. You have means, and from what Roberts has told me, motive." Monk sat across from her at the round table, Kodama, her arms folded, to his left.

"I didn't call you because I didn't know how I wanted to get into this business of what Kennesaw did," his mother started. The door opened and a man in scrubs entered. He took off his plastic hair net, nodding at Monk's mother. The male nurse got a container out of the refrigerator, and sat at one of the other tables.

"Kennesaw was a boot-licking, Mr.-Charley-lovin' Uncle Tom, plain and simple," Nona Monk explained. "It was his testimony that put Damon Creel in prison for more than a quarter of a century now."

"And he was lying?" Monk asked.

"Yes, he was lying," his mother said flatly.

The man in the corner looked up from his salad and the *Newsweek* he was paging through.

"Why'd he do it?" Kodama asked.

"Why does anybody sell out, Jill?" Monk's mother shot back. "Years ago Senator Hiyakawa stated that internment was good for the Japanese; Ward Connerly gleefully working to break up affirmative action programs nationwide; finks in the civil rights movement; other so-called Black organizations being used willingly by the FBI to move against their own. Get a little jive power from The Man, I guess." She shrugged, looking at Kodama unblinkingly.

"Was Kennesaw an informant for the Bureau?" Monk's own opinion of the organization, given his actual experience with its agents, was not high. And the history of the FBI under J. Edgar Hoover's COINTELPRO, an all-out effort to destroy the civil rights movement and the Black Panther Party, didn't win them many fans in several quarters of the African-American community.

His mother yawned, holding the back of her hand to her mouth. "Excuse me. No, your cousin had his hat in the Southern Citizens League."

"The buttoned-down Klan," Kodama said.

Nona Monk stretched. "You know how they got their start?" She gave both of them an inquisitive look. "The Mississippi and Alabama Southern Citizens Leagues were started because of Little Richard and Chuck Berry."

"Race music," Monk said.

"Sweet little white high school girls getting all worked up

over these velvet-voiced, pompadour-wearing, hip-shaking, long lean Black men hollering their hoodoo songs."

"Chuck wasn't wild like Little Richard," Kodama pointed out. "He made rock and roll ballads like 'Roll Over, Beethoven' and 'Johnny B. Goode.'"

"And 'My Ding-A-Ling,'" Monk laughed. "But I guess they all can't be prize winners."

Nona Monk said, "That's true, Jill, but the white teenagers lined up to see him like they did Little Richard, Frankie Lyman, all of them. You can imagine the fallout up north, let alone the absolute stark panic it must have caused in the deep south. 'Nigger bop music' they called it, jungle rhythms enticing their womenfolk to do God knows what devilment." His mother yawned again. "They would have these huge bonfires where hundreds of forty-fives by Black singers and musicians would be thrown in. You'd have sheriff's deputies and assorted crackers standing at the edge of town with shotguns to keep out touring R&B acts."

"And from this the Southern Citizens League grew?" Monk asked.

"Oh yes," his mother said vigorously. "The men who organized their own associations in various states were the downtown business interests and the big landowners. Many of these men were college-educated, had been to the war and so forth. They understood that some kind of change was going to come. And that the Klan had its uses, but used like a scalpel, not a hammer. In the long run, it was better to cultivate good, friendly Negroes willing to work at a snail's pace rather than create a bunch of martyrs with dynamite and rope."

"So what did Kennesaw get out of this arrangement?" Monk leaned forward on his elbows.

"He didn't get any of his white pals to sign with his wife's insurance company," his mother said defiantly, as if her cousin were listening in. "What he got, or rather what he hoped to get by being a turncoat was some under-the-table money and a pat on the head for being a reliable nigra." The venom in her voice cut through the room. The man in the corner pretended he hadn't heard.

"Just for money? Come on, Mom, how much were they paying him?"

"Honey, I don't know and I don't much care."

"He was murdered, Nona," Kodama reminded her.

Unconsciously, Ivan gauged his mother's body language.

"Now I already told you about sizing me up, Ivan." She wagged a short-nailed finger at him. "Ain't a whole lot of us in the family had much to do with Kennesaw after that damned trial. How he'd go around saying he'd done it so as to make things better in the long run. That somebody like Creel was just gonna bring down the wrath of the almighty white man and something had to be done. Shit," his mother snorted, "I guess the poor fool actually started to believe his own bullshit after a while."

"Do you know if he and Dora had any children?"

"I've made some calls, Ivan, and can't get one straight answer. AC down in Corpus Christi swears she knew the child. And Louise in Yellow Springs claims Dora fooled around on Kennesaw as much as he boasted he did on her. And that if she had any child it was mama's baby and papa's maybe."

"The errant offspring returns to slay the father?" Kodama glared at the other two.

"It has happened before." Nona Monk got up, placing her wire-frame glasses back on. "Listen, Ivan, I realize it's serious that apparently somebody overdosed Kennesaw. Who's to say one of those old-timers at the barber shop on Saturday didn't do it? Maybe one of them had an old grudge to settle for some other reason."

"I can't see one of them being that subtle."

"So you're telling me not to leave town, McGarrett?" She laughed hollowly.

"Roberts has an interest in this, Mom. And he ain't slow."

"Well, I am, baby." She patted his cheek, and picked up her forms. "He can catch me 'cause I ain't running." She walked on dead feet to the door. "I've got to get the schedules posted for the weekend. Bye, Jill." She waved and exited.

"Sweatin' your own mother," Kodama admonished mockingly.

The man in the corner grimaced at Monk with disdain.

# CHAPTER 6

"Where you going?"

Monk, in his boxers, had one knee on the bed and his other leg trailing. He leaned over and kissed Kodama's shoulder. "I want to check on something at Spears's house."

"Can't it wait?" She slid across the sheet and took a playful bite on his leg.

"It's been on my mind all night." He moved out of the bed, grabbing his 501s off the floor. "I won't be long."

"Hey, if I get inspired, I might even make breakfast." Kodama wafted a lazy hand onto the nearby radio, and clicked it on. Scott Simon's voice, of National Public Radio's *Weekend Edition*, filled the room.

"Interesting." The preparation of food was not an attribute the judge would go down in history about.

"All right," she warned, hearing the hesitation in his voice.

"Yes, dear." He patted her butt and walked out of the bedroom.

He took the Ford over to Apex, then down to Glendale Boulevard. Monk was proud of himself that after months of living with Kodama in Silver Lake, he'd finally mapped, after much experimental trailblazing, the various byways and their permutations in his head. He'd learned the streets and terraces that dead-ended, those that became another street on the other side of the hill, and those that one could take to and back from his pad to avoid the jam-up Silver Lake Boulevard invariably became during rush hour.

He got to Spears's house on Stanford in less than half an hour, the Hollywood and Harbor freeways postcard-perfect in their light traffic. It was only early hours like this on a Saturday or Sunday where one could effortlessly navigate the massive moving infrastructure of cars and trucks on L.A. freeways.

The freeways were a conduit to the myriad neighborhoods jig-sawing the greater Los Angeles area. There were eighty-eight incorporated cities in the county, and hundreds more enclaves distinct from one another in character and karma. Silver Lake, with its funky tchotchke shops and markets whose isles brimmed with fresh tabouli and feta cheese, seemed remote from South Central's *camecerias* selling carne asada. But such food items were symbolic of the cultural diversity, and separation, of the town.

As he'd suspected, Spears's duplex had been broken into. A rear window on the side of the house, next to the high shrub, had had its bars pried out of the wood. The window's sash, apparently unlocked, had been lifted and the killer had gained entry. The bars had been bent back into position, so as not to make it so obvious to a casual observer.

Monk used his keys and entered. The rooms were in order: No drawers had been dumped and left upended, nor was there overturned chairs or ripped-up upholstery. But the place had been searched. The killer was an efficient, tidy bastard, he reflected.

Fortunately, when he'd picked up Mr. Dellums last Sunday and dropped him off, he had stopped here and taken the

Bekins box of photo albums and clippings—including Spears's file on Damon Creel—from the closet. It was his way of keeping the items safe, seemingly the only thing of sentimental value in the duplex. Knowing he had to leave town to finish up a case—and Sikkuh said she would be going away, too—Monk had wanted to make sure he didn't leave the stuff in the empty apartment.

He let himself out and debated knocking on the door of the two-story house on the other side of the shrub. It wasn't yet eight-thirty. No, he reasoned, he'd come back and complete that task later and then call Roberts. Driving back home, he wondered if Dellums had mentioned the box to Roberts. If so, he'd better say something. Not that Roberts could make much of a claim on the contents as material evidence. The cop might even rationalize the break-in as unconnected, but he doubted the burly detective would. He sure didn't.

KODAMA MADE a breakfast of scrambled eggs, salsa, cinnamon-raisin English muffins and *marguez* sausages. Monk topped it off with coffee and two large glasses of orange juice, his appetite increasing as the case took on added dimensions for him.

Afterward, they lounged around the house, reading and skimming various articles in the *LA Weekly*, the *Sentinel* and the *L.A.* and *New York Times*. A little after eleven, they took a shower together. They made love on the unmade bed, their slick bodies dampening the peach-colored sheets.

Still later, Monk went back to Stanford to talk with whoever he could find at the house next door to Spears's place.

"No, no," the middle-aged Latina said, standing on the porch. Monk had interrupted her sweeping the steps. "I only saw you come by last Sunday and use the keys you had, Mr. Monk. Sundays is when I sit in the front room and have my tea."

"Nothing else, huh, Mrs. Robalos?" He stood on the walkway, the sun shining through the big maple on Spears's yard promised another sweaty day.

"No, I'm sorry." She made an expert twist with her wrist and deftly piled her grit on the top step right at its edge. "See, I cook and clean in a couple of houses up in Brentwood. Sometimes I don't get home until eight at night."

Monk got the dust pan and placed it in position for her. "Thanks." She swept her dirt into the pan. "Now maybe my son or daughter heard something, but neither one of them is here now. They're teenagers, you know." The statement covered a plethora of unfathomable behaviors.

"If you could ask them, I'd appreciate it, Mrs. Robalos." He thought it best he not insist he do the questioning. She was a woman of responsibility, and would interpret such a move by him as crowding her territory. The house was her sanctuary against the petty caprice he imagined she regularly put up with dealing with westside folks' demands.

"Sure," she smiled. She put his card in the pocket of her housedress. He Left as she used the hose to water down the just-swept porch.

Not finding Dellums at home, he swung by Lordain's Hardware. There he found the old gent engaged in a discussion of Kennesaw Riles's recent departure from this oh-so-imperfect world.

"This here is his cousin," Dellums introduced him to the man he'd been talking to. "He's a sure nuff private eye just like on TV."

The man he'd addressed, a lanky sort with an unkempt salt-and-pepper beard, looked at Monk dubiously.

"Got a minute, Mr. Dellums?" Monk touched the retired refrigeration mechanic on the elbow.

"Sure. Did that cop come by to see you?"

"Yes, he did."

"Yeah, that Roberts said he knew you." Dellums wandered over to a spot by some buckets of plaster set against a wall. "So you looking into who killed your cousin?"

"Exactly. Did you see him at all this past week? Before you found him, I mean."

"I talked to him real quick-like on Wednesday over the phone, just like I told your friend Detective Roberts."

"How was he then? Was he still going on about something bein' after him and whatnot?"

Dellums rubbed a callused hand across his deeply lined brow. He tilted his head in close to Monk's. "I know it sounds like a bunch of spirit-talk my granny used to spout, but there's something to it, I tell you for sure, Ivan. My granny used to see the ghost of the slave owner who owned her folks come around the house on holidays. She got me to spread blood and urine on them steps now and then to ward off the evil voodoo."

Dellums stared at Monk expectantly.

"You ain't saying that's what got Kennesaw, are you, Mr. Dellums? He was purposely given more than his normal dose of his heart medicine. And you're the one who pointed out his fire box was missing."

"Uh-huh, I'm aware of that. I'm just saying there are more things to what he was going on about than sometimes we can make out on this earth."

"I can't hunt ghosts, Mr. Dellums. It's the wrong we do to each other keeps my hands full."

"Only the wicked, huh?"

Monk liked the old man and clasped him on the shoulder, smiling.

"He sounded like he wanted to get things settled, you know?" Dellums hooked his thumbs beneath his suspenders. "He said he was waiting for you to get back into town so he could talk with you."

A stab of disappointment went through Monk.

"That Saturday when you dropped us off, he was talking about his testifying in that trial down south. About why he'd done it not for himself but for the good of the Negro community. It wasn't the liquor talking. I feel it was what was in his soul. What he was hearing was Charlie Patton's wail haunting him." Dellums paused, assessing his own words. "I ain't saying what he did, or at least what they say he did, was right. But in the short time I knew him, I can say he wasn't without some hurts of his own."

"Maybe they were of his own making," Monk ventured.

Dellums slid his thumbs up and down behind the suspenders, his eyes focused far away.

"When you went over there on Thursday, was that for a specific reason?"

Dellums refocused. "Nothing, really. We were gonna watch the Angels on TV together." The thumbs worked the leather straps of his suspenders again. "He did say he'd been talking things out." Dellums sucked in a cheek. "I'm not always on top of stuff like this, but it seemed to me he was a lonely man, Ivan. I know he wanted to patch things up with your mother."

"When he said talking things out, did he mean with you?"

Dellums stuck his hands in his pockets. "No, not me. He kinda laughed when he said it though, like it was a joke only to himself. I figured if he wanted to talk we'd do it over a couple of Budweisers and the baseball game." Dellums grinned, showing whitened dentures. "Maybe he meant he'd been conversin' with Patton's spook."

"Could be," Monk said. "You see anything that morning you found him? Something that you may not have thought about before, but now with what you know strikes you as odd?"

Dellums jingled change in his pants. "Like I told Roberts, I got there, and the screen door was shut, but not locked. The front door was shut, but I got the man who lives in the apartment next to Kennesaw to help me jimmy the door open with a screwdriver. We went inside and found him there in the bathroom. I remember thinking it was funny to me that all the plates and glasses were clean in the kitchen."

"Like he hadn't done them," Monk remarked. The Saturday before, he'd noticed a pile of unwashed plates in the sink.

"The place looked neater, too," Dellums offered. "But we got busy with calling the paramedics. It's just now as you ask me that I recollect back on it."

"Like somebody had cleaned up for him?" Monk wondered. "Could be he had somebody come in now and then. Or he cleaned up once a month."

Dellums nodded his head up and down.

"But you immediately looked under the bed."

"Something about how he was . . ." Dellums made a futile gesture, unable or unwilling to articulate the rest. He pulled in his bottom lip, biting it gently with his upper teeth. He pointed a finger at Monk and was about to speak when the man he'd been talking with came over.

"You gonna jaw all day with Magnum there, or we gonna play us some dominoes?" He scratched at his tumbleweed of a beard, shifting from foot to foot.

"Okay, okay." Dellums started to move off. "I'll talk to you later, Ivan."

"Sure, thanks, Mr. Dellums."

Monk left and called the photo agency from his donut shop. It was the only number he had to try to reach Sikkuh, Spears's great-niece. He got a machine. He wanted to tell her about the murder and break-in, and discuss what to do with her Uncle Marsh's artifacts. He called Abe Carson, but he was out, too. He took the file out of the box, and this time, carefully read the clippings Spears had gathered about the Creel case, in particular, the portions that talked about how Kennesaw Riles testified that Damon Creel had come to him, giving him the knife he'd killed Ava Green and Sharon Aikens with in a motel room in Memphis. A knife that he claimed he'd thrown off the docks into the Mississippi River outside Dixonville, Mississippi. Creel, it was pointed out, had been having an affair with Ava Green.

The testimony and miscegenation was enough for an all white jury to assure conviction. Creel was convicted of second-degree murder of the two girls from Brandeis. The two young women had come down south to help in Creel's campaign for mayor. Their summer of justice became their season of death. The piece went on to mention that though it was never proven, the talk was that Riles had been pressured, some said, by the Southern Citizens League to testify. None of the clippings contained any direct quotes from his cousin.

There was also an interview with Bernie Descanso, a criminal defense attorney known for taking cases challenging law enforcement misconduct. He was in L.A., and for the last ten years had been heading the attempts to get Creel a new trial. Monk knew the man slightly.

Another article mentioned Malachi, but not the book of the Bible. It seemed to be a legend in the Delta, dating back several decades. Malachi was the swift and unseen hand of white justice that would come out of nowhere to smite down the colored boy who was uppity or would dare lay his hands on white womanhood.

Monk finished reading through the file and closed up. He drove home, thinking about the past and how his cousin's had finally caught up to him. And how his ballplayer's legs must have been too far gone for him to cut and run, dodging responsibility as he'd done for the years since he'd testified.

# CHAPTER 7

"Mr. Dellums, I'm surprised to see you here," Monk said to him as he sat in the rotunda after entering the area via the stairwell. The older man sat on a lone tube chair, drop cloths and plastic tarps at his feet. The rotunda was part of a suite of offices Monk shared with an architectural and rehab firm called Ross and Hendricks, two women partners.

The duo had convinced him to go for a re-designing of the place, and there were now sections of wall and tile stacked about. Delilah Carnes, the admin assistant he also shared with the two, had her work space moved into what had been the copier and storeroom down the hall. At the moment, she was standing in the doorway to the room, leaning against the jamb.

These days Delilah favored head scarves and retro bell bottoms. The new look was due to her taking twenty pounds off her formerly large, but well-defined frame. She had a swatch book in her hands.

"I think I like the burnt bronze for trim." She waved the rectangle of color at Monk.

"Whatever you like. Can I get you some coffee, Mr. Dellums?"

"No thanks. I stopped drinking the stuff before I retired."

"Come on in and take a load off." Monk poured himself some coffee. The carafe and coffee maker rested temporarily on a pallet of glass bricks.

The older man got up and followed Monk into his inner office. Dellums walked around, assessing the various photographs Monk had along the walls. "You were in the merchants, huh?"

"Yeah." Monk hung up his sport coat on his artifact of a coat rack.

"Where was this taken?" Dellums pointed at a black-and-white on the wall of some dark men sitting and laughing in an open-air cafe made of corrugated metal. They drank from small, yellow ceramic cups.

"Blufields in Nicaragua."

"These cats look like Blacks or half-breeds."

"They are mixed. Blufields, like a lot of places in Latin America, has a history of African settlement."

The older man kept looking at the picture. "I sure wish I'd done more traveling. That's the problem with our people. We don't know how strong our line is. Wine heads on the corner just think their genes only go back to when their people came up from Georgia."

Monk sat behind his desk, stirring his coffee. "I was a ship's engineer."

"No joke," Dellums said, finally turning from the photo. He touched some carved letters in Tagalog that meant "Luck is Found" mounted over the filing cabinet in one corner. Monk kept the thing empty save for back issues of *Popular Science* and the *Atlantic Monthly*.

"Is there something I can help you with, Mr. Dellums?"

The old man eased onto one of Monk's Eastlake chairs. He glanced at the Javanese-batik-covered couch set perpendicular to his Colonial desk. "You got some interesting ideas on decorating."

Monk scratched an index finger on the side of his goatee. "The old lady helps me out."

Monk knew Dellums was tempted to ask if she were Black, but he probably reached his own conclusion.

"I came over this morning 'cause I didn't want to try and tell you this the next time you dropped by to see me at Lordain's." He scooted the Eastlake closer as he talked. Then he got out his wallet and removed from the cracked billfold a cut-out newspaper article. "When I looked under the bed and saw the fire box gone, this was sticking up in the slats of Kennesaw's bed. See, I'd gotten flat and just happened to look up and spot it."

Monk unfolded and read the section. The piece was bylined AP, and related the near-fatal auto accident of Hiram Bodar, a state senator from Mississippi. "The paper's not brittle, so this is a recent clipping," Monk mused aloud.

"I thought it best not to go blabbing in front of them fellas down there. Some of them got loose gums worse than church women."

"You don't believe any of them had anything to do with my cousin's death?" The idea of a plumber being the killer almost made him chuckle. Except who better to do the deed than someone used to working methodically? He had more coffee to calm down.

"Not really, but why not be careful?"

"True, true," Monk responded absently, reading more of the article. Apparently the alcohol level in Bodar's blood qualified as being over the legal limit. "And"—he read silently—"they say here he was alleged to have been returning from a lunch with a woman in Memphis who was not his wife. An assignation is alleged."

"I read that three times. Are they saying he was screwing around?" Dellums asked, running his tongue over his front teeth.

"Oh certainly." Monk flipped the article over and read part of a story about a sniper killing in Belfast. "Can I hold onto this?" He waved the piece.

"That's why I brought it, brother. I ain't looking at this advanced stage to be playing Nick Carter."

"I'm pretty sure you're in no danger."

"Fine." He got up and so did Monk. "Oh, your friend called me yesterday."

"Roberts, on Sunday?" Monk asked.

"He wanted to know if I'd seen a tan-and-yellow Grand Am near Kennesaw's house. I told him no, but he wouldn't tell me why."

Monk's mother drove such a car. The sleepy-eyed sonofabitch was still working his theory about her. "Cops are always asking something. I'm glad you got this to me. Did you mention the clipping to Roberts?"

The old man batted the air with the back of his hand. "Naw. See, I stuck the thing in my pocket, and forgot it was there. Guess I was more shook than I knew. Then when I realized later I had it, I was scared that cop might think I was holding out. You seemed to be the best one to tell."

"We'll keep it between us for now." Monk walked him to the door, then headed over to Eso Won bookstore on La Brea near Coliseum.

Inside, the store's co-owner, James Fugate, was delightfully telling someone on the phone that a recently lauded book was absolute dribble. Monk bought a copy of Creel's collection of essays, *Slipping into the Abyss*, and a biography titled *Damon Creel, Last Round for Justice*.

He also leafed through a few books on the Delta blues,

but could find no reference for Patton's "Killin' Blues." Although he did come across a passage stating the actual count of songs recorded by Patton would vary from list to list. The writer suggested Patton, like several blues artists, may have secreted away some of his songs like one would deposit money in a bank, thereby to have something of value in case hard times hit.

Monk dropped by the Mayfair market on Hyperion on the way home and bought food for dinner. He arrived to an empty house and prepared a supper of potato and fish cakes and grilled portobello mushroom salad with corn muffins. Fleetingly, he'd considered getting a bottle of wine, but its myriad variances were lost on him. He could make a decent choice when it came to brew, and had done so. He'd chosen Saparro Black, and was enjoying one while at the stove when Kodama came in.

"Darling." She put an arm around his neck, smooching him loudly.

"Baby, baby." He plopped his freshly patted fish cakes into the hot oil.

Kodama wore a knee-length red Chanel skirt and matching tunic with matte-black buttons. She undid the top buttons on the blouse and got a beer for herself from the refrigerator. She sat at the table in the breakfast nook, examining one of Creel's books.

"This what everything's about?" She opened the collection of essays, reading the introduction by the late radical defense lawyer William Kunstler, whose funeral she'd attended in New York at the Riverside Church.

He flipped the sizzling patties over, savoring the smell. Monk told her about the clipping Dellums had brought him that morning. "My cousin seems to have spent his last few years either trying to reconcile his cowardice, or looking for some evidence that he did what was right for the cause." He shook a fist in the air in a quick power to the people.

Kodama crossed her shapely legs, her hand supporting her chin as she gazed at him.

Monk removed the fish cakes with a spatula and lifted them onto doubled-up paper towels. The rest of the food was already on the table and he transferred the patties onto plates. The phone rang.

Kodama got up and plucked the handset from the wall phone. "Yes . . . Oh, hi, Dex . . . Uh-huh. Listen tough guy, you caught us as we were just sitting down to eat . . . Of course Ivan cooked. What do you mean by that? . . . Sure . . . Yeah, I'll have him call you after dinner."

They ate and Kodama read Kunstler's foreword aloud. She bit off a corner of a muffin, and said, "Listen to what Bill wrote here, 'I stand firm in my belief of Damon's innocence. Let me be perfectly clear, the testimony of Kennesaw Riles was spurious from beginning to end.'" She looked at Monk for a reaction, then resumed, "'I am assured by parties who will never enter a court of law who the guilty bastards are. Who it is who impeded Damon Creel that evening, and who it is, who's still alive, still running the show from his mansion in the woods, who calls the shots, so to speak.'"

Monk thoughtfully chewed on a thick slice of mushroom. "You implying we should try to contact our Bill through one of those psychic hotlines and see if he'll come clean?"

"What if the murder is somehow tied to something that's happening now with Creel's case?"

Monk swallowed. "I checked. His last bid for a new trial was turned down three years ago."

"But there's an active defense committee in Atlanta. And Creel remains on Amnesty International's list of political prisoners." She sopped up salad dressing with a piece of her muffin. "Anyway, aren't you burning up with the need for retribution for your cousin's murder?" She ate her dripping muffin with relish.

Monk made fitful gestures with his hands. "I wasn't close to him, Jill, so honestly, it doesn't make me angry that he was murdered. I don't have an emotional connection to the man. But he was family, even though he deserved to be an outcast. He was a sell-out, and I despise people like that. I can see rolling over on your friends if your children are threatened, something like that. But to be one of those who was, apparently, willing to be used as a tool by racists to hold us back . . ." Monk went silent, smoldering.

"Yet you still feel the need to find out who killed him?"

"Maybe I feel sorry for him."

"Maybe." She winked at him.

Over coffee the phone rang again and Monk picked it up.

"Ivan, it's me, man, Marasco," Seguin said after Monk spoke.

"Yo, what it is, what it could be." That room in the Rancho where the fire and bullets had stormed materialized in his head at the sound of his friend's voice.

"All of the above," the Detective Lieutenant joked hollowly. "I didn't catch you during dinner, did I?"

"Just finishing."

"Yeah, same here." There was a quiet each let drag on.

"You been watching any of the women's basketball games?"

"I watched a little of the Sparks game the other night." Kodama started to clear the plates. She smoothed her hand on the side of his head as she walked past.

"I had to work a double that night. Had a stabbing over in a bar in Pico Union. Seems some *companeros* who had split off into two different Central American organizations still patronized the same watering hole. They then get into a disagreement over the direction the immigrant rights struggle should be taking. Add some Pacificos and Negra Modelos, and the old bit about booze and politics proves itself right every time."

"I'm hip. How're the kids?"

The cop didn't answer right away, and Monk imagined Seguin was back in that dark room, the heat and fear swarming over him, like it had Monk. "Frank and schoolwork are like strangers sometimes," he answered without emotion. "I swear man, me and Gina must be arguing about this boy every third night. Why the hell pay for a Catholic school education when the boy could be getting his C's and D's for free at a public school?"

Monk dabbed at a damp spot on his temple with a paper napkin. "Maybe it's not just him that's got you bugged." The clamminess on his forehead wouldn't go away.

"Good thing Juliana is the smart one," Seguin went on like he hadn't heard. "I don't know what we'd do if both of them were mess-ups."

There was a rustle of cellophane and Monk could tell Seguin was shaking out a cigarette. He had always been a light smoker, mostly when he worked. The last few times they'd talked on the phone—they hadn't seen each other in person for at least a month and a half—Monk could tell Sequin had been smoking heavily. "You going to take the captain's exam?" He didn't know why he blurted it out. Seguin had been a lieutenant for eight, nine years now. His close rate was above average and he was respected by those under him. The first month after the shootout, studying up for the captaincy had been his constant topic of conversation. In subsequent months, his interests in doing so varied from high to low.

"I haven't made up my mind yet, Ivan."

"Thought you wanted that desk duty in your advancing years."

Seguin laughed gruffly. "Look, I called to see if you're free for a Dodger game tomorrow afternoon. I'm using some of my comp time."

Monk was inclined to say no. The momentum of the case was beginning to gather, and you had to let it roll along to see where it took you. Conversely, he would like to see his friend. Not that he figured they'd get into a psychoanalytical session among the bleachers, but a couple of Dodger dogs and beer, and smoggy sun just might be a poor man's rejuvenation formula. "Okay if I ask Dex to come along?"

"Sure," Seguin replied vigorously. "I haven't seen him since I don't know when. Fact, I might ask Juliana. It's some kinda school-free day for her class. Why don't you ask that hulk of a nephew of yours to come, too?"

"Okay."

"I'll meet you guys at the stadium around noon, okay?"

They said their goodbyes and Monk leaned back in the bench seat of the breakfast nook. His face felt numb.

"How's Marasco?" Kodama asked. She was loading a large clear glass bowl into the dishwasher.

"Same, I think." He touched his face to reassure himself it was still attached to his head.

Kodama stood over him. "How're you?"

"Most days all right." He reached out for her arm, which felt warm and reassuringly alive.

"What about nights? I watched you last week, Wednesday, it was. You woke up 'round two-thirty and went downstairs." Concern colored her voice and softened her eyes. She bent down, holding onto his knee.

"It comes and goes, that's all."

"You want to see Melissa again?"

Dr. Melissa Nankawa Hirsch, therapist, was a college friend of Kodama's. She was a tall, round-shouldered woman who favored metal bracelets and necklaces of various designs. She maintained an impenetrable countenance, yet balanced it with the right amount of understanding in her comments and observations. She had listened and had been useful in helping Monk gain a perspective on what had happened to him. That beyond the obvious threat of death and its import, she wanted him to wrestle with "what did his choice of profession say about him" as a person.

"Arrested development," Monk blurted.

"Huh?"

"What your buddy inferred in one of our sessions. Maybe the reason I like running around, skulking in the shadows and getting sucker-punched by hardheads all the time is 'cause I'm a big kid who likes to still play war."

"Are you?" She smiled.

"Probably." He kissed her.

They went into the den and each had a neat glass of Johnnie Walker Black. They watched some TV and Kodama fell asleep halfway into an episode of *ER*. Monk turned off the set and read some of Creel's biography. After some time he too got drowsy, and dozed off, after finishing a passage in which Creel wrote about a confrontation with some crackers outside a store in Tunica.

In his half-sleep he was on the steps of that store, mosquitoes buzzing around him. One of the good ol' boys had made a crude joke and the others were laughing. Over this one's shoulder, through the ripped screen of the store's door, he could see his mother. She had a finger to her mouth signaling for him to be quiet, as she spiked each of the good ol' boys' RC Colas with some liquid from a vial.

# CHAPTER 8

"Nuts, get 'em red hot, nuts, nuts." Dexter Grant held up a hand and the wiry vendor with the beak nose and bowlegs pitched a bag to the retired cop. He caught the bag in his left, and passed a dollar along through the crowd.

"Thank you my wise connoisseur," the vendor replied, continuing to rattle his sales call up and down the section.

"Chan Ho Park looks good today," Coleman Monk Gardner said. He propped one of his size-fifteen Grant Hill Filas on the back of the empty seat in front of him. He was dressed in stovepipe straight black jeans and a white T-shirt hung loose over his developed upper body. "That boy's smokin'." He unwrapped and nearly inserted half his extra-long Dodger dog, sopping with relish and onions, in his mouth, all the while never taking his eyes off the field.

"Wow, Coleman, didn't you just eat one?" asked an awed Juliana Seguin. She was twelve, with a gap in her front teeth and her lustrous hair braided down the back. She wore a Dodger baseball cap and designer label overalls. Her parents allowed her to wear fingernail polish but no lipstick. The color she had on today was a purplish black called Civilization Decay.

"He's got to eat like that to keep the blood circulating in those gunboats of his," Grant opened a shell between his teeth, pointing at the young man's oversized shoes.

The Braves' batter got a hit and the ball went high and midway toward left field. Karros snatched it down and threw the runner out at second, ending the fifth inning. Ripples of applause erupted from the crowd. As the giant screen instantly showed the play again, a couple a few rows down from Monk in matching Teamster windbreakers high-fived each other.

"So you said your cousin knew Ardmore Antony?" Grant plopped in more peanuts.

"Yeah, they were kinda chummin' it up at the wake," Monk said. "The wife seemed put off by Kennesaw. Now I know that was because of what he'd done down south. But he seemed sincere in wanting to talk with Kennesaw."

Grudzielanek from the Dodgers was at bat.

Grant slowly chewed his peanuts on one side of his jaw. "Back in my time, you'd hear a few stories about Antony. He had this club over on Slauson, right?"

"Yeah, the Nile," Monk confirmed. "He and another cat named Harvey Lyle, a numbers man, bankrolled the baseball team my cousin coached."

Grant shook his head in ascent. "That fits. I know the club was raided a couple of times for operating numbers out the back. I also know it was a place to see and be seen like Hill's Hideaway and Tommy Tucker's Playroom were in their time."

"Dang, y'all going back beyond old school to the olden days," Monk's nephew commented, flabbergasted.

Juliana giggled.

"Even I've heard tales of the Nile," Marasco Seguin piped in.

"Ardmore also had a record label for awhile."

Grudzielanek got a hit and got on first.

"I know," Monk added. "He recorded local doo-wop and R&B acts under the Garden of Wonder name. Hell, I have a few of those forty-fives. Apparently that's how he met his wife Clara. And I've come across rumors of him ripping off some of his acts, but that's all it's been, random talk." He worked his hand like it was a spastic claw, dismissing such conjecture.

Grant scratched at his whiskers. His experienced face was topped with silver-gray hair, a little long along the nape of his neck as it always was. Together with his saddle-tramp build and gruff voice, there wasn't a week went by he didn't get stopped in the street, people sure he was the wraith of the returned Brian Keith. One night in the Satellite, having a beer with Monk, he told one inebriated chap he was the actor and had come back to get some residuals owed him by a producer.

"It might behoove you, old son, to do a little prowling around and see if you can find one of those artists he recorded. All of 'em can't be dead yet."

The Braves' pitcher struck out Beltre and a groan went up from their section.

Monk asked seriously, "Is the Ancient One suggesting Mr. Antony might have a hand in my cousin's death?"

"If my fevered brain doesn't deceive, I do seem to remember an incident his wife was involved in."

"Rat poison. A lover of hers," Seguin commented. "That's the story I heard at a barbecue last year at Sergeant Silva's house. His dad had been in the department, and he was telling us about his old man's days on the force." Seguin turned at the sound of a crack of a bat. He turned back as the man got tagged out. "That bit about Clara and the rat poison was one of the cases he worked."

"She stand trial?" Monk asked.

"No," Seguin drawled, recreating that period in his head. "I can't recall how it was resolved, only that he said a lot of people thought she'd done the deed."

"Was Roberts there at this barbeque?"

"He sure was, home savings."

Monk said, "Now ain't that sweet."

"I'll find out more if you want me to," Grant offered.

"I'd appreciate that, Dex." He settled back in his seat. "Say, youngster, how are you and that history study buddy of yours doing these days?" He winked at Seguin.

His nephew gulped down a quantity of his soda. "We kinda had a falling out."

"Not over a pregnancy, I hope," Grant whispered too loud to Monk.

"Naw, ain't nothing like that," Coleman protested. "Safety first, safety always."

"Safe about what?" Juliana wanted to know.

Monk and Grant looked whimsically at Seguin. The Dodgers got a man on second in the top of the sixth.

"He means when you have a boyfriend or girlfriend, you tell them to put on their seatbelt like we always do, dear," Seguin answered, absently pulling on his mustache.

Grant said to the teenager, "You're studying computers?"

"Actually, designing software for games and doing animation. I want to try to go to Cal Arts maybe next year."

"What about basketball?" Seguin asked. "You were alternate AU-City last season."

Coleman mumbled a noncommittal sound somewhere between a growl and a huff of air.

"That's the school Disney gets its animation talent from, isn't it?" Monk asked.

"Some, yeah."

"Expensive, isn't it?" Monk also asked.

The younger man twitched his head and shoulders. "It ain't like going to Southwest Junior College, if you know what I'm sayin'."

"They have scholarships?" Monk knew what his sister made as a public high school teacher. Plus she had a mortgage and car payments to meet. He also knew what he could afford to contribute toward his nephew's goal.

The Dodgers took the field without scoring.

"Sure, but everybody and his brother are trying to get in that bad rascal. Half the students at the place come from out of town, even from other countries, too."

"We'll work on it, if you really want it, Coleman," Monk said emphatically.

The teenager shifted his head to look at his uncle but said nothing.

"Dad, I have to go to the bathroom."

Seguin, who was savoring a now-warm beer, let out an exasperated grunt. "Aw, honey."

"I'll take her. Old folks and youngins got something else in common besides a love of Nick at Night." Grant made an excessive amount of groans rising from his seat. He led Seguin's daughter down the steps as the Braves got a man on first. Grant cracked peanuts for her as they descended.

"You don't think Grandma did this dude in, do you?" Monk's nephew commented as he watched the field.

"He was our cousin; naturally I don't think she did him in. And"—he hit Coleman lightly with his rolled-up program—"would I admit that in front of a cop?"

His nephew cackled. "Right, right."

Seguin shook loose a Camel filter cigarette from a fresh pack.

"You enjoying them a little too much, ain't you there, Red Rider?"

"I guess." He lit up, defying the California law against smoking in public.

Monk sucked in his cheeks, watching his friend smoke. "Look, don't you get going like the old lady, *comprende?*"

"What I say?"

Seguin tapped an index and forefinger to his temple. "I'm psychic." He took a long drag, and blew out a stream through his nose.

"Sleeping okay."

"Mostly."

"Me too."

Monk's nephew, who was hunched forward, elbows on his knees, pivoted his head in profile, listening.

Seguin narrowed an eye as he lodged the cigarette in a corner of his mouth. "You trying to tell me something?"

"It hit me sitting in a movie with Jill the other night. The feeling came over me like an invisible sheet suddenly being thrown over my head. Then just that quick, as I'm squirming, trying to get air, the sheet was taken off."

Seguin's cigarette burned down some more. The crowd yelled their approval for a catch by Green. "I was," he started haltingly, "I was on my way to pick up Juliana from her soccer game when I started sweating like I was in a sauna."

He looked at Monk's nephew, who was transfixed. "I just had on a shirt and it was an overcast day. There was this clammy feeling like a pound of dough had been pressed against my forehead. Then the water started and wouldn't stop. By the time I got to the field, my shirt was soaked in the back. It wasn't like I felt somebody was after me . . . I know that feeling. But the sweats . . ." he reached for another cigarette.

Monk put a hand on his arm. "Let's you and me go fishing next weekend."

"You don't fish," Seguin pointed out.

"You can teach me, Marasco."

Grant and Seguin's daughter, who was making a face at her father, were coming up the stairs.

"I'd like that, Ivan," He hid the pack and called out to Grant, "You didn't fall for her 'we always get candy at the ball game,' did you?"

Grant settled in his seat. "She wanted to buy me a beer, but I told her next time."

"Good, glad to see you're maintaining those family values, you old croaker sack." Seguin looked panicked as his daughter sniffed the air around him.

"Dad," she wagged an accusing finger at him.

They watched for another inning and a half, Juliana asking her father questions about bunting, what does a manager do, and why did the man standing next to third base keep touching his face in funny ways.

"Excuse me, now I've got to go the restroom." Coleman Gardner unlimbered his lithe body and stepped over his uncle's legs.

"I'll go with you." Downstairs, walking out of the facility, Monk put a restraining hand on his taller nephew's packed shoulder. "I need to ask you something, 'cause we're family, dig?"

The male half of the Teamster couple ambled past them, giving a little salute as he went into the toilet. The teenager leaned against the pockmarked concrete wall, folding his arms as if to ward off his uncle's inquisition into some sector of his private affairs. His face was a mask of quiet defiance.

A wistful look composed Monk's own countenance. He had the impression, more than actual memory, of a similar look Coleman's father used to get. "This may not be what you think, Coleman." Monk shifted on his feet, the scuffing of his soles suddenly very audible. There was an outburst from the crowd, but they seemed to be leagues away, under great depths of heavy gauze. "I want to ask you about your mother and Frank."

The defensiveness of his nephew's body language didn't let up. "How do you mean? What do I think of Frank? He's all right," he went on without prompting.

"I want to know what's up with them. Why does she dote on him so much?"

"She's your sister, Unk, you ask her. Come on, we gotta catch the rest of the game."

He started to walk away. Monk wasn't moving. "This is important to me, Coleman," he said quietly.

The young man halted, his head down, his shoulders slumped. He put his hands on his hips like a ball player waiting to get in the game. "Look, it ain't healthy for me to be talkin' about my mom's sex life, don't you think?"

Monk came closer. "I've seen this kind of act before, that's what I finally figured out." He got in front of him, not blinking. "You know that I used to do some bounty hunting, in my twenties?" His nephew indicated he did. "I did a good deal of bail-jumping work. Bullshit stuff like a bust for traffic warrants, a dime bag—that was marijuana in those days—house burglary, stuff like that."

Coleman waited patiently for his uncle to get to his question. He could take all afternoon and it would be okay with him. Somebody must have got on base because a cheer went up from the crowd.

"Which meant working with and hunting people on the margins, walking the razor blades. So it happens you get to hanging around the kind of folks you won't find featured in an issue of eligible bachelors in *Jet*. You see what I'm saying?"

"I do."

"So here it is: I've seen working girls who were knocked around by their pimps, beat with wire hangers, threatened with hot crimping irons—"

His nephew flinched at his uncle's words.

"—and they over-compensated in affection, attention to these bastards." Monk was having a hard time talking. "Classic abuse symptoms. The more crap they had to take, the more they put out in love for their 'daddy.'" He almost choked on the word. "As if that would soften the bastard's heart."

Coleman, who'd been hunched against the wall, straightened to his height. He loomed before his uncle like an apparition bound by ancient spells whose job was to hold back anarchy. "You're puttin' me in a bad spot, Unk."

"This is you and me talking."

He rubbed both his hands over his long, slim face. The crowd booed. "I only know this one time, all right?" He paused, walking in circles. "I came in the pad unexpected-like about four months ago. I was supposed to be on a date with Vanessa, the history chick, but we had one of our set-tos. So I stroll in all mad like and straight up there's Mom lying back on the couch with the lights off."

Involuntarily, Monk made fists. "Go on," he said quietly. "She had a washcloth over part of her arm. At first, she tried to play it off like she always sits around without the lights on, a bruise on her and all."

"You saw it?"

"I'd put on the light. I kept buggin' her, but kinda kiddin', you know? I really didn't think what it was. It was just so weird her sittin' around like that. She finally took the washcloth down." He made the motions with his own hand. "And there it was." He rubbed the underside of his upper arm.

"Like a hand print?" A harsh anticipation shaded Monk's question.

"No, it was a bruise, looked purple, like spilled ink." He looked off for several moments. "She said she and Frank had been fooling around, wrestling she said. Said she took a fall and hit her arm on one of the small tables in the front room."

"And Frank wasn't around." Monk sounded too calm.

"No. But Mom seemed embarrassed about what she told me. She made me promise not to mention it to you though."

"Any other times you see anything Like this?" Monk kept replaying how his sister had acted around Harris during dinner at his mother's house.

"No other times, Unk. That's why I'm not too sure what she said wasn't true, you know what I'm sayin'? I've never seen him raise a hand to her, even yell, really."

Monk patted him on the shoulder. "It's cool, Coleman, it's cool. Everything is going to be all right. Let's get back."

He knew his attempt at sounding relaxed rang false to his nephew as much as it did to him. They walked without speaking, peanut shells crunching beneath their leaden feet.

"Hey, you two build a new wing on the joint?" Grant cracked.

"Socializing," Monk slapped Grant's knee and sat down.

Coleman Gardner glanced at him, a worried expression creasing his youthful brow. His uncle either didn't see it, or wasn't bothered by the young man's concerns.

White stole second in the bottom of the eighth and got batted in by Cora. The Dodgers won two to one. Monk made plans with Seguin for a fishing trip as the cop took the quintet down Scott Avenue, descending from Dodger Stadium. After saying goodbye at the stadium to the lieutenant and his daughter, Monk, his nephew and Grant went to get something to eat. It was a day for junk food.

They took Grant's pristine '67 Deuce-and-a-Quarter over to the Tommy's, a burger stand on Beverly and

Rampart. The big machine's V8 430-cubic-inch power-house bellowed sweetly as dusk settled over Echo Park. During weekend nights, the tiny stand and its lot would be packed with cars and patrons, its heart-stopping chili a lure for everyone from housewives from Eagle Rock to executives from the studios.

"You okay?" Grant munched on his chili dog with pleasure.

"Uh-huh," the stretched-out teenager replied. He scooped some chili on the end of a clump of French fries.

Monk ate his chili cheeseburger voraciously. "Go on and eat, Coleman. Keep your energy up." He chomped down on a hot pepper, shaking its juice onto his patty.

The younger man laughed and bit off part of the fries he'd been using as a shovel.

Grant pretended like he didn't notice the tenseness in the teenager's frame. He sipped his soda, watching Monk eat with the vigor of a starved tiger.

Later, Dex took them back to Monk's car at the stadium and then Monk took his nephew home. On the way the teenager said, "You're not going to do anything crazy?"

A pained smile creased his uncle's face. "I just want my sister to be happy."

"That's not exactly answering my question."

"Now you sound like a lawyer. I get enough of that from Kodama."

"I'm serious, man. I don't want you goin' off on Frank over a humbug. Look, she's always calling him. They go places together. I'm sure what she said happened is what happened."

"No doubt."

Coleman slumped into the seat. "Oh, I really feel better the way you said that."

"Sarcasm becomes you." He parked in the driveway of his

sister's house in Inglewood. The house looked serene, inviting. "I'll walk with you to the door."

"Frank ain't here, I know his car."

"I can walk my favorite six-foot-four-and-seven-eighths-of-an-inch nephew to his house, can't I?" Monk bounded out of the Ford.

Some time after that, he lay awake next to a quietly sleeping Kodama. Monk enjoyed the sight of the rhythmic rising and falling of the light blanket covering her. But for him, sleep was not forthcoming. He couldn't separate his creeping anxiety, the legacy of the Rancho shootout, from what Coleman had told him. He wasn't sure he wanted to.

# CHAPTER 9

The Rodcore Container factory was a series of structures laid out in what reminded Monk of Soviet factory architecture like he'd seen in film strips in junior high. The company was a series of rectangular buildings with saw-tooth roofs situated on nearly five acres of fenced-in asphalt in Santa Fe Springs. Monk had taken the 5 Freeway east through a brown and gray layer hugging downtown L.A. His car was buffeted by a morning traffic of trailer trucks barreling along to destinations in other states. He parked on the open lot and walked through an old-fashioned wooden door set with a thick window into a brightly lit shop floor of activity.

"Excuse me, could you tell me where I might find Frank Harris?" Monk asked a large man pushing a long cart of deformed aluminum cans.

The bearish individual had shoulder-length brown hair parted in the middle and a drooping mustache hiding part of his mouth. He pointed toward a section of the building. "He's probably in his office back there." The man rattled off with his bounty.

"Thanks." Monk moved uncontested among the men and women as a large apparatus, like something from a Terry

Gilliam movie, hummed in the center of the room. The machinery turned out bright shiny aluminum soda cans that passed near him on a conveyor system. The workers serviced the massive contrivance in a choreography of efficiency. He found the office.

"Is Frank Harris available?"

The young Latina in the satiny shirt behind the beat-to-hell metal desk was reading the sports page of the *Press-Telegram*. She looked confused, blinking at the new arrival. "Do you have an appointment, sir?"

"Would you tell him it's Ivan?" he asked in his best casket-salesman voice.

She sighed with effort, folding the paper as if it were made of the alloy used in the cans. She smoothed the *Press-Telegram* out on the desk. "All right." She walked to an inner door, and opened it to stick her head inside.

"Frank, there's—"

Monk stepped from around her, striding into the office.

Harris had been making notations on the top sheet of a substantial packet of forms. He held the pen still in his hand upon seeing Monk. "Come on in, Ivan."

Monk moved a chair in a corner near Harris's ash pine desk. He sat down without a word. Along one wall was a long window, its blinds up. The view was of the shop floor.

The young woman glared at him and then at Harris, who smiled awkwardly. She shut the door with another sigh of exasperation.

"What brings you out here, Ivan?" Harris intertwined his fingers together on the desk top. "There's nothing wrong with Odessa, is there?"

"That's for you to convince me, Frank." Monk crossed his legs.

Harris's calm demeanor didn't waver. "I'm not sure what's

got you so uptight, man. This seemed to start with dinner the other night."

"Maybe it's when I got hip."

"To what?"

"You've been knocking my sister around." He uncrossed his legs.

Harris undid his hands, and began to fool with the form he'd been working on, keeping his head down. "You better put the brake on that, brah."

"Why?" Monk burned, standing up.

Harris swiveled his head up. "It's not like that, Ivan." He also stood up.

"Then what is it like?" He moved around the desk, coming closer.

Harris laughed nervously, trying to hide it behind a hand like an adolescent. "You just don't get it, man."

Monk shoved him. Harris teetered back on his heels and righted himself easily. "Feel better now?" He squared his muscular shoulders.

"Not yet." Monk came forward and Harris shoved him back with two hands on his chest. Monk had been braced and suddenly lumbered forward, ramming Harris in the abdomen with his elbow.

"Ease off, man," the supervisor clamored. He tried to pry Monk loose.

"Don't you fuckin' put a hand on my sister again," he hollered. Monk propelled the two of them against the wall, beneath a calendar with a photo of a gleaming gear.

"Goddamnit, Ivan, I don't want this to happen."

"Don't think your age gives you shit," Monk said, releasing Harris and backing up, fists ready.

The door to the office popped opened and two men rushed in. One was the cart-pusher, the other a gangly Asian kid with pimples. The first man yanked Monk's arms back, attempting to throw him across the desk. Monk resisted, and wound up in a slightly bent-over position, head up, teeth bared like a cornered animal.

"Who the fuck's this chump, Frank?" Bear-man asked.

The kid took hold of Monk's left arm, squeezing it anemically.

"If he'll behave, let him go." Harris looked ashamed for Monk.

"I'ma call the cops on this *bendejo*," the young woman advised from the doorway.

"No," Harris said. "He's my girlfriend's brother."

That information didn't make the man who had the restraining grip on Monk ease up. "So fuckin' what?"

"Ivan?" Harris asked.

Monk's anger told him to say nothing and let them call the law. Yet somewhere behind the irrationality, he knew his actions would not look good to his nemesis in Sacramento, Mrs. Scarn. He'd never met her but had communicated for years with the bureaucrat via phone and taxed memos. She worked in the Bureau of Consumer Affairs, the state bureaucracy that oversaw his PI license. "Okay," he said hoarsely.

Nothing happened for several moments. Monk breathed hard in and out. Outside the office window, the workers had gathered to see what was the deal. They all wanted to see the asshole going off in Harris's office.

"What should we do with him, Frank?" Bear-man asked. He pulled back on his grip.

"Let him go." Harris's demeanor was that of a psychologist used to the antics of his most troublesome patient.

The mental image made Monk mad all over again, but he forced himself to maintain. "Yeah, I'm sorry." Reluctantly he was released, the men and woman in the room murmuring and watching him closely for his next outburst. Monk put his hands on his hips, eliciting a nervous jerk from the bearish cart-pusher.

"We should talk about this some other time, Ivan." Harris folded his arms, staring unblinkingly at his girlfriend's ill-tempered brother.

Monk couldn't talk and didn't want to meet anyone's gaze. He exited, a mortified feeling consuming him like a flu. His neck was hot and he wished he could simply become invisible. Standing next to the driver's door of his Ford, he knew he would be the subject of lunchtime talk, and after hours ridicule at the local watering hole. He felt cheap.

Back in L.A., he pulled off the freeway and walked into a dumpy topless bar somewhere on East Fourth near downtown. The establishment was called the Tamal Haus, and was located in an industrial section a throwing distance from the Fourth Street Bridge. The facades of the brick-and-stone buildings in the neighborhood had been unnaturally grayed from the countless plumes of smoke from the countless trucks that had traversed this section since before Monk's folks came west. It wasn't yet eleven in the morning.

He stepped through a curtain. A heavy, not-so-young black-haired woman with a pot belly sat on a stool inside the doorway. She wore black briefs, an open, fringed western vest and purple high heels. She also had a surprisingly fit pair of breasts. The woman worked the side of her mouth with a matchbook cover. "Table," she managed, slacking her tongue against her big front teeth.

"I ain't entertaining today."

"Too bad."

At the bar were three other men, the only other patrons in the happening joint. Two of the men were in workman's attire. The other could have been anybody in pressed

Dockers and a cotton shirt buttoned at the wrists. Monk avoided his reflection and ordered a shot of rum.

"We fresh out of that, brah." The bartender was a tall Latina in a top hat and white bikini pants. A long, dyed-orange peacock feather sprouted festively from the hat band. "How 'bout scotch, honey boy?"

"Whatever." The booze arrived and he drank it without enjoyment. She didn't ask, but refilled the glass. He took it to his mouth, momentarily stopping. He then took a taste as if liquor were new to him. He set the glass down, sliding it back and forth between his open palms like a puck.

Here he was having discussions about being a father with the woman he loved, and he was acting like some OG straight out of Pitchess Honor Rancho Jail. He sniffed his glass, the stuff in it little better than bat urine. It suited his mood. He downed it and asked for another jolt.

"Hope you become a regular, doll," the dark-haired one said to him as he ambled toward the exit. The noontime crowd was beginning to wander into the Tamal Haus. And the decibel level of men wanting to get in some midday oohs and ahhs of breast-bearing bored women was too much for the lulling funk Monk wanted to maintain.

"Could be, if I keep doing what I'm doing." He ogled the area between the opening of her vest.

She noticed. "Well, don't you stop, you big-neck thing you. One of my boyfriends played semi-pro down in Yuma." She shifted to give him a better look. "I always did like a fella who could put me in a clinch." Two men in wrinkled Men's Wearhouse suits waltzed in, laughing and hew-hawing. One of them stopped to talk with the greeter, and Monk gave her a half wave as he walked out into the sunlight.

With the steady hands of a fighter pilot, he inserted his key in the Galaxies lock, not scratching its cobalt blue finish.

He flopped inside on the driver's side, resting his sweating forehead against the steering wheel. He wrenched the door shut, catching the engine on first crank. Monk considered driving over to the courthouse to tell Kodama what a stupid morning he'd had.

*Oh yeah, smelling of bad scotch and old flinty broads would garner a lot of sympathy.* He wanted to be doing something normal, like work the goddamn murder of his cousin. The Ford drifted left and the driver in a Suburban honked, shaking a finger at him. Monk righted himself, aiming the car forward, sweat running down the sides of his face. He didn't dare the freeway, but did manage to carefully guide his vehicle to his office.

He tried to ease past Delilah, hoping she didn't hear him from her temporary room.

"Ivan," she called. She stepped into the rotunda area as two workers were erecting some glass bricks into a semicircular room divide.

He just knew his drunk was on his face. "Yes." Oh God, he sounded like Lurch.

"I forgot to put these on your desk." She came over to him. "A woman calling herself Sikkuh called a couple of times for you." She handed him two telephone message slips. "Dex called, too."

"Thanks, D." He kept his head down, but he knew the liquor was seeping from every pore. He felt as if he were a member of some untouchable caste.

"Uh-huh." She retreated.

"I don't want to be disturbed for a while, okay?" Did he say that clearly?

"Uh-huh," she repeated, glancing back at him.

Monk slunk into his office, closing but not locking the door behind him. Yawning, he unplugged the phone, and stretched out on the couch. The black-and-white photo of the *Achilles*, the last freighter he served on, hung off-center above him. Idly, he wondered what had become of Captain Yavros, the ship's master. He seemed to remember he heard something or another about the man not too long ago. But his recall wasn't exactly functioning at the moment. He fell asleep, a lascivious scenario involving himself, Kodama and the woman in the fringe vest occupying his fuzzy nap.

He awoke sometime later, his shirt sticking to his front from sweat. The windows in his office were shut, the afternoon heat making the room stuffy and uncomfortable. The headache throbbing along one side of his head was intensified by the whine of the power saw beyond his door.

More or less sober, Monk traipsed into his private bathroom, washed his face, and popped three Tylenol capsules. He got a gray T-shirt with a FATBURGER logo on it from a closet in the conference room. The thing felt tight around his middle. Making time to get a workout in the Tiger's Den was one more addition to his list of short-term goals. Avoiding the place advertised on his shirt might be a sound notion, too.

Back at his desk, after stretching and scratching before wide open windows, he returned calls. Neither Spears's great-niece nor his mentor were in. Grant's answering machine was now playing parts of Elmer Bernstein's score from the old John Cassavetes detective show, *Johnny Staccato*. The number Sikkuh left was to a modeling agency in Torrance.

He mucked around with some mail, but was restless. It was only three, and there was still time left in the day to go around and shake down some school girls for their lunch money. Jesus, what the hell was his sister going to say? Maybe Harris would be so embarrassed for him he wouldn't say anything. Oh sure.

Monk looked for Delilah but she wasn't around. Ross was in her back office, piling material into a plastic crate.

"Hey, what's up?" she asked.

"Nothing really. Delilah out?"

"Yeah, she went to pick out some new furniture with Hendricks."

In all the time he'd shared the office with the two business women, he'd never heard either one refer to the other by their first name. "Well, I may not be back, I guess I'll catch her tomorrow." What he wanted was to explain himself to Delilah.

Hendricks was dressed in '60s-style bell-bottoms with silver dollar-sized dome caps three in a row along the outward seam. A plain white T was tied at her trim waist. The woman's customary look was trendy but sedate outfits. When Versace had been boldly gunned down by Andrew Cunanan, she wore a different outfit of his each day for two weeks thereafter. She'd been a basketball star in college, and was two inches taller than Monk. She floated near him, reaching for a model of a building on a shelf behind his back. "Don't forget you're going to have to pack up your stuff next week; your office is getting painted."

He had forgotten. "I know. I'll catch you later."

"And you still haven't told us which design you like for the conference room."

His right eye was starting to get an ache behind the cornea. "The Bauhaus version as opposed to the retro late fifties."

"Yes," she said drolly. "After winnowing down from five styles, we'd greatly value your point of view on these last two, Ivan." She moved the model with ease.

"I shall have your answer in the morn, madam." He bowed and backed out. Then he went downstairs to his car, and drove off with no particular destination in mind. Eventually Monk took the 10 East toward South Central.

"Is Mr. Antony around?" The cargo-carrier-sized brother in the extra-large Homburg he addressed was mackin' on a young woman of undetermined race. She was golden-toned and had short hair virtually the same coloring as her skin. She wore shorts and a shirt open over her midriff to the breast bone in an inverted *V*. The garment was designed so there were no buttons along the front of the satiny red material.

The annoyed man lifted an eyebrow, acknowledging Monk's presence. He pointed at a room to the left with an arched entrance, and continued on his goal of impressing the pretty woman.

Monk stepped through the opening. Antony, in shirt sleeves and suspenders, was circling his desk, talking on a cordless phone. Behind his green-lacquered desk was a poster announcing an upcoming R&B review at the Olympic Auditorium. Several artists, including the Bone Shakers, Etta James and Big Jay McNeely, were on the bill. He realized this was the show he'd seen the ad for the day Spears died. Antony sat a half-empty liter bottle of orange Cactus Cooler on a coaster. He settled his bulk in a well-worn wing chair.

"No, no, it has to be there by ten A.M. at the very latest." Antony looked at Monk, showing no recognition. "The sound check will be going on, and I don't want that display to get in the artist's way." Antony listened some more and said goodbye. "What can I help you with, my man?" He got up, knuckling a hand on top of some invoices.

"We met briefly at the barber shop on Broadway the other week. You were friends with my cousin."

"Oh right, sorry, got so much on my mind." He touched

his temples and came around the desk's corner, hand extended. "Promotion is a young shark's game, but some of my old friends been bugging me to do this thing, so what could I do?" He indicated the poster.

"It should be jumping," Monk predicted. "You heard what happened to Kennesaw since you saw him?"

A quizzical look on Antony's face indicated he didn't. He dove a hand at his desk, snatching up a supply of phone messages. "That's why this dude called for me earlier today." He shuffled through the messages. "Sergeant Roberts."

"Yeah," Antony chimed, finding the right slip. "What went down?"

Monk told him.

"Christ," Antony exclaimed, sitting down again in a chair near a window overlooking Central Avenue. "What in the hell is that about?" He looked at Monk, the message slips bunched in one hand. The phone rang. "Get that, will you, Bonnie?" he hollered into the other room.

Monk didn't know if Bonnie was the man or woman until he heard the low grumble of the cement-mixer-sized chap.

"I'm trying to find out," Monk said, aware his response was inadequate.

"Damn." Antony squirmed in the chair, seemingly wanting to do something, but unclear on what action to take.

"Did you hear from Kennesaw last week?" Monk sat down, not wishing for the other man to see him as confrontational.

"Naw, I mean yeah, I did." Antony's voice went in and out of Black southern dialect by way of Chicago in its intonations. "That is, I got a message from him on, shit, it must have been Tuesday or Wednesday last week."

"You call him back?"

"Of course." He halted, blinking and thinking. "Which side of the family are you from?"

Monk explained.

"All right," he nodded, as if that settled some inner debate. Antony exhaled, putting his head back. The young woman stepped sideways into the arch. "That was Buddy Collette. He wanted to know about the interview for that radio show on KLON. Can he do it from his house? Call him back, etcetera, etcetera." She swayed her lithe form to her words, smiling. Her speech patterns provided no clue as to her race or heritage.

"Thanks, Dollink. I'll get it straight with him." She stepped back out. "I called Kennesaw back, but got no answer. I would have gone over, but I didn't have an address for him." He plucked at his beard. "Of course, I expected to hear from him again. The two of us would go out and hoist a few to the bad times and in-between times." A tangible melancholy descended on him, pulling his thoughts inward.

"What kind of man was Kennesaw?"

Antony said declaratively, "You didn't really know him."

And again Monk felt inadequate.

"I'll tell you this way: Your cousin was the kind of man when a ballplayer had drunk up, gambled away or screwed away his dough, Kennesaw Riles would get him an advance. And sometimes, baby, that meant a dig in his own pocket, too, like seeing to the rent for some of these cats. And don't forget, Kennesaw's salary was dependent, in part, on the gate same as the backers."

"Could be that was incentive to make sure his players had nothing but the game on their mind. Maybe he saw it as long as Black folks were entertaining that was cool. But raise some sand and get in the Man's face . . ." Monk let it trail off, not sure why he was trying to goad the ex-club owner.

Antony stared at Monk as if a third eye had sprouted in his forehead. Then he cracked up, slapping his substantial thigh. "Oh, baby. You roughnecks today think you're all that. Don't take no shit from nobody no how. Well, let me hip you to something, *hombre*. There was a not too distant time in too damn many parts of this country if a Black man was ready to throw down with the ofays, well, he might not be around to sit down to his biscuits and grits on Sunday."

Antony was about to proceed when his wife walked in. "Honey, come meet Ivan the Terrible Monk," he roared gaily. "The man who's gonna show all them house niggahs how it's done." He laughed and sputtered.

"Good to meet you again." They shook hands as Monk rose. She moved a chair and sat down next to the shiny emerald desk. Clara Antony laid a Ralph Lauren handbag on its glasslike surface. "Having a good time planning the concert?"

Antony coughed, and undid a top button on his shirt. "No, actually it's kinda serious. Seems somebody did Kennesaw in."

After she'd closed her mouth, her husband brought her up to the point when she'd entered. "Are you supposing that one of them folks he double-crossed in Mississippi did him in?" She had a swig of her husband's Cactus Cooler.

"Wouldn't there have been some kind of confrontation at the barber shop?" Antony piped in.

"Unless they were at the funeral and didn't come by," Monk tried out. "Or didn't show up until now."

"Is Creel out?" Clara Antony asked.

"He's still inside," Monk said.

"One of his running buddies then," Antony pointed out forcefully. "Back when the Black power movement was on, them brothers would get their point across to a pusher or snitch with serious emphasis, if you dig what I'm saying."

"Why wait until now? Why all this time?" Monk was

ready to dismiss the idea, but tucked it away for further examination.

"Yeah, especially when he's an old man. Unless," Antony snapped his fingers, "he was on to something about the trial and wanted to tell you. Maybe the somebody found out you were in the picture and that made him kill your cousin."

Clara looked dubiously at her husband. "I know you want to believe the best of Kennesaw, Ardmore. But history is history, and he was a turncoat." She enjoyed some more Cactus Cooler.

"Then why was he poisoned?" Antony asked testily.

"What about this 'Killin' Blues'?" Monk interjected.

Now it was the wife's turn to get in a good laugh. "That story has been going around since I was at Jefferson High. And I ain't saying when that was." Her eyes twinkled and she smiled warmly at her husband.

"I went to Jeff," Monk said. "And it wasn't too long ago an unknown recording by Clifford Jordan was discovered and released on CD."

"True, true," Ardmore agreed. "That too had been rumored for years. But this 'Killin' Blues' is like the so-called thirtieth song of Robert Johnson, or 'Stormy Weather' on seventy-eight by the Five Sharps, ya dig? It's a legend, and over the years there's been enough half-truths whispered that it keeps people looking. I mean, man, collectors in Japan and Germany are crazy for blues and R&B originals from the states.

"Collecting used to be a quiet little hobby for geeky fans, cats prowling swap meets, garage sales and old records shows. Or going down south and chancing upon a Son House record in some backwater grocery store in the used bin. But like comic books and baseball cards, it just got bigger and bigger, all them baby boomers getting gray and wanting to spend their money on something to invest in for the future.

"Look, Monk, a forty-five by a one-hit wonder group like the Hornets recently sold for eighteen grand. So imagine what an undiscovered album by a blues giant like Patton would be worth by itself, plus all the ancillary junk."

"Like it's magical or something," Clara Antony waved her fingers in the air. "Patton was one of the originators, Johnson an interpreter. Though one hell of one. I heard that a seventy-eight of him singing 'Stones in My Passway' sold for six grand."

"So if the 'Killin' Blues' did exist—" Monk began.

"Then whoever found it would have a money-making machine, baby." Antony stared into the distance. "The CD, some kind of book deal, probably a documentary about finding it, maybe be a consultant to a TV movie." He clucked his tongue.

"If my husband was an envious man, I'd be worried," Clara Antony snickered sarcastically.

"Worth a million?" Monk asked.

"Probably double that if you played it right," Antony allowed. He brought himself out of his daydream of plenty. "On the other matter, see my wife was a singer, Ivan. She and some girlfriends from school and the choir formed a group called the Torches in the fifties."

"'Flame of Love' and 'Main Street Man.'" Monk could hear the tunes in his head.

"Our hit forty-fives. We went on tour with Johnny Otis and played the Five-Four Ballroom on a revue with Dinah Washington." She pointed toward a poster in a corner. The thing was laminated in thick plastic, and was the ad for the musical bill at the L.A. landmark she'd just mentioned.

"Had us a few more hits, a little glitter, but then"—she

gestured with a hand like a baroness dismissing a serf—"I guess we really don't do anything but repeat bullshit from decade to decade."

Monk encouraged her to continue with a look.

"I was the lead singer," she said, pausing as if that explained all the rest. "I guess I got caught up and all."

"You guess," her husband kidded.

She drank more of his Cactus Cooler. "I had a few mikes stuck in my face, an interview in the *California Eagle*, got on KGFJ, even had a beauty supply man put my face on one of his products."

"So you wanted to go solo," Monk commented. "The others holding you back."

"Sounds so cliché, doesn't it?"

"The ego game keeps repeating itself over and over, and forevermore." Antony touched his forehead with two fingers.

"Yeah," Clara Antony added, sighing loudly. "Mary hasn't talked to me in over, my goodness, twelve, fifteen years. And Donice—" She shook her head in remorse.

Antony presented his defense. "So you see why Kennesaw might so badly want to make up for a mistake of his past."

"Getting too big for your britches isn't the same as being a snitch."

"But you see my point," Antony persisted.

Before they got too far on that course, Monk spoke again. "I don't have any delicate way of asking this, Clara, but it's important to me I find out as much as I can about Kennesaw's murder."

She reared back, a sardonic grin contorting her mouth. "I know what you want to know. I'm sure you've asked around and heard those stories about me and Ardmore from the bad old days."

"Look, you don't have to do this," Antony said protectively.

He set a hard glance on Monk, his attitude stiffening. "You think you're some kind of sharpie, don't you?" He got up and pointed, "You can get out now." He inclined his head toward the arch, a second away from summoning the behemoth in the Homburg.

"No, let it alone, Ardmore," his wife said softly. "It isn't like he won't go on and find out."

"They always like to hear you tell it," Ardmore said from experience.

"That's true," Monk admitted. "But I'm not trying any tricks here, Clara. I heard the story about you and poison, and wanted to know what there was to it."

Clara Ardmore stuck her legs out and crossed them at the ankles. "I was going around with a couple of smooth operators. This was around '55 or '56, 'cause I remember one of these fellas loved that *Davy Crockett* show on TV."

Monk caught Antony dipping his head.

"One was him," she pointed at her husband, "and the other was Howell Exum."

"That's a hell of a name."

"I guess. Ex, as we called him, had a job down at the Continental Trailways depot downtown unloading the buses, and doing some light mechanical work."

"But his real work was the ponies and craps," Antony put in mildly.

"Both showed a girl a good time,"

"However, both didn't have chicks packing cardboard suitcases taking the all-nighters from Woodstomp, Georgia, up to L.A. to settle old debts." Antony got up and retrieved his soda, finishing the bottle.

Clara crossed her feet the other way as her husband sat back down. "See, what went down is Ex had run out on this girl's baby sister. Not the first such time he'd done that you understand. So Inez Jackson Shuttlesworth packed her bag with a butcher's knife with one side of its handle missing, some changes of clothes, and a map of Los Angeles."

"You saying this is the woman poisoned Howell Exum?" Monk catalogued the names in his mind.

"When you check, you'll see." Antony used a paper towel to wipe at sweat under his chin.

"Me and this hard-headed dame, Inez, got into it one night at the Barrelhouse out in Watts. We traded some blows, baby, like Ali and Frazier, I'll tell you." She related her ring experience proudly. "Ashtrays and pressed hair flying, upended a table with plates of food." She boomed with a hearty laugh.

"Yes, buddy," Antony clucked his tongue again. "Some kind of woman."

"About three days later, I get hauled in by a couple of detectives over to Seventy-seventh. They're yammering at me about do I have an alibi. Where was I at three that morning, what kind of poison did I use on Ex. The whole bit, man."

"And you did have an alibi," Monk stated.

"Me," Antony declared in a defiant tone.

"That and the bottle of Duniger's rat poison the cops found in the cans behind the rooming house Inez was staying at on Maple."

"This Inez go to prison?" Monk asked with interest.

"They brought her back from Georgia, and charged her. But there wasn't anything concrete to pin the deed on her. They got her for a bench warrant and evading arrest." She pushed out her lips. "I think maybe she did a year in jail."

"Ever see her since?"

"Surprisingly, yes. Ex had a daughter who got in a bad way, financially. Me and Ardmore were helping her out, and who shows up one week but Inez. We kinda stared down each other, then all we could do was hug."

"This daughter Inez's niece?"

It took a few moments for his question to sink in. "Oh no, this child was by some other woman altogether. Not from Inez's little sister. I've seen her a few times after that. Seen her more than I've seen Mary." She drew her legs back under the chair as if a sudden chill had descended on her. "Or rather, I've seen Mary, she just doesn't want to talk to me."

Monk got up. "I appreciate you talking so frankly, Clara." He started to go, then realized the obvious. "Say, did the cops ever talk to the younger sister?"

Antony too was standing. "Her name was Mardisa. Yeah, they grilled her, too. She claimed she was ironing clothes in her apartment and listening to shows on the radio. You know, the *Whistler, Gangbusters,* jive like that. She told the cops what was on when, and given her quiet nature, they had to let her go, too."

"She wasn't sharing rooms with her sister?" Monk got interested again.

"No," Clara said bemusedly. "Inez liked to entertain and her demure sister was one to complain. Inez got that room she was staying in because a childhood friend from Woodstomp lived there, too."

"How in the hell did the tame Mardisa get hooked up with this hustler Exum?" Monk stood directly under the archway, a cool breeze blowing against his back.

"Another old tired story," Clara Antony said. "Fast man puts the whammy on country girl, promises her everything, then cleans out her savings."

"So Exum wasn't that fascinating," Monk remarked.

"Hindsight gets pretty clear over decades," the woman observed.

"Thanks for the history lesson." Monk went downstairs onto the sidewalk in front of the office. Did Clara and her husband give his cousin an overdose, maybe having wrangled a clue to the "Killin' Blues" location out of him? Kennesaw had desperately wanted to talk to the man, so access wasn't a problem. And Antony could parlay such an album, if it did exist, into quite a hunk of cash for his golden years. He worked it over in his head, his hands in his pockets, standing in front of Antony's office.

The space occupied a portion of the front and corner of Somerville Place II. It was a mixed-use building with businesses and retail on the ground and second floors, and low income housing above those. This was on the northern end.

To the south was Somerville Place I, a similar construction. In between these new buildings was the Dunbar Hotel. Originally the hotel was called the Somerville, after the Black doctor who built it in 1923 to service a dusky clientele. The hotel, along with the Clark and the Golden West, were the places Black travelers, from Pullman porters during down-time to entertainers like Lena Home and Cab Calloway, could stay in when in town. L.A. in the '30s and '40s was known for its orange groves and its legal housing apartheid.

Monk's headache had devolved into a steady annoyance, and he remembered something about a bar being in the Dunbar's basement. He was crossing the street and working on the name when Antony called to him. He looked back at the rotund man leaning out of the window.

"Hey, I know you want to do right by your cousin. To make up for coming at you like that, let me comp you a couple of tickets to the revue. Just show up and you'll be on a list at the will call."

Monk waved thanks and drove off. He used the

after-work traffic as an excuse not to drive home. He had a bad feeling his sister had burned up the answering machine and he didn't want to face her transmitted wrath. He went to the donut shop and was surprised to find Curtis and Lonnie Armstrong at work on a Bluebird yellow school bus.

He decided to bug Curtis and started to walk over. Lonnie was on a short ladder, bent over the engine compartment. He had his perpetual cigarette stuck behind his ear.

"I heard from Lonny J.," Lonnie of the "ie" said without turning. "Lonny" used to work for Monk part-time. That Lonny was in his twenties and played in a band called the Exiles. They'd evolved from a rap act into real musicians playing a blend of socially conscious rap, ska and rock. The group had cut a CD on an independent label, and were on a tour.

"Tell him I know he and the band are gonna do it." Monk tapped the fender. The mechanic Lonnie was the play uncle to the younger Lonny J. He'd gotten the job because the singing Lonny had told him Curtis was looking to hire another mechanic. Curtis had a silent partner, a co-owner of the shop, but neither Monk, nor anyone else he knew, had ever met him or her.

Curtis, the beefy one, let loose in his Mike Tyson squeak from down below. "Ain't this some fucking shit." The front end shook as he worked to loosen some particularly stubborn fitting.

"This be our contract with the school district," Lonnie said without being asked, engrossed in his work. "We gets the overruns. Good money, but that mean we gets the buses at all times, days and weekends."

Monk hadn't heard Lonnie string that many words together in half a year. "I'll catch y'all later."

Lonnie grunted and Curtis banged some part of the

frame with his tool and hand. Monk's ears were seared with the mechanic's swearing as he crossed the lot and entered the donut shop. A couple of the regulars were there. Teresa, a good-sized woman given to mammoth necklaces, who worked graveyard at the county morgue, was playing chess with Elrod in one of the now pristine booths. Andrade, a sometimes accountant when he wasn't on the juice, was at the counter, studying a racing form. He swirled the contents of his coffee cup listlessly.

"Monk," Andrade managed in a bored tone.

"Peoples," Monk said, walking past them to his office. He unlocked it and entered the room. Getting online, he searched around in various newspaper archives. He retrieved some cursory pieces on Senator Hiram Bodar's accident and alleged affair from the *New York Times* and the *Boston Globe*. He printed out hard copies, and read them more carefully.

He wanted to read the past articles from *The Jackson Ledger*, but only a smattering of their pieces were online. Rereading one of the *Globe's* accounts, he noted the name of the assistant editor of the *Ledger*. He got out the clipping Dellums had saved. It had been written by the assistant editor, a Todd McClendon. Typing McClendon's name in HotBot, he came up with several matches. Monk whittled it down to the McClendon he wanted in a piece in the *Wall Street Journal* from earlier in the year.

This article talked about McClendon's firing, and interspersed statements from the former editor. McClendon alluded to the fact that Bodar had been stirring up old sins, that his accident wasn't one, and McClendon's subsequent firing was connected. There was a response from the management of the paper which went on about the usual restructuring, that McClendon was a sound editor, the fit wasn't right for the new *Ledger*, blah, blah, blah. Reading between the lines, Monk had the distinct impression that once McClendon broke with the established line about Bodar's accident, his tenure at the paper was time certain.

He made a note on one of the printouts to hunt down Bodar. He went out front and helped Elrod and Josette, another of Monk's staff, prepare dough for frying fresh donuts early tomorrow morning. The three locked up, and he got home to find Kodama sprawled on the couch in the den. She was watching the late afternoon news, her shoes off, feet on the coffee table. Next to her toes lay a picture book of I.M. Pei's architectural projects.

"Baby doll." He sat on the coffee table, massaging her feet. The answering machine had contained no message from his irate sister.

"What you do today, handsome?"

He told her, leaving out his tirade at Harris's job. He'd tell her eventually, he knew, but he just wanted to pick the right time. But for now, as he settled beside her, putting his arm around her, watching the lack of progress of peace talks between the Israelis and the Palestinians, everything was just fine.

# CHAPTER 10

Nona Monk extricated herself from her Grand Am with great effort. The sun wouldn't be up for another twenty minutes or so, but she could hear that damn woodpecker doing his mischief on her maple tree high up on the trunk. She liked her little house on Stanley, on a nice section between Packard and San Vicente. She was active in her block club, and it only got noisy on the weekends. And even then not every weekend.

When Josiah was alive, they lived on McKinley off Thirty-Ninth. In those days, South Central was solid working class, her neighbors toiled in the post office, at the railroad, and as skycaps, bus drivers, teachers, and nurses. Her children may not have had everything, but they didn't want for the basics of clothes, shoes, decent food, or a bike when they outgrew their previous one. Now that they were quite grown, getting gray themselves, it seemed like someone else's life to think about when Ivan and Odessa were growing up.

These days, Nona Monk was working hard to remain a size ten, when for most of her life fluctuating between size seven and eight had been the norm. Her feet ached and there was that twinge again in her right elbow. Yeah, the next checkup she'd bring it up.

She was also worried about her son. She'd noted the new lines on his forehead, and detected the occasional dread moving behind his eyes last week at dinner. The after-effects of the shoot-out in the Rancho Tajauta were as apparent to her as the tribulations of Vietnam vets she'd cared for decades ago. Ivan's state reminded her of the constant quiet anguish, intensified by the racism back home, that had eaten at her husband, a Korean War–era sergeant. That gnawing of the way things were, and how hard it was to change the unfairness, tore at him until his will and heart gave out.

At first the jerk of her left shoulder had her thinking she too, like her departed Josiah, was having a heart attack. But she was already dismissing that idea by the time the hand spun her around, and shoved her back against her car. The thing at the other end of the arm was wearing overalls, fur-lined gloves, and a Creature of the Black Lagoon mask. Behind the eye slits, some kind of mesh obscured the masked man's race.

She'd been mugged before and calculated this wasn't the same thing. Street thugs had very little imagination nor aptitude for advance planning. She threw her purse at her attacker's feet. "Take it and go. I'm getting off a double shift and too tired to spit."

Nona Monk wanted to sound brave and defiant, despite what her son had told her to do in such a situation: to as much as possible go along with the bad guy's demands. If she didn't, he'd warned her, defiance would result in angering the crook. And that would be a challenge to his misplaced manhood, thereby compelling him to up the ante into violence.

The Creature kicked the purse back toward her and pointed at her.

Scared and confused, Nona Monk could only gape as the

Creature rushed her, forcibly clamping a hand over her mouth. With the other hand, the attacker reached for her hand, the one holding her house keys. "You ain't going in my house," Nona Monk said more to herself than in any clear, audible fashion. She started to squirm and got a bop upside her head for her efforts. She sagged against the passenger door, and slid to the grass next to the driveway, near her purse. Dizziness gripped her head, and she felt her stomach lurch.

The Creature bent down, and gurgled, "Look, Nona, let's get inside and get this over with."

The gruesome realization of being raped and murdered, particularly in her own house, channeled the fear coursing in her veins. In a strange third-person way, she floated outside her body, watching the gun as it pressed against her temple. The Creature roughly tugged her upright. Reflexively, she swung the can of pepper spray she'd pulled from her purse. She let it go at the eye slits, and prayed as she did so.

"Motherfucking bitch," the Creature wailed as she emptied as much of the stuff as she could at his face. The Creature put its gloved hands over its immobile face, tearing at the rubber mask. She was on her knees, and tried to stand. Weakness and terror had her disoriented.

"I'ma fix you, you old ho," the Creature yelled, stomping around, trying to aim the gun at her.

Nona Monk went down on all fours, crawling toward the end of her car. A shot went off, and she didn't know if it hit her or not. It was so damn loud. All her energy seemed to be leaving her like water out of a pitcher. She blew the whistle on her key ring. She kept blowing it even after she heard a couple of doors open and feet scuffling across manicured lawns wet with dew.

# CHAPTER 11

Monk, his sister, his nephew, and Kodama bunched in Nona Monk's semi-private hospital room. She was propped up in bed, an IV running into one arm, an oxygen hose clipped to her nostrils. There was gauze holding a bandage around her head. She smiled weakly, her daughter crying softly, holding her hand.

"Mama, Mama." Odessa Monk put a hand to her own face in a useless effort to halt the flow of her tears.

Monk gripped the railing at the end of his mother's bed, looking at, but not focusing on her. Kodama rubbed his back with an open palm, comforting him.

"She's got good neighbors," Kodama said.

"And the family's hard head," he said dryly.

Odessa, who had made a thing of not looking at him since arriving, spoke without turning her head. "What in hell was this crazy bastard after?"

"I'd like that answer my damn self," Sergeant Roberts said from behind them. "How is she?" he asked no one in particular.

"Some clotting under the scalp, and we're waiting for the MRI to come back," Monk answered, straightening up.

Roberts made a motion with his head and Monk followed

him out into the hallway. A tall doctor with steel-gray hair rushed between them. "You think maybe this was one of your old homies you got the goods on, lookin' for some payback?"

"It doesn't seem so, coming so soon after my cousin's poisoning," He had toyed with the idea that the attack also came right after his set-to with Harris. There was a perverse reason to believe he was responsible, but logic made him dismiss the notion. "Although the Creature did know Mom's name, and he sounded Black."

"She seems coherent enough that I can take a statement."

"I think so, yes. You should know he wanted to get inside the house." Monk let it hang there, neither encouraging or refuting Roberts's possible scenarios. Nor did he feel in any way obligated to tell him about the clipping Dellums had given him.

Roberts went inside and Monk stood there momentarily, unsure of how to proceed. His sister came into the hall, the whites of her eyes red and wet, but more composed now that she knew her mother was going to be okay. Angrily, she turned on Monk and poked him in the shoulder. "What is wrong with your mind, Ivan?" she snarled in a lethal whisper. She poked him again, harder.

"I thought he was abusing you."

She looked like she was going to hit him again, but started blinking rapidly. "Wha—What made you think that?"

"I've seen bruises on you." It was a lie, he only had what he'd forced out of his nephew, but he'd see where it would get him.

"No you haven't." She got close.

Kodama watched them from the doorway to their mother's room.

"You mean he usually works you over so it *doesn't show*? Wraps a coat hanger in a towel so the welts don't rise?"

Odessa bit her bottom lip as Kodama led Coleman out of Nona's room and toward the vending machines at the other end of the hallway.

"You don't know what you're talking about, Ivan. We are not in high school anymore like when you took on Joey Palmer for slugging me in the back." She looked back into the room as Roberts hovered over their mother, making notes on his steno pad. "I'm a full grown woman, and Frank and I are very happy together."

"Don't let me find out different."

"Now look," her voice notched up, "don't you use that tone with me, Ivan. You can't get shit straight in your own life, stay out of mine. Just keep being a good uncle to Coleman."

"I am, that's why I'm concerned about his mother."

She did a tight back and forth movement like a track star keyed up before a meet. "There's nothing wrong, Ivan." His sister touched his upper arm tenderly. "Everything is fine, you have my word on that. Abuse is not in the picture."

Monk wanted to pursue the business of the bruise Coleman saw but realized that would implicate the young man. Not that she probably didn't suspect he'd told since she knew they'd all gone to the ball game. But there was the more immediate concern of finding this killer stalking the family.

"Whatever, Odessa," he relented—if only momentarily.

Kodama and his nephew were walking back. As they pulled close, the young man scuttled past the three. He stood next to a painting of fishing boats bobbing in a calm harbor. He leaned his back to the wall, examining his large feet.

All four took up their respective positions in the hallway as hospital personnel walked past, all moving at fast clips. They were busy with the business of healing or administering finality. Monk had been looking out on another wing of Cedars when Roberts came over to him.

"She was pretty good on the description of what the attacker was wearing, and what few words he said. Unfortunately she didn't see his getaway vehicle."

"She was a little busy on her hands and knees trying not to get popped there, Sarge." It surprised him how dispassionate he made it sound.

If a comeback was forming, Roberts didn't let on. "Unfortunately, I'm not going to be able to spare the man—or should I say, the people—power to keep a guard on your mother. You know, no ID on the crook, not too much interest from command staff. But this ain't no gangbang play, so there's little chance some eight-bailer will come waving a rod and shootin' up the hospital."

"That's what I figured, too. This punk wanted inside because whatever he thought my cousin had, and he couldn't find, he assumed my mother would have."

"Does she?"

"You know what I know."

Roberts scraped his note pad against his unshaven face. "Certainly. I'll be in touch, thanks."

"What are we going to do?" His sister had walked up behind Monk as Roberts departed.

"I'll find out who it is. I haven't lost all my faculties." He put his hands in his pockets, gauging her reflection in the window.

"I hope that's so." She went back into their mother's room.

OVER COFFEE and seven-grain hot cereal at Jerry's Deli, Kodama stroked Monk's hand. "You sure you're all right?"

Monk dug small trenches in his food. "I realize I can't take back what I did, but she's my sister, Jill."

"Honey, I know that. And I know you to be an honorable

and true man. But I also know you operate with logic and
the dynamics of reason, tempered by your passion for bal-
ancing the scales."

"'. . . Of solitary beds, knew what they were, that passion
could bring character enough.'" He had a spoonful of his
cereal.

She frowned, unable to place the quote. She had some of
her own breakfast. "And you got a mind to go with those
shoulders of yours." She smiled sweetly, but got serious quick.
"I just want to make sure you're not going to be so wrapped
up in this you'll make mistakes."

"At times this gig does have its dangers."

"As long as you're not out there instigating when you need
to be investigating."

He considered being obstinate but having one loved one
mad at him was enough for now. "Yes, dear." He ate like a
man rescued after a week in a mining shaft.

LATER, AT Continental Donuts, sitting in the front, Monk
again went over the things belonging to Marshall Spears.
He examined all the photos, looking for some visual clue
that would trigger the alarm in his brain. No such item
appeared, though he did identify a few familiar faces in some
of the shots. He was sure he'd spotted Black aviatrix Bessie
Coleman in at least two photos. There was a young Louis
Armstrong in a suit of wide pin stripes blowing his horn on
first base. And he was pretty sure that was W.E.B. DuBois
at a game the Grays had against the Birmingham Barons.

Whoever killed his cousin apparently didn't get what he
wanted when they stole his mementos from his duplex. Yet
it seemed whatever they were after wasn't in Spears's effects,
either.

Underneath the scrapbooks Monk found a ball

autographed by homerun king Josh Gibson. It was wrapped in dry burlap and tied with twine. He hefted it against the light. This memorabilia had value, but only to a connoisseur. Was there some incredible artifact the killer was supposing Kennesaw possessed? People had been killed for rare coins and old books, so it was possible. Yet it also seemed to tie into the Creel case. Or maybe that too was not really what it was. Maybe the killer left the clipping in the slats on purpose to make it seem Kennesaw's death was revenge for him testifying, when that wasn't it at all. So the murder had to be tied to the "Killin' Blues."

Monk felt rudderless. He poured two twelve-ounce Minute Maid orange juices into a large cup with ice. He slid into a booth and lit a Te-Amo Maduro. He smoked and ruminated while several customers came and went, the brass bells over the front door jangling each time the door was opened and closed.

The bluish-white plumes of his cigar obscured his face at times from all others in the corner. The cigar was down to the red-and-white band when the phone rang behind the counter.

"For you," Josette said, after answering. She grimaced at the sight of the stump in his mouth as he approached. "This ain't gonna be a habit, is it?"

"Thanks," Monk said, taking the handset. "Hello?"

"Ivan, this is Sikkuh. Your secretary gave me this number."

"I've been trying to find you."

"My part ran longer than I figured. I got back yesterday. Ah, say, is there a way we can get together later? I have a few things that need doing. But it's important I see you."

"It's a little more involved now," he went on. "Somebody poisoned Kennesaw."

"Are you kidding?" she said, aghast.

He told her what happened, including the attack on his mother earlier that morning. "Can we get together today? I'll bring your great uncle's goods; you might have some idea on what's going on." He clamped the dead stump back in his mouth.

"Oh sure, we have to," she said urgently. "I have something to tell you, too."

They arranged a time and place and he severed the connection. He then called Dexter Grant and managed to reach him at home.

"Jesus, Ivan," the former LAPD plainclothesman exclaimed after being filled in. "How long is Nona gonna be laid up?"

"Her doctor should have gone over her MRI by"—he looked at his watch—"'bout an hour from now. I'll call and see what she says. If everything is cool, she's to be out tomorrow."

"You want me up there?"

"I'd like that, Dex, if you could. I'm not a hundred percent sure right at the moment, but it looks like I might need to take a trip down to the Delta."

"What for? The killer is loose up here."

"Yeah, but everything points in that direction. And maybe if I move that way, he will too. I don't think he's a stranger to those parts."

"But down there you are," Grant pointed out.

"It's where the case takes me, Dex."

"So it would seem." He breathed heavy for several moments. "Say, I got a coupla things on that Ardmore Antony of yours."

"They told me about the Shuttlesworth matter."

"Well, ride this mule, Fosdick, did they tell you that Antony once put two from a Luger into a guy who said the impresario ripped off some songs from him? He was a writer-singer by the name of Slim Willie T."

"That particular gossip didn't come up," Monk admitted.

"Antony got off 'cause the other dude had a bowie knife he was trying to bury in your portly pal's belly-button at the time."

"Anything to the song business?"

"Hard to say. The ASCAP registration has both their names on it, and only Ardmore's around to tell the tale. I looked in an R&B history book, and the writer was non-committal on the subject."

"Maybe he figures Mr. Antony's kept his German heirloom oiled." Monk stuck the cigar stump in a corner of his mouth, chewing on the stalk.

"Whatever. This couple's got death following them around."

"People might say the same about you and me."

He laughed briefly. "You must be reading your B. Traven again."

Monk tugged on an ear. "Listen, Dex, I know I seem to take you for granted, but it ain't like that, man."

"I'm a dependable guy, right?"

"You're more than that."

Grant let some time gather. "Look, Ivan, how long we been saddle tramps?"

"You remember when I first came into your office? That walkup you had over that radio-TV repair place?"

"Stoddard's, on Overland. Had a view of that goddamn water tower on the MGM lot. You'd been tracking some stickup clown who'd knocked over a couple's ice cream parlor."

Monk grunted. "It was his second offense, so the bounty was good."

"You were a fuckin' hound dog, right out of one of those Fred Williamson movies. All hot on guns and stopping power."

It was embarrassing to hear him tell it. "But as usual you had the goods, Dex. LaSalle had hipped me you'd run the kid's father in for grand theft auto. He figured you'd know his haunts since he'd gotten his son started on the path to ruination."

"LaSalle. Christ. That corner-cutting bail-bonder still kickin'?"

"Retired, got a little plot of land up in Hesperia, I heard last."

"Built on all of them poor folks' collateral." The line buzzed for a few more moments. "When you want me at Nona's?"

"Day after tomorrow, assuming her tests are okay. I'll call you *mañana*, Sarge Steel."

"Be looking for it." He replaced the receiver gently.

Monk rolled the stump to the other side of his mouth, chewing on it and assessing what he knew so far. Later, forty minutes after sunset, he walked into the Grassy Knoll coffeehouse on Coldwater. It was "open mike" night, and a reedy yellowhaired youngster in a watch cap and overrun jeans was swaying before the microphone stand like a hip-hop version of the late Frank Sinatra. He was reciting a bit about driving his mother's Plymouth Fury to Arkansas, while popping Percodan. Sikkuh stood and waved to him from a tiered rise to the right.

"What in hell happened to you?" He indicated the double ace bandages around her wrist. He sat, his view of her and the performance area unobstructed. The front door was at a diagonal from him. When was the last time he sat with his back to the door? Old habits.

"That's why it was so important we have a face to face,"

she whispered. "I got thrown around my apartment last night when I got back to town."

A waiter with an earring piercing the middle of his nose wafted in front of them. They ordered and he snapped his fingers twice in appreciation and drifted away.

"What'd this attacker look like?" Monk leaned forward.

"Overalls and a Halloween mask of some kind." Her hand shook on the table as she talked, and she clasped one over the other in her lap.

"That describes the fool who assaulted my mother earlier this morning. How'd this go down?"

She ordered her thoughts before speaking. "I got back to my apartment around seven-thirty or so. Put my key in the lock, and walked inside, beat. Suddenly this hand gripped my arm, and wrenched me around. I went back against the wall, thinking this was some kind of burglary and rape. I was mad terrified."

"I can believe that," he sympathized.

"This man growled at me: 'Where is it?'"

"He didn't specify?"

"He might have, but I wasn't paying that much attention. I ran into the bedroom, slamming the door. Fortunately, the apartment has solid, not hollow-core doors. While he was hitting it with his shoulder, I hit the panic button next to my bed, praying."

"He split then?"

"Yes, thank the Lord. Here's a Xerox of the police report." She got a folded copy out of her purse at her feet and handed it across.

Monk perused it and tucked it away without asking any questions.

"What does he want, Ivan?" Her eyes got wide with anxious uncertainty.

"Something that either your great-uncle or my cousin had."

"What, old baseball jive?"

The waiter eeled back to their table, delivering Monk's café mocha and her cappuccino. The server set the cups down and twirled the tray on an index finger as he walked away.

"Your great-uncle ever mention the 'Killin' Blues'?"

"The what?" she asked, scrunching up her face.

"Never mind. You know he had an autographed ball by Josh Gibson."

"Who?"

"He was a homerun king who never got his chance in the majors. It's worth something to the collector, but not, you'd think, to a murderer."

"Or maybe something's hidden inside." She got excited like a ten-year-old on a pirate treasure hunt.

"That's possible," Monk grumbled doubtfully. "But it seems farfetched. Are there other items you or a relative have from your great-uncle?"

"That's funny you bring it up. I was racking my brain at the emergency room and remembered I already had some of his things. This is stuff his sister used to have and I got when he was moving around. I've had it in a safe deposit box for several years, with some other family things."

"Can we take a look tomorrow?"

"Hey, baby."

Monk cocked an eye in the direction of the voice coming over his head. The newcomer was a sturdy fellow in tight, coal-black jeans and a shirt sans sleeves. All the better to show off his rippled triceps and deltoids, Monk noted. He was bronze-skinned with dreads pulled back in a ponytail.

"Hey Indigo," Sikkuh greeted.

"How are you, sir?" The man stuck out a hand toward Monk.

He must have been no more than twenty-five. "Just fine there, son." Monk accepted the handshake; each applied subtle pressure to show how manly they were.

"Hey, how 'bout we catch Ben Harper at the Palace on Saturday?" Indigo addressed Sikkuh.

"Well," she hedged, "I might have to get up early for a shoot with *Car and Rims magazine.*"

"How 'bout you call me on Friday?" He shifted his glance to Monk, then back to her.

"Sure, that's a good idea."

"Awright . . ." He let out in a guttural hiss. "Friday." He bobbed his head and flexed as he strode away.

"Lovely fellow," Monk raised his cup in a salute.

The pretty model laughed genuinely. "He's just trying too hard. Like all of us, he wants to be something in a town where everybody's got to have a title."

"Reminds me of a saying my dad used to repeat now and then." Monk sipped thoughtfully. "Three-dollar job descriptions and twenty-five-cent pay checks."

"He still around?" She perched her pointed chin on a sturdy-looking hand.

Monk shook his head.

"Sorry for your loss."

"It's been a while."

On the stage area a petite woman in a leopard-print dress began reciting a piece about killing her landlord with gusto.

He stirred his coffee and had some. "Can we go to the bank tomorrow to look at those other items from your great-uncle?" he asked again.

"Absolutely. I want to stop this horrible person."

"And find out what he's after." Monk tipped his cup in her direction.

"Yes, that is so." She showed great teeth and tipped her head slightly.

"You sustain any other injuries?"

"You're sweet," she purred. "No, just this." She held up her arm.

They sat, talked, drank and listened to several poets and writers do their thing at the mike. Some were okay and some were too paralyzed by angst and self-pity to produce work of any reflective nature. But all at least had something to say.

Monk checked his watch. "I better be getting along. Can you stay at your friends' place in Sherman Oaks for a few days?"

"Yes, I've already talked to them and they said cool."

"What about some clothes and towels and such?"

"Come back with me to get them?"

"Sure." But he felt a tug in a place he shouldn't. Monk forced himself to remember she was a client, and he was living with a woman who knew how to use a gat.

They started walking out. A wiry-built dark-skinned Black man with high cheekbones in oversized gabardine shorts and a tight black T with gold epaulets was coming through the entrance. His eyes were lidded, and he smelled as if he'd just smoked a joint.

"Zup, girl? What's your hurry?" He snagged her forearm, tugging and moving his body as if his spine were a slinky.

"Jing," she said tonelessly, removing her arm.

He made another grab and Sikkuh's face got hard.

"Excuse us, okay?" Monk inserted himself between the two.

Unfocused orbs swam before him. "You her daddy?"

"You ought to listen to yours, and learn some manners."

Jing stood defiantly, arms loose but ready at his sides. "You motherfuckin' Martha Stewart now?"

Monk was about to get further in the young man's face when Indigo stepped over. "Come on, let me buy you a raspberry frappé." He put an arm around the belligerent younger man's shoulders.

Jing snarled, "Aw, man, Pops Racer here don't raise no water on my balls."

"I know, my brother. Come on, let's talk about it over here." Indigo winked at Monk and led the surly and high Jing to a table near the kitchen.

"Who in the hell was that?" Monk asked, walking with Sikkuh to her car across the wide expanse of Coldwater.

"Jing's done some acting on a couple of episodes of the Wayans Brothers' show."

"That explains everything." Monk scratched his cheek. "So the cool thing these days is to have one name?"

She giggled, touching his arm. "Pretentious, isn't it?"

They took her Probe to her apartment on a dark street where the leaves of the maple trees bristled in the night wind. There was a security gate on the entrance and one on the underground carport to her complex.

There was a locked door off the garage and Sikkuh explained tenants had to use their key to enter through that door, and the door beyond to the elevators. "Of course the intruder could have hung around the entrance until someone came in or out and slipped inside." Monk knew this could be the case since he'd done just that himself in the past. "Then the attacker changed into his work uniform once in the stairwell."

Upstairs, Sikkuh got some clothes together. Looking around the living room, Monk noted the lock to her apartment door was nothing special—not that he was a lock-picking expert. He studied the mess the intruder had made of her place. He crouched down, holding pieces of a broken CD case. It was an album by James Cotton.

"You dig the blues, huh?"

Sikkuh stepped into the room from her bedroom. She was holding onto some clothing. "Don't everybody?" She held aloft some black lace panties in one hand, pinkish silk ones in the other. "Which ones should I wear tomorrow, Ivan?"

Monk managed to convey his opinion without taking her up on the offer to see how each one fit. Afterward, she drove him back to his car parked near the Grassy Knoll. "Two o'clock tomorrow," she said, running her hand on his upper thigh as he sat in the passenger seat.

Gently, and with some hesitation, he removed her hand. "Until then, ma'am."

"Nice ass for an old guy," she laughed, driving away into the humid Valley evening.

"Kids," Monk grumbled, admittedly flattered a gorgeous young thing would flirt with him. He managed to cease fantasizing by the time he rolled home and found Kodama replacing a washer in the bathroom sink's faucet.

AT ELEVEN minutes after ten the next morning, Monk was standing in the Southern California Library for Social Studies and Research in the 6100 block of South Vermont Avenue. The Library was a nonprofit Kodama had belonged to for a number of years.

The nonprofit was housed in a two-story, large rectangular structure. The building had been an appliance store during the Watts Riots of 1965. The holdings of the facility included pamphlets from the Industrial Workers of the World, the Wobblies, in the '20s; the End Poverty In California campaign of Upton Sinclair in the '30s; more than

26,000 volumes of books on history, women's studies, the Chicano civil rights movement; the Unemployed Councils that operated in the South in the '30s, and many other paeans to the strugglers who wanted to make a better world.

"This Freed cat secreted a lot of material away during the McCarthy era, didn't he?" Monk was leafing through an anniversary publication and had stopped on a photo of Emil Freed, the library's founder, and his wife, Tassia. He and the wife—he was squat and squarish like a high school football coach—were marching with others brandishing placards demonstrating against the Smith Act. The repressive law was a Congressional measure used to round up radicals and Progressives in the late '40s and '50s.

"Like a man hiding pieces of the Grail, Emil hid people's books and papers in garages and apartments all over town," Sarah Cooper said. She was the director of the library, and looked like any casting director's idea of a librarian, complete with glasses on a chain around her neck. She wore little cows for earrings, and could recite the Ten Point Program for Progress of the Black Panther Party, backward and forward.

He closed the booklet and set it down on a long counter. "And after things settled some, he gathered this material back together?"

"Yes. Of course Emil had this material jammed in boxes, crates, grocery bags and whatever else he could use to keep them together. It took a long time to get things catalogued and situated." She pointed toward the open upper level where a couple of oldsters were shelving stacks of newspapers. "And the work still goes on."

Monk, his hands thrust into the back pockets of his jeans, nodded his appreciation.

"Come on, I'll get you the Embara tape," she said.

He followed her around several stacks to a door located

down a hallway with a plaque tacked to it announcing it as the EARL ROBINSON Room.

"Who was that?" he asked as Cooper twisted the knob.

"Composer, 'Ballad of the Americans,' made famous by Paul Robeson."

There were shelves of audio and videotapes neatly arranged and labeled in the room. Equally important, there was a monitor and a VCR. "Since I knew you were coming, I got her tape out and had it ready to go." Cooper turned on the power.

"Thank you."

"No problem."

She closed the door behind her and Monk hit PLAY to get the tape going. Entitled *Fire and Justice*, the video was a documentary about Damon Creel by independent filmmaker N'Kobari Embara. There were a couple of '60s-era kitchen table seats in the room. Monk put one in place and sat down.

He watched the absorbing story of Creel's life and times. From his days growing up in a white, lower-middle-class neighborhood in Culver City, to his volunteering for Vietnam, and his politicalization while in the service during his second tour. There was also a fairly recent interview with Creel conducted at the federal correctional institute at Millington, Tennessee. Creel was over six-two, with a runner's sleek build. He had an expressive face, and a full mustache that he'd apparently worn for more than twenty-five years. Though the brush was now salt and peppered with gray, the hair on his head was still black and full. When he spoke, there were pauses in his speaking voice attesting to the weight he gave each question from Embara.

"You have to understand, when we did the campaign, Jackson State had gone down." Creel was sitting in a metal chair in a sterile room, looking ahead intently. His speaking voice was hoarse but steady. "Four Black students gunned down, protesting racism on campus and the war was a very big thing in Mississippi," he went on. "The repression that was unleashed was fierce. Conversely, the national attention built up by the work since Freedom Summer in '65 had inspired do-good foundations and even some corporations to start feelin' guilty and donate money to us." He tapped the table with the side of his hand several times underscoring his words.

The interview cut to a clip of Bernie Descanso, the attorney who'd come to fame during the Days of Rage as a leader of the SDS, and who had championed Creel's case for more than twenty years. He said some supportive words, working his hands in big circles as he did so.

Then on to a scene of people walking around holding their heads and some others shouting and still others crying. In voice-over, a woman stated there was a loss of student life at Jackson State on May 7, 1970, when highway patrolmen indiscriminately opened fire on unarmed students. "Later," the narrator intoned in the voice-over, "the authorities would claim there had been sniper fire. The same unproven assertion the National Guard made at Kent State in Ohio that same year."

For several moments, the image froze on a young woman with a puffy Afro, her finger held to her mouth as if holding back recriminations. She stood at a window that had been shot out, bullet holes from large-caliber weapons dotting the wall around her.

Monk watched more of the film, then halted the video. He left and walked over to get an early lunch at Goss' Seafood You Buy, We Fry—two blocks north of the library. He returned with his lunch of cornmeal-breaded catfish, fried shrimp and potato salad. Dousing his fish with hot sauce and ketchup, he worked out his next steps in his head. After he finished eating, he watched the rest of the documentary and shut off the monitor. He sat still for several beats, then got up.

"Thanks for letting me see the tape," he told Cooper.

"Are you looking into his case?" She was in a room fronted by large glass panes, working on a computer.

"Not directly," he said. "But it seems current incidents keep revolving around Creel and the trial. I was hoping to find out details that might help me with what I'm trying to solve."

She murmured an assent. "We had a half-day conference on him and other political prisoners like Leonard Peltier, not too long ago."

Nobody had said it, but Monk felt a burden to do something right for Creel, if only to allay his own suspicions. Yet he also had to be realistic. "What I'm looking into may help Creel—"

"Or may not," she finished. "I understand." She put on her glasses, though she looked over them at Monk. "Want to talk to N'Kobari?"

"Sure," he said.

Cooper wrote down an address and phone number. He thanked her and drove out to the Valley to meet Sikkuh at the Glendale Savings on Ventura Boulevard. His temperature gauge drifted past center. As usual, the Valley was hot and dry and he could not see why in the hell people lived out there. The streets were over-built, and the houses all had that ensconced neo-Brahmin pseudo-ranch look he found so infuriating.

Marshall Spears's grand-niece was cheerful and optimistic in a plaid, pleated skirt and green velveteen top. She had on a pair of lace-up burgundy Skechers boots, and waved at him as he pulled into the parking lot.

She wrapped an arm around his and they walked that way into the place. Soon they were sitting in the private cubicle examining the contents of the large safe deposit box.

"It must be seven years since I put this stuff away. Every now and then I get a notice from the branch telling me I have to sign the form so they don't throw out the box."

Monk was examining the objects he'd taken out of a large manila envelope folded over and held in place by rubber bands. There were three rail spikes stamped with dates on their heads, baggage claim tags, decals from several cities like Yazoo and Greenville, postcards not filled in on the back, and some photographs. The postcards had various locomotives chugging along, The Atchinson, Topeka and Santa Fe, the Reading, Southern Pacific and so on. Among the photos, there was a slightly out of focus shot of a picnic scene that garnered a second look from Monk.

"I think this is Damon Creel sitting at this table, your great-uncle on the other side." He peered close and handed it to younger eyes to judge. He'd put off the visit to the optometrist last month. In the photo people were eating and talking. Off to one side was a barrel barbeque pit and a man hard at work grilling some Q. He was sweating like Hercules on his seventh labor.

"Yes, it is," Sikkuh confirmed. "Who's Damon Creel?" She handed the photo back.

He explained who he was and the connection to Kennesaw Riles. Then, "Damn," Monk said faintly.

She hovered a black-nailed finger over the man doing duty over the pit. "That's your cousin, isn't it?"

Monk glared at her questioningly.

"I saw his picture on the funeral program, slick."

"Let me hold on to this for awhile, okay?"

"Certainly. Do you think those tags are any use?"

Monk picked them up. They were for depots of numerous cities. He'd only heard of about half the towns, all of them, he assumed, scattered through the deep south. There was no tag more recent than 1974.

"If he was hiding things in each city, it woulda been long since cleared out by now." It wasn't too much of a strain to fancy Spears operating like Emil Freed behind enemy lines, hiding away the precious works of generations to keep them safe.

"So what does this mean?" She pushed the aged receipts around like Jigsaw pieces.

"I can stand still and see if the Creature comes for you or my mother again."

"You mean set a trap." She almost bounced in the seat.

"Slow down, Honey West." Monk patted her arm. "The killer may be a cold-blooded thug, but the bastard's also smart. He's moving around, knowing things about us that only an insider could know."

"So you're going to pretend like you found this thing he's looking for, and he comes after you."

"He would know I hadn't," Monk had already decided. "Plus, how would we do it? Go to all the old-timers at the wake and drop hints like we'd actually found this whatzits?"

She twitched her shapely nose. "Where'd you get that term, out of a old movie on AMC?"

"Regardless," Monk said dryly. "We have to assume the killer is connected to someone who knew one or both of our relatives."

"Maybe someone in this picture." She pointed at the indistinct figures in the picnic shot.

"Another reason to head to Mississippi." He stared at the photo.

"And the killer will follow you? That seems pretty shaky to me, Ivan. Plus, how's he gonna know you left town?"

"'Cause if I bang enough bells down there he'll know."

"And come after you 'cause he'll think you're on to something? Why wouldn't he just wait until you got back here to town with your whatzits?"

"Sikkuh," he said patiently, "this thing might be information and not an object."

She bobbed her head to an inaudible beat. "Something to prove this Creel's innocence." She leaned to one side, hand under her chin, regarding him with amused interest. "But what you really want to be is the mack daddy player, the man who makes things happen." She put a hand on his cheek. "You're so cute, Ivan Monk."

"Damn, girl," he admonished.

She laughed and slapped his arm. Leaving the bank she said, "Maybe you'll get lucky and find something out about Patton's record, too."

"Maybe." He got in his car and drove away.

THE NEXT day Monk went to see N'Kobari Embara at her office/workspace on the lot of the Las Palmas studios in Hollywood. The studio was a collection of large work areas rented out to concerns as diverse as prop shops to interactive game production. Each office was fronted with graying wood decks. The filmmaker was on the tall side, with frizzed-out hair and three wide silver bracelets along one muscular arm. Monk guessed she was about his age since there were bags under her eyes.

"I was down in Texas getting some information on this private prison company called Percival Facilities Management. They're looking to take business away from UNICOR, the Bureau of Prisons' whacked-out labor scam." She was fiddling with a camera mount. "Innocent sounding, aren't they?"

"Everybody's trying to make a buck." Monk crossed his leg at a perpendicular angle to his knee.

She leaned the collapsed mount in a corner. "Uh-huh, taking federal dollars out of our pockets for doing the job of warehousing on the cheap. Symptomatic of the further abandonment of compassion and responsibility our politicians should be exercising."

"I'm not arguing with you."

She laughed heartily and lifted a pile of books and papers from one part of her desk to another to get a clearer look at her visitor. "You want to see what wasn't in the film?"

He uncrossed his legs. "It won't be sold to *Hard Copy*, N' Kobari."

She vibrated an open palm in the air. "I know, I know. I called around about you. You'll be happy to hear some folks actually think you're a down brother even though you're a semi-cop."

"What do the others say?"

Embara belted out another gust of her infectious laughter. "Could be I'll use that in the documentary. I'll do one day on capitalism and the underworld, and the role of the private eye who maneuvers in both arenas." She picked up a set of interlocking gears and sprockets and idly manipulated the device. "To get the first unstated question out of the box, yes, Damon Creel was having an affair with one of the white girls from Brandeis." She stared straight at him, adroitly twisting and turning the gears as she spoke.

"But you wouldn't say he had an insatiable sexual appetite, would you?" Monk left it to her to add or defer information on the topic.

"Should I feel a need to defend him?" She kept working the gears.

"Just understand him. I'm going to try to talk to Creel when I get down there."

"Damon liked the center ring and what came with it. In that regard he's no different than many of those throwing stones at the system from the left and right in the name of being the vanguard. Those who always manage to get their names in the papers."

"Your film implied that, but also balanced it with his sincerity for the movement."

"As I hoped it would." She finally set aside the gears. "I think Damon's a for-real, hope-to-die revolutionary who wants to alter the nature of power in this country."

"But you assess him honestly," Monk admired. "Faults and plusses."

"And I firmly believe then and now that he was railroaded into prison. Damon admitted in court seeing Ava Green earlier that evening. Hell, we all knew they were getting it on."

"According to his book his car broke down on the way back from Memphis to Mound Bayou," Monk filled in. "By the time he got it going and got to his destination, the two young girls had been slaughtered."

"But the breakdown is a big gap in his time. It is an unaccounted whereabouts."

"That and the testimony of my cousin." Monk got depressed.

She clasped a hand around the bracelet on her wrist, the harsh light of her office giving her skin a sheen like burnished copper. "I want you to see this," she said firmly. "I was going to use this in the documentary, but, well, you'll see." She wheeled in a monitor and commercial deck on a cart from another room and searched for a 3/4-inch tape among a stack of them on a bookshelf. She found what she was looking for and popped it in the machine.

The tape fuzzed for a few moments then there was a pixilated face of a man in short sleeves. He was sitting in a straight-backed wooden chair and he was fidgeting: his leg pumped up and down, his shoe arched upward, his butt perched on the edge of the seat.

"Oh, wait a minute." Embara, who was standing next to the set, stopped the tape and fast-forwarded it. "This was the version I'd messed with. Let me get to the original." She got to the appropriate place on the counter, and set the tape to play again. She sat down at her desk. Monk had edged his chair closer.

The initial scene was the same except the pixilation affect was absent. The subject was an older white man in clip-on suspenders and a straw, snap-brim hat. He had a lean sagging face, vestiges of its once rugged good looks hinted at beneath the myriad lines. His nose had a groove of a scar along the length of the bridge. The old wound was purple with age, and broken blood vessels rivered on either side of it.

"The Citizens League wasn't a bunch of night riders swilling hooch, running around excited to kick some Jew's ass." He whipped his face toward some unknown source, then back to the camera. "We were the thin white line of Anglo-Saxon culture against the disorder being rent upon us by them professional coons and their benefactors, the liberal she-he's running those foundations in New York City."

"Were you the one interviewing him?" Monk asked.

She indicated she had. "Wallace Burchett was not given to immodesty." Embara put a finger to her lips.

"We had served in the Big One and in Korea. We had seen what the Red Chinese had done to brainwash American prisoners of war, and how they wanted to take away our free thought. We weren't brownshirts, no sir.

"But then we get back here and you got all that race mixing music with them pedophiles Chuck Berry and Jerry Lee Lewis. Juke songs right out of joints with nigger tunes and dago singers was being played by blossoming white girls right here in Decatur, goddamnit." He gyrated on the seat, his shallow cheeks puffing.

"Decatur, Mississippi," Embara illuminated.

Burchett's head was hanging low, moving from side to side. He talked down toward his shoes. The camera pulled back to accommodate his pose as he went on. "It was about your whole god-fearin' way of life could be ripe for spoilage if those Castroites had their way.

"And they say we were wrong, that we went too far. Just look at the evidence. What was Cambodia? What in the name of sanity was Rwanda or Kosovo? And now, Jesus and the blood of Christ, Hong Kong belongs to the Reds, good Lord almighty." He waved an arm in the air as if he were a referee trying vainly to call foul.

Burchett's voice was steady, clear. Yet both his legs were going up and down now, and a desperation had crept into the corners of his pupils, which had constricted. "You asked me about certain activities I don't rightly think a young gal like you should be pursuing." There was a jump in the tape and then Burchett was speaking again.

"Yeah, yes, I've heard that plenty of times." He wiped at his brow with his palm, which was suddenly glistening with perspiration. He upset his hat and it fell to the floor. He leaned down to retrieve it and stopped to look halfway up at Embara, who was out of the shot. "You expect me to tell you how we arranged the removal of no-goods like them two in that pickup truck over in Yazoo City?"

Embara remarked, sotto voce, "You mean the murders of Yost and Hiller in the fall of 1966?"

Monk remembered the crime. Yost, a white high school teacher from Philadelphia, Pennsylvania, and Hiller, a young Black man from Biloxi, Mississippi, had been doing voter registration. They'd been forced into the woods by Klansmen or cops, what difference did it make since they never got out again?

"Yost was disemboweled, Hiller had his penis severed and stuffed in his mouth. And both had their heads caved in with sledge hammers." Monk had a cold fascination for Burchett.

"Here," Embara said, pointing at the monitor as the Citizens Leaguer continued telling his tales.

"That Riles loved money and pussy, shit, what nigger doesn't?" He leered at where Monk presumed Embara sat. "Some white fellas too, I guess you could say." There was another jump cut and now Burchett was erect in the chair as if he were bound with invisible chains. His arms were tight against his body, his neck pulled in as if to ward off blows, his hat pushed far back on the top of his head.

"He loved his money, but he wanted his pride, too. That Riles had the right idea, yes sir. He knew the coloreds had to bide their time and be patient; they couldn't rush things and get all out of sorts like they had no sense."

Monk was angry at the way Burchett referred to his cousin, and angry his cousin had been so weak.

Burchett was now jerking his body about in a violent fashion. Since the interview had begun, these movements had been slight, and had continued building into exaggerated spasms. His hat remained on his head.

"What's wrong with him?"

"Watch."

Burchett launched himself out of the chair, the camera losing him momentarily. The camera operator found him rolling and writhing on the floor. "Malachi knows as did

Riles, turning in that rabble rouser. Ye must tithe to Malachi, ye must make amends sometimes in blood."

The old man, who'd had his arms outspread, slapped them against his sides again. He gurgled and snaked himself along the floor like a circus geek. The camera was now behind him, recording his antics from a low angle. "Those girls were needed for the work ahead for they chose to stand on the border of wickedness."

Embara shut the tape off. Neither said anything for several moments. Monk was taking time to consider the import of the man's words—or ravings.

"So what was the deal with Burchett?" He knew he wasn't going to like the answer.

"He had lung cancer and was taking powdered morphine sulfate. Don't ask me how he got hold of it, 'cause I don't know. For a chaser he was apparently also imbibing some backwoods moonshine."

"How in hell did he get up in the morning?"

"Yeah," she commiserated. "Burchett died five months after I taped this interview with him. Initially I was going to include him in the documentary, what with his inferences to Damon being set up."

"What changed your mind?"

"How would it be?" She tucked in her lips and widened her eyes. "I run this segment where he's talking about Malachi and the girls having to be sacrificed. Granted, he's scooting around like a goddamn slinky, but I hoped to account for that in the narration. Yet the more I wanted to do it, the more I hit the wall."

"Nobody would cooperate," Monk noted.

"He has a daughter, Nancy, but I couldn't locate her."

"And who would believe a dying man's rantings on his homemade anesthetizing cocktail?"

"Right. Even though supposedly the files of the League have been made public, there's a lot of talk down there that that was more a publicity stunt than anything. That some things, the real dirt, were kept secret."

"The League kept double sets of files? One different from the other?"

"Something like that," Embara said.

A young woman in a Speedo cycling outfit entered without knocking. "Hey, Harlen moved the meet up to three if you can make it." She handed a set of stapled pages to Embara. "Here's the list you asked for."

"You know he's always doing that kind of shit. Gotta be the cock of the walk."

"Yakkity yak, and blah," the other woman responded, rotating her hand in circles.

"Fine, fine," Embara conceded, knocking against her gear apparatus with the back of her hand lightly. The woman left, leaving the door partially open.

Embara leaned forward on the table, dangling the papers. "Here's my list of former Damon Creel Defense Committee members I assembled for the film. Some may have moved on since then." She set the list down. "See, I think the League couldn't help but let some of its files come out." She made concise movements with her hand as a professor might illustrating a point for a student. "It's not like this stuff hadn't been leaking out for some time in memoirs of civil rights people and so forth."

Monk stroked the sides of his goatee between thumb and index finger. "But like the CIA, you allow some bloodletting to appease the hounds, meanwhile the dirty work goes on. You're not suggesting the League is still in existence? They were officially defunded in 1974." It sounded naive as soon as it left his mouth.

"There's a kind of Delta Godfather down there, Manse Tigbee. He's got farm land and textile mills all over the place, freighters on the docks in Biloxi, and his catfish farms sell to restaurants as far away as France. He also runs a philanthropic venture called the Merit Foundation."

"Meaning he finds merit in white projects?"

"No," Embara corrected, "the Foundation has given money to inner city public schools and private ones too." She made a face and Monk didn't know how to interpret the expression. "By trade he's a structural engineer. His name came up during Damon's trial. But that's all it did, come up."

"So he still wields considerable power."

"In a quiet way, *Señor* Monk, a quiet way. This is the modern age after all." She glanced at a clock set in a brass cathedral arch on a marble pedestal. "You know about Nixon's Southern Strategy, his plan of splintering off Dixiecrats through racialized appeal and patronage?"

Monk indicated he did.

"Okay, Nixon knew Tigbee, had met with him and other southern leaders over a period of time to devise and carry out this realignment of electoral power. Men who Nixon knew could get the votes together in their counties and districts."

"Tigbee having plausible deniability concerning the more nefarious doings of the Citizens League," he observed.

"Yes, Tigbee's always managed to maintain an arm's length from the League in public much like P.W. Botha did with his security forces that engaged in political assassinations during apartheid in South Africa," Embara said. "And peep this," she added, "the feeling among some in the know is that Nixon got the idea for his covert operations against his real and imagined enemies, the break-ins, wiretapping, Plumbers Squad, and so on from Tigbee."

Monk was floored. "You mean he and of Manse were sitting around jawing one night and Tigbee suggests ..." He let the rest go unsaid but implied.

"Exactly, taking lessons from what the Citizens League had been doing for years against uppity Blacks, outside agitators and soft-headed whites. Look, I have to get ready for the bowing and scraping I gotta do for this guy who might shake loose some bank for us."

"I'm really glad you could spare the time." Monk got up. "Say, you ever hear anything about Hiram Bodar in all this?"

Embara was looking for something on her desk. "I know he initially campaigned as a Gingrichite Republican who wasn't squeamish to talk about race."

"Think his principles are what led to his accident?"

"Could be." She found the notes she'd been hunting for. "You might want to talk to that editor—what was his name—from the Mississippi paper?"

"McClendon." Monk told her he'd retrieved some of his articles online and that he intended to talk with Bodar. He thanked her again, picked up the list, and left the studios. Not too far west was the Formosa Cafe. The landmark was a stop for Gen-X and Y-ers and some old-school screenwriters and character actors. Also in the mix were the kind of people who could drop into a joint a little past two in the afternoon and slide into a booth in the back: those who seemed to have no set job, but always enough money to be going out.

The rear portion of the bar and grill had originally been a Red Car, one of the trolleys of the Pacific Electric Line whose tracks back then were the inter-urban line crisscrossing the city like Martian canals.

Monk ordered a Bud, some vegetable fried rice and a plate of popcorn fried shrimp. In the old days, food was not why you came to the Formosa. The quality of the chow then was fair at best; you came for the ambiance. The pictures of the old-time stars along the walls; the cracked carmine leather of the booths; the long, scarred bar, and those who lurched up to it had made the grub's ingestion passable. But the menu had been upgraded for the less hardy.

Dexter Grant had introduced Monk to the Formosa, and the bartender in the bow tie, who mixed his drinks adroitly all the while telling you a story about the days of L.A. when orange groves outnumbered people. The bartender had passed on some ten years ago, walking home one night as he'd done for more than forty years. He got to the top of the steps to his apartment on Fuller, breathed his last gasp into the early morning air, and sank down, holding the rail. The cops found him like that, his one hand frozen like statuary on the peeling paint of the wooden railing, in a kneeling position.

Silently Monk saluted the man. He hoisted his glass of beer to the photo of the guru of bartending residing over the window where he sat. The bartender's crooked smile hinted but did not reveal the grand joke only he knew the punch line to. Paying his bill, Monk wondered when it would be his time to find out the answer for himself.

"EVERYTHING COOL?" Kodama was eating a double cone of Tahitian Guava and Rocky Road.

Monk was hanging up the receiver at the pay phone. "Yeah, she's got a male nurse who's going to follow her home and see her inside."

The couple strolled again along the Third Street Promenade in Santa Monica. The walking thoroughfare was a post-industrial marketplace with a virtual reality store, sunglasses shops, record stores, bookshops, coffeehouses, toy emporium, movie palaces and an omnipresent Disney store.

"Look, the killer knows you're stirring up shit, he's not going to take another run at her now." She put an arm around his waist, tugging him. "Plus, Nona's got that Beretta of yours you insisted she carry."

"And she knows how and where to shoot it." Monk clasped her hand and brought the cone up to his own mouth. He took a big bite, chewed, then swallowed the lump of creamy goo.

Kodama winced. "You're the only person I know who never gets those headaches from cold stuff. Why the heck is that?"

They got closer to the Midnight Special bookstore.

"Fumes from old carburetors have given me certain powers."

They looked at various books displayed on a long shelf in the plateglass window. One row contained copies of a book Monk had a particular interest in, *City of Promise: How Los Angeles Destroyed Public Housing.* "Now in trade paper," he said admiringly. The book was authored by Fletcher Wilkinson.

Kodama peered closer, holding her cone close to the glass. "Have you talked to Fletcher recently?"

"No, I should give him a buzz, though." Wilkinson had been in the city's housing department decades ago. He'd been run out for his left-wing ideas like integration and providing decent housing to low income and working families. He'd also been instrumental in Monk solving the murder that led to the shoot-out in the Rancho Tajauta Housing Projects.

"Shall we browse, my love?"

"Just let me finish this," Kodama said.

By the time Kodama was done with her cone, a sax player

and a violinist had set up in front of the bookstore. As was the custom along the Promenade, various street musicians and performers did their thing at all hours to earn a few dollars from passersby.

The musical duo were doing a melodic version of "Stella by Starlight" as Monk and Kodama entered the store.

# CHAPTER 12

An elliptical pane of leaded glass was set above center in the front door. The house the door was attached to was a modified '30s-era Hansel and Gretel design set at the crest of a sloping, sparkling green lawn. Monk parked his Ford and got out, proud it had only taken him three false turns to find the place among the convoluted streets of Baldwin Hills.

The homes of Baldwin Hills were strewn up and down land rising between Coliseum Street on the north, and Stocker to the south. La Brea Avenue, which ran north/ south, was the main drag bifurcating the mostly Black middle-class area. The Hills had been named for E.J. "Lucky" Baldwin, an Irish immigrant who'd come to L.A. during the real estate boom in the 1880s. He had a yen to make money and his fame.

Lucky was known to have an eye for younger women, fast horses, and throughout his life was involved in a series of financial and morally suspect escapades. Yet he died very solvent in 1909, after settling not only the section of town bearing his name, but also Santa Anita, and naturally, its racetrack.

No doubt Lucky's ghost smiled as dozens of automated

oil pumps these days worked continuously in fenced-off lots near Stocker. The land Baldwin developed was still producing the black gold as if fossil fuels would never run out.

Second-tier entertainers, upper-level city bureaucrats, and some music people claimed residence in the hills on streets with names such as Don Lorenzo, Don Quixote and Don Zarembo. In 1985, a massive fire had wiped out more than fifty homes, and before that, there had been a bad flood when the hills' concrete reservoir had burst in the '60s.

If there was something symbolic about both flame and water having wrought destruction in Baldwin Hills, some biblical sign the homeowners were meant to have heeded, they apparently had not. Or at least chose not to. For Baldwin Hills was still a place one could find the strivers, the strata of Black folk one also found in nearby Windsor Hills and Ladera Heights, who asked for no hand out, worked hard at their jobs, and kept their wet bars well stocked with premium liquor.

Not too far down below in the flatlands, Monk glimpsed the contours of the jungle. Coliseum Street sliced through this compact area of low- to moderate-rent apartment buildings landscaped with overgrown shrubs, wildly sprouting rubber plants, and towering eucalyptus trees. When he was a kid, he and his friends thought the place was called the jungle by whites because it was an all-Black enclave. As it turned out the area had gotten the nickname when it was still white because of the amount of topiary.

Monk ruminated on the intricacies of Los Angeles' demarcations as he strode up the walk to the door with its unblinking single orb. Next door a woman in a shapeless housedress was on her knees digging at a brick-lined flower bed running along the base of her home. She pushed back the floppy brim of her sunhat at the sound of his footsteps.

Monk knew she was giving him the once-over through her shades, what with him dressed in off-white jeans, striped shirt, with sleeves rolled up and scuffed Timberlines. She also shot a glance at his restored '64. Had one of the graspers from the crowded apartments down below dared to journey beyond his station? Monk smiled.

She turned her head back toward her zinnias and marigolds, the trowel in her hand moving listlessly. She appeared to be deep in thought as Monk rang the bell.

"Yes?" came the question from the indistinct shadow beyond the opaque glass.

Monk told her his name and why he had come.

"Really?" the woman said as she opened the door. She was somewhere in her mid-fifties and her dark brown hair was cut close and straight to her roundish face. She wore a loose silk T and a blue and orange print skirt. "A real live private eye?"

He could tell his outfit didn't fit the expected image. "I can show you my ID if you like."

"Oh, I believe you." She stepped back. "Come on, we're in here."

He followed her through a deeply carpeted foyer past a flagstone fireplace and a big-screen TV set diagonally from it. "Okay, ladies, clean up your language, there's a man in the house," the woman joked.

Monk could hear hearty laughter and the unmistakable slap of cards on a table top. He came around a corner to see an enclosed patio where three other women were playing bid whist.

"Uptown, girl," one of them said, tossing down a seven of hearts. She glanced at Monk.

"How'd you find me?" Clara Antony asked pleasantly.

Grant had found out her haunts. "Denise Rutledge's

sister-in-law knows somebody I know." That was more or
less accurate.

She nodded appreciatively. "You want to play a hand?"

The owner of the house touched Monk's arm. "Would
you like some iced tea?"

"He's a beer man, Jeri." The woman who said it was about
Monk's complexion, wearing a red sweater top, matching
pumps, and had on too much blue eyeliner. Her hair was
coiffured in layers and he could tell she worked out regularly.
She kept her eyes on the only man in the room as she laid
down a three of clubs.

"I'm fine, thanks." He wasn't sure whether he should sit
or stand. He didn't want to seem awkward.

Clara Antony explained who Monk was. "And what can
I help you with today?" She indicated a couch set in front of
a sliding glass door. Beyond it an old golden retriever
lounged and scratched.

Monk sat down, suddenly wishing he had accepted the
beverage as it would give him something to do with his
hands. All the women were now sitting at the table, looking
at him. They were all middle-aged Black women dressed
casually but expensively. They gave him the impression of
having reached a certain station in life but they were not
"siddidy" about it, as his mother would say.

"Normally I don't bust in on people like this," he began.

The one in blue eyeliner said, "You look like the kind that
busts 'em up regularly, sugar."

Clara Antony gave her a look but said nothing, then
glanced at the hand she held. "Who bid five?"

"It's just that I'm on short time and need to get as much
done as I can in the next coupla days before I light out."

"Down to the Delta," the former singer guessed.

Monk confirmed that and told her about the attack on

his mother. He was careful not to draw too fine a line
between the last time he'd seen Clara Antony and the assault.
His moving about town, dropping the news he was going to
Mississippi, was a way to see if he could draw the killer and/
or his partner to him. He wished Jill would pack that Smith
& Wesson .38 she had, given all the attacks on the women
around him.

"Like I said, I may be a little rude here, Clara, but I wanted
to ask you a few things away from your husband."

Blue Eyeliner made a face. And a serious-looking woman
in oversized glasses opened her eyes wide.

"Ardmore may have had his rough edges, Ivan, but he
wouldn't truck with anything like murder." She crossed her
legs, her fingers pushing several of her cards face down on
the table. "The club game in those days wasn't for the faint-
hearted. I'm not saying he was always a gentleman. But—"
She shook her head as a way of completing her sentence.
"And he's too old to be jumping ladies in their driveways."

"She'd rather he jump her," the one with the mascara
snorted. Big Glasses giggled and the one who had opened
the door slapped her friend on the arm.

Monk asked, "How about Harvey Lyle, the numbers man
who sponsored the All-Stars with your husband? He and
Kennesaw ever have a run-in?"

Clara Antony considered his question. "Yeah, probably,
but who didn't with someone so foul tempered as Lyle?" She
flicked her hand at the woman in blue eyeliner across from
her. "Course Gloria here had a thing for him, didn't you
Glo-glo?"

"Careful," she advised. She turned her eyes on Monk.
"Harvey had at least two sons I knew of." She played clubs.

"They grow into their old man's business?"

"One went back east, Boston I think, he's legitimate,

works for a sportswear manufacturer, I believe. And the other, Trent, he was involved in some shady stuff." She looked at the others to fill in. The homeowner raised an index finger and spoke.

"Trent wound up involved in drugs, no surprise there. I hear he's been in and out of jail several times."

"Anybody know what firm the one back in Boston works for?" Monk asked.

"Oh, now, why would Stewart be a suspect, what would he be after?" Clara Antony continued to move her cards around on the table in circular motions.

"Maybe Lyle and Kennesaw had some deal going back-then," Monk said. "Something behind your husband's back."

"And the son is out to collect?" one of the women suggested.

"Can anybody find out for sure where Stewart is?" The women's hesitation was apparent. "I just want to close all unnecessary doors."

Eyeliner looked at her friends, then said, "I can find out. But I'd want to talk to him first. Give me your card and I'll have him call you."

"He's going to be out of town," Clara Antony reminded her.

"My office will forward the information to me." Monk got up and handed her one of his cards. He remained standing.

"Why don't you ask him to put his home number on it, Glo?" the one in the glasses goaded her.

Glo showed horseteeth and tucked the card away in a clutch bag at her feet.

"I appreciate your time, ladies, especially yours, Clara."

"I hope you find this nut, whoever he is, Ivan."

He said his goodbyes and wound his way back down to

La Brea and headed north. The sky was uncustomarily clear and the San Gabriel mountains stood out sharp and bold beyond the high-rises of downtown.

Monk had a chicken omelet and fries for lunch at Roscoe's House of Chicken and Waffles on Pico. Afterward, he headed north again. He had an appointment with Bernie Desconso, the lawyer who'd been involved in Creel's appeals for the last twenty years. He knew Desconso, a gregarious man, slightly, having met him once at a garden party his own lawyer, Parren Teague, had given. He'd also run into him at some National Lawyer's Guild dinner or ACLU fundraiser that Kodama had dragged him to over the years. Desconso was a partner in a law firm that had offices in the Equitable Building on Wilshire near Normandie.

He was standing and staring at a Basquiat print in the men's waiting room when Desconso came out to greet him.

"Ivan, long time no see, man. Come on back." Desconso shook his hand, clasping his left one over the top like a ward healer on his rounds. He was in rolled-up shirt sleeves and tailored slacks. His longish hair was fast receding from his unwrinkled brow, and his waistline was trimmer than Monk remembered.

"You been working out," he commented.

Desconso touched his head. "If I can't keep this, might as well lose the other. Hell, it's been five years since the divorce, might as well get in a few more innings until I need Viagra. How's Jill?"

"Busy." He was going to go on about them talking about having children, but decided against elaborating, that maybe telling him would jinx the possibility.

They sat in a corner office furnished in sterile modern. The personal touches were the photos of Descanso's teen-aged children on his desk in Plexiglas holders. Behind his chair, the vertical blinds had been drawn back to reveal a view to the west.

Monk filled him in on his investigation.

Desconso whistled. "I wouldn't doubt that the Southern Citizens League was behind the attack on your mother, Ivan. I'll maintain till the day I die their reach has been far more insidious, far deeper than anything they revealed in the files they released or the so-called in-depth pieces on them the news magazine shows have done."

"They've officially disbanded," Monk ventured.

"And the CIA never partnered with drug dealers," Desconso countered derisively.

Monk held up his hands like he was under arrest. "I'm with you, brother. I faxed you that list I got from N'Kobari Embara of some of the folks who've been involved in Creel's defense committee. Any one of them in particular you think I should talk to before I get down there? Or anybody else you can think of?"

"Yeah, I gave that some thought. None of them jumped out at me. But there was this one woman we came across during one of our appeals. She'd been Ava Green's roommate that first semester at Brandeis."

"You never deposed her?"

"No," Desconso was looking for something in the piles of files and notepads on his desk. "One of my investigators talked to her, and it turned out she'd had to come back home at the end of that semester; out here to LaCanada-Flintridge, actually." He pointed north while still searching his desk. "Her mother had taken ill, and she was needed back home to help care for her." Desconso found a torn half sheet of paper. "Here's the note I made to myself." He held the sheet aloft quickly, then read it. "Helena Jones is her name. See, she never did get back to Brandeis or join Green in Damon's campaign. So really, for our purposes, she could offer nothing of value." He handed the note across to Monk.

He stared at what passed for Desconso's handwriting. "Why do you think I should talk to her?"

Desconso made a face. "You asked for others, she's another. That's an old address and phone, the family's house."

"Can you set it up so I can see Creel when I'm down there?" He folded the paper and slipped it into his pocket.

"Sure, we'll tell the prison authorities you're working for us." Desconso stared at him evenly, leaning back in his chair, "Now if I get you in to see Damon, I hope you'll share anything relevant should you uncover something."

"Sure, Bernie, why wouldn't I?"

Desconso's brows went up. "I've been convinced of Damon Creel's innocence since the second day I became involved in his case. Some nights I can't sleep right because I know that this country has cavalierly and repeatedly locked Black men like Damon Creel away for what they stood for, what they tried to do. He is a political prisoner in a class and race war that's been going on since the first Pilgrims arrived, and the rock Malcolm talked about landed on the Indians."

Monk was uncomfortable. "You want me to be a true believer, Bernie?"

"I don't know the relationship you had with your cousin. I heard from an attorney at the courthouse the other day about his poisoning before you phoned me."

"And you know he had a snitch jacket," Monk leveled. "I won't hold out on you, man." A pigeon flitted past the large window, settled on the ledge and pecked at something as the two men stared at each other.

Desconso rose and they shook hands again. "The best huh?"

"Thanks."

MONK TALKED with several people on the list Embara had given him over the next two days. One was a woman named Reily who, along with her husband, owned a print shop in Culver City. She related that she still believed in Creel's innocence, but what with the kids and the business, her activist life was severely curtailed. Another committee member named Franks was a practicing Buddhist, but his striving for inner balance didn't temper his bitter feelings that he felt he'd been taken in by the Creel Defense Committee.

"I'd be interested in knowing why," Monk remarked. He stood next to Franks in the art gallery/bookstore/coffeeshop the latter owned in a shopping mall near King Harbor in Redondo Beach.

Franks regarded Monk for several moments before speaking. "Let me put it this way, Mr. Monk. I think Damon Creel is the biggest fraud to come along since the three-dollar-bill. He's a self-aggrandizer, an egotist who only wanted to advance his book deals, and of course, nail some college-educated pussy."

"Tough words from a man into brown rice and inner peace. So you think he murdered those girls?"

Franks shifted on his feet, lightly touching the frame on a Betye Saar assemblage. "I know he was bopping one of them at least, probably both."

Monk enunciated, "Do you think he murdered them?"

"I do," Franks said softly. "I think he did it because Ava Green was going to expose him for the fake he is, and I think things got out of hand. "Franks's eyes bore into Monk's, daring him to question his judgement. "I think people like Creel used good-hearted white liberals like me. And too many of his brethren are still doing it today rather than getting on with their lives."

"Don't a lot of us come up short, Mr. Franks? Does that mean Creel's goals are less worthy?"

Franks snorted. "Figures you'd defend him."

Monk was getting worked up but decided to let his irritation at this man simmer. It wasn't as if he wasn't ambiguous about Creel's guilt or innocence himself. And Franks had been through the experience of being on the defense committee, not him. "Thanks for your time, Mr. Franks." He started to leave.

"Hey," Franks called to him as Monk made the doorway. "If you find out something when you're down there, let me know, okay?"

"Why?" he asked, not looking around.

"Maybe you'll restore my faith."

"I look forward to it."

THE NEXT day, the day before he was to leave for Mississippi, he had a talk with Helena Jones. They had agreed to meet for lunch at the Koo-Koo-Roo on Santa Monica Boulevard in the City of West Hollywood. Jones was a professor of urban planning at UCLA, and worked part-time as a consultant for the small city of gays and Russian emigrants.

She was on the lean side, her upper body defined in angular lines with a full bosom. Her face broadcast her Slavic origins, and her smile was infectious. Jones wore dark wool pants and a satiny purple shirt with shiny black buttons. Gray was edging its way into the roots of her auburn hair.

"So you and Ava talked over the phone from time to time when she and Sharon Aikens were down there working on the campaign?" Monk ate a forkful of creamed spinach.

"Yes, that's right," she said, using her fingers to pick up her skinless chicken drumstick.

"I've talked to several people who used to be active in the defense committee," Monk continued, "And I've been told that it was Ava who was big on going down to Memphis that summer. Why was that, a kid who grew up in Scarsdale?"

"It was an adventure," she said lightly. "And she was a young woman with her own mind looking to make her mark." She chewed with vigor.

"She wanted to change the world and herself at the same time," Monk empathized.

"You gotta remember Herbert Marcuse had been a big influence on the campus then. His classes were always packed. And him being a mentor to Angela Davis only increased the allure of his writings. Hell, in those days, Brandeis was considered Berkeley East, for goodness sake. All the smart young women had the desires Ava expressed before the onset of kids, and arguments over bullshit at three in the morning with your husband." She appraised him. "You married, Ivan?"

He'd noticed the band on her finger. "I live with my"—he worked his hands—"well, whatever the word is these days."

"Children?"

"Not yet."

"Then you better get on it, huh?"

"How about yours?"

"Thirteen and ten. And you don't know what it's all about until those teen years hit, baby." She had some of her cole-slaw, her eyes gleaming mischievously.

"When was the last time you'd talked to Ava?"

"About a week before she was killed." She must have said those same words several times over the years, but there was still emotion behind the repetition.

"You think Creel did it?"

"Which case you trying to solve?" She pulled the straw

out of her glass and gulped down her soda. She wiped at her mouth with a paper napkin.

"Did I hesitate too long in my answer?" Monk smiled.

"What else you want to know about Ava?"

"She ever mention that Creel was knocking her around, being abusive?"

"No," Jones opened her purse, looked inside, then closed it decidedly. "She knew enough to know it wasn't Donna Reed time, dig? But he cared for her, was respectful and talked about strategy with her. She wasn't just his squeeze."

He halted his fork midway to his mouth. "Any mention of threesomes?"

"Uh-uh, no way with Ava, see?"

"You ever meet her folks?"

"No. We'd talked about me going out with her to Scarsdale, but I had to go home that January, and see about my ailing mother."

"That was the last you two actually saw each other?"

"Yes."

"You wouldn't have an old number for her folks? And remember their names?"

Jones made a motion with her fork like a conductor. "Oh, God, that's been so long. But I think they're still there." She frowned, "Or maybe at least the father; seems I heard somehow they'd had a divorce. I don't recall his name, his first name, I mean. But I think the mother's name was Allison or something like that." She ate some more, then said, "Hey, what kind of detective can't use the phone book?"

"I'm lazy."

"Like hell."

He grinned again. "I did call some Greens in upstate New York. People who've been bothered over the years by reporters and such. But no parent of Ava, at least no one who would admit that over the phone."

They finished their lunch and Monk walked with the professor out to the parking lot. She fetched the cigarette she'd been coveting out of her purse and cupped her hands to light it. A restored maroon 1947 Ford F-1 pickup with hot pink fenders drove past them toward the exit, a drag queen with a beehive hairdo at the wheel. "Do you think you'll find something out nobody else has in all this time?" She sucked on the cigarette like it was manna.

"Think I'm that arrogant?"

She touched his biceps. "I didn't mean to make it sound like that, you brat. You know what I mean." She looked into his face, the cigarette bobbing from her lip, movie-tough fashion.

"Yeah, well," he said dismissively. "If you could make a few calls to some of your old college friends, see if you can find a current number for one or both of Ava's parents, I'd appreciate it." He gave her one of his cards. "I'll get the message if you leave it with Delilah."

"Sure, Nash Bridges." She put the card in her purse. "So, do you want to know whether I think Creel did it or not?"

"Tell me when I get back." They shook hands and parted.

FROM HIS office phone, Monk talked with several other former members of the Damon Creel Defense Committee scattered throughout the Southland and the nation. It was past seven-thirty when he finally got over to his mother's house on Stanley. She hobbled about due to her recent assault.

"Shouldn't I go with you to Clarksdale?" Nona Monk asked.

"You could be his back-up, Nona." Dexter Grant was

rummaging through one of the soft-sided bags he'd recently brought inside. "A mother-son detective thing, now we might be able to sell that to Showtime or HBO and get some money out of the deal." He put bug eyes on Monk.

Monk had his legs stretched out before him on the couch, his arms spread along the back. Kodama sat next to him, thumbing through the *TV Guide*.

"No, Mom." He smoldered Grant with a death stare.

"But I know them folks down there, Ivan. Country people got their own ways of going about things, their own pace. You come there with that hurry up and do attitude, you liable to make 'em nervous or they'll clam up 'cause you come off like a slicker trying to be smarter than them."

"Your son's the people's servant, Nona; he's always humble to the will of the masses." Kodama kept reading listings in the *Guide*.

"Say, baby," Monk teased, "shouldn't you have your glasses on to make out the small print?"

She hit his leg and he chuckled.

"Y'all makin' sport of this, and this is serious," his mother said. "That New South them crackers flouting ain't nothing but window dressin', baby. Look at all that craziness that's been going on, that Satan-worshipping teenager who shot up his campus in Arkansas, and all those supposed suicides of Black men in the jails down there."

"I don't believe those incidents are related, Mom." Since this business started, her Southern accent, which had never been that pronounced, had been getting thicker. A defensive mechanism, he figured, a psychological comfort in this time of stress.

"I'm just saying I know you're an operator, but Clarksdale, Mound Bayou, Shelby, and what have you are not your stompin' grounds."

"I got it, Mom," he rasped.

Grant extracted his ancient Police Special revolver from his bag, and carried it into the bedroom he'd be using.

Nona Monk tracked the ex-cop with an even look as he did so. "You just remember when to ease up, Ivan. Your father let too much eat at him, son." She put her arms around herself. "Sometimes, you must let what can't be changed go."

Ivan said, "I know, Mom."

LATER, MONK and Kodama were in each other's arms in their bed. Cassandra Wilson was singing "My Funny Valentine" on the radio.

"You set the alarm?" He rubbed the small of her back.

"Hmm," she purred. "How are you getting your gun through the check on?"

"That's a surprising question coming from you, being an officer of the court."

"Don't try to misdirect."

"Dex is sending it via express."

"Don't they check that?"

"Says he's got it covered."

"I'm glad you both use your powers for good, and not for evil."

"Ain't that the truth."

They held onto each other as they slept.

# CHAPTER 13

Monk dozed on the smooth Southwest flight to Memphis International Airport. Upon landing, he made a call to Bernie Desconso's office, and was informed by one of the assistants the interview with Creel had been arranged for tomorrow. He rented a five-speed Dodge Ram 2500 ST pickup complete with a highway emergency kit in the rear bed. Monk briefly considered hanging around town, taking in some blues clubs on Beale Street later that night.

Well, he concluded, there'd be time for that later. He headed south on Highway 61. As he crossed the state line into Mississippi, the scenery appeared more full and verdant.

Monk drove past vast fields of soybeans, cotton and wheat, walnut trees and groves of pecan trees, maples and sweeping oaks. The land of the Natchez and Chickasaw was first plundered by the Spaniard Hernando De Soto in 1541. The conquistador demanded slave labor from his generous Chickasaw hosts, who promptly attacked the Spanish garrison in retaliation for De Soto's bad manners. But 'Sippi wasn't known for that battle. Indeed, the Magnolia State's profile had nothing to do with the fight of the red man against European colonizers. No, its legacy of Black and white animus was forever burned into the nation's, and the world's, consciousness.

The first African slaves were brought to Mississippi in 1720, long before Eli Whitney introduced his cotton gin in 1793. The machine sped up the process of separating the seeds from the cotton bolls. The slaves could now produce much more than their upkeep—slavery finally started to turn a profit.

And so began the torturous existence between the races in this small state that even now seemed to not have been fully reconciled. But why should Mississippi be any different from the rest of the country? Sure, in the bad old days the folks up north could point to Mississippi and look down their noses at the rednecks and their backward ways and their efforts to halt the inevitable dynamics of history—that somehow those forces believed that through will and chicanery they could forestall social progress forever.

As late as 1964, less than eight percent of the Black population had been allowed to register to vote. Conversely, Mississippi was now home to the highest number of elected Black officials than any other state. Maybe change was possible—at least on the surface.

Outside Robinsonville, Monk spotted a white farmer in a cowboy hat riding a tractor, tilling an iron-rich patch of earth. The man tipped his hat as Monk drove past and he returned the gesture by touching his forehead. He chuckled to himself in the air-conditioned comfort of his cab, and passed the welcoming sign into Tunica.

The last memory he had of the town from years ago was a visit he'd taken with his mother and father. Then it was only miles of flat land and sugar ditches undisturbed by anything more than a two-story structure. Now Tunica was a happening place with several casinos dotting the landscape.

The buildings ranged from red-bricked structures with cheap awnings tacked on the fronts, to large structures built in what seemed to be giant Lego pieces fitted together. These structures squatted close to the roadside like fat, indolent spiders waiting for their next feeding.

Monk went on into Clarksdale and pulled into the gravel lot of a small motel called the A-Model Lodge. The place was a one-story series of rectangular rooms with fake hitching posts spaced evenly along a wooden walkway beneath an overhanging roof. Red curtains hung in the windows. He went to the manager's office, which was situated in one corner of the motel.

"How long will you be staying with us, sir?" The young woman standing behind the counter was East Indian. She was dressed in form-fitting bicycle pants and a long-sleeve shirt, tail out.

"I'm not sure, but at least a week." He handed her his credit card as he began to fill out the registration.

"Come to gamble?" She passed his card through her machine.

"A little maybe. More than anything, I want to enjoy the sights."

"You might try the Nova Express Casino, they have a floor show of local talent. Me and my girlfriends like it okay."

"This local flavor include the blues?" He nudged the registration card toward her.

"Naturally, showgirls, too." She read his card and smiled at a joke to herself. She picked up the form and his credit card slip and put it somewhere below the counter. "We ain't got what you call room service 'round here, but there's some good eatin' spots, though."

"You bring on that southern accent on all the out-of-towners?" He picked up his bags.

"Only when I want to." She produced a key with a bronze-colored tab attached to it. A gold numeral 17 gleamed dully on the fob. "Here you are."

Monk exited and made his way along the wooden walkway, which creaked. A white woman in a tube top, JC Penney Arizona jeans, with curlers in her hair, came out of number 15. She had a purse tucked under one arm like a running back and dark splotches were beneath her bleary, but expertly mascara'd eyes.

She gave Monk a weak smile and he nodded going past her. Her footsteps pounded on the walk as she went away and Monk unlocked the door to 17. He let air in on a clean room of beige walls. In its center was a queen-sized bed with an aqua-and-black quilt. A peeling walnut desk and chair were in the corner. A so-so painting of a catfish, suspended in a void of bright orange, hung on one wall. The TV was on a cart, the top of the set crisscrossed with light chains, the links wrapped around the cart wheels.

He put his bags on the floor and opened a built-in closet next to the tiny bathroom. There was a recent *Newsweek* and a brochure from the Nova Express Casino lying on top of the desk. Out of habit he opened the drawers, frowning at dried rat droppings in the lower left one. Hearing no scurrying in the walls, Monk took off his shoes and lay on his back on the bed.

He napped and awoke to footsteps creaking along the walkway. He'd left the curtains open and felt embarrassed for sleeping in the daytime like a nursing home resident. The footsteps stopped before they got to his window, and he heard a door open and shut forcefully.

Monk phoned Malus Locke's house, the farmer who rented out his mother's land over in Mound Bayou. He was informed by a woman's voice her father was out and Monk left a message. Then he walked south of the motel and passed the famous crossroads where Highways 61 and 49 met. Residing at the four corners were a Kentucky Fried Chicken outlet, a power tool rental, a chain-linked lot and a coin laundry. This was where blues great Robert Johnson, who learned his initial licks from Charlie Patton, was to have sold his soul to Legba, the devil, so as to play his starvation box like no other.

Of course, his mother had told him several times, the actual crossing of the highways in the '30s was in a different location. But Clarksdale, like Robinsonville up the road, had a blues museum, so it was understandable if the town officials saw the need to be creative in their geography. After all, there was only so many blues tourist dollars to go around.

He finally wound up walking along Sunflower Avenue that paralleled the Sunflower River. At various intervals along this stretch were metal signs on dark green poles. The stenciled messages warned the traveler that sight-seeing in certain parts of Clarksdale should be done with the same amount of care one would do in any big city. You've come a long way, baby, Monk reflected.

At Third, he stopped in at Stackhouse Records, an emporium that any true aficionado had to visit to purchase a blues map and independently produced cassettes of local Delta artists. He was considering which Frank Frost tape to buy when he noticed a wooden crate on a counter near him. Stamped into its soft wood on one end were the words TIG-BEE MILLS, ROBINSONVILLE. The crate was old, and filled with LPs in worn record jackets. He touched the letters on the crate as if to absorb some knowledge of the entity to which they belonged.

Monk bought his tapes and got a hot beef sandwich and mustard potato salad at the Burnside Cafe a few doors down from JJ's Social Club, which fronted the train tracks. The day was waning when Monk left the cafe and walked across the tracks, taking in the sights. The long shadows of approaching evening engulfed the buildings as he finally walked slowly back to the motel.

A little later, he was enjoying a bottled beer at a corner table in a roadhouse pushed back on bleached gravel from Highway 61. The establishment was called the Tornado Lounge and Game Parlor, and currently both its pool tables were occupied. There was an empty parquet dance riser trimmed in duct tape, and the CD juke was playing a Ray Bailey number, "Blowing Satan's Horn."

Men and women sat at the bar and the tables, talking and sipping beer; one cosmopolitan woman was drinking wine. Just as the steady chatter of the place wrapped comfortably around Monk's psyche, another anxiety attack overtook him. He fought against a strong urge to shove his chair back, hoping the legs wouldn't stop until it rammed against the wall.

He hunched over his beer, protecting the brew as if it were liquid silver. His stomach felt like there were hooks latched onto the lining, and an abusive sprite was tugging on them while straddling his spine. The beer was becoming bile inside him and he could no longer discern or care what was playing on the juke.

The apprehension was like warm hands on his heart and Monk considered rushing out the door. He restrained himself, clutching the bottle before him like it was a life preserver, and he sucked the brew down, his forehead wet with the terrors.

"Can I get you anything, shuga?"

Monk couldn't look up.

"Hey, you been nippin' at somethin' other than beer, Mr. Big-and-rough-lookin'?"

Monk tried to teleport the waitress away. "I'm all right," he croaked, staring at the Budweiser label. He didn't hear her footsteps leave over the wailing of Johnny Shines, but he was aware he could once again distinguish the music from the conversing and movement of bodies in the club. It was as if Shines's moanful inflections were a call pulling him back into the world of familiarity and relative safety.

Monk was finally able to sit back in his chair, and let go of the bottle, his mooring. A young woman with Afro puffs in a pleated mini-skirt and platform shoes gyrated on the dance floor with a man in overalls and a canvas cap with a CAT logo on it. He watched the couple move about for awhile, then examined the others in the place. There was a middle-aged woman in a loose vest leaning over the pool table to make her shot, and two men laughing and slapping each other's shoulders at the bar. A smallish man in an out-of-date suit, the coat buttoned, entered through the front door.

The newcomer walked directly to the bar, leaned on it and signaled for the bartender. He was noticeable for his preserved attire, and because he was the only white customer in the Tornado Lounge. He didn't appear uncomfortable, and none of the other patrons seemed to take any particular notice of the man. His beer arrived and he turned, to lean and sip and watch. He undid the button on his coat.

Monk had lost interest in his beer and rose. The man in the suit tipped the stem of his bottle at him slightly before quaffing an amount. Monk walked out into the humid night, the wetness under his arms and chest chilling him even though he wore a jean jacket. He was cold all the way back to his room.

# CHAPTER 14

Damon Creel had lost some of his hair since he was last seen in Embara's documentary. His shoulders were squarish, and his midriff was thick, but solid. He wore a gray shirt, the flaps of which were buttoned over the twin breast pockets. His blue khakis were shapeless, the bottoms cresting worn work boots. He and Monk walked in the small peach orchard behind the Unicor wire-harness and aircraft-assembly building, as they talked.

UNICOR was the federal prison industries program for the Bureau of Prisons. The enterprise was mandated to make a profit, and it was doing quite well, never at a loss for idle hands. Inmate labor in public and private prisons earned more than two billion dollars a year, and UNICOR was carving out a sizeable niche of those monies along with private firms such as Wackenhut and Corrections Corporation of America.

In the age of punishment, the idea was that convicts could serve a useful and thrifty purpose by undercutting the wages a local worker might get on the outside in offering services such as airline reservations, manufacturing steel security doors and making mezzanine systems. In this advanced stage of capitalism, a sound work ethic was no doubt instilled in men doing long years for ounces of crack, interstate flight, or bank robbery.

Creel was a shift foreman, and his lunch time had been moved around so he could have this meeting.

"I guess it'd be fitting for the legend if I was mellow and philosophical about being shut down for more than twenty-seven years." Creel stopped, leaning his back on a slim peach tree, his hands in his pockets. Since meeting him ten minutes ago, he'd only taken one of his hands out to shake Monk's. He wore rimless glasses, his eyes alive with inquisitiveness, yet his voice was prison-guarded, betraying little in the way of emotion.

"But that would make you a goddamn fool," Monk finished.

Creel nodded his head quickly. "You're on your J. Everybody's read my bio, a lot less bothered with my collection of essays." He looked up into the tree's boughs. "So you think I had your cousin snuffed from inside?" He reached up and plucked a peach free.

"I don't, not really. But aside from hating him, I was hoping there was something in both of your pasts I could use now."

Creel examined the peach and carefully placed it in the crook of the tree. He then put his hands back in his pockets. "I wasn't sleeping with his wife, if that's what you're hinting at."

"No, it's not."

Together, they moved off at a diagonal out of the orchard and toward an area where several guards congregated. There were ten redwood picnic benches on a cement pad, and a bunch of Millington's prisoners sat and talked.

Monk resumed, "Something's been stirred up by Marshall Spears's death."

"You mean the wrath of Malachi?" Creel asked.

"That still going around?"

"Naturally; we talking about Mississippi, man. Her public schools are still considered the worst in the country. And you been through Tunica, seen all those casinos? The school system there is seen as one of the worst in the state. In 1995, Tunica's school district ranked one-fifty-two out of one hundred and fifty-three in a statewide literacy exam. Illiteracy's very high among the Black population of the city." Creel shoved his hands deeper in his pockets, like he needed to keep them in check.

"Hey man, you gonna tighten me up on that legal brief thang, right?" Another man in gray and blue, his hair braided in cornrows, asked, moving past both men.

"Most definitely," Creel answered. He inclined his head back toward a building and Monk walked alongside him. "The casinos, along with catfish and cotton and soybeans, are the economic engines of the state. Management of the casinos hinted that the local Black population was only prepared for low-level jobs in their industry, that positions such as dealer are not possible, given the lack of math and reading skills.

"There's been an ongoing fight by Black parents to get the casinos to allocate reasonable portions of their revenues for the school system. There had been a suit to force the casinos to pony up more to the local economy. But that action ran up against the desires of the majority white county board of supervisors who wanted the casinos to invest in the infrastructure, and thereby be able to attract more businesses. And modern Mississippi was once again engaged in a fight of who got what resources, and when did they get them."

They stood in front of another unmarked brown brick

building. "Another UNICOR enterprise," Creel said sardonically, jerking his head at the structure. "PC repair."

"Ain't that something," Monk commiserated.

"What you want to know about Ava, man?" Creel leaned
against the brick wall. "I know that's what you really want
to find out about."

"Among other things."

Creel laughed, scratching the back of his head on the
brick. "The eternal seeker. What happens when all truths
are told, Monk?"

"Peace or chaos."

"You could write one of those self-help books for prisoners with thinking like that."

"You the one who brought Ava up," Monk emphasized.

"Indeed," Creel said, looking off. "You wasn't in the service, were you?"

Monk told him about bombing out in college football,
being a bounty hunter and then signing onto the merchant
marines.

Creel took a hand out of his pocket and undid one of the
flaps on his shirt pocket. He didn't take anything out of
the pocket, and returned his hand to his pants pocket. "Yeah,
everybody's been through some kinda fire fight, I guess."

"That go for Ava, too?"

"She wanted to burn down the walls, man. The walls I
saw out there in white soldiers' eyes while we were out on
patrol. The walls that been holding Black folks back here
since before Reconstruction. She was real, man."

"And you came to save us?"

"Naw, Monk, I don't have some Black messiah jones. I
came to do my part like Ava did and hundreds of others,
Black and white."

"And Sharon?"

"She was here 'cause of Ava, whose passion for justice was enough, at least for awhile, to carry her friend along too."

"Until . . ." Monk prompted.

"Until Sharon saw the honkies down here wasn't playin'. That they weren't about to hand over local power, no matter how symbolic, to a bunch of burr heads."

Monk knew from Creel's book his campaign office for mayor had been shot into more than once, and several of the volunteers were run off the road and beaten up. "So she wanted out?"

"And others, too." Creel straightened up. "But I didn't do it, I couldn't kill Ava, and damn sure wouldn't have killed Sharon. You read my book?"

"The live version is always so much better."

Creel was quiet so long Monk assumed the meeting was over.

"I was driving to the Mason Lodge in Mound Bayou from Memphis. I had a '63 Falcon I'd bought in Long Beach when I'd been discharged. I was on my way to see the Delta Dukes, this blues an' rock band, to line them up for a benefit concert for the campaign.

"The Falcon had been running funny that day, but like who had time to fix it with all the other stuff that had to be dealt with? Anyway, somewhere out around Gator, the damn thing quits. Now you understand, Monk, this is in the day before call boxes and cell phones, let alone some Dixie matron stopping to help a Black man stuck out on the highway."

"The prosecutor claimed your unaccounted time was a convenient cover to commit the murders."

"And your cousin testified I'd given him the knife."

"A knife the state never produced." Creel's face was blank. "You and Ava had been at the Crystal Spur Motel that afternoon?"

"No. We had on previous occasions, so it wasn't no big secret. Everybody around the campaign knew we was getting it on. Which meant the Citizens League knew, too."

"And you finally saw the crack in your distributor cap?" Monk went on, recalling the passages from Creel's book.

"I didn't have a flashlight, but I had taken off the air cleaner housing, and some of the sparkplug wires and whatnot. I was using the glove compartment light to examine the items and spotted the crack. I did have some electrical tape, so I taped it up so the rotor wouldn't short out and I was off."

"How come your lawyer didn't present the cap as evidence?"

"The judge wouldn't allow it."

Monk asked, "Who could have lured Ava and Sharon to that motel? Was Sharon seeing anyone?"

The question caused Creel to narrow his eyes, taking his hands out of his pockets. "Like they came because they knew someone?"

Monk said, "I've been thinking a lot about the murders. In your book, you said the motel's manager and co-owner, Charlie Crowther, testified he didn't hear or see anything. Neither you nor anybody else."

"He was a boozer," Creel added curtly, "he'd be passed out half the time you'd come to the front desk, have to pound on it to wake his sorry ass up. He died years ago from a spongy liver."

"He could have been lying," Monk pointed out.

"Me and Bernie discussed that, but what was the use? Crowther's dead and his widow lives in a old folk's home in Athens. And in them days, if you was white and wanted to keep your business going, you didn't fuck with the Citizens League."

"But let's say both things are true," Monk went on,

absorbed with his own theories. "Crowther's sleeping the sleep only Jack Daniel's can provide. I bet once or twice you or Ava grabbed a key out of a slot without waking him." Creel nodded in ascent. "Charlie's out, the murderer, who knows his habits, shows up and grabs a key. He then calls the girls from the room—there's phones in them?"

"Nowadays. Then it was a pay phone in the rear of the courtyard."

"Okay, he buzzes them, saying he has important information to relay to them about the Citizens League. Information he will only tell one of them, and the other brings her girlfriend for protection."

"And one man knifes both of them. That's OJ action, Monk," Creel commented sarcastically.

"There's an accomplice," Monk surmised.

"Then that could mean your cousin was in on this from the beginning," the prisoner observed without rancor. He shrugged his shoulders with his hands in his pockets. "But so what? There are several scenarios we could create, but what good does it do me?"

"Hiram Bodar was involved in a supposed accident. Has he talked to you?"

"Not directly. One of his staffers called me and he asked me the questions you're asking."

Neither man commented for several moments. Creel checked his watch. "Gotta be back in a few."

"Did you know Marshall Spears?" The picture from the safe-deposit box hovered in Monk's mind.

"Yeah," he acknowledged warmly. "He was kind of a local hero, what with his baseball career. When he came down here, he worked as a distributor and spokesman for Red Devil Soda Water in the Black sections in the tri-state area. That's actually why he'd come south. The job had come about because the Red Devil owner had remembered Mr. Spears from the old days and wanted to boost his Negro sales."

Creel started walking back to his job. "Marshall helped organize, Monk. He could carry sensitive messages to local SCLC or NAACP chapters, words not meant for phones that may have been tapped, because he was naturally on the road for his job. Plus, when things heated up after Freedom Summer, he got bolder like a lot of folks, and helped put together meetings in local churches, American Legion Halls, jukes, whatever."

"Jukes?"

"That's where the colored folks be, man."

"He and Kennesaw get along?"

Creel put a hand to his jaw, smiling ruefully. "You should know Mr. Spears had a long affair with Kennesaw's wife."

Now it was Monk's turn to blink. "Kennesaw know?"

"He must have after awhile, you just kinda get hip, right? But dig, Monk, your cuz was no Ozzie Nelson. He ran his wife's family insurance business, and worked the field, just to keep limber, right," Creel winked, "making those policy calls on grieving young things or middle-aged sisters whose husbands just lost an arm in the saw mill, or holding hands and quoting the Psalms with left-alone housewives with long hauling husbands."

They'd arrived back at the UNICOR wire-harness building. Several men, Black and white, filed inside.

"Husband and wife each knew the other was foolin' around—"

"And it got to be convenient, I guess. My dad played a couple of years with the Towne Avenue All-Stars. When I got down here, it was Marshall Spears who showed me what's what." Creel looked over his shoulder. "I better get back in. I get a little slack 'cause of my notoriety, but I don't try to abuse it, dig?"

"Of course." Monk shook Creel's hand. He wanted to tell him something might break, that some kind of justice might finally be delivered to this man who'd been waiting more than twenty-seven years for re-trial on a suspect conviction. That the system didn't always grind up the outspoken. But they both knew that'd be like wishing on a star in a heaven where the lights were going out, one by one.

As Creel walked off, Monk asked again, "Did Sharon have any boyfriends down here?"

He paused, hands in his pockets, turning in profile on his heel. "She was a Plain Jane, bro', living wallpaper, dig? Really, she existed in Ava's shadow. If she had one, I didn't know about it." He stopped again. "I suppose she would have come into her own though, had she lived."

"I'll try to see you before I leave," Monk promised.

Creel waved back and returned to his shift working for the prison industrial corporation.

MONK WENT south back into Memphis to pick up his gun at an express office. Grant had phoned him early in the morning, and given him the location. He missed the place twice as he drove by. The business was on Walker Avenue, a street of packed-in shops and bars not far from the Liberty Bowl Stadium. It was the address Grant had given him for Mercury Cartage. Over the door was their logo, a faded rendition of Flash from the Golden Age of comic books. His lightning bolts jutted proudly from his doughboy-style helmet as he ran with a large package under his arm. The art was flaking off the transom above the entrance, but the Flash's broad smile was still discernible.

Unlike its global competitor, FedEx, Mercury Cartage did

not go in for the slick image. The interior of the storefront had cheap wood paneling, a wooden counter painted industrial white, and a thrift-store coffee table for decor. There were no chairs for sitting.

Monk came up to an older white woman in a photographer's vest and flower print shirt standing behind the counter. She wore half glasses and was earnestly leafing through a copy of *Playgirl*.

"I'm here to pick up a package sent by Dexter Grant."

The woman kept perusing the magazine. She paused on an upshot featuring the thighs of some young stud from a daytime soap.

"Excuse me—" he began again.

She held up a hand, absorbed in studying the lad's form. "Hold your horses, trooper." She put a subscription postcard on the page to mark her place, closed it gently, and left the counter. She went through a wooden door behind her that rattled on its hinges, its ancient glass doorknob nearly falling off. She returned momentarily with a squarish package wrapped in ordinary brown paper. She placed the box on the counter and returned to her lusting.

"Want to see some ID?" he goaded her.

"You want me to remember your face?" She managed to turn to the next page.

Monk exited and drove around, debating whether to hang around Memphis and get lunch, or head on back into Mississippi. As of yet, he'd not been able to speak with Todd McClendon, the former editor of the *Clarion-Ledger*. The woman who answered the phone at his home had been evasive as to where and when McClendon might be around, but she had taken his number. He stopped and called the man's home in Jackson again, but got no answer, not even a machine.

Getting gas at a BP station near the highway, he spotted a rib shack across the way. After parking on the eatery's lot, Monk ordered fried turkey, barbeque sauce on the side, beans, corn on the cob, and a bottle of beer. He ate and reviewed his notes.

There was information on everyone in this case, this bifurcated case, except Sharon Aikens. As Creel had said, she existed as an extension of Ava. She was always the one who got less ink in the news accounts of the murders. Why was that? he wondered, dipping a piece of turkey in his sauce. In the articles he'd found online, he remembered a profile of Ava Green from *The Progressive* and there had been a mention of Aikens, but what had it said?

He shook his head and had another beer. Then, feeling lazy and sleepy, he dialed Delilah from a pay phone using his calling card.

"Hey, D.," he said once they'd taken care of pleasantries, "at the donut shop I've got a file of stuff I found online about the Creel campaign and trial."

"Yeah," she said expectantly.

"Would you look up what's there on Sharon Aikens? She was at Brandeis, too. I want you to give that stuff to Dex."

"Why not the whole file?" she suggested.

"Yeah, you're right." A bus cruised by the rib joint. Painted on its side were the words Graceland Tours. In the windows, Monk could see some of the people admiring the gewgaws they'd bought at their sequined ashram. One child, about ten or so, held up an Elvis doll in a sequined outfit and shook it at Monk, smiling eerily. He couldn't tell if it was meant as good or bad juju.

They said their goodbyes and Monk dialed his mother's house. He got her answering machine and left a message for Grant to see if he could track down any of Sharon Aikens's family or friends. Next he called Dr. Jones and found her during office hours at UCLA.

"Hercule, 'zup, cutie pie?"

"You and Ava ever talk about Sharon Aikens's love life?" He covered his ear as several semis roared past on the highway.

"Funny you should bring that up, slick," Helena Jones said, a seriousness working its way into her light tone. "I was thinking about that after we talked. Seems to me Ava and I were joking over the phone about a month before the murder and she said this cryptic comment concerning Sharon."

"And that would be?"

"Ava and I were, ah, well you understand this was the era in which women felt liberated, indeed compelled, to discuss sexual matters."

"Don't be shy now, doc, we got wires between us." And your kids and husband and my old lady who can bust a cap in my ass, he didn't add.

"I'm not being coy, I just don't want you to picture me as one of your skank chippies."

"Can we quit digressing?"

"I make you stutter?"

"The conversation." He didn't sound as professional as he wanted, or needed to be. What? Did he have a sign tattooed on his forehead, Committed Man, Let's Mess With Him? Or maybe he was leaking psychic come-ons.

"Hey, you fall in a vat of chitlins?" Jones kidded. "You there?"

"Jet lag."

"So you say. So yes, Ava and I were comparing the sexual athleticism of our respective lovers at the time, Damon for her and a rather spry fellow for me, when Sharon came up."

"Her being the retiring sort." He wondered who was the spry chap, but refrained from pursuing that particular inquiry.

"That's right, since it was known the permissiveness index seldom had her included in that curve."

"But this time was different?" Monk asked.

"I want to say this right," Jones let out an amount of air. But I've been trying to reconstruct Ava's words since it came back into my head. Unfortunately, I was drinking wine and tolling on some weed when I was on the phone with her."

Impatience gnawed at him. "The gist, Helena, was Sharon seeing some good ol' boy? Or one of the campaign workers?"

"What I remember," she responded, her classroom demeanor apparent, "was Ava and me cackling about why men didn't go down unless you berated them. I mean if you told a guy you were going to give him a blow job at two-oh-five on the dot, then he'd race five miles driving backward the wrong way down a one-way street to get there on time."

"Okay," he drew out.

The smile was in her voice as she spoke. "And Ava saying that Sharon was content to have this dude slip a hand up her dress and rub her thigh."

"Who?" Monk shouted as another tour bus belched past him.

"I'm sorry, Ivan, I really don't recall exactly. I have the impression it was a Southerner though; that was an aspect both of them found interesting."

"College boy?"

"Could be, but that's reaching for tadpoles in a muddy lake. Isn't there anyone left around there who could answer that?"

From the way Creel had talked, it didn't seem he knew about Sharon's beau. "Maybe Ava was high and she was only referring to an incident in a bar and not some steady guy."

"Maybe," Jones allowed.

"Anybody you can think of from the old college days might have been buddies with her besides Ava?"

Quiet, then Jones said, "I wish I could tell you, but she was one of those who was always around, but not making much of an impression, like an extra on a TV show."

"That's rough, doc," he responded. "Did Ava take a liking to her, or did Sharon just attach herself?"

"No, no it was genuine. Ava didn't have any siblings and sorta saw Sharon as the younger sister, show her the world thing."

"Sharon was younger?" A kid walked by him bouncing a basketball and rhyming a rap song.

"Yeah, she'd graduated high school at sixteen, which only added to her feeling awkward." Another drag of silence ensued where no words were spoken. "Does any of this help?"

"Damned if I know, Helena. Thanks for your time."

"Bring me back some crayfish."

"On it." Monk stood at the pay phone for a few moments after he hung the handset up. He wanted to talk to Hiram Bodar, the state senator who apparently, according to the voice of the honey-dripping woman in the state capital who answered his call in Bodar's office, was still away recuperating. Healing from his car accident or hiding out? He got back in his car and was going to head back into Mississippi, then decided to turn around and catch some blues on Beale Street.

AROUND TWO the next morning, he was on Highway 61 driving back into the Delta. He'd called Kodama from a place called the Alphonse Club earlier, and told her how much he was already missing her. Monk had a couple of beers and listened to a band whose idea of blues was loud licks and a screeching harmonica.

Leaving the mainstream section of Beale Street, he'd wandered into a hole-in-the-wall joint where the windows were grimy and the chairs were lopsided. This band, however, played some down-home gut-bucket blues. The woman singer, thin as a clump of reeds, had mastered renditions that tickled the tailbone and blew smoke across your soul.

He knew he shouldn't have had those Wild Turkeys on ice, but what was the blues without whiskey, he'd reasoned stupidly, the cold wind numbing his face. Not having a supply of Vitamin B with him to cut the hangover he knew he was going to have, he'd powered down the window so as not to get too warm or comfortable, and therefore drowsy, on the way back to his room. A headache was already festering somewhere behind his left eye, but he managed to get back to the A-Model Lodge without running into a pole or wiping out a litter of raccoons. Monk got to his door and absently pulled off two messages that were taped to the panel. Inside, sitting on the bed, Monk was pleased to read that Todd McClendon had called him back and had left a number.

The second message, again in the feminine script of the manager, simply read: *Welcome to Mississippi, Mr. Monk.* At first glance he assumed the message was from her; he fantasized a sweet, innocent flirtation. Then he looked at the note closer. She'd taken a message. The caller had said those words and left no name.

He was tired and drunk and his come down from his drinking should have zonked him out. But the "welcome" message had set him on alert. He dozed, snapping awake off and on for hours, propped up in bed in his clothes and shoes. The package from Mercury Cartage was open, his father's gun at the ready next to him on the bedspread. He was happy Grant had also sent a box of Hansen shells with the shipment.

# CHAPTER 15

"Judge Jarius Malachi Forrest was hard but fair, at least to white defendants. Black men coming before him, that was a different story, yessir. The judge was the condemnor, the embodiment of the unforgiving hand of the state exacting every bit, and more, from the brawn and sweat of poor colored boys he'd put on the chain gang for years on end for such heinous misdeeds as being drunk in public or late on their sharecropper's rental."

Todd McClendon was short and stout and solid. He had the body of a college wrestler. He had large hands, and deepset eyes that held steady on you like a doctor observing suicidal patients. He was dressed in light-blue, pressed jeans, linen coat and overrun loafers. The lower part of his face was tinged with bluish shadow.

Somebody whooped, and Monk clamped his teeth.

"And God forbid it be a real crime like theft against a white merchant or the soiling of southern womanhood, well, *white* southern womanhood," McClendon said dramatically, making his eyebrows go up and down.

A gleaming white monster truck rolled over a black Falcon stationwagon, and the crowd yelled with great pleasure.

"Or should Forrest hear of some miscarriage of justice in

a fellow jurist's court, then the judge would round up a few bailiffs, a shoemaker or two, and let righteousness be served at the end of a rope and tree limb."

Monk's throbbing hangover, and the lack of continuous sleep, had made for a joyless, and long, afternoon drive to the meet with McClendon at Smith-Wills Stadium on Lakeview in Jackson, the largest city and capital of Mississippi. Numerous confederate battle flags were being waved around, and more than one set of blue eyes had fixed on Monk as he'd found McClendon at a prearranged spot. They'd entered the Harkins Sisters Truck and Tractor Demolition Derby Spectacular as it ramped up full tilt.

There was beer flowing and whooping and hollering as everybody's favorite driver named Clint or Bobby Lee ground up passenger cars underneath their two-story tires. This was goddamn redneck heaven.

"This Forrest related to the ex-Confederate General Nathan Bedford Forrest who militarized the Klan to use them to halt Reconstruction?" Monk was surprised that question had managed to form in his troubled brain.

"Possibly, or at least the judge encouraged such thinking." McClendon spooned up more of his red beans and rice. The concession stands offered the tasty fare in wide-mouthed Styrofoam cups, along with catfish and home fries, collards and red-eye gravy and ham, and hot dogs and hamburgers.

Monk was earnestly working on some catfish doused in hot sauce. "Was this judge in the Klan, too?"

"Yes, a Grand Wizard," McClendon confirmed.

A woman in a nylon windbreaker, her dirty blond hair piled high, went past them toward the aisle, bumping Monk's knees. She didn't say anything and Monk glared at her, chewing.

"The myth goes that Forrest disappeared in the woods

off the Natchez Trace, leading men and hounds chasing an escaped convict."

Monk ate and waited.

McClendon delivered his punch line. "The real story is Jarius Forrest died in a sanitarium in Chattanooga blind and half mad from untreated syphilis in the fall of 1933. His idea of rehabilitation for young ladies picked up for solicitin' or vagrancy also had to do with him gettin' out from behind the bench. In this regard, and this only, he did not discriminate between Black nor white." McClendon finished his snack.

"An activist jurist," Monk saluted the memory of Jarius Malachi Forrest with a tip of his cup of water. "So Forrest's exploits are glorified, and Malachi becomes a ghost—no, make that a spook story—to keep the superstitious darkies in line."

Out on the dirt floor of the stadium, a souped-up tractor, its silver mufflers looking as if designed by the late great comic book artist Jack Kirby, spewed nitro flame into the air. The thing reared up on its hind wheels, and the driver waved his Stetson over his head as his mechanical steed did wheelies. The crowd went nuts.

"Exactly, " McClendon concurred. "If a Black man were to get off, even if the evidence was overwhelmingly in his favor, well sir, maybe the Hand of Malachi had to come down and maybe that poor soul would find himself disemboweled, his bloated corpse floating down the Yazoo. Better yet, the supposed malefactor might disappear altogether, the more to heighten the reputation of the compone avenger of white rights." McClendon dabbed at gravy on his chin. "As it says in Malachi, Chapter Three in the Bible, 'And I will come near to you to judgment; and I will be the swift witness.'"

The nitro-burning tractor took off from a ramp, and

landed on a row of Japanese cars. Again, there was the vigorous waving of confederate flags and a general cacophony of giddiness.

"And Manse Tigbee and his Southern Citizens League kept this legend alive?"

"And thus we come to Hiram Bodar, the new breed of deep-fried Republican, fiscal conservative, racial healer."

The woman in the windbreaker returned, holding a large cup of beer. She went past the two, spilling some on Monk's leg. She went on.

McClendon noticed, holding the rim of his cup to his mouth. As Monk smoldered, he proceeded. "At first it was just a story about Bodar's crack-up on the highway. I assigned a reporter who regularly covers political stuff here in Jackson. But this woman, Selma Portofino, has got the nose, you see? She'd no sooner filed her first report, when she got word that Bodar had been seen doing the ogle eyes in a Memphis restaurant in the company of a redhead—his wife is brunette."

"In her follow-up piece," Monk began, using his paper napkin to wipe the sweat, produced by the hot sauce and remnants of alcohol, from his forehead. "She hinted maybe the heretofore straight-arrow senator was waxing his shaft in another quill."

"We like a salacious story as much as the next province, Mr. Monk. Really, we went with that slant on the story because it was a way to keep it alive, and not incidentally build circulation, I'm not too proud to admit. But more than that, it was the extra information Selma had."

Monk nodded in ascent. "The identity of the woman."

Two Peterbilt cabs were growling, churning up waves of earth while the vehicles played chicken with one another down on the track.

"The big payoff being the woman was the daughter of Wallace Burchett, a hardcore member of the Citizens League."

Monk told him about seeing the odd interview with him in Embara's film.

McClendon took a breath. "Did you know he was rumored to have done killings on orders of the League's inner council? That in effect he was one of the ones chosen to be Malachi?"

Monk's jaw dropped partially open.

McClendon threw his empty containers down on the concrete riser, and laced his fingers before him. The stadium lights sprang on as evening overtook the festivities.

"Several years ago, the files of the supposedly defunct and various Citizens Leagues were released from Mississippi, Tennessee, Alabama and Arkansas. It made national news."

"Oh, I know," Monk agreed,

"Well, you probably know the one here in the Magnolia State was the originator, and the headquarters for the various branches. Like"—McClendon used his hands, one as if it were holding a globe, the other circling over the imaginary sphere—"like here was the boss of bosses, and the others were the lieutenants."

"The underbosses," Monk amended, to better fit the analogy.

"Absolutely," McClendon said, pointing at him emphatically. "The Citizens Leagues have been compared to buttoned-down Klansmen, and there's some truth to that. But the Leagues, that is to say the inner council, the leadership, was always about the future, not about bringing back some lost white paradise that didn't exist anyway."

Monk was feeling better and feeling scared. "This is what Bodar was trying to get at?"

"In a way," McClendon yawned. "Excuse me, I've been doing some copyediting and clean-up work for a corporate website designer over in Canton. After all, I gotta keep up my end of the mortgage."

"No need to apologize for that."

"You're all right, Monk. Anyway, like any clandestine organization, like any outfit that had burrowed deep in the political and social structure, the Citizens League had strategized plans for the long term."

Monk saw where McClendon was heading. "The files were released, after much wrangling. And more than thirty years after the little girls were bombed in the Birmingham church, and Schwerner, Goodmen and Chaney were murdered leaving the Philadelphia jail. Those files were made public."

"Conveniently found under the floorboards of a rickety smokehouse over in Wiggins, and then some more contributed by retired businessmen. These papers detailed illegal electronic surveillance, beatings, character assassination campaigns, even named some sell-out Uncle Toms, who for money, did their bidding. Our own version of the East German Stasi."

Nausea made saliva gather in Monk's mouth as he thought about his cousin. "But there must be other files that reveal who carried out the sanctioned hits ordered by the inner council."

A Mack cab with three engines mounted over the rear wheels was dragging a large cage on wheels. Inside the cage, buxom, bikini-clad young women gyrated. Some waved U.S. flags, and others the stars and bars.

"These files named who in local and state, and sometimes even federal authority, looked the other way, or obfuscated the investigation. Don't forget that old queen Hoover had a pathological hatred for King and anything smacking of Black self-determination. The FBI down here wasn't nothin' but some regular fellers from 'round here who knew how to knot their ties properly,"

"This what you were getting close to before the publisher canned you? That you were on to actually producing these secret files?"

McClendon squinted into the artificial lights. "We looked for Burchett's daughter, Nancy, once we got onto her. She used to have a typing service she ran over in Brownsville for something like ten years. A week after the accident, she was nowhere to be found."

"Killed?"

"Or running scared, what happened to Bodar a warning to git and stay git, man."

The truck and its cargo of busty bevies had made its last circuit, and now another customized tractor spewed chunks of stadium floor and bleated thunderously as it roared into view. A glass-walled tank of sharks had been brought in and twin thin metal planks were now being placed parallel across the tank. A ramp was pulled into position to allow the tractor to get up to the planks.

"That's the hombre I gotta interview." McClendon pointed at the souped-up tractor, then removed his press pass from a rear pocket and put the laminated card on its chain around his sweaty neck. "Pickin' up some extra scratch from *Babes & Rigs* magazine." He assessed the look on Monk's face. "You'd be surprised at the size of their readership."

"You got any pull with Bodar or his wife?"

"'Fraid not. We tried for weeks to get him to talk, but no go. The missus, Cassie Bodar nee Ibers, and me went to the same high school, but that didn't get me anywhere either." McClendon stood up. "You goin' out there?"

"I'll take a run at 'em, Can you give me the address?"

McClendon did and Monk walked with him out of the bleachers and down toward the rear of the stadium. The driver was adeptly maneuvering his tractor over the sharks, screeching and belching smoke and fire. People were yelling and the stomping of their boot heels all over the place was like listening to a stampede of bison.

"Well, I wish you luck, and hope you can shake something loose. If you do, remember me for the book rights when you walk out arm-in-arm with Creel."

"You got it, Todd." He shook the man's hand and made his way to the exit. Three good-sized men in Ts and open shirts were talking near a display of various tractor- and truck-pulling paraphernalia. The three bunched together as he got nearer, and Monk flexed his shoulders, refusing to slow his gait in the least.

"Enjoy the show?" one asked, the other two snickering. Two of them were holding beer cups.

Monk got close. "Real fine. I especially liked the girls dancing in the cage."

The one who'd spoken was taller than Monk, thinner in the arms. He grinned down at him maliciously. "Like that white pussy, do you?"

In a very measured tone Monk said, "I like it any way I can get it." He returned the smile with a gleeful one of his own.

Neither one said anything as the pulse in Monk's neck intensified.

"Come on, Barry, we gotta get movin'."

"It'll keep."

"Sure it will," Monk agreed.

"Come on," Barry's buddy insisted. "You want another beef to contend with now, when you tryin' to get the visitation rights with your kids back?"

"I guess we can find out how much tough boy here really likes that blond southern snatch another night."

"I'm holdin' your boy, Barry."

The two backed off. Barry and Monk stood looking at each other for several minutes until the former walked away with his friends. Monk was glad he'd left his gun back at the motel—along with his good sense, it seemed.

# CHAPTER 16

Grant and Nona Monk walked up to the woman sitting in the open doorway of the house. The abode was, appropriately, done in the Monterey Revival design. There was a second-floor maple balcony running the horizontal length of the front, its wood lustrous in the bright sun. The original wood shingle roof, according to the listing, had been replaced by unblemished terra-cotta tiles. Though they were several miles inland, the smell of the peninsula was keen in the morning air.

"Come on in, folks." The woman stood up, smoothing her business skirt, a practiced, but sincere smile on her handsome face.

"Actually we didn't come to see the house; we came to see you, Ms. Allen." Grant stopped at the doorway, indicating that Nona Monk should go through first.

"And why is that?" The smile now had creases in each corner.

"About your older sister, Sharon, and that time," Nona Monk said, taking some of the edge off Grant's harsh delivery. Man wouldn't know subtle if it smacked him upside the head, she noted. "My son is a private detective, and he's in

Mississippi looking into matters that touch on your family's history."

The woman looked beyond the bogus couple as if in hope of spotting genuine potential buyers, someone who would relieve her from engaging in what was clearly a painful subject. There were no people coming along the segmented walkway, and she drew her shoulders in like a boxer ready for a savage round. "I was just a kid; there isn't much I can tell you."

Grant rumbled, "Listen, young lady—"

"Is it okay if we sit?" Nona Monk interrupted him, and swept her hand toward the large living room and a couch covered in throw pillows.

Lindsey Allen was resigned to saying something. "Why not, it's not as if you're interrupting the morning rush."

"We won't be long," Grant blurted, boring Nona Monk with a look.

He and Monk's mother sat side by side on the couch after Grant made room for his bigger frame by stacking some of the pillows to one side.

Allen sat diagonally in a cabriolet chair with red velour padding. She crossed her legs, tightening up her face as she examined the pair. "Let me get this right: You two are some kind of modern age Nick and Nora, and your son is a sleuth, too."

Nona Monk explained the permutations of what brought them to Monterey after Grant had quieted down from his laughing jag.

"I'm sorry to hear about your cousin—Nona, is it?" she asked. "But, like I said, I wasn't even ten years old when my sister was murdered. And well, Mom and Dad didn't go on a lot about what happened . . ."

"I understand they got divorced not too long afterward," Grant put in.

"How did you locate me?" Allen asked in a collected voice. She'd reconstructed her professional demeanor, and easily modulated her words.

"I've been finding one person or another, in a fancy house or a cheap back room for more than fifty years, Ms. Allen," Grant answered wearily. He turned his head toward Nona Monk, a thin smile compressing his Lips. "Good, solid citizens like you, who pay their taxes, and join their neighborhood watch, send their twins to private school, always leave a friend in one place, a satisfied client in another, you're easy to find. And once we found out you had a real estate license, we traced you to when you lived in Chicago, and started from there with a forwarding address search at the post office."

Allen leaned forward. "I can see it in your face, and hear it in your voice. Kansas or Oklahoma, right?"

"An oil lease Daddy went bust on in Oklahoma," Grant admitted. "You went to live with your mother after the divorce in Madison, Wisconsin."

She sat back. "Yes, Mom's side of the family was from there, some had even worked in the LaFolette administration."

"Dexter had an uncle who was an organizer for the Wobblies," Nona Monk mentioned. "We came here to fill in some background on your sister, Lindsey."

"I know," she shook her head, "Sharon has become the footnote to the story of firebrand Green, the white Angela Davis who came out of the ferment of Marcuse and Markowitz. But to me she's still the smart-ass sister who tortured me to learn long division, and who took me to see *I, Monster* and *Planet of Vampires* because I begged her to." She stared beyond the room, then adjusted her vision back to the present. "And stayed up with me that night until I could get to sleep."

Grant asked, "Did your mother or father ever mention anyone she was seeing during the Creel campaign?"

Allen batted her lashes like she'd taken a blow on the nose. "When I was fifteen, Mom and Dad and I had the big talk, the one we'd been dancing around for several years. We talked about the summer before Sharon left for college, how they were so proud because she'd gotten a partial scholarship because of her grades."

"Had your parents gone to college?" Nona Monk asked, crossing her own legs.

"Dad, some on the GI Bill; Mom was a bookkeeper. We were all rooting for Sharon."

Grant was antsy, he wanted something to happen, to get something out of his long drive up north to Monterey. "We now know Ava's mother, Sara, died a few years ago and her father is retired, living somewhere in Spain." At least that's what Grant had been able to determine. "But I haven't been able to run him down there."

"He was an academic," Allen verified. "I think he taught at Antioch in Yellow Springs. His specialty was Marxist economics, I think. I remember reading that Sharon had been very impressed about that."

"You mean your sister kept a diary from that time?" Nona Monk's excitement was obvious.

"Yes," Allen hesitated, "but there's nothing in them that can help you."

Grant pounced. "How do you know, Ms. Allen? When's the last time you gave them a careful reading? Five, ten years ago?" A sound made them turn their heads. A couple and their two small children stood at the door. Tentatively, the adults stepped into the room, the kids hugging their legs. Sharon Aikens's sister looked relieved. She started to speak but Grant cut her off.

"If we could just look through the diaries . . ."

All three were now on their feet.

"When we finally got her things back, there were pages missing from the last one, Mr. Grant. The authorities in Jackson said it had probably been Creel, trying to cover his tracks."

"Do you think he killed your sister?" Nona Monk put a hand on the other woman's arm.

Casually, Allen picked up a set-up page for the new hopefuls. "I've stopped trying to answer that question."

"But my son hasn't," Nona Monk implored. "How about you re-read what's left of that diary, with the eyes of someone who's older than the last time you read those passages. Maybe you'll see something differently this time."

"You folks start looking around," she said to the couple, "I'll catch up in a minute." Allen began to move away. "I won't promise anything. Sometimes it's best not to walk too often past the headstones."

"I understand, Lindsey, yet don't the dead deserve an answer, the knowledge that the ones who did her harm pay for their misdeeds?" Nona Monk handed her one of her cards from Cedars. "This has my work number and pager. Call me, okay?"

She took the card without committing herself to any future course of action and went to show the house to the newcomers. The sounds of the children giggling and running around could be heard from upstairs. Grant and Monk's mother left, a wind bracing them as they walked back to his car.

"How about we go check out that new John Steinbeck Center over in Salinas?" Grant asked, getting in behind the wheel. "Last time I was up here it was just a room devoted to him at the local library."

"Sure, but let's get some late breakfast or early lunch first, this detective stuff gets a girl hungry."

Driving off, Grant nodded appreciatively at his passenger. "You did good back there, Nona. If I'd been alone, I'd have probably raised her hackles and she'da froze me out. I think she'll call."

Nona slumped in the seat, suddenly looking her age. "I was being real with her, Dexter. I feel," she searched for the word, "obliged. Kennesaw wasn't my responsibility; he was his own grown man and made his own decisions for whatever reasons. Yet I feel the damage he did is somehow my responsibility to atone for. If Damon Creel is guilty, then, fine. But this hanging in the air, it's every Black person's business . . . it could be that, it could be this." She made gestures. "Look, there're enough people around tearing down the good that was done in the civil rights movement, hijacking King's words to suit their purposes as they go about getting rid of any of the gains." She scratched at the scalp beneath her short hair. "Shit, ain't it about our turn to kick some cracker ass?"

"Amen, sister."

"Shut up and drive, Dexter."

"Yessum, Miss Monk."

# CHAPTER 17

Monk was in someone else's body and he couldn't make it respond to his commands. The hands fluttered when he badly needed them to ball into a fist. His legs jerked spasmodically when in fact he wanted them to swing out and over the cot filled with bramble onto the floor. He came fully awake and realized he was having another post-traumatic attack. Only this bout had blended with the last stages of a nightmare. And he was having difficulty deciphering his present reality beyond his psychological state. Whose bed was he in? And why was it so fucking hot?

He glanced around the room, locking on an indiscernible object located on the wall. He stared hard at the thing, trying to adjust his eyes in the velvety darkness. Leaks of light like inert gas hung below the crack of the door and haloed around the curtained window. As if he were an amnesiac, or a visitor stranded on this planet, Monk searched for the names of the other items in the black room.

A mosquito landed on his sweating bare chest and he slapped at the insect on automatic response. The creature took off, buzzing around his left ear, taunting him with its superior mobility. There was a creak on the walkway outside, and his consciousness dropped fully back into his body, his skin alert like an organic sensor net. He was in the A-Model Motor Lodge, and he was slick from disorientation and heat.

The gun? Where had he put his .45? He scrambled and plucked it out from beneath the mattress near where his head had rested. Another creak. He got out of bed—was he naked? He felt downward with his left hand and tugged on the stretchy material of his sweat pants. That's good, he'd hate to be laid out in the local funeral parlor bare-assed. His mother would be chagrined.

Monk had his ear to the door, his eyelids nearly shut so as not to distract his sense of hearing. There was some rustling and the clink of metal. He twisted and yanked on the knob, and it wouldn't give. His breathing stopped, and he assumed someone was holding the knob on the other side in big corded hands that would soon be locked around his neck. He tugged on the knob again, hard. It finally occurred to him in a bolt of clarity to unlock the damn thing. With measured movement, he undid the tab, the anxiety pumping his heart starting to subside.

"Hi," the woman said. She was the one he'd seen going off to gamble when he'd first arrived at the motel. Now she stood at the door to Number 15, her key in the lock. Her potato sack of a purse was draped across her like a bandoleer. Apparently she'd just returned from another battle of lone woman versus the dreaded gambling empire. The green-blooded octopus that at first caressed and soothed you with its embrace, but invariably drew you closer and closer, until it devoured you whole, waiting for the next morsel to temporarily satisfy its hunger.

"Hey," Monk answered, the .45 down at his side, hopefully obscured in the low wattage of the red lights hanging over the covered walkway. "Have any luck tonight?"

"Okay," she said, getting her door open. She started across the threshold, then paused. "You some kind of salesman?"

"I go from door to door, but too often find the occupant running out the back." Out on the highway, a late model car—was it a Sable?—turned into the courtyard, the cone of its lights illuminating both of them. The car completed its U-turn and drove off in the opposite direction.

"Well, goodnight." He closed the door on her quizzical frown. He stood against the inner door, reassembling his mind. The thing on the wall was that damned cavorting catfish. His mental state was better but now his lower leg, the one that had been shot, was hurting again. Great. He prowled the room, massaging his thigh. Eventually he clicked on the TV, and sat on the bed, his leg lying flat on the covers. On screen a preacher in a lightning blue jacket with rings on each hand and a tsunami of white hair, tearfully cajoled his audience to seek the counsel of Jesus, the greatest prosecutor of evil in the universe. The devil—and by inference, the criminal lawyers who served as his minions—was the source of all mendacity and afflictions.

Monk fitfully found his way back to sleep, the muscles in his lower leg finally subsiding to a rhythmic throbbing; a lullaby of pain. Half awake, in his head he could hear the telegenic holy man screaming that Jesus was going to present a bill, and too many would not be able to afford the payment.

A dark-skinned Jesus answered the door to the house in the valley of sorrow as an exhausted Monk knocked. The Lord was holding a photo of Monk's cousin in blackface, with wide white lips. God's son laughed at the joke. He had real nice teeth.

# CHAPTER 18

"You got to get from 'round here, mister."

"How about Mrs. Bodar, she available to see me?"

"Mister," the housekeeper said, grinding her teeth, "you don't listen too good. Mr. Bodar is recuperating and Mrs. Bodar has things that need takin' care of." She was a good-sized woman whose arms were more muscle than flab. Her biceps were pronounced as she stood in the foyer, hands on hips. "How in hell did you get this address?" she fumed.

"I'm all the way from L.A.," Monk said, trying to make it sound bright and cheery as if he was delivering a million dollar check.

"I don't give a hoot if you took the express from Timbuktu, mister. The Bodars ain't seeing no reporters today."

"I'm looking for a killer, not writing a story."

She looked him up and down with a steady gaze. Momentarily, she announced her findings. "Man, you ain't no policeman, you ain't law of no kind."

He liked her. "How do you know that?"

"You miss the mirror this morning?"

Monk had been looking around the entranceway. The house was not the stereotypical plantation colonial affair he expected a Mississippi state senator, a senator with old

familial ties in the state, to own. It was more Renaissance
Revival in appearance, with quoins going up the corners of
its two stories, and pedimented heads over the windows.

"I'll only come back."

"I'll get you arrested," she promised, what little tolerance
she had for him having dissipated. "We don't play around
with snoops in Vicksburg."

"Would you tell Mrs. Bodar that I'm the cousin of Kennesaw Riles, and that he was murdered in Los Angeles."

The housekeeper, who'd been holding a dishtowel, began
to knot the cloth in both of her capable hands. "You is Riles's
kin? For real?"

"Yes, ma'am."

She looked off toward the staircase, then at the front door.
"You hold on." She didn't take the stairs, but went through
a walnut swing door that led to some other part of the house.

He came in and stood in the entranceway, looking around.
On a circular Chippendale table there was a vase sprouting
morning glories and violets, a Merit Foundation annual report
next to it. Black-and-white Nike running shoes, fresh red clay
crusted around the soles, sat on a step of the stone composition
stairs leading to the second floor. In the dining room, he could
see an oil painting of a patriarch in a suit with wide lapels. His
hands clutched small globes at the end of the arms of the
ornate chair he sat in. The expression captured on his face
suggested only he knew how to get things done.

Soon, a smallish woman with wide hips in a plum-colored
sweat top with a CAMPBELL COLLEGE logo on it and faded
jeans came back through the swing door. Displeasure was
plain on Cassie Bodar's face.

"Will you please get out of here?" She pointed toward the
front door.

"I'd just like to know if your husband had been in contact

with my cousin prior to, or after his accident." He was well aware he was a stranger, a smart-ass Black man from out of town refusing to leave the house of a white woman well connected in Mississippi's social and political circles.

She stood close to Monk to show him she would not be intimidated. "Whatever happened to your cousin in California has nothing whatsoever to do with us."

"Why can't I have a few words with the senator? He's not infirm from the accident, is he? I know he was looking into the Creel matter and the Citizens League involvement in his frame-up. I know too he was talking with Wallace Burchett's daughter."

"You've been listening to fanciful stories from ex-newspaper editors known to get their best stories out of a bottle of Early Times. I didn't tell Todd McClendon anything, and I'm damn sure not telling you anything, either." She stood under his nose, her chin and head thrust upward. If she'd been a fox, she'd have gone for his throat. He wasn't too sure she still might not.

"I'll be around, Mrs. Bodar; there're still a few people who might enjoy my company. Might even turn up those missing pages from Sharon Aikens's diary." He knew neither he nor Grant wouldn't, let alone that the pages would be of little significance, but would they mean anything to her or her husband? "Be seeing you."

Monk's heavy-soled shoes made clunking sounds as he made for the door. He could feel her stare x-raying into his spine and he wondered if she could will its too-fragile connection of bone and tissue to sever. Outside, clouds had gathered and the air was wet with the anticipation of rain. He looked back at drawn curtains in the upper window. If there was somebody peeping around them, he couldn't detect anybody.

He got into his rented Dodge pickup and drove back onto 61, heading north. He stopped once at a roadside café, and had a meal of oxtails and green beans cooked with fatback. Monk got back to Clarksdale ahead of a new threat of rain. He decided to take a look at the Delta Blues Museum. Originally, the museum had for twenty years been housed in the Carnegie Public Library. The street in front of the library had been renamed John Lee Hooker Lane in honor of the great bluesman. But the museum had been moved to larger, more spacious headquarters in the converted freight depot a little over a year ago—the same station Spears had tags from back when it functioned. The refurbished station was now part of what was called Blues Alley. There was a concrete stage out in back, and local acts performed there, and at the Do Drop Inn in next door Shelby.

Clarksdale had originally been a lumber camp in the late 1880s. Later, it had also been the residence of playwright Tennessee Williams. And it was said that he modeled Blanche in his famous *Streetcar Named Desire* on Blanche, the daughter of the town's founder, John Clark. In the 1920s, the town became known as "little New York" due to the presence of men who'd made their money as railroad barons. These days, though, Clarksdale had the distinction of being one of the poorest cities in the poorest state in the nation. In the summer of 1999, President Clinton had stopped in town on his four-day poverty tour to draw attention to its plight. Yet Clarksdale was rich in blues history.

There were large painted depictions of blues musicians who had been born in and around Clarksdale and other parts of the Delta, including the R&B singer Sam Cooke who, along with Son House and Ike Turner, had come from Clarksdale itself. There was a large rendering of Hooker handling his guitar like it was a pick axe just finishing a long

day of digging trenches; a moaning B.B. King, and a sly
Howlin' Wolf. Off to one side there was a life-sized manne-
quin of Muddy Waters in a white suit and a crisp Panama.
Over the left shoulder of the blues man's dummy was a
photograph of the fake Muddy and the live ZZ Top in their
bearded days.

He paid particular attention to the material on Charlie
Patton. There was a shot of a two-story cotton gin with
lettering on its side. The script read from the top: DOCKERY
FARMS, and centered under that EST. 1895. The next line
down was WILL DOCKERY, 1865–1936 AND RICE DOCKERY,
OWNER. The plantation still existed, located on Highway 8
between Cleveland and Ruleville. It was there that Patton,
born in Edwards, Mississippi, would lift the blues from
merely juke music—played up until then, as far as whites
were concerned, by interchangeable Black men—and stamp
it with his individual style.

Patton learned how to play the guitar from Earl Harris
and Henry Sloan, and somewhere around the age of seven-
teen, or it may have been a little later, he was already getting
a following. Patton and Sloan lived on the plantation, their
families sharecroppers, though Patton's father would eventually own his own plot near Dockery.

Charlie Patton had attended several grades of school,
but trying his hand at the starvation box was preferable to
scratching out a living chopping cotton or clerking. His
father, Bill Patton, was a big man, a lay preacher, and was
not so inclined to see things as his son saw them. He dis-
couraged young Charlie from spreading the Devil's music
with thunderous lectures, and sometimes with the switch.
This repressive hand on Charlie might have also been
because the older Patton had harbored doubts in being his
son's biological father. Charlie looked much like his mother,

herself Indian, white, and Black. Their appearances, Bill, dark and big, and Charlie, light and wiry, had spawned rumors in and around Dockery that didn't subside, And as he got older, Charlie Patton embellished those whispered conversations.

If WC Handy was the father of the blues, Patton was the godfather of the Delta blues. He incorporated Ragtime, hillbilly and folk into his brand of the blues, and some sixty years before Hendrix, was known to play the guitar between his legs and behind his back.

Monk conjectured if it was Natchez or Chickasaw that was part of Patton's roots. He stood looking down at what was apparently the only extant photo of the progenitor who influenced Robert Johnson, Son House and so many others. A man who died relatively young at forty-five, or was it fifty-two?—his birth date wasn't a certainty—of a heart condition. Other stories claimed what killed Patton was a knifing and still others a poisoning. The poisoning story may have been inspired by Robert Johnson's death, because old Johnson had been done in by a jealous husband.

Could that have been the cause of Kennesaw's death? If Spears was messing around with his cousin's wife, and his cousin was known to tip out himself, had some son or daughter he sired finally found him and exacted a revenge for him wronging the child's mother? Given the history of the blues and its practitioners, the notion might not be that far-fetched.

He pushed the new theory to one corner of his brain, and concentrated on Patton's photograph. He had protruding ears, light-colored straight hair and, it seemed, tawny-colored skin. There was a studious schoolboy look to him reinforced by the bow tie he wore in the picture. That image belied what Monk knew of Patton's wicked ways.

Like many an archetypal blues man, or blues woman such

as Bessie Smith and Big Mama Thornton, Patton had a reputation for sin and folly. Son House was quoted as saying the singer and writer of songs such as "Mean Cat Blues" and "Prayer of Death" was "a bad plantation nigger." He would beat his eight or so wives regularly, on the off occasion when he was not idle. Patton, Son House went on, "would lie about his love for any female listener, and was tight with his money. His only daughter, China Lu, disavowed him."

Patton survived getting his throat cut a year or so before he died, though it did effect his singing a might. Patton's voice on those scratchy records was a belly-to-the-ground stalking growl filled with menace and raw whiskey. He played slide and would use syncopation and beat rhythms on the back of his guitar as part of his performances. Like his father, he did some jack-leg preaching, but only, it was noted, to entice women into his arms. Though not a physically big man, his deaths-head voice bellowed up from some depth in an earth soaked with slave sweat and the Red Man's lament. His songs told of incarceration in "High Sheriff Blues," and travel in "Stone Pony Blues." Patton drank and screwed and played, and dodged the law by dint of a power he may or may not have been fully aware of. He had etched his place in the cultural history of a state and country where it was only many decades after his death that his contributions to this most peculiar of American music forms had been acknowledged.

"Not too many ask about the 'Killin' Blues' anymore." The young white woman proprietor behind the counter in the Delta Museum arranged some harmonicas for sale in a glass case. "I guess it's been three years now since some fellas from Boston came down here with a supposed letter from one of Patton's kinfolk that they claimed provided clues to this mythical lost recording." She straightened up, "Like if it was around, we wouldn't have been looking for the album ourselves. If Robert Johnson's thirtieth song, or a wax cylinder of Buddy Bolden playing coronet existed, someone would have found it by now."

Monk smiled. "How do you think the rumor got started?"

"This is the Delta, mister, we full up of spook stories and whispers among the willows and oaks. And God knows, it ain't like Mississippi has a virgin past, am I right?"

"Yes, that's so."

"Try this," she went on, "Patton was known to rework his songs from time to time. He was an innovator, always trying out some new twist as he traveled around, sometimes just steps ahead of some woman he'd taken advantage of, naturally. Anyway, it wouldn't be much of a surprise if one night he's playing some barn dance and retools one of his songs, or makes up something on the spot and calls it the 'Killin' Blues.' Maybe he even sang it in several more towns; hell, for all I know it could have been a hot request number."

"Yeah, I could see that happening," Monk agreed. "People start talking about it after he died, and the story gets changed after time."

"See?"

He bought some blues maps, a baseball hat with the museum's logo on it and thanked the young woman. A chill had swept in across Clarksdale, and the clouds once again looked heavy with moisture. By the time he got back to his motel, the rain had started again and was coming down in a steady drum. Monk got to his room. There was a neatly handwritten note from the manager on the panel again. She'd taken down two numbers for him. The first was to his mother's house. The other was a local exchange. He sat on the bed and dialed the latter number.

"Merit Foundation," the recorded honeysuckle of a voice on tape fluttered. It asked him to leave a message.

"This is Ivan Monk returning Mr. Tigbee's call." He hung up and called his mother, but also got a machine. He checked his watch. It was past nine in L.A., where were Grant and his mother? A brief horror gripped his heart and he prayed a heathen's prayer they weren't out somewhere on anything that might be construed as a date. He called Kodama. She'd been reading her notes from a current trial involving millions of dollars in land rights out in the Mojave Desert.

"I miss you when I don't see you, baby."

"Ain't that the truth? What you got on?"

"I better not tell you, or where my other hand is right now. It wouldn't pay getting either of us too excited, " Monk rasped.

They bantered for awhile then he asked her, "You talk to Dex or my mom today?"

"No, is there something I should be worried about?"

"Oh, nothing like that, I tried to reach them, but no one was there."

"Your mom's probably at work, and Dex no doubt tagged along or is out with one of his troglodyte retired cop pals."

"He ain't got too many of those guys left," he remarked pointedly.

The two talked a little more about his progress, or what passed for it, until Kodama began to drift off. "Well, how should I take you yawning in my ear?"

"I'm so comfortable with you, Ivan, the sound of your voice is soothing. Its deepness wraps around me, and I wish you were here next to me."

"So do I, Jill. I'll call you tomorrow."

"You'd better."

Monk cradled the handset and got off the bed. Keyed

up, and wanting to be doing something, he put on his jean jacket, and trudged over to the Tornado Lounge and Game Parlor. Encamped there, he had a can of beer and smoked a cheap cigar, the rain patting the windows in steady beats.

# CHAPTER 19

"G oodnight, sweetheart."
    "Goodnight, Mama."
Lindsey Allen kissed her son Jarred on the cheek. Her
daughter Sharon had fallen asleep on the couch as the family watched *Toy Story 2* on tape for the third time. Across
from Jarred's bed the girl lay sleeping, snoring lightly.

Soon, she reasoned, she and her husband Terry would
have to reconfigure the room upstairs so Sharon could have
her own space. It wouldn't do to have a preteen boy and girl
sharing the same digs. What would child welfare think, she
mused, going back into the living room downstairs.

"You have a seminar on Saturday, right?" Her husband
was sitting in the big club chair leafing through a copy of
the *San Francisco Chronicle*.

"Just till one, I can pick them up from swimming," She
crossed in front of him, touching his leg as she did so. Lindsey Allen straightened and stacked items on the glass-topped
coffee table in an effort to occupy her mind.

Her husband peered at her. "I got it out of the closet; it's
on the dining room table."

She gave him a kiss. "Thanks."

In the dining room, she pushed in the dimmer switch,

turning the overhead light up all the way. The dinner table had been cleared of the dishes, and a week's worth of opened envelopes and magazines had been stacked on a Japanese tea cart in the corner. Allen opened the large cardboard box containing her sister's photographs, letters and diaries her husband had placed on the table. Also inside the box were the trophies her mother had kept when Sharon was a sprinter in high school.

In her hand was a photo taken when she couldn't have been more than four or five. The family had gone to the Grand Canyon, and had taken a donkey tour of part of the big hole. There she was, making faces at the camera, a goofball cowboy hat on her head, sitting in front of Sharon on the same burro. Her older sister's arms were around her, and she was squinting into the sun.

Bookending them were her parents, her father tall and lean in the saddle like one of those bronc busters on that old rerun show, *Gunsmoke*. Her mother looked uneasy on her mount, but her hands were relaxed, loose on reins entwined in her strong fingers.

She spent some time smiling at the snapshots of her big sister and her at the beach, the time she broke her arm or Sharon dressed up pretty for the prom. Lindsey Allen had those quiet moments of dread, as her own children began to sprout, realizing they had already formed their own ideas and interpretations of life independent of her or their father. You could see that individual thinking on her sister's face in the Grand Canyon photo.

Yet she knew, going back upstairs, holding onto several of her sister's diaries, psyches were made up of various components glommed from those who influenced us, positively and negatively. At certain stages of development we might consciously use the same phrases as a teacher we liked, or sit in a chair and cross our legs the way our mother did. But she also was sure there were some things one couldn't explain through social science.

She had seen characteristics in Sharon, her sister, that had been replicated in Sharon, her daughter. And the two had never met, at least on a physical plane.

It's not like she was a nut for that kind of mystical clap-trap, although she did read a self-help or business motivational book occasionally. And there was a new book she'd been considering buying, *The Shackle of Dreams*, by one of those gurus of inner peace, a woman whose name she couldn't remember at the moment. A couple of people in the office had been raving about this woman's book and her tapes.

She got undressed, put on her night slip, brushed her teeth and gargled. In bed, she carefully read through the dairy Sharon kept when she'd been in Mississippi. Lindsey Allen couldn't remember the last time she'd read the dairy, but guessed it must have been when she'd been in college. Sharon's infatuation with Ava was evident in her writings. Her script was in blue pen, a feminine handwriting replete with large circles for dots over her I's.

Her sister recounted various activities of the Creel campaign, and her impressions of the then young revolutionary's reactions to the racist attacks in the press and by the business community. She also told of an incident where Creel stood down four whites who had cut the three of them off—Sharon, him and Ava—on a street in Memphis. Sharon observed in her diary that Creel seemed full of himself, but he was also brave and driven to make something better for Black people; and that he knew he'd never be elected mayor, but the campaign served to highlight the enforced division between white and Black voters in a South being dragged and brow-beaten to change.

There were several long and convoluted passages describing the relationship between Ava and Creel that only a nineteen-year-old girl from a proper home, yet hinting at her hominess, could produce. Lindsey Allen plumbed the writing for evidence that her sister was or wasn't a virgin, but there seemed to be no definitive writing on that personal aspect. She fingered the section where the missing pages had been torn out of the book. The time period in the book stopped two days before she was murdered.

The last full page recounted a long staff meeting where Creel shouted at Ava that maybe she ought to take her pale little dilettante ass back to mommy and daddy. What happened immediately after that outburst, if her sister had written about it, was now gone. The supposition could work toward his guilt, or she supposed his innocence since Creel's side would no doubt maintain the people who slaughtered the girls removed the pages to further incriminate him.

"Find out anything new?" her husband asked her, settling in bed beside her.

"I got to know my sister again," she said fondly.

"Good," her husband said, kissing her and rubbing a hand in the small of her back. "But nothing about, well, you know."

Inspired by her journalistic archeology, and the answers that might be there, Lindsey Allen catalogued the material in her head. "She does mention she and Ava were out one night in Memphis' Pinch section and got to talking to two apparently prim young college men. What had prompted her to write about it was one was Black, the other white. The Black one was from out of state, Ohio, she wrote, 'cause she overheard him talking about the Buckeyes with someone at the bar. The white one was a Mississippi boy."

Her husband motioned for her to continue. She started again, "So of course she and Ava got to talking to them about how interesting that they were friends, did they know about the campaign, stuff like that."

"What do you mean 'of course'?" he asked.

She moved her shoulders. "Ava's mother had some relatives in Akron, that's what Sharon wrote in parentheses here."

Her husband didn't hide his blank expression.

"It was something they sort of had in common," she elucidated. "I gathered from what she wrote, Ava had initiated the conversation with the two."

Her husband yawned. "These two college boys become involved in Creel's mayoral race? Did Sharon go out with one of these dudes?"

"I don't know," Lindsey Allen admitted. "Sharon calls the white one by his nickname, Rusty, so you might assume she was interested in him, but who really knows?"

"You gonna call the couple?"

"They're not a couple, exactly. But yes, I'll give them a call tomorrow with this tidbit."

"Could be useful," Terry Allen speculated. "A white and Black pal'n around together in the early seventies, maybe a set-up to lure the girls in or something."

His wife raised doubtful eyebrows and turned off the nightlight.

"Mom, Jarred won't turn his radio off," their daughter yelled five minutes later.

"Shut up," their son warned his sister.

"You go see about them," his wife said to her husband.

"It's not my turn," he said, but was already putting his feet on the floor.

# CHAPTER 20

Monk left Mercury Cartage with his letter pack and drove until he found the rib joint he'd eaten at the other day. He ordered food and a beer, and sat at the same corner table, the sun beaming directly on him. He opened his pack and took out the background papers sent to him overnight from the Southern Poverty Law Center in Montgomery, Alabama.

The Center, founded by white Southerner Morris Dees— an attorney who first made money selling birthday cakes through the mail in college—was a research and legal facility dedicated to an aggressive defense of civil rights. The organization had successfully sued Klan Klaverns and skinhead groups, and produced various publications, including the *Intelligence Report* magazine. The publication was a roundup of hate groups, examining their activities and the forces behind them.

He'd requested information on Tigbee and his foundation before leaving L.A. through Kodama, a contributor to the Center for more than a decade. Now he sat and sipped and read through the information. Some of it was compiled from what public records existed on the Merit Foundation, which was a family foundation, and so was not required to divulge assets and what groups they'd funded.

But the Center had done a great deal of detective work over the years on the Merit Foundation. Backtracking through the records of various organizations and charities which the Center concluded might have received Merit monies—organizations such as political campaigns and charities required by law to disclose their funding sources— they had amassed a comprehensive list of possible and certain recipients.

As Embara had told him, Merit gave money to Mississippi public schools and private ones, to homeless shelters, literacy programs, and other venues to advance the public good. There were also grants to several out-of-state groups Monk didn't recognize. But the groups were broken down by ideology on an annotated sheet. Not surprisingly, they were either religious conservative or right wing, like the group of zero-population advocates who blamed America's pollution on unchecked immigration.

Of much more interest was a reprinted article from the *Public Eye*, a newsletter put out by a left-wing think tank in Massachusetts that monitored the right. The piece listed Merit's current and past board members. Among the names were a couple of Black conservatives with national profiles, a politically narrow Latina Judge Kodama had debated once, and several CEOs of intermediate and large corporations.

Monk ate and continued perusing the material. Another reprinted piece written some years ago, by the truck-pulling aficionado Todd McClendon, was an interview and profile of Tigbee. His picture, taken in 1991, was of a stern-looking man with a lean face, a prow of a nose, and close-cropped hair. He was sitting in a padded chair, and behind him was a window overlooking downtown Oxford, Mississippi.

Accidentally, Monk dripped barbecue sauce from his beans on the photocopy. He blotted it with his napkin.

The piece revealed something of Tigbee's philosophy. McClendon had asked him pointedly about Creel and the Citizens League's possible involvement in Creel's trial. Tigbee point-blank said the League, which he characterized as having been well-intentioned, but admittedly some of its less involved members may have committed some excesses, had no knowledge or connection to the incident. He maintained that Creel was guilty, having been convicted by a jury. An all-white jury, McClendon pointed out.

Tigbee replied that it was a Black man who testified for the prosecution, someone who was himself a civil rights activist. Monk felt bile mixing with his meal and had to halt his study and eating. He sat back, letting the sun beat on his face, the brew soaking his brain, until his stomach settled. He'd have to take the quisling nature of his cousin less personally, he knew that. He wasn't sure when or if he could.

The piece stated that Tigbee had been married twice, and had three children, all grown. Looking back through the material again, he noted there was a Cullen Tigbee on the Merit board, but he couldn't tell what relationship he had to Manse. He finished his lunch and made some calls from a pay phone using his phone card.

"Only thing I got from Lindsey Allen was the first name, Rusty, of that white kid Sharon might've been seein'," Grant said over the wire, after recounting what Lindsey Allen had told him earlier.

"And my mother's fine, right Dex?"

"What, you got short-term memory loss? How often I gotta tell you Nona's just swell? She's at work, and I got one of the guards, a guy who used to be with the sheriffs, escorting your mother to her car in the parking structure. I didn't start doing this yesterday, youngster."

"Being thorough, Lord Peter, just being thorough."

"Checking how I tie my saddle's more like it."

"Whatever." Monk filled him in on who he'd talked to and where he'd been. "It don't look like much to show, Dex. I called Tigbee back this morning and he was out, but once I see him, I guess that's it."

Grant breathed on the other end. "What do you think about this Rusty lead?"

A splash of sauce was drying on Monk's shirt and he picked at it. "I could spend another month down here trying to question every cat named Rusty or some sumbitch who knew a Rusty."

"Or find his Black friend. These two could have been plants by the Citizens League," Grant surmised.

"But the only two who met them that night, who knew what either of them looked like, are dead. At least the two we know about."

"Maybe this Black one turned up in something else like your cousin. You know, he might have testified in some other trial or some such."

Monk bounced his head side to side briefly. "I'll bite, Dex. I will look into that."

Grant said excitedly, "Hey, Tigbee contacted you after you saw the senator's wife."

"Yeah, I been running that around in my head, too. Looks like the Bodar residence is a house divided."

"Unless Bodar's hiding out 'cause Tigbee threatened him or his wife," Grant commented.

"Either way, I'd like some ammo when I go to see the man. But looks like I'm going to enter the tiger's lair butt naked. But go I must." Monk had a sudden thought. "What about his

family? I've found the high and mighty especially don't like
to be shamed by the doings of their progeny or wives. You
said he was married twice."

"I know one son is named Cullen. And the second wife
is named Harper, I mean that's her first name."

"No way."

"Way." Grant shot back. "Harper Jenny McBride was her
maiden name; she was ten years his junior. It seems Tigbee
had three children altogether, one by the first wife, Dolly
Lee, and two by Harper. But let me see what else I can find
out. Give me the name of the researcher at the Southern
Poverty Law Center and I'll talk with this McClendon fella
you said wrote this piece," Grant said.

Monk consulted his steno pad and gave Grant the numbers. "Tell you what, 'cause I'm the paranoid type, if you find
out anything, call me at the motel and say something about
my Ford."

"You think your room's bugged?"

"Tigbee had it done in the old days, and for all I know
he might actually own the place. Fax any info to your girl
Smiley at Mercury Cartage. Push come to shove, I'll call
her from somewhere if I can't get back up here to Memphis."

"I got a story to tell you about her sometime."

"I'm sure. Tell Mom hi. Odessa been around?"

"Came over night before last." The old pro could hear it
between the spaces of the question. "Why?"

If there had been bruises, he knew Grant would have said
so. Unless his sister had pleaded with him not to. "Nothing.
I'm out."

"What is that, hip talk?"

Monk hung up and decided not to call Tigbee back until
tomorrow. He didn't think Dex would find anything that

soon, but figured that would give him another day until he had to see him.

With nothing particular to do, Monk decided to take the bus tour offered in town. The tour took you to Sun Studios, then to where Stax Records had been, WDIA radio, and other points of interest in the city's musical history. Monk had carefully salted away his Otis Redding Stax albums in the bedroom closet at home. The superstar R&B artist's rough-hewn voice and command of lyrics was a direct lineage to Patton's unpolished, driving style. And Carla Thomas's "Time is on My Side" still gave him a warm memory of the garage party where he first heard the song, and had his first slow dance with Tina Chalmers.

LATER, AT night, he sat on the enclosed porch with Malus Locke, the farmer who rented out the land his mother owned in Mound Bayou. The town had been settled after slavery. In a reverse of the usual white municipalities practices, the officials of Mound Bayou had turned down federal aid in the old days so as to not be forced to meet Washington's standards of integration, and thus keep the city's political infrastructure Black.

Monk sat in a decrepit metal tube chair with a folded blanket for padding, Locke in his hickory rocker. The farmer was in his sixties, and wore thick lenses. He was Black with Chinese mixed in on his father's side of the family. Several African-Americans with Chinese descent could be found in various parts of Mississippi, a reminder of the days of railroad expansion and the import of cheap Asian labor. At their feet between them was an open bottle of Ballantine's scotch whiskey, the only liquor Locke drank. The market he traded at in Shelby ordered it specially for him from Jackson.

"How were those pork chops, brother Monk?" In his

pressed blue khakis and short-sleeved shirt he sipped from a red plastic cup. A pale yellow porch light caused more shadow than clarity for the two sitting figures. Locke called people brother not in the Black bonding sense, but as in all men were brothers in the eyes of God. He'd been a deacon ever since Monk could remember, at the Mount Olive Holy Redeemer Church.

"Too good," he admitted guiltily, pork being one of the things he was supposed to be eliminating from his diet. But damned if no sooner had he walked in the house when the irresistible smell of the smothered chops, simmering in brown gravy and onions, hadn't triggered forbidden desires in him. Add the mashed potatoes and fried okra Locke's grown daughter had prepared, he knew he had to get in a double workout at the Tiger's Den when he got back home.

"That's okay you had three," the older man said by way of a dispensation for gluttony. "I won't tell 'em up there in California where you got to be chawing down on them sprouts and what y'all call them cubes they make from soybeans?"

"Tofu," Monk said, smiling and enjoying his own scotch. "But I ain't big on that jive."

"Good to hear it, brother Monk." The rocker creaked and a lightning bug landed on the porch screen, flashing some insect code in its rear end for the benefit of the human onlookers. "Got a cigar if you'd like."

Well, no sense tiptoeing into vice's embrace. "Sure, if you're having one."

"I'm a pipe man myself, but I can blame you for my smoking to my daughter," he said, getting up. Locke went inside and returned shortly with the goods. He eased the screen and front door open, moving quietly for a man his age. His small movements were meant not to arouse the suspicions of his daughter. The farmer handed Monk a cigar, which he was surprised to see was a decent Robusto. He also gave him a book of matches.

"I get a few in with my orders of scotch," Locke answered Monk's unspoken question. He sat down and began packing his pipe from a worn tobacco pouch.

The men lit up and smoked for a while, the cicadas' hind legs rubbing and humming in the fields beyond the porch. "You do all right with your detective work?" Locke eventually asked. His head was momentarily shrouded in blue smoke, as if he were a supernatural being come to puzzle mortals with riddles.

"Some years good, some years so-so, money-wise."

"But you satisfied with it, ain't you? It's what you want to do, right?"

Monk took the cup away from his mouth. "I wouldn't know what else to do, Malus."

"You choose it, or it choose you?" Creak, creak.

Monk laughed. "I answered her call."

The older man didn't respond, there was only the sound of him drawing in on his pipe like a well-oiled respirator running in a small, closed-off room. Finally he said, "You makin' headway in this thing about your cousin?"

"Not especially," he said frankly. Again silence, and Monk figured what little image the man had of him as a PI had been shattered.

"You say something at dinner about going to see Tigbee?" Locke asked after a few moments. He was fooling with his pipe, which had gone out.

"Yes sir, big daddy himself."

Locke got his pipe relit and puffed into the air. "He's a slick old boy, but I guess I don't have to tell you that."

"You ever meet him?"

"Interestin' enough, I have. He gave some of the farmers around here a hand when the big frost hit in '92, wipin' out portions of a lot of good crops."

Monk puffed too. "That include you?"

"Yeah, but I made sure it was a loan, brother Monk. I'll be payin' it off next winter, God help the rhubarb to rise." They both laughed softly, several lightning bugs zipping by the porch's screen.

"He's a respected man around here, by Blacks and whites?"

"We ain't all book learned, brother Monk, but that don't mean we got amnesia. There's plenty know his past. But he wasn't the first one, you know, like George Wallace did later on, who ain't changed a few spots." He let that linger, then added cogently, "Or at least the leopard appeared to." Creak, creak.

Monk stated, "This money must have come from something other than his foundation."

"That's right. Tigbee set up a kind of relief fund with some other business fellas," Locke said. "But his son administered it through another branch of that foundation of his."

"His son Cullen?"

"Yeah, that's the second oldest. He was a starting forward at Mississippi Valley State."

Because Grant had made him itch about the family's affairs, maybe Locke could scratch the curiosity. "The other two children also involved in Tigbee's businesses?"

"The youngest son, Daniel, I believe has some kind of TV station he owns down in Florida."

"Seed money from dad?"

"Believe so."

"And the third one, that be the oldest daughter?"

"What you on to?" A defensive tone had suddenly risen

up in him as if Monk were probing an open wound with tweezers.

"Don't know until I get there, brother Locke."

Locke rocked, holding the cup in his hand on the armrest.

"You know the Lord don't tolerate a gossip."

"I wouldn't want you to speak out of turn."

They smoked and drank a piece.

"The oldest is in fact a daughter, Merrill," Locke said from around the stem of his pipe.

"But she didn't stay close to her father?"

In the weak light, Monk watched Locke tap the bowl of his pipe against the leg of the rocker, "From all accounts she was very much her mother's daughter."

Now Monk was following. "The first wife."

"Dolly Lee," Locke provided. "She left Tigbee."

"How you come by all this, brother Locke?"

Locke rocked and puffed on his pipe. "Mind you, you got me gossipin' like some ol' hen at a beauty parlor."

Monk toked on his cigar. "This is helpful information. This isn't just idle chatter to amuse the devil. You're helping me with my case." That might not be quite accurate, but he wouldn't lose too much sleep over small inaccuracies.

Locke weighed his guest's comments and took a sip from his glass. "Seems like it was a member of the church, a rightful sister who used to clean the Tigbee house from way back. Seems like she got to tellin' the missus had left with the young daughter back in '52 or so." He rocked some more and the country noises blanketed both of them.

"This sister say where Dolly and the daughter lit out to?" Monk ventured after a fashion.

"Yep," Locke drew out, then rocked some more.

Monk puffed and listened to the night.

"Ohio it was, Youngstown, Akron, may have even been Yella Springs. I can't rightly recall now exactly where. Someplace she had relations. I believe this church woman I'm speakin' of overheard one day as the missus was on the phone. 'Course that good sister went to meet the Lord in '69, so's she ain't around for you to cross examine." His easy laugh originated in his throat and stayed there.

Monk held the Robusto up to his eyes. "Fine cigar there, brother Locke."

"Thank you, kindly. Uh-huh." He rocked some more.

"People still come around here looking for the 'Killin' Blues'?" Monk belched, the taste scotch and tobacco heavy in his mouth.

"Oh yeah, you know they put up a marker for Patton over there in Holly Springs in the graveyard of the New Jerusalem Missionary Baptist Church."

"Like to see that 'fore I go." Monk was getting very comfortable slumped in the chair, his leg up on the porch railing.

"It ain't buried 'neath him nor stuck behind the cupboard in the church's kitchen, if that's what you're ponderin'," Locke advised.

Monk grinned. "I really didn't think so."

"They caught a couple of fellas from Milwaukee a few years ago diggin' up 'round Patton's grave. The church made 'em weed and reseed the whole plot as their punishment."

Out on the access road, an engine's transmission could be heard straining to get into a higher gear.

"You ever look for the album?" Monk inquired.

"When I was comin' up, the way I heard it was Patton recorded this 'Killin' Blues' album when he was preachin'. You know, like Swaggart used to when he was bangin' out a tune on the piano, Patton would serenade the congregation with one of his songs while he played guitar."

"With his wild-cat growl, I don't think serenade is what you'd call it." Monk puffed.

"Right you is, brother Monk. Anyways, the way I understand it, and this came from a play uncle of mine who was a friend of my mother Coretta, he told about some fella from New Jersey had come down here to record Patton live. He made his recordings, signed a contract with Patton—you know he had some book learnin'—and was on his way back up north when the bus he was riding in skidded off the highway somewheres outside of Nashville. So he and some of the others are dazed, see?"

"I do," Monk said, suddenly alert.

"So he comes to his senses and scrambles outside. Now the luggage compartment flew open, and this fella looks all over the spot where they'd landed, and the suitcase he had them disks in was gone. Only that particular case, see."

Monk digested the tale as best he could. "That's kinda amazing, brother Locke."

"It is indeed. Want a refill?"

"Well, I . . ."

"You can sleep in the front room, wouldn't want Nona's boy roamin' 'round these parts liquored up, not knowing east from west, now would I?"

"You're mighty generous with your accommodations," he praised his host, half dozing again.

"Ain't I though?" Locke ambled back inside quietly.

Out beyond the porch screen four lightning bugs zoomed up then down as if dive bombing in formation. The Robusto had nearly burned down to his knuckles, and Monk took his feet off the railing, stretching his legs out. His lower right leg, where he'd been shot, had knotted and he leaned over to knead the muscles. He fretted that in the years to come his collected injuries would stove him up, as his dad used to say. It would be just his luck to have children with Jill, and they'd have to roll the old man out to their softball games in his wheelchair. Suddenly cold from the certainty of his advancing years, Monk went back inside, shutting the front door in a futile effort to ward off inevitability.

# CHAPTER 21

Monk shaved languidly, standing in the small bathroom in his boxers. He'd done several rounds of crunch sit-ups and push-ups and had even jogged through town, gathering several intrigued looks from working folk on their way to their jobs. It wasn't like Mississippi hadn't been touched by the health craze, but Clarksdale, where you could get grits and biscuits and gravy for lunch, probably wasn't the next town on the list for a Bally's outlet. He didn't believe he'd totally burned off the calories from the pork chops and booze, but the exercise did alleviate his guilt.

After the workout he'd walked over to the Laundromat and put his clothes in the wash. From a pay phone he made a call to his mother's house and talked with Grant. The older man had found out from McClendon that Dolly Lee Ryshell had obtained an uncontested divorce from Manse Arnold Tigbee in 1954. She then went to live in Akron, Ohio, with a half-sister, the sister's husband, and her and Tigbee's daughter Merrill. McClendon had used a friend still on his old paper to get the information from its archives.

"Of course in those days a southern woman getting a divorce was somewhat scandalous, particularly from a powerful man like Tigbee," Grant had said. "By then he and his father were running the family textile mill over in Robinsonville, plus they had a large farm. And you know he saw action in the Normandy invasion."

"Anything else on the ex-wife? Is she still alive?" Monk worked a kink out of his neck.

"Nothing else from the archives, according to McClendon. You think there's anything here worth pursuing? Like maybe Tigbee called his former wife after Creel's trial and confessed to rigging the whole thing?"

"I guess we couldn't get that lucky," Monk allowed. "But the two sons seem close to the old man. The daughter Merrill isn't mentioned in anything I've read. Like he cut that part of his life off."

"As if he disowned his own daughter," Grant postulated.

"Or she him. Anyway, if you can't go in one direction—"

"Go in the other," Grant finished the saying he'd repeated often to his pupil.

Monk said, "Ask Coleman to dial up Rook Securities, one of the search firms I use. He's got my password and my PI number. See what they can get us on an employment record for Dolly Lee or Merrill. Given the time period, I would guess the daughter used Tigbee as her last name. And see if there are parking tickets or a change of address by the half-sister or her husband."

"I know how to do this, Junior," Grant said testily.

"Yes, wise one."

"That's better. Your mother went to the store, but you'd better call her back later, she wants to hear you're all right."

"I shall." He hung up and went out to check on his wash.

Now Monk examined his handiwork in the bathroom mirror. Using his trimming scissors, he clipped a loose thatch under his chin. He was pleased he'd managed to even out the sides of his goatee. Now that the fad had faded, he felt

the need to keep the thing as a sign of . . . what? Commit-
ment? He'd first grown the goatee in '91 as it became an in
thing. Now, past the end of the century, and the demise of
the look, did he hope by keeping it as a relic to be a statement
of individuality? Pushing his face closer to the mirror, he
noted the puffy areas under his eyes, and the new lines at the
edges on his face.

Maybe for the shindig he'd been invited to he ought to
just wear a mustache. More and more gray hairs kept spout-
ing in his beard anyway, so why not get rid of it? As he
contemplated the momentous act, he spotted several gray
hairs at the sides of his head. It seemed he and the judge
better stop contemplating children and get to stepping, as it
were.

Putting his jeans on, Monk decided the mustache look
could wait. He sat on the bed and read the invitation again.
The cream-colored envelope had been under his door when
he'd rolled in early this morning. He'd slept on Locke's
busted, body-contorting couch until rising at four in the
morning. Fortunately he hadn't been greeted with a hangover.

Wasn't, he reminded himself buttoning his shirt, last night
the second time since being down here he'd drunk too heavily? One more vice to overcome before the grave. He sighed
wearily.

His name had been handwritten in a hand he couldn't tell
was feminine or male, including his middle initial, which he
never used. A subtle but clear point from the sender telling
him he'd checked on who he was. The card inside announced
an afternoon of frolic and fund-raising on the *Belle La Rouche*
riverboat this Saturday. The boat was to glide up and down
the St. Helena River while a Dixieland band played and the
guests were to mingle and no doubt laugh gaily. Cuisine was

to be Chinese, braised rib tips and fresh seafood. The event was a fundraiser for a school of the blind over in Meridian, sponsored by the Merit Foundation.

Monk was going to meet The Man.

THE ST. Helena River was ruddy brown with sea green foam brimming along the banks. The *Belle La Rouche* was a fine old ship redone with dark marine varnishes rubbed into its woods and fresh white paint slathered on from top to below the water line. The engines hummed authoritatively, and the twin paddle wheels, one on each side toward the stern, slapped the water in soothing syncopation.

On its third level where a pilot house might have been was a dome with windows.

A knot of people were discussing the pros and cons of doing business in China. The band, headquartered on the fore section of the top deck, played Scott Joplin's "Maple Leaf Rag."

Monk was holding a glass of papaya juice and watched as the landscape of Tunica went by as the riverboat navigated its way from the St. Helena River south onto the Mississippi River.

"Who do you know?"

The questioner was a slimly built, pretty Black woman dressed ten years younger than her age. The hemline of her skirt rose above muscle-toned calves and hard knees. She had on lipstick the color of bruised peaches and Egyptian motif earrings hung from her lobes. She made no attempt to hide the country in her accent.

"I'm a stranger in town."

"Chicago?" she guessed, cocking her head at the sound of his voice. "No"—she held up a hand before he could speak—"farther west."

"L.A.," Monk said.

"I lived out there for a while," she admitted, "but honey, them drive-bys you got get on one's nerves, you know what?"

"It can be troubling," he said. The boat sounded a horn as it rounded the bend. A gambling vessel passed them on the portside. A redhead in a black sequined dress on the other boat was hiking up her skirt and wiggling her butt as she backed to the rail. It looked like she was going to pee but they'd gone past her before Monk could determine if that was so.

"People are acting up all over these days," Monk retorted.

"Ain't that the case. What do you do?"

"How about you," he lobbed back, wanting to avoid long explanations.

"The tall oblique type, huh?"

"I'll work on polishing the image."

She laughed, revealing several silver fillings. "I'm employed by our host."

Monk's eyebrow went up.

"I'm a program officer there, my docket is civil rights and civic participation."

"How long have you been at the foundation?" he asked seriously.

"If I told you that, I might give away my age."

"I keep many secrets." The two scrubbed white guys who'd been pretending not to be looking their way went into motion. They were the same two white guys he'd made when he first drove to the landing and parked. The duo had been standing midway on the upper deck as the riverboat lowered its ramp, eagerly engaged in conversation. But he'd caught the flick of their eyes, the sudden drop of their voices as he'd filed on with the others. There had already been some people on deck, so evidently the *Belle La Rouche* had made a previous pick up.

"I wonder," she said.

"Enjoy what you do?" Monk asked.

One of the men on this level, dressed in a Moschino sport coat of dark serge, had come over. He touched Monk's elbow gently like he was docent pointing out an artwork of special interest. "Excuse us, Darisse, I was hoping to steal Mr. Monk away for a few moments." The man had good-sized shoulders and thick legs. Crow's-feet webbed out from the corners of his blue eyes, and his brown-blond hair was turning gray like it was dusted with ash.

"As long as you bring him back, Cullen."

"Promise."

The woman and Monk exchanged smiles and Monk followed the younger Tigbee across the deck to a side door near the paddle wheel. As they did so, the son nodded at this person or that one, or murmured an assurance to look into whatever matter. They also walked by an open-jawed Cassie Bodar, who glared at Monk like he was a leper. He waved at her as if they were old friends.

The second man came in behind the two as they entered the passageway.

"This way if you would, Mr. Monk." Cullen Tigbee stood to one side and indicated a flight of polished wood stairs leading up to an opening in the upper deck. The second man, smaller than either Monk or Tigbee's son, stood with his arms loose at his sides, one foot cocked at an angle to the other. Some kind of martial artist, Monk surmised.

"Thanks," Monk said, turning abruptly and thrusting his glass toward the martial-arts specialist.

"Kanner doesn't usually take away the drinks," Cullen Tigbee commented.

But Kanner didn't miss a beat and casually accepted the glass. "My pleasure. Always like to see guests treated right."

His voice was tight and throaty. What might have been a sneer contorted his lips for a brief second.

Monk went up to find himself before the door built into the dome structure. The door was the same maple as the stairs, in contrast to the dome, which had a burnished steel finish.

"Go on in, sir," Cullen called from below.

Monk entered the dome. As he'd expected, the interior was a combination office/retreat for the man standing and talking into a cellular phone. He was looking out of one of the windows, and turned at the sound of his visitor's arrival. Manse Tigbee indicated a Swedish Modern leather-and-wood chair for Monk to sit in.

Tigbee had to be in his mid-seventies, about Grant's age, Monk calculated. He was six-foot even, on the thin side, but seemed in good health. He stood erect and his hair was a virtual match of his son's hue. He was dressed casually in an off-the-rack sport coat and open collar. He'd been speaking in an even tone into the cell phone and soon clicked it off.

"Good to meet you." Tigbee extended his hand.

Monk half-rose and returned the handshake. "Glad you invited me, Mr. Tigbee."

"Can I get you anything, water, whiskey, or both mixed together?" He didn't make a move toward the wet bar. It was trimmed in turquoise marble built into one part of the room's wall.

Monk was going to say no, but was curious to see what would happen if he did want something. "A splash of Maker's Mark if you have it."

Tigbee walked to the bar. "Ice?"

"Neat is fine."

Tigbee poured the drink and walked back to Monk with the squat tumbler. "How about a cigar? I'm going to have one."

"That'd be fine," he said, accepting the drink. In France, the condemned would get a shot of rum before getting his head lopped off by the guillotine. Monk didn't see anything suspended from the roof, but you never knew.

"I've got some Cohibas and Padrons, Churchills in fact." Tigbee was reaching below the bar and Monk estimated he could cut the distance between them if he leaped immediately. Just in case the old boy pulled out a gun.

"A Cohiba would be great." Monk's triceps tensed.

"Very good." Tigbee produced a walnut humidor fitted with yellow ivory along its edges.

Monk stood as the older man approached with the box and he extracted one of the valued, and contraband, Cuban-made Cohibas. Tigbee severed the ends and the two lit up. Tigbee fanned flame from an electronic lighter on the tip of Monk's cigar. The desk in the room was empty except for the cell phone, the lighter and two books stacked one on the other. The sounds of the revelers were muffled through the walls of the steel igloo, and Monk realized any sounds from inside the structure were bound not to be heard, either.

Tigbee moved an old-fashioned brass stand-alone ashtray and placed it near Monk. Then he wheeled his plain office chair from around the desk, and indicated for Monk to take his seat again. Monk did, and Tigbee sat too, diagonally from him.

"You get some big private detectin' cases?"Tigbee allowed his accent to drip over his words. "I was curious, and ran across your name in several write-ups we looked up."

Monk blew a cloud into the air. There was a ventilation vent over the bar, and he could hear the quiet whirl of its blades behind the metal slats. He watched the smoke drift toward the fan. "I don't try to grandstand."

Tigbee tapped the end of his cigar over the tray with a

blunt finger. "I like a man who does his work quietly. It's them pesky paper people who like to make stories sometimes out of nothing. Diggin' and snoopin' like hounds with their ribs show'n', goin' through a mess of garbage cans."

"Sometimes there's something there that needs to get dragged out into the open."

Tigbee pulled on his cigar, looking at Monk down the length of the shaft. He let the bluish-white fumes pour from around his open mouth, and he talked with the Cohiba latched in the corner. "You think that's the case in this matter?"

"Don't know until you lay out the pieces on the table, sorta like rebuilding a carburetor. Have to see what fits together, and what doesn't." He tasted the Maker's Mark and it went down warm.

"Only them old jalopies got carburetors these days," Tigbee pointed out.

Through the vent, Monk could hear a clarinet reach higher octaves. "Don't mean it won't work once it's put back together."

Tigbee crossed his legs, placing his glass at his feet. "Mississippi has always moved at a different pace than the rest of the country."

"Meaning there's truth, then there's Mississippi truth?" Monk set his glass down, too. If the strong-arm Kanner was going to give him the bum's rush to the door, Monk didn't want his hands busy.

Tigbee examined his cigar. "I know there's been much about my past that's been misunderstood. I also know there's been mistakes made, but the future is what's important." Unblinkingly, he looked across at Monk.

"We all have to account."

"You think the Citizens League was a buncha shiny suit

Knights of the White Magnolia who blew up little colored girls in church basements or took some fourteen-year-old out into the woods to torture and castrate him?" A tremor rose in his voice, and it seemed he was trying hard to stamp it down.

"The files speak for themselves," Monk said, easing back into the chair.

Tigbee uncrossed his leg, pivoting his body back and forth slightly on the chair's ball bearings. "Know what they used to call the NAACP 'round here?"

"Niggers, Apes, Alligators, Coons and Possums," Monk said.

"A man who knows something of history." Tigbee nodded appreciatively, tapping his cigar this time against the ashtray's rim. "You think us monsters, Mr. Monk?"

"What does it matter what I think?"

"Obviously something gets you going in the morning."

"Obviously."

Tigbee grinned, showing natural teeth. "I'm not looking for absolution; I don't shirk from anything I've done in this life. Whatever it is, whatever you imagine I've done, the reality is it was done with good men with good intentions to keep this a good state."

"And whites should be on top because it's the natural order of things." Monk blew smoke.

"The wheel always turns, Monk. Look at where we're at these days. The Yellow Peril may not have happened as an outright invasion of planes and tanks, but you can't tell me they ain't anglin' to get us by the short hairs. You know, just look at the place you come from." He pointed with his hand holding the cigar, and he picked up his drink with the other. "Asians knocking Blacks out of higher learnin' faster'n a dog scratchin' off a tick."

Did all of Tigbee's similes revolve around canines? "So now it's us against them?"

Tigbee thumped Monk's knee with his cigar hand, and leaned closer. "Black and white is the two sides of the equation, Monk, we made this country. More Black folk are movin' home, Monk. The African-American population in the South has steadily gone up in the last six, seven years. Now why is that?" The older man's eyes twinkled; he had his answer: "'Cause up north and in the southwest the Mexicans and Central Americans are making more babies than you and me combined. By 2020, whites and Blacks are gonna be strangers in their own land. Except here." He pointed the cigar at the deck.

"You can't tell me that some Black fellas standing out on corners looking for work—and I know more of them are, I read through ten papers each morning—don't feel funny when the man pulls up in his car and hires the Mexican. He hires him 'cause he knows unlike the Black man, the immigrant will work for less money, and longer hours. Work that should be going to us Americans."

"So this is a new day, when we can come together against our mutual Spanish-accented enemies." Monk took a look toward the door but the latch wasn't twisting. "What happens after the natural order of things are restored, Mr. Tigbee, does it go back to like it's always been? Black man scrambling to get a little something from the white man whose reins of power we just helped him hold onto?"

Monk knew this was a useless debate, but he couldn't help himself. It wasn't as if he and Tigbee would solve this country's race problems, it wasn't as if he and Tigbee were even dealing on the same level. Tigbee could call out the hard boys on him at anytime.

Tigbee looked offended. "Against incredible odds, the

Black man has made many strides, Mr. Monk, you certainly know that. History is an inter-connected set of tracks upon which our train is forever barreling."

A new simile, Monk noted archly.

Tigbee was still talking. "The civil rights movement didn't start with Miss Parks refusing to sit in the back of the bus in '55." He drank some more and wet his lips with the tip of his tongue. "And it ain't like she was the first. Hell, there was a case in '55, back before I got out of the service, where a Black woman named Sarah Mae Brown, who had some sand, got in the face of a bus driver right on the corner of Dexter and Lawrence and refused to budge and go to the back."

Tigbee leaned his rangy frame forward for emphasis. "And who inspired Miss Parks?" Now he was the teacher, testing the knowledge curve of his one, less-than-eager student.

"She'd attended classes at the Highlander Institute in Tennessee." Monk rewarded himself with a sip and a toke.

"Where she'd met Septima Clark," Tigbee added. "Who somebody ought to build a statue to. And it was fellas like E.D. Nixon, a Pullman porter who received his political education under that Randolph fella, who organized the Montgomery bus boycott coming offa Miss Parks's arrest."

"So you know more than a whole lot of Black kids coming up these days about the movement." Trying to stay cool, Monk could nonetheless feel the edginess working its way into his voice. It bothered him this Mississippi mover wasn't as one dimensional as he'd assumed.

"Right," Tigbee said, smiling and touching Monk's knee again with the glass in his hand. "And we could go on talking about the ones who sacrificed much here in this state: T.B. Wilson who organized the National Progressive Voters League, or certainly, the Delta's Amzlee Moore."

Monk knew about Moore from his teen years when his

mother made sure his school work was supplemented with
the books she had him and Odessa read. They had objected
then, but he was glad now she had made them learn the
"other" history. "He and Reverend T.R.M. Howard founded
the Regional Council of Negro Leadership in 1951. A coun-
terpoint to the white Delta Council," Monk said forcefully.
"The same Council which had been the engine driving the
attacks on returning Black servicemen, some of whom were
murdered. The good Christians were scared these brothers,
who'd fought for freedom in foreign lands, might actually
have the audacity to demand the same in their own country."
Monk made a tsk, tsk sound, loud and dramatic. "The same
Council that was the basis for your Citizens League. Imagine that."

"We sometimes learn something from the past, Mr.
Monk." Tigbee was maintaining his layer of civility, but the
comment had gotten to him. "The recording of history is
the book of the tyrant, the future is the bible of the free."

"Melville, more or less," Monk said, recognizing the para-
phrasing.

"You a man of the sea, Mr. Monk?"

He realized Tigbee knew he'd been a ship's engineer. "I
served some time in the merchants."

"Grand, grand," Tigbee spouted eagerly. "My oldest son
served in the Navy."

It was an opening to bring up the daughter, but there'd
be another opportunity. Monk merely nodded slightly.

Tigbee tipped his glass up, then said, "I'm a man of progress, Mr. Monk. Now, understand, all things cannot be
accomplished at the same time. Of course, our country finds
itself at an exciting and dangerous juncture in her history."
He stood abruptly, going to one of the windows. "Not too
far from here," he began, pointing with his cigar in no

particular direction, "the Germans have built a car plant. It means jobs for the area, sure. But what does that say about American workers when we're considered cheaper labor than the goddamn krauts?"

"The chickens always come home to roost."

Tigbee turned as if slapped. "What are you saying?" he sputtered excitedly. "You think somebody like Malcolm X had the answers? Or are you a Karl Marx man?"

"I mean," Monk said, taking the cigar out of his mouth, "that the interests of big business have always been the same. That Blacks, whites, Asians . . . whoever, who have to hit that gig every day to survive so they can buy their kids food, have been divided since this country began—over language, over skin color, over the texture of hair and the thickness of lips. Over bullshit, Mr. Tigbee. Bullshit men like you perpetuate."

The *Belle La Roache* shuddered on the river and a bottle of cognac slipped from the shelf on Tigbee's bar and crashed to the deck.

Monk went on. "More than fifty years ago the anthropologist Ashley Montagu wrote that race was a social construct, not a biological reality."

Tigbee scoffed, "He was a Jew, you know. Changed his name from Aronberg. That's how much he believed in his own theories."

Monk made a tick sound with his tongue. "I know. What I was going to say was that Montagu was right, of course, in the abstract. But we humans can't get that high on the evolutionary plane. In the context of how we deal with each other, how we perceive each other, race certainly exists; it's a tangible force in this country and the world. But the hell of it is, it ain't the only thing keeping us apart. A guy working at one of those chain department stores here in the Delta has something in common with a Southeast Asian immigrant doing duty in a restaurant's kitchen in Orange County. Only they can't see it."

"That all-is-one crap was tried before, Mr. Monk, back before your time with the anarchist Wobblies and the communist-dominated Unemployed Councils that used to be 'round here in the thirties with all that Angelo Herndon stuff." Tigbee sounded satisfied, as if the matter was settled.

"That don't mean they were bad ideas," Monk remarked. "I never boogied to the Party's beat, but goals like national health care, a decent wage for a decent day's work, what the hell's un-American about that?"

"It's how we get there," Tigbee said tonelessly. "That's what it's always been about."

Monk was feeling frisky. "You mean get there at a proper pace."

"Look, we are at the barricades, and it's going to be all of us working together, shoulder to the wheel to make us strong again."

Gravely, Monk asked, "The question is: Are your enemies mine?"

"They ain't your friends, Mr. Monk. That rainbow coalition shuck Reverend Jackson goes around getting money from guilty whites to give to his PUSH organization hasn't materialized and it won't. Multiculturalism is a fraud, and you know it. The Brown man don't need you 'cause he's producing numbers faster than any of us. The yellow man thinks you're lazy and stupid." He swayed slightly in the seat, and Monk could see Burchett flopping out of his chair and squirming on the floor in the video.

"Black and white," Tigbee touched his fingers together.

"We need each other, Mr. Monk, in these uncertain times."

There it was. Manse Tigbee, the power behind one of the

most devious and powerful whites' rights organizations of the civil rights era, a man who had reinvented himself as a genteel southern philanthropist, was the last true integrationist. He almost burst out laughing.

"Mr. Tigbee," Monk said, wishing to make himself clear and uncluttered in his response. "As long as we only talk about race, as long as we only point fingers and beat our chests saying we suffered the most or we deserve to be on top 'cause God or genes intended it to be that way, then we ain't getting anywhere. It's about how we see the many get screwed by the few. And how racism keeps us apart from seeing where we might have some issues the same, like schools for our kids, good jobs, or bowling, for God's sake." Despite the circumstances, he laughed.

He paused, the smoke from his cigar congealing around a portion of his face. Tigbee waited. "People are dying every day because of the skin we're in or how somebody speaks, so I guess we'll never get to that other discussion." He puffed on the cigar a little longer and had another sip. A melancholy had suddenly descended on him.

"You think your friend Damon Creel believes in this grand and glorious vision of yours?" Tigbee took a long pull on his Cohiba, which had burned halfway down, specks of ash like dirty snow flitting to the shiny deck.

"The thing is, Mr. Tigbee, it's not just me who sees an America like this. And I think that's what's got you worried."

Several degrees more of Tigbee's civility slipped from behind his eyes. "What do you want, Monk? You want your name mentioned on the news at ten? You want money enough to buy a rack of suits and put away enough for retirement?"

Monk put his drink down and left the cigar in the ashtray. "I'm not opposed to being comfortable. But like you said, it's how ya get there, that's the trick."

Muffled sounds of clinking glasses, and people laughing and talking came through the vent. It was as if he and the older man were spinning toward the stratosphere in a hermetically sealed chamber, the invitees and the ground crew celebrating a successful launch.

Tigbee clasped his hands on his forearms and lowered his head as if in prayer. Finally he said, touching his lip briefly with his tongue, "I wish you luck, in whatever endeavor you might pursue."

"How about putting in a word with Cassie Bodar so I can speak to her husband?"

Tigbee laughed softly as he stood. "One tries not to interject themselves in things best left to husband and wife."

Monk was also up. He retrieved his cigar, which had gone out. "I suppose."

Tigbee walked with Monk to the exit. "I need to go out and see a few people, but I'm a private man at heart." The two stopped at the door. "You must have matters you'd want best kept alone."

"Only on Tuesdays. See you around, Mr. Tigbee." Monk stepped back out and into a waiter carrying a tray of beer in highball glasses and a bowl of shelled pistachio nuts. Monk took some pistachios, and looking back, saluted Tigbee. Then he descended the stairs. The inference about the old rascal wanting to maintain his privacy wasn't lost on him. Monk just didn't give a damn.

# CHAPTER 22

There was a message from Grant posing as a mechanic when Monk returned from his riverboat ride. The note stated the Galaxy needed a ring job. He'd crossed the highway and phoned him back from the Tornado Lounge and Game Parlor after laying a ten on the proprietor. What the ex-cop told him had made his heart thud against his breast bone and he refused the beer the lounge's owner offered as a way of change for his money.

After getting some initial information from Rook Securities via Coleman, Grant had flown the red-eye out to Akron. The city had remained the home of the half-sister of Dolly, the ex Mrs. Tigbee. There, on microfiche, he'd found an obit for the half-sister, Edna, in the *Akron Beacon Journal*. Rook had supplied the information that she'd retired in 1974 after years as a records supervisor for the County Building and Safety Department.

Edna Clavert Hayden had been something of a minor celebrity, too. For more than a decade she'd written a gardening column for a throw-away weekly. Shed died of pneumonia in the Silver Crest Rest Home on May 9, 1991. The husband, Charles Hayden, was still alive, but pretty much out of it after three successive strokes.

The same day, Grant paid a visit to the rest home claim-
ing to be a long-out-of-touch relative and learned the name
of the assistant director, a nurse, who'd since left, who used
to be friends with the woman. Finding her by phone was not
too hard. As a nurse she still did home care work from time
to time, and had signed on with several nurse registries.
Monk's mother, back in L.A., had helped with that task.

Grant found the nurse, Shana Harvey, working as a shift
supervisor of a home care business in the Detroit suburb of
Beverly Hills. This after he'd first followed the lead back to
southern California; the name of the town had confused
him. From Harvey—he told her up-front why he was calling
her—Grant got the information that Dolly Lee Clavert had
re-married and moved away sometime in the early '60s. Edna
had been particularly talkative about the past and her family.

Harvey also remembered Edna's niece, Merrill, coming
to visit shortly before Harvey herself had moved on. She
didn't remember much, though the niece had mentioned that
Edna's sister, her mother Dolly Lee, had passed on some
time before. And no, she didn't remember what city Merrill
was visiting from, but she was a pleasant woman, Harvey
mentioned. After Grant segued into a story or two about his
days on the LAPD, Harvey loosened up.

She did remember one additional fact: Merrill had flown
in. And that the younger woman had mentioned there was
snow already on the ground where she'd come from. It had
been fall and cold, but there'd been no snow in Ohio yet,
Harvey recalled.

Working backward, Grant developed a profile of eastern
states with snow in that year, in that month of mid-November.
Then he set the Rook Security Agency in motion again to
track down Merrill Sarah Tigbee through change-of-address
cards, employment records, DNW records, all the manner

in which modern humans mark the compartments of their lives in the age of the number.

But more importantly to Monk, along the way Dexter uncovered a new fact that gave the case a whole new spin. Grant hadn't actually located Merrill yet, but he didn't have to. Not right then, anyway.

MONK STOOD moving side to side in the just-breaking dawn morning of Vicksburg in his Levi's 501 jeans, watch cap and buttoned-up jean jacket. He was glad he'd put on a sweater underneath too, A police car had glided past him and he walked along like he always took his constitutional this time every day, even though he must look like what they figured OJ was wearing that fateful night.

Their stares said they didn't quite buy it, and he assumed they'd roll back his way soon. But the man he'd come to see was coming from around the rear of his house. He was dressed in dark blue cotton sweat pants, a tri-colored nylon top, with a matching hooded sweatshirt underneath. The soles of his black-and-white Nikes sounded like the fingers of hands in wet rubber gloves tugging at each other as he trod over the dewy lawn. He had on the same pair of shoes Monk had noticed the other day on the steps. The shoes that were too big for Cassie Bodar's smaller feet.

"Senator Bodar, I'm Ivan Monk." He'd fallen in step beside the man as he began his jog.

"I was hopin' you were a persistent reporter, or just an early-rising mugger," he said adroitly. Bodar kept his knees moving, and Monk was hoping he wouldn't take off. The senator was a tallish, solidly built man with a graceful build. If it got to be a foot race, Monk knew he'd lose. Good thing the lawmaker stopped.

"I haven't much to tell you, Mr. Monk."

"Then if you don't mind, I'll try a few theories on you."

A Corsica went past them and the driver honked. Bodar waved at the retreating vehicle. "Save it for the lecture hall, my friend." He turned, preparing to take off.

Monk said simply, "I know who Ava Green really was." A bird chirped in the tree above them.

Bodar snapped his head around at his unwanted workout partner. Finally, he said, "Let's go over to the park where I ran, all right?" He didn't wait for a response, and began to walk briskly in a westerly direction.

"Why have you been lying so low?" Monk asked, concentrating to keep up. "You definitely seem to be back in the groove," he huffed, condensation clouding from his mouth.

"Reasons," Bodar replied tersely. He kept moving as if late for an appointment. Occasionally he'd look back and Monk would get nervous.

The two crested a low hill of wild grass and red clay and before them was a baseball field, basketball court and a well-maintained jogging track. Bodar descended the hillock and walked onto the basketball court. He circled about, hands on his hips like waiting to get called in. "What do you intend to do?"

"At the least try to get Creel a new trial."

Bodar kept pacing. "That may not happen."

"You wishing for that or assessing the situation?"

"This is not a chess game."

"It's people's lives, Senator; I know exactly what it is," Monk scolded.

Bodar passed a hand through his hair. "This is one of those matters that requires our delicacy in handling."

"We've had four hundred some odd years of delicacy in handling the racial matter in this country, Senator. Besides, I am not one of your voters." Monk was angry Bodar was pulling the politician's trick of seemingly chummy inclusion to throw him off guard. He pointed at the man. "And this isn't a matter for a senate committee; this can't be punted to them in order to bury the information. Somehow you found out about Ava, right, which put you onto Nancy Burchett who told you about her father's connection with the Southern Citizens League?"

Bodar gave a camera smile to a couple walking past them who were heading for the track. "Have you talked to Merrill?"

"I will," Monk promised.

"She has no direct knowledge, you know, about Creel's case." He was doing the elected official slip-and-slide.

"Really?" Monk whispered doubtfully.

Bodar shrugged. "It appears Merrill never told Ava. Or at least she does a good acting job."

"So you told Cassie about your investigation into the Creel case?"

Bodar didn't say yes or no.

"Is your wife protecting you from yourself, Senator?"

Bodar scratched at his unshaven face. "You wouldn't believe this, but I set out to show that Mississippi could right its own racial wrongs, Monk. I set out to prove to the self-absorbed pundits on the Sunday shows and the smug columnists in *The Nation* and *Emerge* that being from Mississippi, and being conservative, didn't automatically make you a Kluxer."

"And what better way to prove that than the Creel case?" Monk concluded. "Just looking into it got you national attention. And it was so long ago, who could find anything of value anyway?"

"You can be cynical, Monk," Bodar said without animosity "And yes, I'd be less than truthful to say I didn't have my eye on higher goals." He was poised to go on, but held himself in check. "But that doesn't diminish the attempt." He said it more to convince himself than the private eye.

"Speaking of your significant other—I love that term, don't you?—what's her deal with Tigbee? I checked with this trade newspaper called the *Chronicle of Philanthropy* and found out she's on the board of a Merit-founded organization for youth interracial relations. It's doing quite well it seems, with multi-year grants."

"You'd make a good living inside the Beltway, Monk," the senator said appreciatively. "Contrary to opinion, there's some poor white folks down here, too." Bodar began to walk again, and Monk followed him. The other couple was now circling the track. "My wife was one of them. I don't believe they had carpeting until she was twelve or thirteen. And the phone was off and on so much, she assumed it was that way in everybody's home."

"It's you family-value boys who keep saying poverty is no excuse for crime."

Bodar flared, "My wife has not committed a crime. It's not a certainty that Creel didn't kill those girls," Bodar shot back. "Who Ava was doesn't answer for the deed."

"But it does put into question the official story," Monk corrected. "At least enough to look at it again."

"I thought you wanted to find out who killed your cousin."

"This looks to be in that direction, too." They walked along on the outer edges of the track. "You get a call after your supposed accident? That's what scared you off?"

Bodar pulled on his bottom lip with his thumb and index finger. "As I said, my wife came up hard. We met in college, Ol' Miss. Me, I was there because of family connections; she got there on actual ability. I'd never met someone with so much drive, vision really, I guess you'd call it."

Monk let him talk.

"We went crazy for each other." Bodar crossed his arms, looking off in the direction of his house. "I always knew what I was going to do, due in no small part to what my parents had set out for me as a child. Cassie's mom figured she'd do good to complete high school and maybe get a job with the city. It's not 'cause she didn't want better for her, it's just what she'd come to expect from this world."

"She's not the only one not to expect more."

"Yes, I know," the senator concurred. "You see, Monk, what I'm trying to say is Cassie and I are quite attached to each other. We both want to see that our work has value."

"Do the demons of racism burden you more than her?" he asked sarcastically.

"That's not so surprising, is it, Monk? Haven't all the revolutions in the past century been led by members of the middle class? Aided by those of the upper class who turned their backs on their privilege, to rail against injustices." He snorted self-mockingly. "Isn't the white working class of this country a contradiction in how it resonates with reactionary politics, yet any objective analysis would see they are in the same economic boat as working-class Blacks?"

"Whites don't see themselves as working class. Anyway, all that class analysis is outdated, isn't it, Senator? Plus, aren't you biting the hand? Those reactionaries voted you into office."

"One can lead by example, Monk. That's what a politician should do, not simply play to the less sophisticated instincts of the electorate."

"We have no argument on that. So what's been stopping you?"

Bodar clucked his tongue. "My wife and I have tried to have children for some time. You have kids?"

"No, I don't."

"She finally got pregnant three years ago." Bodar wiped at one eye with his fingertips. "The child, the fetus, wound up in her tubes. Needless to say, we were devastated." He walked in big circles. "The child was going to be our anchor, Monk. We've been either shouting or avoiding discussion of race relations in this state for sometime. And the avoidance of that subject has become the unsaid subtext to me and Cassie not dealing with the matter of children, either. I guess if we can't discuss what kind of society we want, we can't separate out our entropy on the matter of children."

Several more people were now jogging around the track.

"But when I latched onto the Creel case, well, that touched an unhealed wound."

"But you'd sponsored legislation on racial tolerance; you yourself called for federal intervention when a number of questionable hangings of Black and white prisoners took place in Harrison County jails a few years ago, and your wife's group helps kids of different races."

Now it was Bodar's turn to remain quiet.

"Unless of course you're telling me she . . . No"—Monk snapped his fingers—"somebody she *knew* was involved in the Creel matter."

Bodar pulled at his lip again. "I'll tell you, 'cause I can see the lid is off the box, and if it's not you, it's going to be somebody else who will spill the goods. Cassie's older brother was a hellraiser, had more than one run-in with the law. And it's fair to say, he never met a Black person who could do anything for him 'cept stay out of his way.

"Well, it seems there was a rumor going 'round among some of them ol' boys he hung with. Some were Klan, some just your regular fatback-and-greens-lovin' crackers—and some of these boys had done strong-arm work for the

League. Now this is right after Creel was sentenced you understand, and the word was the girls' killing had indeed been a job sanctioned by the Citizens League." Bodar fixed an eye on Monk. "That four men had done the deed."

"And her brother is supposed to be one of these four."

Bodar wrung his hands despite the sun having risen and the onset of the morning heat. "I didn't hear this from my wife, at least not initially. Remember, she was still a gap-toothed kid when he was damn near grown, and had already done a juvenile stint for assault."

"But you got this from Burchett's daughter," Monk said. "And what was Burchett's role in this?"

"She told me her father, as he died, confessed to her he was the strike leader, as he called it. He said the captain called the mission, and he'd followed orders like a good soldier."

Monk knew Tigbee had been a lieutenant in World War II, and a captain when he'd re-upped in Korea. Burchett had also served in Korea. He'd also been, according to the service record Monk had read, in a prisoner of war camp called Chi-Han near the province of Tunghwa.

"And Burchett named your wife's brother?"

"Yes. Rusty."

Monk's head got light, and he tried to sound detached, professional. "Where is Rusty these days?"

"Doing ten to fifteen on what would have been an easier sentence for selling illegally converted guns, but he shot and wounded an ATF agent in the raid, so he's doing serious time down in Pensacola. And he's as hard as they come; he's not telling anybody anything."

"Nancy Burchett name anybody else?"

Bodar shook his head. "She told me he went into another of his deliriums, and that was that."

"Why she tell you this?"

"Nancy had worked in my campaign. She felt too burdened when her father had told her what amounted to his death-bed confession."

"Was your accident rigged?"

"The Highway Patrol inspector can't rightly determine foul play. The steering knuckle had come undone, but it's not unheard of, them separating on that model of mine. Fact, they'd been recalled for that defect. I haven't received any calls at night, or gotten any unsigned letters since then."

"But it was after your accident that Nancy got scared and split." Monk put his hands in his back pockets. "And when you told your wife, she no doubt felt very conflicted, and has let you know that."

Bodar gripped his temples in one hand, massaging the areas.

"Consciously or not, she also hasn't been pursuing the idea of children too much since then, either."

"Have you tried to find Nancy Burchett?"

"I haven't."

"But you could if you wanted."

"And what would it come to, Monk? I end my marriage over hearsay and supposition? Burchett's dead and I can assure you, Rusty Ibers isn't naming names this side of the grave. And why should he? There's nothing beyond Nancy's word tying him to the murders."

"But I've just found out who Ava really was, and I intend to let it be known."

"You don't live here, Monk. You aren't going to bear the brunt of your reckless actions. And believe me, it will be your people who will feel it the most in the long run."

He was tired of white men telling him how careful you had to be about exposing racist crimes. It wasn't as if Black folk weren't already bearing the brunt of inaction. It was as if he should just let the wickedness slip by him like newspaper carried on a sudden gust of wind to clog a drain already clogged with weak excuses to let it be. That somehow if you just did nothing, it would all work out on some future unspecified date, when the reality was that history only moved forward when you made conscious effort, and sacrifice, to make it so. Yes, he didn't live here, yes, he could in a sense walk away, and goddamnit, probably nothing would happen to Tigbee. The irony being if there was truly justice in this world, something should happen to the old cracker— something of a violent and painful nature for all that he'd caused to others over the decades.

"The whispered dwell here in Mississippi, Monk. Older than the Natchez, more ancient than our mighty river, or before anyone chopped the first tree here. What has been kept hidden has festered and infected us. We have been among the worst when it came to race relations. I only wanted to see if we could be among the best, too. But it's so hard."

"Thanks for your candor, Senator." Monk began to walk away from the man, the joggers and their cozy park.

"You going home, Monk?"

He knew he didn't mean his motel room. "Yes, I am." He didn't add that he was going to call McClendon before he left and tell him what he'd learned about Ava Green. Monk looked up to see Cassie Bodar coming over the hill. She looked svelte in her coordinated workout sweats and running shoes that matched her husband's. There was a ruddiness in her cheeks which dissipated as she saw Monk.

"What the fuck are you doing here?" she all but screamed.

Her eyes became slits and her right hand a shaking fist.

Monk looked through her. Silently, he walked past the woman on the hill, and down toward their house, where he'd parked his car.

# CHAPTER 23

"This is Nancy Burchett. I need to see you."

Monk sat on the edge of the bed, the phone next to him, the handset in his left hand. "I'm surprised you called me."

He'd placed his father's .45 close by on the night stand. He'd lubricated the rebuilt parts of the ACP 1911 model late in the afternoon after talking with McClendon and getting a 4 A.M. flight out of Memphis. The Colt was in cocked-and-locked mode, the hammer pulled back and ready to drop should he have reason to pull the trigger. He'd noticed some pull with the slide assembly shooting at the range a few weeks ago. Therefore, he'd paid close attention to any burrs along the edges of the metal or fatigue in the spring when he'd disassembled and oiled the weapon.

"I gotta talk to you, Mr. Monk. I gotta be done with this." Her voice had a slight quake in it from apprehension.

"Bodar call you?" Outside, the floorboards of the walkway creaked. Muffled voices floated in to him through the walls.

"He said we couldn't duck this any longer." There was a resigned quality in her voice. Like she'd reached a boulder in the road blocking her after a long and fruitless journey. There was something else there, too, a suggestion in her tone that one of McClendon's reporters was right about his hints concerning Bodar's crack-up.

"Are you two lovers?"

"What you want to know, mister? You want to know what my daddy told me or you want to be on Jerry Springer?"

"So you decide to call me now at"—he glanced at his watch—"damn near nine-thirty."

"Shit, mister, I didn't call you up just to hear you be sour. Frankly, I think it does make better sense for me to stay gone."

It was a chump play, but what if she was for real? He couldn't let a chance at a valuable link in this affair simply slip away. "Come on out to the airport in Memphis."

"All right," she agreed, surprising him. "It'll take me a couple of hours from where I'm at. Make it twelve-thirty, tonight, okay?"

"I'll be at the Southwest section. How will I know you?"

"I'll know you." She severed the Line before he could say anything else.

He wondered who she'd talked to, but would go with the flow. Monk finished packing and, having settled his bill with his credit card, exited the room. He put his bags in the back of the pickup truck and got out on Highway 61, heading north. He'd wait around at the airport to see if the woman would actually show. As he drove through Gator, a station wagon pulled out from an access road behind him. The car remained steady on him and Monk periodically kept watch on the vehicle in his rearview mirror. Crossing the state line, the wagon's driver put on his turn signal, and went east. The rest of the drive was uneventful.

He returned the truck at the National stall set aside for afterhours drop-offs. The shuttle took him to his terminal. He was walking in just as a kid with long stringy hair, a baseball cap emblazoned by a silver AC/DC logo jammed on his head, came toward him. The teenager had been standing in the recess of the automatic doorway. He was sniffling like he had a head cold, and had passed Monk before he spoke.

"This is for you."

Monk whirled, dropping his bags as his right hand went for the belt holster beneath his jean jacket. The kid wasn't facing him and was trotting away across the lanes toward the parking structure. Near where he'd been was a six-by-nine manila envelope on the ground.

Inside the envelope was a single Polaroid. The woman sitting in the chair in the shot had her top ripped off, in shards about her waist. Her mouth and eyes were covered over by duct tape. A gloved hand was grabbing one of her breasts in her plain bra, the fingers sunk deep in the ample flesh. The arm extended into the frame of the close shot, the face, of course, not seen, but he didn't think this was Nancy Burchett's idea of fun. He went inside.

He was being paged to a courtesy phone over the PA system.

"She gets butt-fucked with my shotgun, then her brains will be blown out, nigger boy," the voice on the other end of the line gleefully informed him after he'd picked up. "You got an hour."

"I turned in my truck." Monk was calculating how long it would take him to convince the cops to believe him.

"You got fifty-nine minutes, Snowball," the voice advised. "Go back south on 61."

Monk got back to the rental stall and shot the lock off the strong box holding the keys. He took off in the pickup truck. Back below the border the same station wagon that had been behind him earlier—a '70s-era LTD Country

Squire with numerous rust spots and peeling fake wood grain—got close and zoomed ahead of him. It was a moonless night, and the lights along this stretch of the road were spaced far apart. The wagon took a turn onto a gravel road barely discernible among the maples and poplars, and Monk followed.

The car went deep into the woods, passing an occasional mail box staked at various intervals along the edge of the single-lane pathway. The wagon made a sharp left and the route took them deeper into the gloomy topiary. Monk bounced along not too far behind. They were heading west, in the direction of the Arkansas border. The wagon took another turn and came to a stop at a series of low buildings spaced at numerous angles to each other. A halogen light was on over one of the buildings in the center of the yard. Several tractors, a grader, a combine harvester, a manure-spreader and a tandem-disk harrow were also about. Another car, its lights off, had pulled in behind the pickup truck. It was the cream-colored Taurus Monk had seen several days earlier at his motel. Grinding the clutch's throw-out bearing, Monk forcefully reversed the Dodge's gears, violently plowing into the Taurus. The grill and upper hood crumpled as that car's front end went under the truck's higher bumper.

"Fuck," someone yelled over the grinding of metal and molded plastic.

Simultaneously, Monk tumbled out of the truck on the passenger's side, two lit flares in his hands that he'd retrieved from the highway kit in the truck's bed before leaving the rental depot. The pickup truck's windshield exploded from a shotgun blast. He threw the flaming sticks over the roof of the truck at the driver's side of the Taurus. Then he pivoted and cranked off two shots at the wagon.

"Get down," the voice screamed again.

Monk ran and dove beside the manure-spreader, which was positioned near the right rear of the Ram pickup.

"Blast his monkey ass," the voice bellowed.

Three more shots in rapid succession from Monk's .45 rang out, and the halogen light was extinguished. Blackness caressed the area, the buildings and farm machinery becoming murky forms seemingly strewn about by a capricious baby titan.

"Scared, nigger?" one of the men from the wagon taunted evilly, crouching near the vehicle on the passenger's side.

"Shut up," the wagon's driver hissed, also crouching down.

"Smart bastard," the one who had driven the Taurus summed-up quietly. "We can't see him, but he can't see us clearly neither," the wagon's passenger said unnecessarily.

"Find him," the quiet-voiced one commanded. "He can't be allowed to say anything to anybody."

"Who in fuck put you in charge?"

"Who do you think?" came the assured reply.

Cicadas made their whines and frogs did their croaks. Nothing human talked nor moved for several moments. There was no gravel or leaves in the clearing and the footfalls of the killers would be hard to discern, if at all.

Monk had moved off from the manure-spreader, belly crawling across the moist ground. He'd noticed tall poplars among the heavy undergrowth bordering the clearing on its eastern end as he'd driven in behind the wagon. He made for their relative safety, and came to rest beside a tree. The automatic was in his hand, shells stuffed into the front pockets of his Levi's. He got his breathing under control in an attempt to hear the men.

Was it three hitters? Or was there a fourth like the ones who'd done the girls decades ago? One to watch out, two to hold the young women, their callused hands gripping them hard, gags tied excruciatingly tight around their mouths. And the last one to do the cutting. Burchett must have been the knifer, proud to do his bloody duty for the cause.

A flashlight's beam probed the dark, some yards from where Monk had kneeled down. The owner of the flashlight was moving about tentatively, aware his light could also pinpoint his existence. Monk obliged and clipped two off at the point of origin.

"Goddamnit," the man yelled, clicking the light off.

"I told you not to use it," the other one snickered from the other side of the yard. Monk recognized that voice—Kanner, from the riverboat.

Monk went flat again, scratching his face and hands as he burrowed through some low shrubbery. Absently he wondered if the stuff was poison ivy. He needed to draw the one nearest him closer. The fact that his eyes had adjusted to the dark mattered little. Everything was hulks and amorphous blobs, the night sky only slightly darker than his surroundings.

He could hear footsteps in the brush, legs sweeping past the calf-deep foliage covering the floor of the wooded area he was in. Monk felt about him and closed on a loose branch. It was a hefty piece of wood and he tried to snap it by leveraging it against the soft earth, bending it in his left hand. The bough wouldn't break. The footsteps were now moving away from him. He didn't want the men regrouping.

Hurriedly he put the gun under his chin, holding it there propped against his upper chest. He got in a position on one knee, making too much sound. He snapped the branch and squirmed away to his left, the opposite direction he guessed the man with the flashlight to be, A shotgun blast boomed, wide and way off target to where he'd been. He could hear some of the shot hit a tree.

Monk moaned loudly, cupping a hand to his mouth.

"I bagged that nigger," the shot-gunner declared proudly, clicking on the flashlight.

"Idiot," his friend warned.

Monk, both hands supporting his handgun shooting-range style, sent two toward the light, higher and to his right. The man would be holding the flashlight in his left, the gun in his right. The clip was now expended, and he didn't bother bringing the hammer down on an empty chamber. The light had fallen into the broad expanse of leaves and plants, its owner down.

He could hear the wounded man sucking in air. "Fuck, fuck," the man he'd shot gasped. "Help me, Grainey."

Grainey either wasn't that good a friend or that kind of fool. Monk took a chance and, crouching and scuttling, made for the point where the flashlight partially shone through the underbrush, the sounds of the fallen man coming from close to the beam.

Monk got there as the man, holding both hands over his stomach, suddenly focused on the figure before him.

"Nigger shit," he screamed. He made an attempt to reach for his shotgun, a Browning with walnut stock Monk could see in the cast-off light coming through the brush. The substantial weapon was lying across the man's lower legs, but when he removed one of his hands, viscous fluids seeped from around his fingers. He quickly put his hand back, doing his best to press his intestines, or what was left of them, back into place.

The man rocked back and forth and from side to side, wailing and writhing and cursing Black people, God for making Black people, and some woman named Linda who'd left him. Monk scooped up the Browning, and took shells for the weapon out of the man's Army jacket pocket. He tried to grab at Monk's arm, yelling for Grainey to come. Monk knocked the weakened hand away. The shotgun-wielder wouldn't last an hour like he was without medical attention. But an hour right now might as well be forever.

Monk had to push any empathy he might work up for his would-be executioner out of his mind. He could not afford to focus on anything but wanting to see his mother, and Jill and his sister and everybody else who meant anything to him again. Monk wanted desperately to be able to walk through the door of his donut shop and see Elrod's impassive face. And he wanted more than anything to be swamped by the aroma of fresh glazed donuts and brewing coffee. He had to survive.

Monk plowed deeper into the woods, tripping over some roots. The .45 went out of his grasp and landed somewhere among the thick leaves and vines. The shotgun was beneath his body, the barrel pressed under his chin. He was thankful its owner kept it in condition, since it hadn't gone off and blown his brains out through his ears.

He felt around for the pistol, hoping to latch onto its familiar casing with the gouge in the finish, a legacy of a deflected bullet his father, the sergeant, had earned in Korea. Of course, his dad's re-telling of how the nick happened took on different details each time. No time for reminiscing. Footfalls were getting close. One man, light on the tread and moving easily. He must know these woods. That was not good.

Without his automatic, and clutching the shotgun like it was a broom handle in his right hand, he scrambled forward, then zigzagged right, into another part of the forest. A gun-shot went off, but struck nothing near him. From the echo of the report, Monk guessed the gun was a large-caliber pistol, a .357 or maybe a 10-MM Desert Eagle, all the rage since their use in movies and TV as the latest weapon of choice. Monk slammed against a tree, momentarily stunning himself.

He steadied himself. Not too far away, he could hear water, a stream he reasoned. Beneath the sound of the running water, he couldn't discern a human one. His tracker must be an experienced game hunter. Or for all he knew, this might not be the first time he'd pursued a victim in these woods. Monk considered hunkering down and waiting, but he didn't think he'd catch this one off-guard like he had the first one. No, Grainey would be different, more calculating and more patient. And more careful after Monk had dropped his buddy.

But even he was not as patient as the one he thought was Kanner, who must be circling around. This one, and Monk assumed it was the martial artist from the river boat, would understand there was no rush. That there was very little chance Monk would reach any help before he got to him. He might even have a pair of see-in-the-dark binoculars or goggles to give him an added advantage as he stalked his prey, until the right moment to get his sights lined up on Monk's form in his night scope.

Monk moved off toward the creek. Branches and dead leaves crunched underneath his feet as he plodded toward the water. He heard brush give way as the second gunman came for him. He probably knew where this stream was in the map in his head. Monk trotted, holding the shotgun soldier-fashion, one hand around the stock and trigger guard, the other supporting it by the barrel grip. He fell again, over a tree trunk, and slid into a clump of leaves. Their dry odor filled his nostrils, and he fought the terror increasing his heart rate, knowing the gunner had heard him crash.

He got up groggily, and did his best to weave through a

stand of tall trees that he judged, from the amount of fallen leaves about, to be oaks or maples. Monk halted, kneeling down against a bulk he could feel was the log of a fallen tree. The stream was behind him. Something moved in the brush and the hot sweat on his face went cold. Reflexively, Monk flung himself forward but no shot rang out. The noise persisted and listening closer, he guessed it was a smaller form, a squirrel or possum. Hopefully.

DESPITE HIMSELF, Grainey smiled. Sure, he'd probably be sad later that Lester was lying back there dying, might even kick the bucket. But the goon was always so cocksure of himself—he always gotta be the man, the one to drink the most, the one to do the most shitkickin'—Grainey knew something like this was going to happen to him sooner or later.

Anyway, the motherfucker had been fucking Linda, filled her full of lies about him, and he'd been seeing her first. Lester always did think he was smarter than him, getting the swank jobs from the big boss and all, now who was top dog?

The Black boy was no knock-over. He was seasoned; Grainey could tell he'd been in tough spots before. He wasn't running around panicked-like, he was trying to move with purpose through these woods. But Grainey had grown up around here, still hunted venison and rabbit. They were on the outskirts of the St. Francis National Forest, and that city coon didn't know his right from his left out here. Grainey did.

He stopped and listened. He knew exactly where he was. There was the fallen log with the sunflowers growing out of its end just to his left. The stream was about three yards in front of that, and it flowed diagonally through several patches to the east where Grainey figured he'd catch up with his intended target. If he didn't get him before. Damned if he was going to let that weird bastard Kanner plug the jig. He really didn't Like Kanner.

Best to concentrate, Grainey admonished himself, cautiously prowling forward, his Desert Eagle at the ready. He wished he had his Winchester, but goddamn Lester had insisted he only take a pistol. Telling him why did he need his hunting rifle since Monk would drive up, they'd box him in, and that would be that. But the sumbitch proved to be wily, and now your smart ass is breathin' through your stomach, Lester. He knew Lester had figured Monk would run, and that Lester'd be the one to cut him in two with his Browning. The funny thing was, Monk now had the shotgun.

Yeah, he told himself, easing along, he'd better be wise. That dinge might not be familiar with these surroundings, but he was still armed. Grainey reached the section of the woods where the rise of Wacha Mountain caused the river to bend, and veered off to the southeast. Nothing. No sounds except the usual night noises. Where'd that porch monkey get to? He couldn't be moving that confidently in all these unfamiliar surroundings, especially at night. Shit.

And where in the fuck was that Chuck-Norris-wannabe Kanner? When the shootin' started, he just kinda disappeared. Making all mysterious with his kung fu bullshit. Shit. Now what should he do? Keep going. He knew Monk would follow the river, figuring it would take him to clearer ground, and it would. But as there were several tough spots along the way, like where the small mountain was, that would slow the darkie up. Had he gone on, thrashing through the forest, lucky not to bang into a tree or trip over some roots? Or had he not gone on at all?

All right, he should find Kanner. Fuck. It was his idea that they should take some cellulars with them, but no, Lester had nixed that, too. It was only because he'd suggested it that the small-minded asshole had said no. Grainey moved back the way he'd come, slow and steady, his ears pricked for anything out of the ordinary. At some point Kanner would find him, and together, they'd smoke the Black boy into the open.

He got back to the tree trunk and called out. "Kanner, it's me. I'm over by the log with the sunflowers." No answer. Slope-thinkin' motherfucker. "Come on, Kanner," he shouted, exasperated.

Something rustled and for that single moment he turned toward the area directly in front of him, straining to see Kanner's form. Almost as quickly it occurred to him the sound wasn't quite leaves crunching underfoot, but something else. He aimed the gun at the log and fired. At the same moment, hands clamped on his ankle and he was upended. "Kanner!" Grainey hollered. He was bringing the pistol up, firing as Monk's fist struck him in the windpipe.

MONK PRESSED his attack. He leaped and landed on the man named Grainey, who was trying to get to his feet. They became entangled, and Monk could feel the hot muzzle of the man's semi-auto press against his groin. He ducked, and in the same motion, shoved the heel of his hand against the bottom of the other man's chin. The gun fired.

Grainey let out air in a rush, the gun going momentarily slack in his right hand. Monk's shoulder blade burned where the second shot had clipped him, but he couldn't let up. He wasn't going to die.

"Kanner!" Grainey cried hoarsely, his windpipe severely damaged, slamming his knee into Monk's kidney.

His back up against it, Monk became more ferocious. He got on top of Grainey, their arms intertwined. Having no hands free, he used his head to try to butt the other man. But Grainey had anticipated such a move, and kept his own head moving.

Driven by the certainty Kanner would be arriving at any second, Monk notched up his attack. He let his grip go on Grainey's forearm, where his pistol resided at the end of it. As the pistol hand came up, Grainey twisted his body to get in position to blast Monk in the head. In a blink, Monk shifted, crabbing forward over the man, freeing his left arm. Monk hit him again, stunning the man, temporarily halting the ascent of the gun. Monk latched both his hands around the man's throat, squeezing with as much force as if he were molding clay.

The gun hand, and he could sense this more than see it against the darkness, was at an angle to their bodies. Monk let go of Grainey's throat with his right. He grabbed the gun hand and brought the piece down against the middle of the man's face as he tried to orient himself. Monk then boxed the man's head with his right in two rapid blows.

Grainey moaned and Monk lurched to his feet, wrenching the gun away from the man. Monk kicked him in the face with his heel, ceasing the moaning. He paused, bent over, hands on knees, taking in air rapidly, and looked around. The clearing and the buildings lay behind him. It made sense for him to try to reach their respective shelter. If Kanner was the third and last man, that would make him come to him. Even if he wasn't, it was the smartest thing to do, even though it meant crossing the clearing. His breathing somewhat regular, he retrieved the shotgun from where he'd placed it next to the log.

Monk had resigned himself to being cocooned in his

canopy of leaves and earth all night. The ground near the river was soft, the leaves over it had kept the moisture tamped down. Like a mole, he'd clawed his way beneath the leaves and dirt next to the fallen tree trunk as much as he could. He knew he was giving fate the finger, traipsing around in these woods with at least two men after him. And that inevitably, he'd be caught.

When he heard the footsteps return, he'd had no choice but to take a chance and spring himself on Grainey.

Moving back toward the buildings, he concluded that's where Kanner had been all the time. Lying in the cut, he could have had the two country boys do the dirty work. If they were successful, fine. He was the cool, level-headed administrator. If they failed he'd be Mr. Clean-Up.

Monk was returning to the buildings like a salmon swimming upstream. Reaching the area where the machines were, he hunkered down, the pain along his shoulder blade starting to effect his endurance. Cold made him shiver and he hoped he wasn't hyperventilating. The bullet seemed to be in muscle and not in the bone, so that was good. But it was in him nonetheless and you couldn't just jump around with a foreign object in you and not notice.

His jacket and shirt were wet from sweat, mud and blood. He had to keep going. If he slowed down too much, if he stopped to rest, he'd become too aware of the fatigue starting to corrode his energy. He reached a large machine, the harvester. Fantastically, Monk figured how long it might take him to get the thing going and drive to the buildings. He just as quickly dismissed the idea. Stuck in the cab, fumbling with the levers and buttons in the dark, was putting himself in too vulnerable a position.

Going around the machine, a bolt of pain lanced his side. He sagged against the harvester, pinwheel bursts going off behind his eyes. Come on, Monk, don't let yourself down now. Come on, breath in, breath out, legs up then down. He got up, the butt of the Desert Eagle pistol digging into his back where he'd tucked it snug in the waistband of his ruined Dockers. He listened and of course there was no sound of another human. No creak of feet on leaves or the click of a gun's hammer.

Monk was now feeling along the harvester. In front of that was the low-slung rectangular hulk of the main building not more than twenty-five yards away. Its door was probably locked, but that wasn't a problem with a shotgun.

Then again, maybe he wouldn't go there. Didn't it seem the most obvious way to go—for the main building? Why not try one of the ones he'd noticed set at angles to this central one? Whatever he chose, he was going to expose himself. He didn't think Kanner had a high-powered rifle with a night scope. At least, to keep himself from freezing up with self-doubt, he had to believe he didn't; Kanner would have used it by this time. Kanner had to believe he was as alone as Monk was. But Monk had to believe he had more to live for.

Whatever prankish supernatural being rolled the dice to decide his personal destiny, he just had to believe he had one more throw of good luck left. He didn't run straight toward the main building, but toward the one tucked behind a stand of several tractors. A couple of the machines had loaders attached. Several shots cut the dirt to his right ahead of him. Kanner was in the main building, having guessed that would be where Monk would head. Monk dove beside one of the loaders. Kanner didn't waste a shot.

Luckily too, Kanner only had a pistol, judging from the weapon's report. Which meant he'd have to get close to get the job done. Good enough. Monk felt around and undid the wheel locks of the loader. Pressing his shoulder against it, the throbbing steady, he pushed the thing. Designed to be mobile enough to hook and unhook from a tractor, the loader with its slanting elevator leading up to its discharge spout creaked along. Monk had placed the shotgun on a horizontal area of the machine. Having gone several feet with the loader for cover, he was now breathing hard and sweating like a stuck pig, as his dad used to say.

The gun clattered and got caught in something at the loader's base. The wheels stopped turning, and Monk concentrated on remaining calm. In the murk, he felt about and latched onto the Browning, partially jammed against the tilling shaft. He yanked on it, his shoulder blade warm with his blood. Was that footsteps? Come on, please, he pleaded with himself, trying to wrench the shotgun free.

Abruptly it loosened, and Monk staggered backward, bumping into something smooth and cold. It was another piece of farm machinery, the purpose of which escaped him at the moment. He was near his destination and took several moments to get some strength back up.

"Monk," came a quiet voice over the stillness.

Monk cradled the shotgun.

"There's money in this for you, Monk. Two hundred, hell, three hundred thousand for you to make it go away."

"Aw, why didn't you say so before, buddy?" He started moving the loader again toward the smallish bulk of the building. "Those guns going off at me were just to get my attention, huh?" His shirt underneath his mud-caked jacket was clammy and clung like Spandex to his skin. The building was less than forty feet from him.

"Two bodies in the woods, even in Mississippi, are going to take some explaining," Kanner went on. "You've proved yourself a difficult man, Monk. We want to keep things efficient. Money is a great way to achieve understanding."

Monk assumed he wanted to keep him talking as he snuck out of the main building and crept toward where he could hear the loader being moved, the sounds masking Kanner's movements. Monk stopped moving the loader. He was tired and he was getting fuzzy in the head again. He plucked the shotgun off the machine, and sat in the dirt next to the wheels.

"I suppose I'm to wait here while you go fetch the dough." And more gun hands.

Kanner laughed easily. Monk could tell he wasn't calling to him from the building. "I know you're no fool, Monk. I drive off, you drive off. The money gets wired to you where you say."

"You got Tigbee's say-so to approve this?" He got up on one knee, listening for the footsteps beneath the voice.

"You know I do," the other man said with confidence.

Monk positioned himself so the barrel of his Browning was pointing toward the main building. He adjusted, swinging the shotgun left, guessing, if he were Kanner, what path he'd take toward him. Certainly not a straight line from the structure. "Let's say four hundred grand. That way I got enough to set aside, and your boss has made a substantial payment knowing I won't be showing up for another bite."

"Fine," Kanner said casually. "I'm sure you're a man of your word."

Monk let off two blasts, one beside the other to hopefully give the other man pause. He darted for the small building and sank beside a corner and some overgrown grass just as a shotgun blast tore into the air. Kanner had been holding back. Monk crawled on his hands and knees to the rear of the building. He got up and felt along the wall until he clasped a metal knob. The door was locked, but one blast took care of that. Monk plunged inside, closing the metal door behind him.

The Browning was empty but he still had the five shells he'd gotten off Grainey. The room he was in had several low tables at right angles to each other. He felt around and determined the room was for repair and general maintenance. Various parts lay about the tables, and numerous tools were pegged on the walls and encased in their rollaway tool boxes. Monk went to the front door.

The area around his shoulder blade had settled down again to a dull numbness, and the blood seemed to have begun clotting.

There were safety-glass windows on either side of the front door. Crouching down, Monk looked out as he reloaded the shotgun by feel. Gasping, he put one of the rollaway tool boxes, itself about four feet high, against the door. If Kanner blew off the lock, the rollaway would slow him up a few steps.

There was a phone with several lines available on an industrial-type office desk. Picking up the handset, Monk couldn't get a dial tone no matter what line he punched. He didn't expect to, but he had to try. He reviewed the possibilities.

Kanner might have called for backup already, but Monk doubted it. Surely Tigbee had learned from experience that the more people he called in on this, the more chance there'd be a leak about the killing later. Conversely, waiting here until the sun came up didn't necessarily improve his odds. This must be a company Tigbee owned. No doubt he could shut it down for a day or two for some reason or another, and wait Monk out.

No, he had to do something of a more aggressive nature, because Kanner would also be upping the stakes. He would have to show Tigbee, now, after Monk had bested the first two, that he was the man. That he could get the job done.

An engine revved. It must be the LTD since the Taurus wasn't driveable. With icy certainty, Monk leaped ahead in his reckoning as the lights snapped on from the vehicle. The car's lights swung toward the building, then veered off. Monk unlocked the front door and cracked it open a millimeter. He could hear the car circling, the lights off now.

Kanner plowed the station wagon through the rear of the repair building. Parts and tools sailed everywhere as several worktables got shoved toward the front. Monk tumbled out the front door, seconds ahead of getting trapped against the wall. As quickly as he could, he ran around the building. Kanner would think he'd dash away—he was going to catch him as he came around the corner.

The Browning was up and aimed and suddenly Monk was staring at a heavily breathing form also holding a shotgun up and ready. So much for his plan.

"My, my," Kanner proclaimed. The barrel of his shotgun twitched.

"Isn't it," Monk responded, his finger tightening on the trigger. Oddly, he could hear frogs splashing into the stream but not his own heartbeat. The world was Kanner and his shotgun, Time crawled. Sweat clouded his right eye, blurring his sight. The wagon's engine was still running. His finger shook. Monk blinked rapidly, trying desperately to clear his eye. The shotgun felt so heavy.

Both guns went off almost in the same instant.

# CHAPTER 24

Sheriff Brian Lauter of Tunica County scratched at the back of his ear with the blunt end of a pen for the umpteenth time. He and two of his deputies regarded Monk. The three men and the doctor were white. The PI was stretched out on the table, like an exhibit they'd read about, but weren't sure what to make of once the thing had arrived in town.

The doctor finished and stepped back, examining his handiwork. "Not bad, not too bad." He lit up a filtered Marlboro.

"This is nasty," Lauter said, again, not for the first time.

Monk sat up, the cuff around his wrist pulling on the other end that clinked around the railing. "You call my lawyer?" The gauze and tape on his back and the top of his shoulder chafed. He was woozy from the local anesthesia, and he was freezing. He flexed the stiffening muscles in the shoulder and chest the doctor had plucked buckshot out of for the last two hours. He was lucky it was mostly a miss, the bulk of the pellets having gone past him as he'd ducked and dove aside. Had the blast been full-on, they'd be calling him Lefty.

"This office ain't your legal service department," one of

the deputies growled. "Maybe y'all get that kinda treatment
back home, but not down here."

Monk grinned listlessly. "Nice to know law enforcement
is consistent no matter where I go."

"What's that supposed to mean?" The belligerent deputy
took two steps forward.

Lauter tipped his hat up and zeroed the deputy before
turning his glare back at his prisoner. "Maybe you don't
realize what kinda predicament y'all are in, Monk, but lookie
here: You done bored out Lester's guts with your non-
registered weapon. Interestingly, he survived despite the mud
and filth he was wallowing in. Of course, a colostomy bag is
gonna seem like a luxury to him from now 'til whenever.
Then there's Grainey, whose nose and jaw you done broke
and fractured. Now he's probably gonna sue you for all you're
worth."

"That can't be much," the other deputy, a tall balding man,
snickered, his thumbs hooked in his gun belt.

Lauter continued with his summary. "And Kanner was a
licensed private investigator in four states—well, three, you
don't need a license in Denver where he kept a desk and a
phone in the upstairs of a peek-a-boo joint." Lauter got
miffed at allowing himself to digress. "What I'm getting at,
he counted judges and members of the Mississippi State
legislature as his clients and friends."

"And I imagine his wife is going to be real displeased with
the knowledge of you blowing her husband away," the first
deputy prophesied. "He's got more than one friend gonna
cause you to tip-toe around . . . brother."

Monk shivered in the cold room they'd wheeled him into
off the main wing of the emergency ward. His shirt had been
ripped away and his drenched torso and mud-soaked pants
were clammy against his legs. Nobody offered a blanket, and

he wasn't going to give the law the satisfaction of asking for one now.

"Did you call Manse Tigbee yet, Sheriff?"

That surprised Lauter. "Of course, Mr. Kanner had been in his employ for some time."

"Then you should know two lawyers in Los Angeles, a judge, a cop, and a private investigator—who's an ex-cop—know all about the information which made Tigbee send Kanner and those other two after me. Information Tigbee doesn't want known, but it's too late. Even if his hired motherlovers had succeeded in icing me, it was already too late."

"What you getting at, Monk?" the hard-nosed deputy asked. There was the hint of worry behind his tough talk.

"What I just said."

The three law enforcement men stared at Monk. The doctor busied himself lighting another cigarette, a thoughtful frown on his face.

Monk laid back, tired like an old dog.

TWO DAYS later, while Monk remained in jail, domestic and international media camped out near Manse Tigbee's mansion in Oxford and his various businesses in the Delta, in Biloxi, and his other mansion in Plaquemine, Louisiana. More reporters and stringers were checking out the various companies he owned, or had money in other nearby states, including the BMW plant he'd complained to Monk about.

Protected by a barrier of lawyers and spinmeisters, Tigbee did damage control worthy of Bill Clinton. On the fourth day, Tigbee released a half-hour slickly produced video where he explained matters from the comfort of an undisclosed location. There he sat in a modest leather chair, a living room setting behind him, the prop windows letting in carefully modulated stage lighting. His face had a composed, pained look to it. He presented the image that he was stoically bearing the weight of the Jacobeans arrayed against him.

Monk, finally released on bail the previous day—his lawyer Parren Teague in Los Angeles had secured an attorney over in Mound Bayou—watched the taped message first on CNN and then when it aired again on C-SPAN 2 at his hotel room in Memphis. A reporter from the *New York Times* interviewed him over the phone, but several other outlets would have to wait until he got back home.

"It is the doing of irresponsible elements, working in concert with certain forces operating out of Iraq and Libya, that have weaved this vicious, tenacious lie, my friends. Their chief agent is a man who now goes by the ludicrous name of Ivan Monk. He, in turn, has paid off known drug abusers and extramarital fornicators to do his bidding." Tigbee paused in that part of the tape and drank from a glass of water. Then he proceeded to vilify members of the Tunica Sheriffs Department for letting said dangerous agent go.

Tigbee tried to control the fallout, and he certainly had holdings in various media conglomerates to work his will. But the competition for ratings and ad revenues among those conglomerates dictated that at least one of them would pursue the story.

Monk's .45 had been recovered and the Tunica County DA made a lot of noise about prosecuting him for the inter-state transportation of a weapon for the purposes of committing a crime. That was after neither the man with no stomach, nor the one whose nose he broke, would answer the prosecutor's questions, and Kanner's wife and two children had abruptly, and unannounced, left Jackson for parts unknown.

The Tunica County DA impounded the .45 pending a

close of the investigation. Monk's local lawyer obtained bail and permission from the judge for him to travel back to L.A.—since it had a bearing on the charges brought against him. Monk had to surrender his passport. By the end of the week, it became obvious the most Monk would be charged with would be possession of an unregistered weapon in Mississippi. And given all the public attention, he'd be fined and given probation just like any good ol' boy.

Kodama and Teague had set up Monk with several media operations to provide him avenues to put forward his version of events, and to put the spotlight on the law in the Magnolia State. It also didn't hurt that cutting-edge sociologist and writer of the hip Robin D. G. Kelley was doing a major piece about Tigbee and the Creel case for *Vanity Fair*. The magazine put up the money for Monk's bond. He promised to provide Kelley with exclusive information, whatever the hell that would be.

"SO AVA Green was Manse Tigbee's granddaughter?" Geraldo Rivera asked Sheriff Lauter on a remote broadcast of his cable show from Tunica, a shocked look on his bespectacled face.

Lauter tipped his hat way up on his forehead. "Yes, sir, it appears that Mr. Tigbee's first wife Dolly Lee had remarried up there in Akron. Merrill, their daughter, who, mind you, was already a young teenager when the wife took her away, and also went by her middle name of Sarah, had taken the stepfather's name of Green." Lauter chewed his bottom lip in disapproval. "He was a history professor from that college in Yellow Springs."

"She went from being married to a buttoned-down racist to marrying a Jew," Geraldo observed for his TV audience.

Having been coached that something like this might be

said, Lauter wisely said nothing, only stared ahead with a steely look of ruggedness.

Geraldo said, "And Dolly's daughter, Merrill, herself a teenager, gave birth, out of wedlock, to Ava, in 1954. Merrill simply used Green as Ava's last name."

That said something about living up north, but Lauter bit his tongue on providing the obvious.

"Ava," Geraldo said, "it seems, had been raised with a lie, too: She was told her mother's father had died, and of course never been told his last name was Tigbee. Tigbee apparently tried to contact Dolly Lee unsuccessfully several times over the years, so he might not even have known about Ava's birth."

Camera one dollied in on Geraldo. "Not only did Ava's fate return her to her ancestral home to fight injustice, there are those—including the Los Angeles-based private investigator who declined to be on our show—who allege Ava Green's grandfather, Manse Tigbee, may be the man who caused her brutal murder decades ago. And I have it on good authority that this PI was lured by a staged photo to one of Tigbee's businesses in an effort to kill Monk, who had found out the truth." Geraldo adjusted his glasses, "Tragic, tragic. More after this," he said, looking properly forlorn into the camera. The program went to commercial.

# CHAPTER 25

"You killed my cousin Kennesaw because you believed the myth about Charlie Patton's 'Killin' Blues'. Maybe he believed it, too."

"Them peckerwoods did that, honey. That's why Uncle Marshall had all that information about the Creel trial."

"I'm not sure why Spears was gathering the news articles, but they definitely start at the time of Senator Bodar's supposed accident. Kennesaw might have figured if the senator was stirring up the hornets, then some of them might sting him. Could be ol' cuz wanted to be informed and on his guard." Monk felt the setting sun on his wounded shoulder and the warmth was good. "Who knows, Spears might have even convinced himself he could get me to find Patton's album and use the money to re-open the case."

Cheryl Murray, who called herself Sikkuh, allowed the untied robe she was wearing to flutter open. She had on a pair of shiny bikini pants and nothing else. She played with a nipple as the two of them stood between the dressing trailers as the sun set over Zuma Beach. "Is that right, Ivan." She brought a leg up and rubbed it against his thigh.

He grabbed her firmly by the upper arms, holding her back from him. Sharp pain knotted his sore shoulder and lanced down his back, but he willed himself not to show it. One more bullet wound and this business of getting shot was going to get serious.

"Here it is, Cheryl: The sheriff down there may be slow in getting going, but once he's got a direction, damned if he isn't on it like yellow on teeth. He's been sweatin' the two still around after our little party in the woods. Both of them have alibis at the time of Kennesaw's death. One was banging a cosmetologist over in Bovina, and the other knocking over a quickie mart along the road to De Witt. Neither one knew Kennesaw's name."

"They could be lying." Sikkuh put out her bottom lip, letting a slight smile form.

"No, that won't wash." He let go of her arms. "So who could have a motive in poisoning him?"

The bottom lip stopped being inviting and got a tremble in it. "You've been checking on me?"

"Your iron-butt buddy Indigo has worked as a male nurse in several rest homes." Monk didn't go on, not bothering to explain that Indigo—Fred Landy—would be familiar with medication like Digoxin since it was a commonplace drug with the elderly.

He did add, though, "A big LAPD detective named Roberts is going to make inquiries with the production company you said you went out of town with to shoot that bit part. What do you want to bet he finds out you came back earlier than you told me?" Roberts didn't know about her being out of town, yet.

"He did it." She gave up Indigo without hesitation. "It was his goddamn plan." The robe was pulled decisively shut.

"What'd you tell Kennesaw?" he asked. "'Course he had a taste for the ladies, so any thin story you gave him I imagine he'd go for. But he'd seen you at the wake, and he knew you were Spears's grand-niece."

"I told him how exciting it would be if we could find the album. I had him going that a record magazine would pay good money just for an article about our search that I would write. I think he saw it as a way to tell his side of why he sold out Creel." A demure look settled on her face. "Anyway, no matter what their age, men don't mind a good-looking woman paying them some attention."

"A fine woman and the blues myth, unbeatable," Monk said with mock admiration. "So what was it, Cheryl? The death of your great-uncle was definitely on Kennesaw's mind. His own time was dancing before him. But what in hell made you really think the 'Killin' Blues' album existed?"

The model who called herself Sikkuh put the edge of her hand to her brow. She squinted into the sun. The robe parted and she knew Monk was looking. She took her time responding. "Death can give you a funny perspective on life," she began. "I loved Uncle Marshall, I really did, Ivan. After, when I was going through his stuff, I saw those pictures of him and your cousin and remembered him laughing about Kennesaw being like Kirk Douglas and his Golden Fleece."

Monk's questioning look prompted her to elaborate.

"You know, that movie where he plays Jason, and he has his Argonauts. The fighting skeletons, Neptune rising from the ocean. That was one of his favorite movies."

"So you get to thinking about Patton's maybe record. Your great-uncle was dead, and here finally was Kennesaw. With Spears gone I guess you rationalized you had no moral obligation anymore."

She put on the full court press. She got closer, grabbing at his loose shirt, making sure her nails dug into his sides. "This was all Indigo's doing, Ivan. He kept pestering me that if we found the record we'd be set. That what with licensing fees and the multi-platforming that kind of find would be worth, it would generate millions of dollars." She let the rest go unsaid, let it build in his mind like she hoped it would.

"You know your pretty boyfriend Indigo don't want no part of prison." Monk felt a tight pull on his lower face and he didn't know if it was a grin or a scowl. "Roberts is talking to him now."

She fell back against the side of the trailer, tucking her shoulders in as if she were readying for a left hook. With her head down, she looked up at him as if waiting for her opening to get her counter-punches in. She did. "Indigo, that is Fred, was the one who told me to look in your cousin's medicine cabinet on my second visit, and what kind of pills I should look for."

Goes to means and motive, but Monk remained mute and simply nodded his head. "Uh-huh."

"I didn't know what he was going to do, Ivan."

"So you're saying he mixed the lethal dose."

"God, you know I couldn't do that." The robe was held fast to better coincide with her chaste demeanor.

"Here's what I think: You two figured the best way to take care of Kennesaw was to make it look like a heart attack. Take the fire box below his bed, where you must have figured were clues to the record's secret location. You assumed no one knew about the box. Only, Mr. Dellums had seen it that first night he was over there and remembered. You two got even cuter and broke into Mr. Spears's place, even though you have a key. That way, it would look like some outsider was rounding up any information that might lead them to the 'Killin' Blues'." He took a breath. "Including attacking my mother and staging the break-in of your place."

"I told him not to touch your mother, I swear." She didn't overdo it, she didn't get closer this time.

"You sent him after my mother just like you engineered Kennesaw's death."

"How—" she stammered, seemingly hurt.

"I'd asked you about the 'Killin' Blues' at the coffeehouse, and you said you didn't know anything about them. The next day when we were leaving the bank, you were laughing and mentioned Patton. I figured maybe you were just playing the percentages, keeping any knowledge you had of the 'Killin' Blues' to yourself in case the album turned up. But since the men who chased me in the woods couldn't have done the deed to Kennesaw, I quite logically looked closer to home for the answer.

"And I sure didn't see Indigo as the brains of this outfit, Sikkuh. When you got nothing from the fire box, nothing from any of your great-uncle's effects, and the attack on my mother went bust, there was always me. You'd get me to feel sorry for you, mad about getting back at whoever assaulted my mother, and send me off to do your looking for you. You knew Indigo would stumble around like a big clown, and probably not scare up anything of value."

Barely audible, she said, "I don't know how you can say such vicious things about me. You must have a heart of stone."

"But" Monk added, "Kennesaw wasn't so much wrapped up in finding Charlie Patton's album. Or maybe he was, but I heard him that Sunday when he was tight. He'd mixed the legend of the album together with the myth about Malachi and that was shaken up with his own gnawing guilt over selling out. You put more booze in him, and with him smelling you around him he was libel to spin any goddamn tale you wanted to hear. Maybe greed makes you hard of hearing."

She started to respond but Monk cut her off. "I'll go inside with you so you can change and then give you a ride to your lawyer's office."

Venomously she said, "What makes you think I'm going to go anywhere with you?"

"Do I stutter? Roberts is sweatin' Indigo right now. And if you get funny, I'll hook you in the jaw and say you tried to knee me in the balls."

She evaluated what he'd said and the fight left her. "It wasn't my idea to kill your cousin."

"Don't want to peak too soon, Sikkuh. You might want to save some of your act for the jury."

"You're wrong about me, Ivan. All wrong."

"It wouldn't be the first time."

Somebody called, "Three minutes," but they were already moving toward her trailer.

# CHAPTER 26

She pulled the strands across the table top and got on her hands and knees. She giggled as she crawled toward the space between Frank Harris's spread legs. Clad in heels and a G-string, she went underneath the table. Reaching the other side, Odessa Monk got on one knee and bit teasingly into Frank Harris's left thigh.

"Harder," he requested.

She complied like she was eating a raw piece of steak. She laughed and made growling noises, and left teeth marks in his smooth muscle. With her free hand she pulled on his stiffening shaft. She then parted the strands and tied the ends around each thigh. Odessa Monk stood behind him. In the position he was now, Harris, nude, was bent over the table, his arms flat on its surface and tied together at the wrists. The strands then continued to the table's edge, where she'd brought them underneath and tied the straps securely and tight, around his legs.

"Is that okay?" she asked him, running her hand between his legs and up the crack. She let her index finger probe in there.

"That's great, baby." He squirmed against his bonds, the purple vinyl straps pulling taut. Odessa Monk briefly wondered how she might tell her brother that Harris had only bruised her that time her son had seen the mark during one of their cherished S&M sessions. And it had been her fault as she'd been excited and demanded him to hit her harder with a padded paddle as he worked a silver vibrator with a mushroom head in her. She blushed, imagining the uncomprehending look on her dear sweet brother's face.

She bent gently, whipped her man with the cat-o'-nine-tails and kissed and licked his back. Odessa Monk, public high school teacher, nearly naked and slick with sweat, dug her nails into his love handles as he squealed with pleasure.

# CHAPTER 27

Monk and Kodama left the Shur-Cho Korean Bar-B-Que restaurant on the corner of Catalina and Eighth Street full and sleepy. They walked toward Vermont Avenue.

Thinking about how much she'd just eaten, Monk asked, "You're not eating for two, are you?"

"Not yet, smart ass. And if you keep it up, I never will, if you know what I mean."

They took in the sights along busy Vermont. Friday night and the thoroughfare was hopping with a combination of Hangul pouring from karaoke bars, vendors selling ears of corn and *pupusas*, and *norteña* beats pulsing from passing cars. There were also some elderly whites straggling into an event at the Gothic-styled First Unitarian Church on Eighth Street.

Monk tightened his arm around his old lady's waist. "Aw, baby," he jived.

The couple kissed and continued toward where Monk had parked his car east of the Unitarian Church.

"You hear that?" he murmured to the woman he loved.

"What?" she nuzzled his neck.

"From"—Monk stopped, pointing at two apartment buildings sandwiched together in the dense area—"there," he said, pointing at the buildings. "You hear it now?"

"An old blues recording it sounds like."

"That's Charlie Patton's voice." A cold jolt tweaked his cortex. "And it's not a song I recognize, and I've played them all several times in the last couple of weeks."

"No," Kodama disagreed.

"Yes," he insisted, moving across the sidewalk toward one of the buildings. A stout woman with a laundry basket on her head was going through the building's security entrance and Monk, Kodama coming up behind him, put his hand on the edge of the door.

"*Con permiso,*" he said.

"*Gracias,*" the woman said, smiling at the two. She went in and Monk, motioning for Kodama, followed.

The apartment was an older building, originally constructed sometime in the '30s. There was an open courtyard that contained an egg-shaped patch of dirt where only a few undernourished rubber plants remained.

"Listen." He drew Kodama close to him. There was no mistaking Patton's panther voice as he whacked the pine of his guitar.

*I got the ticket from my darlin' gal—she done sent the letter across the nation—gonna ride the train 'til it makes the Clarksdale station—gonna ride that rail even though they's after me—even though them killin' blues is after me.*

"Through there," Kodama pointed toward an open archway containing stone steps leading up. The couple ascended and found themselves in an enclosed hallway. Two uncovered bulbs, one at either end, dispersed their diminutive light in the space. They went down the hall.

*Drop down to the bottom—drop down and see ol' Satan—he got my soul in a jar—say I got to pay my dues—say I got them killin' blues.*

The voice on the scratchy recording yelped and hollered

and then the music faded. Monk paused at a door of peeling ochre paint. The number on it was an upside down seven, loose on its nail.

"Can I help you?" a Latina with curlers in her hair asked, sticking her head out a door near the stairs. "You two looking to rent?" Down at her side Monk could see the glint of the pistol she held.

"Is this one occupied?" He poked a thumb at number Seven.

The woman looked back at Kodama and made the decision the two were either too old or dressed well enough not to "be up to foolishness" as Monk's mother would have said. "Hold on," she said, easing her door shut to a crack. Momentarily she stepped out into the hall, sans the firearm. She marched over to the door where Kodama now stood next to Monk.

Examining the duo she asked querulously, "You two aren't going to run some kind of business out of here, are you? I've already gotten hassled by Building and Safety about that."

"No," Kodama answered.

The woman did a thing with her head and eyebrows and unlocked the door. She flicked on the light, revealing an empty apartment. No furniture, but there was a green shag rug in need of immediate replacement on the floor. Covering the windows were clean, light-blue sheets. Monk stepped inside.

"Who used to live here?"

The manager also stepped inside. "Old man, Black man, I think." She addressed their quizzical looks. "It was hard to tell. He certainly wasn't as dark as you"—she indicated Monk—"he was colored like gold, you know? And his hair was straight, but you know, curly on the ends. The way he talked, he sounded Black." She worked her head up and down. "I guess he must have been Black."

"He have a name?" Kodama asked while Monk prowled around the empty rooms.

"His name was," she searched her memory, "Dockery. Yeah, I called him Mr. Dockery."

"For Dockery Farms," Kodama whispered.

Monk was back in the front room. "When did you last see him?"

The manager scratched at her chin. "It's been some time now." She looked around. "Funny, too, I haven't been able to rent this apartment since."

Monk wanted to wait around for who knew how long, but Kodama made him leave. Back out on Eighth Street, Monk and Kodama sleepwalked to the Ford. Neither one said anything as he drove them home.

Continue reading for a preview of the first
Harry Ingram Mystery

# ONE-SHOT HARRY

## CHAPTER ONE

"Fifteen." Josh Nakano placed his domino tile on the
table with the others.

The raspy voice of comedian Redd Foxx, known for his
blue material, issued from an LP spinning on the record
player. "Yes, ladies and gentlemen, here we are again for the
great racing of the T-bone stakes." An audience tittered in
the background of the live recording. The album was titled
*The New Race Track*.

"Don't stop writing yet, scorekeeper." Peter "Strummer"
Edwards smiled, slapping down a tile. "Ten." He was a tall,
dark-skinned man with large hands, several of his knuckles
misshaped like a seasoned boxer's.

James "Shoals" Pettigrew marked the points on a lined
yellow notepad, then put down his own domino. The hardware store owner didn't score.

Using one hand, Harry Ingram picked up his facedown
tiles, turning them toward his face, studying them. Between
two fingers of his other hand, a cheap cigar smoldered.

"If you blink three times, they still ain't gonna change," Pettigrew joked.

"Got it, Captain Hook." Ingram put down his choice, hoping this time to block Nakano from scoring again.

"Thanks for nothing," Nakano said, playing after Ingram. He was a medium-built man with thick black hair going gray at the sides. He wore glasses and a colorful Hawaiian shirt over casual slacks. He favored loud sport shirts when not relegated to suit and tie, as befitted a funeral director.

"Always at your service, good sir."

When the LP ended, Ingram got up from the card table and went over to his record player, which was set below several built-in bookshelves. Among the books on the shelves were two police scanners and an AM/FM transistor radio. Ingram put the record back in its sleeve, the photographic image on the front a smiling young woman in modified jockey gear straddling a hobby horse.

"Put on the radio, would you, Harry?" Edwards said, yawning and stretching. "Can't have Redd making me too excited before I go to bed alone."

Pettigrew wiggled his fingers. "Alone, you say?"

Everyone chuckled.

Ingram slotted the Foxx album alphabetically among other comedic, jazz and blues albums he kept in wooden produce crates stacked in a corner. He turned the radio on, adjusting the antenna and turning the dial to bring the station in clearer.

". . . and the hunt goes on for the bank robber dubbed the Morning Bandit. But now, my dear listeners," the DJ continued, "we here at KGFJ urge all right-thinking Angelenos to come out and hear what Martin Luther King has to say when he arrives in town less than three weeks from today. As many of us know, his message isn't just for the

South, but for what goes on here in the supposedly enlightened north."

"You covered the reverend when he was in town before, didn't you?" Nakano said to Ingram as he sat down again. King had last been in Los Angeles two years earlier to speak at the Sports Arena. The facility had been filled to capacity with thousands standing outside to hear him over the loudspeakers.

"Yeah, I've got a request in through the *Sentinel* to take shots when he speaks this time too. But they'd already got this reporter assigned who takes his own pics." Ingram made part of his living as a photographer for the Black press.

"What about the march later this year?" Edwards said. In the 1950s he'd been the one to look after the interests of gangster Jack Dragna on the Black side of Los Angeles. These days he had his own interests to see to—some aboveboard and others he didn't file taxes about.

"You going?" Ingram asked.

"Thinking about it." Edwards looked up from his dominoes at the other three staring at him. "What? All sorts of people are going, including Moses." He meant Charlton Heston, who was heading the Hollywood contingent to the March on Washington taking place in August.

"You know this is the second time this has been tried," Nakano said.

"Huh?" Edwards lit a cigarette and opened another can of Hamm's he'd retrieved from Ingram's refrigerator.

"A. Philip Randolph threatened a march back in the forties unless Roosevelt desegregated the armed forces and paid the same wages to Blacks working in the war industries. FDR didn't desegregate but did sign a bill about the fair pay. And Randolph called off the march, though some say he was bluffing all along."

"King ain't bluffing," Pettigrew said.

"Damn, how come you always know more about negro history than me, Josh?" Edwards said.

"Maybe he's just a better soul brother than you," Ingram laughed.

"That's probably true." Edwards had more of his beer.

Nakano said, "The Japanese American Citizens League is sending a contingent. A cousin of mine is going to be in it."

"You thinking about going?" Ingram asked him.

"Yep. For sure I'll be at the rally in town." Nakano looked up from his dominoes, a wry smile lighting his face. "Equal rights is equal rights, isn't it?"

"Across the board," Pettigrew said.

The friends played until a few minutes past ten in the evening. After they left, Ingram folded up the card table they'd been playing on, put the dominoes back in their box and cleaned up in the kitchen where they'd made sandwiches. There was a door separating the kitchen from a compact back porch area. In there was a utility sink for use with a rubboard to wash clothes. Ingram had turned this area into a darkroom with lengths of clothesline strung up to hang drying prints. Back in his apartment's living room, he considered putting on one of the scanners but decided to pour himself something stiffer than beer and sit in his easy chair. The window overlooking the street below was cracked open and the sounds of a quieting city drifted in as he sat and drank. The radio was still on, but he'd turned the volume down.

Ingram had taken one of his file folders from a rack of several and had it open on his lap, looking through his photos. He frowned as if this were the first time he was seeing his work from a critical standpoint. There was all manner of mayhem represented in the black-and-whites, from a man laid out on the sidewalk in a nice suit, two-tone shoes and a knife sticking out of his head to a woman in a beret, hands manacled behind her back as a cop led her away. There was a bloody hatchet in another cop's hand and a bloodstain on the lower part of her skirt.

"No wonder *Look* won't hire me," he muttered, enjoying more bourbon. He closed the file and put it aside. As he began to doze off, Ingram resolved to take more happy pictures, like people picnicking in the park and kids laughing as they flew kites.

At some point he woke up and KGFJ, an around-the-clock station, was playing classical music. He got up and went to bed to the strains of Debussy's *Three Nocturnes*.

In the morning after a sound sleep and a trip to the john, Ingram put on his threadbare cotton bathrobe over his boxers and athletic tee. He turned on one of his scanners.

"...suspect, male, white American, twenties, reddish-blond hair heading north on Bronson from Venice on foot..."

With that as his background accompaniment, Ingram fixed a breakfast that included sausage links from the neighborhood grocery store downstairs, Whitehead's Market. Afterward, taking his second cup of coffee into the bathroom, he showered and shaved. The scanner was still going. Monday morning crime, at least in terms of the Black east side, was limited to a purse snatching and a parked vehicle clipped in a hit-and-run. This wasn't unusual. Ingram knew colored fellas were often jacked up by the cops on Saturday night and were awaiting a hearing or still arranging bail at the start of the new week.

Things would be jumping by nine tonight, he reflected as he got his equipment together, including his Speed Graphic camera. There were two nicks from bullets grooved in its casing and Ingram rubbed one of them for luck, as he always

did. He'd brought the camera home from the war. Fleeting
was the notion of photographing normal people doing normal things. Where was the kick in that? Melancholy
moments like the one he'd had last night he invariably
washed away with booze.

Tweed sport coat on and no tie, slipping a couple of his
cigars into an inner pocket, he quit his apartment, going out
the rear door through his darkroom and down the creaking
wooden stairs. Behind the building his car was parked in one
of the few designated spaces. There was another man downstairs in a plaid shirt-jacket and casual slacks.

"What's happening, Arthur?" Ingram clapped the other
man on the shoulder as Arthur unlocked the back door to
Whitehead's. Ingram's building was made of brick and wood
trim, constructed in the late 1920s. The corner grocery store
commanded most of the space on the ground floor. To the
south of that was the front entrance into the apartments,
stairs leading up to the second and third floors occupied by
tenants.

"Same old sixes and sevens, Harry."

Arthur Yarbrough got the door open but did not turn on
the lights to cut the gloom. He was a light-skinned Black
man about Ingram's height, a little over six feet, though not
as solidly built. There was a zigzag of scarred skin along one
side of his face that gave him an intriguing as opposed to
disfigured appearance. He wore heavy framed sunglasses and
the stylish cane Ingram had bought him some years ago
leaned near the door.

The store had originally belonged to a Caucasian family
named Whitehead. When it changed hands to Black own-
ership, the name was kept, one, because people were familiar
with it in the neighborhood, and two, it was an in-joke.

"Need me for anything?"

"I got it covered, man."

"Yeah, you do."

Yarbrough had been blinded in the Korean War when on patrol he'd stepped on a land mine. It would be another hour or so until one of his sighted employees came to work. In the time between, he'd have gone through the store arranging the items on the shelves, swept the aisles and so forth. There was a blueprint of the store's layout imprinted in his head, Ingram liked to imagine.

Ingram left Yarbrough and unlocked the trunk of his several-years-old Plymouth Belvedere. In here was his traveling photo development setup. When he had to make a deadline and didn't have time to return home to use his darkroom, he developed his pictures in his trunk. He checked to make sure he had enough of the requisite chemicals and that they were secure in their containers.

Trunk closed, he got behind the wheel and backed out of his parking spot into the alley. He righted the car and drove slowly along the rutted, potholed asphalt. He took a left onto Forty-Third Street and headed west, made another left on Figueroa, passing several businesses with a TOM BRADLEY FOR CITY COUNCIL sign in the corner of their windows. He kept on, reaching Imperial Highway, went west again to the municipality of Inglewood and the Hollywood Racetrack. The horse racing venue was miles south from Hollywood. Its name had originated with studio boss Jack L. Warner, who in the 1930s was one of its main backers. Investors included Bing Crosby, Ralph Bellamy and Walt Disney.

The stars still came to the park, but Ingram wasn't here to try for a candid of Doris Day feeding an apple to a thoroughbred. Reaching the track, he turned onto a side road and followed that around a bend to an area most of the patrons didn't venture to, the stables. He parked on an open spot and walked across the hay-strewn ground, taking in the sights and ever-present smell of horse flesh. He passed a teenage stable hand raking up horse droppings and spotted his contact, Dolby Markham. He was washing down a horse in a stall. Ingram aimed the camera strapped around his neck and took a few snaps.

"Hey, Harry," Markham said when he heard the shutter click.

Ingram raised a hand. "Keep working. Looks great, Dolby."

The celebrities who were often photographed in the stands or at the turf club were usually white, though the likes of Nat King Cole and Lena Horne had also had their pictures taken here. The gossip rags weren't interested in the workers behind the scenes. Many of the trainers, stable hands and horse walkers were Black or Mexican American, a few Filipinos too. Ingram had talked with the West Coast editor of *Jet*, who told him he'd pay for some shots of the colored men taking care of the horses. Ingram could also write a few paragraphs to go along with the photos, which the editor figured would be a solid human-interest piece. *Jet* was a weekly digest-sized roundup of news about the Black community. It was published by Johnson Publications, which also put out the monthly full-sized *Ebony* magazine. The digest was not found at newsstands; rather the discerning buyer could find *Jet* on a counter rack at their local market or liquor store. Each issue included a centerfold of a swimsuit-clad young woman as the Beauty of the Week.

Markham took a break as Ingram stepped into the stall. "Don't mind my cold fingers."

They shook hands. "Ain't nothing to it."

The wiry Markham was several inches shorter than the

photographer. Once he'd been a jockey. But a particularly bad spill had resulted in his leg being broken in two places. Not the first time he'd been banged up, but what with permanent injuries having piled up over the years, Markham had retired from the racing aspect of the sport. But horses were all he knew, and he had to be around the animals in some capacity.

Ingram said, "Why don't you introduce me to the fellas?"

"You read my mind."

They exited the stall and Markham first took him to the kid who was raking.

"Yo, Tally, this here's a friend of mine, Harry Ingram. A certified daredevil newshawk of the negro in Los Angeles."

The kid stopped raking and glanced over at Ingram. "Say what now?"

"Dolby's funnin' you," Ingram replied, giving his friend a sideways glance.

"I seen you stand up to them peckerwood cops," Markham said. He tapped a thin scar on Ingram's temple, a present from a nightstick a few years ago.

"Anyway, about them shots," Ingram deflected.

"Shots, like from a doctor, because I'm around the horses?" The young man hooked a thumb at the stables.

"Naw, son, Harry's going to make you famous." Markham clapped him on the back.

The teen grinned. "Then let's get to it."

Ingram spent more than an hour taking photos but mostly hanging with the stable hands and other track workers as they went about their tasks, finding out what brought them to horse racing and so on. He'd filled several pages in his notepad. As he finished up, Ingram wondered if this might not be a piece he could interest one of the white slicks in if he fleshed out the story.

"Thanks for spending time with us never-seens, Harry."
Markham shook his hand again.

"Like I said, I'll get copies of the prints over to you,"
Ingram said. He'd used up two rolls of film.

About to head back to his car, Ingram spotted three men
up ahead in front of one of the stalls. One of them was a
trainer he'd met briefly when talking with Markham and the
others. He wore a sweat-stained hat that once upon a time
had a shape. The white man he was talking to was in his
fifties, Ingram estimated, tailored clothes and a barbered
head of silvery hair. But it was the third one who Ingram
zeroed in on. He was standing off to one side and as he got
closer, he could see this man lean his head toward him.

"Harry, is that you, home folks?"

"Ben? Goddamn, it is you." Ingram set his camera on a
small shelf upon which were bottles of liniment for the
horses.

The two rushed at each other and hugged, slapping each
other on the back.

"When did you get back to town?"

"A couple of weeks ago. Been meaning to look you up,
cousin," Ben Kinslow said. Addressing the silver-haired man,
he added, "We were in the service together, Mr. Hoyt."

The silver-haired man nodded curtly. "That's something.
Korea, was it?"

"Yes, sir," Ingram said, smiling. He took the older man to
be Kinslow's employer, and wasn't going to say something
crude if he could help it.

Hoyt and the trainer walked inside the stall, the trainer's
calloused hand on the horse's hindquarters.

"I'd heard you're still taking them stills," Kinslow said.

"You still tooting the horn?"

"Now and then."

They'd stepped away from the stall, but Ingram had heard enough to know that Hoyt was the owner of the horse being examined. He said in a low voice to Kinslow, "Look, I don't want to get you in Dutch with your boss. I'm sure he wants you paying attention to every pearl of wisdom spilling from his spoon-fed mouth."

Kinslow smiled, looking over at the other man. "Lay your number on me. I'll give you a shout."

Ingram wrote it down on one of his sheets in his notepad, tore it off and handed it over. "Don't be no stranger," he said in his normal volume.

"Never," his buddy said. "Give me some dap."

They slapped palms. Ingram retrieved his camera and walked to his car. Near his vehicle was a coal-black 1962 Lincoln Continental. He whistled at the swank car. Dispensing with his envy, he got into his car and after turning the engine over for several cranks, the vehicle started. He drove off, stopping at a pay phone on Imperial.

"Hey, Doris. Got anything for your favorite runner?"

"I think I do, Harry," Doris Letrec said. He heard her set the handset down, then papers being shuffled before she came back on the line. "Got a divorce case, a car involved in a cross complaint and some kind of suit involving a truckload of refrigerators." She paused, reading the paperwork further. "Oh, but that one's in Glendale."

He almost cursed. "You might as well have said Mississippi."

"I hear you." Letrec was white but she knew about sundown towns like Glendale. If you were Black, it was best you not be caught there after the sun set—by the cops or by the self-righteous residents. Ingram wasn't going to be there during the day if he could help it. "Okay, I'll swing by for the divorce and car."

"See you." She hung up.

Ingram drove back into L.A. proper and the offices of Galton Process Services and Legal Papers on Grand Avenue, not far from the downtown courthouses. Letrec, the office manager, was at the front desk typing a report when Ingram entered. She was a middle-aged woman who lived with a female roommate, a younger librarian, in a garden apartment in East Hollywood.

Her cat-eye glasses were on a chain and she removed them as she looked up from her Underwood. "I've got them right here, Harry." She handed the paperwork over to him.

"Thanks." He glanced at the addresses, then tucked them away.

The main part of the office contained a row of gray file cabinets, a few chairs, two desks—there was a man who came on for the after-hours trade from four to midnight—and an inner office. This had a door inset with a large glass pane, a set of blinds behind that. As usual, the blinds were drawn.

Ingram pointed his jaw at the door. "Is His Lordship in?"

"He was here before I got in," she said, hunching a shoulder. "He did stick his head out once to ask a question."

"Like the groundhog," Ingram mused.

Tremane Galton, the owner of the business, was of British extraction but had lived in the States since his twenties, some thirty-plus years ago. He was agoraphobic, though he managed to drive from his house in Frogtown to the office at least three days a week.

Ingram started for the exit. "I'll let you know how it goes."

"Keep 'em flying straight, Harry."

"Always above the flack."

Glasses back on, she gave him a last look, then resumed typing.

Driving to his first destination, Ingram passed a sharp-dressed teenager standing on the corner hawking copies of the *Sentinel*.

"'Negro Workers Demand Fair Pay at Bethlehem Steel,'" the young man yelled. "Get your *Sentinel* newspaper, get your *Sentinel* newspaper."

Serving the divorce papers was not hard. The unshaven man who answered Ingram's knock was wiping sleep out of his eyes. He worked the graveyard shift at a frozen fish supplier out in San Pedro.

"Mr. Efrain Martinez?" Ingram said pleasantly.

"Yes." He regarded Ingram warily.

"You've been served." Ingram held out the tri-folded papers requiring his presence in court.

"That puta bitch," the man growled, taking the papers, muttering in Spanish and English as he slammed the door.

The disputed car was another matter. The address took Harry to a residential street off of north Western Avenue. On his way he passed by the boarded-up Fox Uptown Theater. A few years ago, he'd taken a date there to see Vincent Price in a movie called *The Tingler*. The movie was pretty tame for a horror show. Ingram had hoped to get his lady friend all clingy. Instead, she'd fallen asleep by the second half.

He slowed as he went past a California bungalow, double-checking the address. The car in question wasn't out front, but there was a detached garage at the end of the driveway. First, though, he drove up and down the surrounding blocks, looking for the car whose plate and other details he'd memorized. Having done process server work for some time now, Ingram knew the tricks drivers used to hide cars they owed payments on—including switching the license plates. He rolled up on a Buick LeSabre, but it was the wrong color and plate. He didn't think the driver, a Scott Jayson, had had the vehicle repainted. If he could afford that, he would have tried to come current on the note.

Ingram parked several doors down from the bungalow and walked back to the house. He took a peek inside the garage. The double doors had a chain through where the locks had once been, and this was padlocked closed. But there was enough play between the doors that Ingram gapped them to shine his flashlight inside. The LeSabre was there.

"Hey, what are you up to?"

Ingram turned around to see a white man in jeans, his shirttail out. He was holding a baseball bat and had come out the back door.

Ingram held up a hand. "Take it easy. You must be Mr. Jayson." This wasn't the first time he'd been threatened with violence when he'd been trying to serve someone. The war had taught him how to handle his fear.

"What about it?"

"Your car is involved in a cross complaint and I'm here to serve you papers initiated from Triton Auto Sales." He'd also read the used car lot was run by Jayson's brother-in-law.

"Ain't no coloreds work for Triton."

"I'm being paid to serve you."

"Yeah, then get in the kitchen and get my lunch ready." The man chuckled.

"No reason to not be civil."

Jayson came closer, waving the bat. "What you gonna do if I don't? What if I use this to teach you a lesson about nosing in business that ain't your concern? How would that be . . . boy?"

"That would be a mistake, Mr. Ofay."

Jayson's eyes popped open as if he'd been struck in the forehead. "What did you just say?"

He swung the bat and Ingram turned his body into it, taking the brunt of the blow on his arm. He was hurting but focused. He got his hand on the bat and at the same time punched Jayson with his free hand.

"How dare you, nigger," the other man said, stumbling back but still holding the bat.

Ingram allowed the other man's momentum to carry the both of them backward, muscle memory dredging up the rudimentary jujitsu he'd learned in basic about leverage. Jayson aimed a fist at Ingram's jaw, but he slipped aside, the jab glancing off the side of his face. Ingram got his foot behind Jayson's heel and shoved. This sent them both down to the ground, Ingram landing as hard as he could atop the other man.

"Get the fuck off me."

They both wrestled for control of the bat, rolling around on the ground. Ingram rammed an elbow into Jayson's face, stunning him. An angered Jayson let go of the bat and got both his hands around Ingram's neck, choking him.

"I'll teach you good, Blackie."

Ingram went flat on his back and as Jayson tightened his hands around his neck, the part-time process server got a knee against Jayson's sternum, flipping him over. Ingram bolted to his feet, snatching the bat up from where it lay. The handkerchief pocket on his jacket was torn.

Jayson was getting to a knee. "You better put that down. I'll get you arrested for damn sure."

Ingram was mad enough to strike him, but feared sending him to the hospital, which would send him to jail quick. When it came to the testimony of a Black man against a white man's word, what chance did he have in a so-called court of law? Still. He jammed the opposite end of the bat into Jayson's stomach.

"You motherfucker," the man wheezed, bending over and holding his middle.

Ingram grabbed him by the shirt front and stood him up. "Listen, gray boy, if I have to come back here I'll set that Buick on fire and you'll never prove it was me. You'll really be in the hole then." He let him go and threw the court order at his feet. "You've been served, asshole."

"What about my bat?"

"What about it?" Ingram started toward him and Jayson flinched. Ingram laughed harshly, then turned, spearing the bat through a bedroom window, shattering the glass with force. "There it is."

Off he went, a tremor in his leg. By the time he got into his car he was shaking all over, tears in his eyes as he gripped the steering wheel. Ingram didn't give a shit about Jayson. It was the violence dogging him he knew. The war wouldn't let him go.

After a few minutes he calmed down. Hand steady, he inserted the key in the ignition, started the car and drove away.

SHOALS PETTIGREW was closing up his store as dusk settled. A late-model, somber-colored Buick LeSabre pulled to the curb and parked. Out stepped a youngish white man in shirtsleeves and tie. He carried an attaché case and stepped inside Shop Rite Hardware.

"Good evening, Mr. Pettigrew," he said.

"Mr. Westmore," the owner said, nodding curtly.

The other man placed his case on the counter. "As I mentioned over the phone, the association we represent is pleased to provide the church another contribution to the building fund." He clicked the attaché's locks open and lifted the lid. He extracted a sealed envelope, placed it before Pettigrew and reclosed his case. "As before, we seek no overblown ceremony. A mention from the pulpit come Sunday is sufficient."

"Yes, sir."

"Have a good evening."

"You too."

The man exited the store and drove away.

Pettigrew, head of the building committee of his church, Ward African Methodist Episcopal, had been tasked by his pastor to receive these particular donations delivered by Westmore. The cash infusion was a one-step-removed protocol being followed. It was understood these funds freed up church monies for stipends and such. These stipends in turn flowed as contributions from individuals to specific previously designated political campaigns in negro neighborhoods. Federal tax law prohibited churches from making outright political donations. Currently the money was earmarked for Tom Bradley's City Council campaign. It hadn't been the pastor who'd explained to Pettigrew how this worked, rather a former church secretary he'd been dating. As far as the books were concerned, everything was aboveboard and legal.

And as far as Pettigrew was concerned, this was how business was conducted in the white world, so why not his church, an entity that was doing right by the community? Bradley was an extension of that as well.

He locked up, taking the envelope with him.

# CHAPTER TWO

Ingram heard from his Army buddy Ben Kinslow, who invited him to a party in the Sugar Hill section of West Adams, among the Queen Anne and Beaux Arts homes. The name Sugar Hill, a tribute to the original Sugar Hill in Harlem, had been bestowed on this neighborhood by well-to-do Black folks: doctors, lawyers and those who owned businesses on Central Avenue. Celebrities such as Hattie McDaniel and Eddie "Rochester" Anderson had homes here. They and other actors were often relegated to stereotypical roles, be it maids and manservants on screens large and small, but in Sugar Hill, they were acknowledged for breaking down barriers.

But even here there was no escaping the onslaught of a white-dominated bureaucracy. The Santa Monica Freeway, begun in 1957, would eventually reach the ocean. It had cut a sizable swath through the neighborhood, leveling homes acquired by eminent domain despite residents banding together to try to alter the route.

Kinslow wasn't here yet but Ingram, used to being an interloper, wasn't feeling self-conscious. He was in the spacious kitchen of a three-story Victorian adding chips to the paper plate he'd stacked with a salami sandwich. He winced, his bruised arm smarting where he'd been hit with the bat. On the table beside the snacks were a few bottles of hard liquor, including Old Grand-Dad and Wild Irish Rose. Beer was in a washtub filled with ice on the tiled floor. The rear door was open and there were people socializing in the backyard—though he supposed in a house like this it would be called the garden. He'd once been told by the staid Charlotta Bass, the former publisher of the *California Eagle,* that back in the 1920s, when the residents had been mostly white, that more than one of these fine abodes around here had been the venue for an orgy. Sizing up the racially mixed but sedate crowd chatting away pleasantly, he didn't figure people were going to be letting their hair down that dang much this evening. He had a camera in his trunk just in case.

"Harry, how's it hangin'?"

Ingram gazed at a familiar face. "Johnny, hey, ain't nothin' up but the rent, baby."

"I heard that." They shook hands vigorously.

Johnny Otis was a vibraphonist and bandleader, and had once been co-owner of a nightclub in Watts called the Barrelhouse. He was of Greek origin, but often stated he identified as a Black man and with the negro's fight for justice. The two stepped out of the kitchen to talk.

"I'm doing a fundraising gig for Bradley if you want to drop by and take some shots," Otis was saying, munching on a handful of chips.

"For sure. When and where?"

"The date's still not settled 'cause of the reverend coming to town and Tom's folks are helping to prep the event. But probably no more than a couple of weeks after that." He added, "I'm trying to get King Cole to drop by and perform as well."

"Y'all got a place in mind for this?"

"Oh yes." Otis rubbed his now empty hands together to rid them of his chip crumbs. "The Hotten Tot has agreed to host the fundraiser."

"He's got a chance, right?"

"Should. Hell, he just might be our first Black mayor if he wins this race."

"Sheet, this is L.A., Johnny."

They both laughed. Otis turned his head slightly, scanning the room, then tapped Ingram's arm and pointed.

"Let me introduce you to this chick, she's got it going on."

"The tall one?" The woman had shoulder-length black hair and had thrown her head back, laughing with the man she was talking to.

"Yeah, come on." Otis held up a hand. "Hey, Anita."

The woman looked over as Ingram and Otis snaked their way through a knot of people. As they passed two of the Dandridge sisters, Dorothy and Vivian, Otis said hello.

When they reached the black-haired woman, Otis said, "Harry Ingram, this here's Anita Claire."

"Hello," she said to Ingram. She indicated her companion, an older white man in glasses and boxy sport coat, and said to the bandleader, "This is Frank Wilkerson, who you might know of."

"My man, yes, sir, know of you and dig you." Otis turned to Ingram. "This cat's been out front on housing issues for us poor folks."

"I know. We've run into each other a couple of times."

Wilkerson regarded Ingram. "Where?"

"The equal rights rally at the 5-4 Ballroom," Ingram replied. "It was right after you got out of the joint for facing down Congress, I recall you mentioning. I was there taking pictures." Wilkerson had been one of the speakers at the event. Ingram knew the photographer, like a waiter or floor sweep, was seen but not seen, his face often obscured by the camera in front of it.

"Right, got it," Wilkerson said, but not really.

"Anita's working on Tom's election committee. She's a wiz with numbers, stats, that sort of thing." Otis beamed at her.

"Pleased to meet you," Ingram said.

"Same," she said.

Ingram wasn't going to get caught staring. She struck him as self-assured, and if she knew numbers, she was smart too. Ingram had painful memories of trying to get through algebra word problems in high school, all those trains leaving opposite stations at different speeds. Of course, if he'd had a teacher who looked like her, his mind wouldn't have been on math any damn way.

He orbited back to the conversation that the other three were having about what sort of programs Tom Bradley might try to institute if he got elected.

"Reining in them damn cops of Parker's should be his number-one concern," Otis said.

"Amen to that," Ingram said.

"When Tom made captain in the Department," Wilkerson began, "no white patrolman would tolerate a colored man as his boss. He was put in charge of the graveyard shift, a command of Mexican and Black officers."

"We still got a long way to go," Otis noted.

The other two nodded.

Milling about later, Ingram struck up a conversation with a white man named Eddie Burrows who did freelance reporting for *The Nation* magazine. He was in short sleeves and his longish hair was disheveled.

"I'm going to cover King at the rally," he told Ingram.

"That's great." Ingram hadn't mentioned what he did.

He didn't want to seem desperate to cover the rally, though he was.

"I think the March on Washington is going to be a watershed event, don't you?"

"Maybe. But crackers digging in their heels to preserve the way of life they like has usually been the response to any forward motion us colored folks have tried."

"That's kind of cynical, isn't it?"

"Or just a realistic observation."

Burrows nodded. "So, what is it you do, Harry?"

They wound up exchanging cards, and Burrows said he'd see about getting Ingram into the rally. *The Nation* wasn't big on photos, but this was a special event, a precursor to August.

"'Course this might paint you as a red," Burrows said. "Hanging out with the people I know."

"I've been accused of much worse."

Not long afterward Ingram was out back catching up with Ben Kinslow, who'd finally shown up. From inside the house, riffs from piano keys carried on the evening's warm breezes. He and Kinslow liberally sipped on the Old Grand-Dad from the kitchen.

"Don't think I'm going to be working for Hoyt too much longer." Kinslow winked at Ingram. The two sat near the rear of the walled-in yard in faded Adirondack chairs. Decorative colored paper had been cut into shapes of the Buddha and Day of the Dead masks and hung from a clothesline.

"You taking up the horn full-time?"

"Maybe—that is, maybe I'll have more time to get my chops back."

"What are you going on about?"

Kinslow said, "Jus' talkin' is all. More of those big dreams we had sitting in a foxhole trying not to shit our britches."

"You were gonna have your own club."

"That's right," Kinslow agreed. That had been the reason he'd come out to L.A. before. He'd gotten close more than once to making it happen, but things didn't pan out. Kinslow sat back, arcing his hands in the air as if revealing a title. "How you like the name Club Central? You can be the house photographer, Harry."

"I appreciate that," Ingram said, drinking more. A tall man with reddish-blond hair guffawed loudly. A woman next to him giggled, putting a hand in front of his mouth to quiet him down. The two old friends let the silence linger, staring at the cutouts dangling before them, until Kinslow spoke again.

"You ever wonder what she looked like?"

"Who?"

"Your girlfriend, Seoul City Sue," he said.

"You the one went to sleep at night dreaming of her in your arms, lover boy."

Seoul City Sue was the name for a propagandist broadcast from Pyongyang in the north during the war. She had a velvety voice and lovingly told the GIs how their cause was lost, read the names off dog tags of dead American soldiers, and spun records like "I'll Be Seeing You." Many simply listened to her for her comforting voice, thinking of the girl they'd left stateside. That was the point, of course, but as far as Ingram knew, no one defected because of her.

"She wasn't Asian," he said.

"Yeah, she was. I've seen pictures," Kinslow replied.

Ingram hunched a shoulder. "That was more jive from the reds, man. Not only was she not Asian, she was as white as they come. Whiter than you even."

"You think 'cause I'm tipsy you can bullshit me?" Kinslow drained his glass and set it down beside his chair.

"Naw, she was a Methodist from Arkansas."

"How you know that, Criswell?"

Ingram held his hands up, swaying his upper body. "I see all and know all." He then added, "Read it in the *Saturday Evening Post*."

"For real?"

"For real. She still lives there in North Korea."

"Of course. She came home she'd be shot for treason."

"There is that little hitch."

"She a knockout?" Kinslow asked.

"You'd sell out your country for a pretty turn of the ankle, son?"

Kinslow affected a commanding officer's tone. "Patriotism or pussy, soldier. Which is it?"

"No wonder I could barely get through the war." Ingram's words came out flat, though he meant them to be light.

Kinslow patted Ingram on the shoulder.

Eventually they wandered back inside. Kinslow didn't say anything else about his plans. He'd brought his horn, which he'd stowed on a built-in sideboard beneath an impressionist painting. Joe Sample, a musician Ingram had seen at clubs around town with a group called the Jazz Crusaders, was improvising a tune. Nat King Cole stood off to one side behind some others, hands in his pocket, his snap-brim hat pushed back on his bopping head.

Kinslow had his horn out, waiting and tapping his feet as he discerned the patterns hidden within the seeming non-structure of the music. He held off for nearly a minute, fingering the horn's keys but not putting it to his lips. He joined in when Sample began pounding out a fast tempo. Together they worked their way into a tune that was melodious and involving. Ingram stood on the periphery, digging what the two were laying down. Improvising using spoons on the bottom of an emptied metal trash can, Johnny Otis joined in with understated syncopations. The groove continued for another twenty minutes or so. When they came to a stop, there was energetic applause. The temporary trio took their bows as the din of conversation again rose in the parlor.

"I saw you and the horn player talking earlier." Anita Claire had come up behind him.

What? Was she checking him out? Keeping his face neutral, he said, "Yeah, we were in Korea together."

"I see. I had a cousin who was there."

"How'd he take it?"

"He didn't make it back."

"Sorry to hear that."

"I didn't mean to be so dour."

"Could be the times we're in, Anita. When I came back from over there, figured me and all them other negro troops bleeding for democracy and all that would be appreciated. How could Mr. Charlie deny us our due on the home front?"

"But then it was the same old, same old."

"What a surprise."

"Let's get a drink."

"I'm gonna have something to eat. I might have hit my limit. Me and Ben catching up, I mean. Not that I drink like this normally."

She was heading toward the kitchen. "Do I look like a nun to you, Harry?"

He almost blurted, "No, ma'am, you look like a dream," but managed to stop himself. Instead, he gave an embarrassing chuckle and said, "That sounds like a trick question."

He followed her, noting that he'd sobered up some. Out of the corner of his eye, he spied Kinslow talking with Sample and Vivian Dandridge.

The kitchen had fewer people in it as the evening wore on. There was, though, a white woman in a green swing dress with eyes that matched her attire. Claire put an arm around her waist as the other woman finished mixing a drink.

"This is my running buddy, Judy Berkson," Claire said to Ingram. Both women showed big teeth at each other.

"Good to meet you," he said, sticking out his hand. She shook firmly.

"Here's how." Berkson tipped her glass to Claire and exited.

Claire got a beer out of the tub, which was now mostly full of water. He handed her a church key.

"So, what is it you do when you're not working to elect a candidate?"

"I'm a substitute teacher. I teach algebra and geometry in high schools and at a couple of community colleges. But I'm doing more of the Bradley kind of work these days."

"How does the math work in that situation?"

"I look for the patterns to develop profiles. Frequency of voters in an area—break it down by those who attend church, go to PTA meetings and so on. It's boring shop talk, but you asked."

"No, I'm digging it. You break down how segments of the voters vote?"

"Exactly. Ultimately what excites them to come out and vote. Now them cigar-smoking white fellas overseeing the state Democratic Party figure just running a negro candidate is enough to get colored people to the polls. Which admittedly is accurate to an extent."

Ingram nodded. "But we don't all think alike. A mechanic might have different concerns than a librarian."

"There you go." She smiled at him. "Really it's about compiling data to predict behavior. In a City Council race it's more concentrated, but Kennedy used a computer in his race to glean that kind of information to his advantage."

"He did?"

"Yep. We're all in this together, but we're not always marching in the same direction."

"Like the differences between King's approach and what Malcolm X is on about?" A year ago, the cops shot up the Black Muslim headquarters, mosques they called them, on South Broadway, leaving one man paralyzed and another dead. Malcolm X had come to town and given a fiery press conference in response at the Statler-Hilton. Ingram had covered the whole thing for the *Herald Dispatch*.

"Which way for you, Harry?" Her question brought him back to the present.

"Me, I'm just trying to make the rent."

"Uh-huh."

"Math is not just abstract formulas on a chalkboard?"

"I know, what does it say about me that I find numbers exciting? But you see, working in local politics is kind of a family tradition."

"Your folks work in politics?"

A cagey look came and went behind her eyes. "You could say that."

"Lady of mystery, huh?"

"That's right."

Later, as the party finally wound down, Ingram said good night to Claire, who'd come to the party with Judy Berkson. Her car, a convertible two-tone DeSoto, was parked under a streetlight. She was standing off to one side, pretending to be looking for something in her purse.

"Am I being too forward if I ask for your number?"

"I'm nothing if not numbers, Mr. Ingram."

Making sure to keep expectation off his face, Ingram

waited as she borrowed a ballpoint pen from her friend. Claire wrote her phone number on the curve of his palm. The blue numerals glistened on his brown skin under the light.

"I'll never wash this off."

"I expect you to be shaved and showered when next we meet, sir." With that she turned and took Berkson's arm. They laughed getting in the car.

"You old hound dog," Ben Kinslow said, walking up, his voice clearer that it had been before. "Bye-bye now," he said, waving at the two women as the car pulled away. His face was sweaty from drinking.

"You gonna make it home all right, soldier?"

"Son, I was knocking 'em back when you were still figuring out your wee-wee from your pablum spoon." He dug his keys out of his pocket. His car key held upright, he touched it to his forehead in a salute. "Okay, One-Shot, let's get us some steaks over to Lo Li's soon. Maybe to celebrate."

"Looking forward to it, Ben."

Kinslow slapped him on the shoulder and walked across the street to where his car was parked down the block. It was a '59 black-and-red Mercury with moon hubcaps. Turning the car around, he drove back to where Ingram remained standing. He slowed, the passenger's side window partly rolled down.

"Keep chargin' the enemy. We do what we do to survive." The admonishment from their Sergeant Jefferson faded into the early morning as Kinslow drove away.

A contented Ingram walked around the corner and unlocked the driver's door to his Plymouth. It took several cranks to start the engine. Getting the car in gear, he once again considered buying a newer sled. But then, hoping he might be seeing Miz Claire again, he figured it was best he have folding money available to show her he was no piker. Not that he took her for being a superficial person. If anything she was the sort to zoom ahead, and he wanted to keep up.

He drove past a line of late-nighters at Johnny's, an around-the-clock establishment on Adams Boulevard. The stand served up not only burgers but hearty pastrami sandwiches, fries and tacos. He resisted the garish neon advertising and made it home.

Not ready for bed, he turned on the radio, tuning in all-night KGFJ. This was the time slot for R&B. From a drawer in the kitchen he got out his S&H green stamps and using a damp sponge to wet the backs, put them in their booklets. Enough filled booklets and he could redeem them for an appliance. Eventually he yawned and switched off the radio, T-Bone Walker's "Mean Old World" still playing in his head as he went into his bedroom.

# Other Titles in the Soho Crime Series

**TERESA DOVALPAGE**
(Cuba)
*Death Comes in through
    the Kitchen*
*Queen of Bones*
*Death under the Perseids*
*Last Seen in Havana*

*Death of a Telenovela Star
    (A Novella)*

**DAVID DOWNING**
(World War II Germany)
*Zoo Station*
*Silesian Station*
*Stettin Station*
*Potsdam Station*
*Lehrter Station*
*Masaryk Station*
*Wedding Station*
*Union Station*

(World War I)
*Jack of Spies*
*One Man's Flag*
*Lenin's Roller Coaster*
*The Dark Clouds Shining*

*Diary of a Dead Man on Leave*

**RAMONA EMERSON**
(Navajo Nation)
*Shutter*

**NICOLÁS FERRARO**
(Argentina)
*Cruz*
*My Favorite Scar*

**AGNETE FRIIS**
(Denmark)
*What My Body Remembers*
*The Summer of Ellen*

**TIMOTHY HALLINAN**
(Thailand)
*The Fear Artist*
*For the Dead*
*The Hot Countries*

**TIMOTHY HALLINAN CONT.**
*Fools' River*
*Street Music*

(Los Angeles)
*Crashed*
*Little Elvises*
*The Fame Thief*
*Herbie's Game*
*King Maybe*
*Fields Where They Lay*
*Nighttown*
*Rock of Ages*

**METTE IVIE HARRISON**
(Mormon Utah)
*The Bishop's Wife*
*His Right Hand*
*For Time and All Eternities*
*Not of This Fold*
*The Prodigal Daughter*

**MICK HERRON**
(England)
*Slow Horses*
*Dead Lions*
*The List (A Novella)*
*Real Tigers*
*Spook Street*
*London Rules*
*The Marylebone Drop
    (A Novella)*
*Joe Country*
*The Catch (A Novella)*
*Slough House*
*Bad Actors*

*Down Cemetery Road*
*The Last Voice You Hear*
*Why We Die*
*Smoke and Whispers*

*Reconstruction*
*Nobody Walks*
*This Is What Happened*
*Dolphin Junction: Stories*
*The Secret Hours*

**NAOMI HIRAHARA**
(Japantown)
*Clark and Division*
*Evergreen*

**STEPHEN MACK JONES**
(Detroit)
*August Snow*
*Lives Laid Away*
*Dead of Winter*
*Deus X*

**LENE KAABERBØL & AGNETE
    FRIIS**
(Denmark)
*The Boy in the Suitcase*
*Invisible Murder*
*Death of a Nightingale*
*The Considerate Killer*

**MARTIN LIMÓN**
(South Korea)
*Jade Lady Burning*
*Slicky Boys*
*Buddha's Money*
*The Door to Bitterness*
*The Wandering Ghost*
*G.I. Bones*
*Mr. Kill*
*The Joy Brigade*
*Nightmare Range*
*The Iron Sickle*
*The Ville Rat*
*Ping-Pong Heart*
*The Nine-Tailed Fox*
*The Line*
*GI Confidential*
*War Women*

**ED LIN**
(Taiwan)
*Ghost Month*
*Incensed*
*99 Ways to Die*
*Death Doesn't Forget*

**MARCIE R. RENDON**
(Minnesota's Red River Valley)
*Murder on the Red River*
*Girl Gone Missing*
*Sinister Graves*

**JAMES SALLIS**
(New Orleans)
*The Long-Legged Fly*
*Moth*
*Black Hornet*
*Eye of the Cricket*
*Bluebottle*
*Ghost of a Flea*

*Sarah Jane*

**MICHAEL SEARS**
(Queens, New York)
*Tower of Babel*

**JOHN STRALEY**
(Sitka, Alaska)
*The Woman Who Married a
   Bear*
*The Curious Eat Themselves*
*The Music of What Happens*
*Death and the Language
   of Happiness*
*The Angels Will Not Care*
*Cold Water Burning*
*Baby's First Felony*
*So Far and Good*

(Cold Storage, Alaska)
*The Big Both Ways*
*Cold Storage, Alaska*
*What Is Time to a Pig?*
*Blown by the Same Wind*

**LEONIE SWANN**
(England)
*The Sunset Years of Agnes
   Sharp*
*Agnes Sharp and the Trip
   of a Lifetime*

**KAORU TAKAMURA**
(Japan)
*Lady Joker*

**AKIMITSU TAKAGI**
(Japan)
*The Tattoo Murder Case*
*Honeymoon to Nowhere*
*The Informer*

**CAMILLA TRINCHIERI**
(Tuscany)
*Murder in Chianti*
*The Bitter Taste of Murder*
*Murder on the Vine*
*The Road to Murder*

**HELENE TURSTEN**
(Sweden)
*Detective Inspector Huss*
*The Torso*
*The Glass Devil*
*Night Rounds*
*The Golden Calf*
*The Fire Dance*
*The Beige Man*
*The Treacherous Net*
*Who Watcheth*
*Protected by the Shadows*

*Hunting Game*
*Winter Grave*
*Snowdrift*

*An Elderly Lady Is Up
   to No Good*
*An Elderly Lady Must Not
   Be Crossed*

**ILARIA TUTI**
(Italy)
*Flowers over the Inferno*
*The Sleeping Nymph*
*Daughter of Ashes*

**JANWILLEM VAN DE
   WETERING**
(Holland)
*Outsider in Amsterdam*
*Tumbleweed*
*The Corpse on the Dike*
*Death of a Hawker*
*The Japanese Corpse*
*The Blond Baboon*
*The Maine Massacre*
*The Mind-Murders*
*The Streetbird*
*The Rattle-Rat*
*Hard Rain*
*Just a Corpse at Twilight*
*Hollow-Eyed Angel*
*The Perfidious Parrot*
*The Sergeant's Cat:
   Collected Stories*

**JACQUELINE WINSPEAR**
(Wartime England)
*Maisie Dobbs*
*Birds of a Feather*
*The Comfort of Ghosts*